The Captive HEART

The Captive
HEART

DALE
CRAMER

BETHANY HOUSE PUBLISHERS

a division of Baker Publishing Group
Minneapolis, Minnesota

© 2012 by Dale Cramer

Published by Bethany House Publishers
11400 Hampshire Avenue South
Bloomington, Minnesota 55438
www.bethanyhouse.com

Bethany House Publishers is a division of
Baker Publishing Group, Grand Rapids, Michigan

Printed in the United States of America

Library of Congress Cataloging-in-Publication Data
Cramer, W. Dale.
    The captive heart / Dale Cramer.
      p.   cm. — (The daughters of Caleb Bender ; 2)
    Includes bibliographical references.
    ISBN 978-0-7642-0839-3 (pbk.)
      1. Amish—Fiction. 2. Frontier and pioneer life—Fiction. I. Title.
PS3603.R37C37 2012
813'.6—dc23   2011035593

Scripture quotations are from the King James Version of the Bible.

Cover design by Lookout Design, Inc.
Cover photography by Mike Habermann Photography, LLC

Author is represented by Books & Such Literary Agency

11   12   13   14   15   16   17   7   6   5   4   3   2   1

For Mary Frost Nolan,
a warrior

Books by Dale Cramer

Sutter's Cross

Bad Ground

Levi's Will

Summer of Light

THE DAUGHTERS OF CALEB BENDER

Paradise Valley

The Captive Heart

THE FAMILY OF CALEB AND MARTHA BENDER
JANUARY 1923

ADA, 28 — *Unmarried; mentally challenged*

MARY, 25 — *Husband, Ezra Raber (children: Samuel, 6; Paul, 5; infant twins Amanda and Little Amos)*

LIZZIE, 24 — *In Ohio with husband, Andy Shetler (4 children)*

AARON, 22

AMOS — *Aaron's twin brother; deceased*

EMMA, 21 — *Husband, Levi Mullet (infant child, Mose)*

MIRIAM, 19+

HARVEY, 18

RACHEL, 16+

LEAH, 14

BARBARA, 12

Chapter 1

The mountain range known as the Sierra Madre Oriental ran the length of Mexico like a bony spine. Bold summits and limestone cliffs reached up among the passing rain clouds and diverted them and frustrated them and robbed them of their moisture so that by the time the clouds crawled out of the mountains, they had been reduced to wrung-out tatters with nothing left to give. In the wind shadow of these rugged mountains, the low-lying eastern coastal plain and Rio Grande valley had become parched red lands of scrub brush and cactus, while the upper reaches of the Sierras held cloud-shrouded pockets of tropical forest.

Nestled between the ridges at the eastern edge of the mountains lay a five-thousand-acre oval of rich pastureland known, in the 1920s, as Paradise Valley. The volcanic soil was black and fertile, the six-thousand-foot elevation guaranteed moderate temperatures year-round and a modest amount of rain fell throughout the growing season.

In the spring of 1922, in response to what he saw as religious persecution in Ohio, Caleb Bender brought his large family to Paradise Valley to pioneer a new Amish colony. Others would follow. Caleb's wife, Martha, his two living sons, and seven of his eight daughters uprooted themselves from the only home his children had ever known, traveled a thousand miles and toiled ceaselessly for a year, forging a new homestead, bonding with new neighbors, adapting to a foreign culture and breaking new ground for crops. It was a monumental undertaking, made even more perilous by roaming bands of outlaws, but the family pulled together through tremendous hardship like a matched team of seasoned horses, and they thrived.

In February of 1923 the Shrocks and the Hershbergers arrived. The population of the Paradise Valley colony tripled overnight.

After dinner that Saturday evening Caleb strolled a little ways up the ridge behind his house and sat down on his private rock to be alone with his thoughts, and with *Gott*.

"Have I been foolish?" he whispered, burdened by his own responsibility for this mad venture, and racked with doubts. *"What have I done?"*

But his eyes roamed over fresh-plowed fields and fat cattle, the adobe house his sons and daughters had built from soil and sweat, the yellow lights of his two married daughters' houses where three new lives had come into the world—the first Amish children born in Paradise Valley—and now the campfires of two whole new families, come to do the same. He saw two of his teenage daughters standing together on the edge of the wheat field, watching the moonrise. Under the full moon he could make out Rachel's flame red hair peeking out of her white prayer *kapp*, and Miriam, the dark one, the serious one, arm in arm with her gregarious sister. The mere sight of his daughters, beautiful and whole and happy, filled him with light. Caleb Bender was not a prideful man, for he was Amish to the bone, but he was bursting with pride in his children.

When the chill of the evening began to seep into him Caleb buttoned his coat, snugged his wide-brimmed hat on his bald head and started down the ridge smiling, with a renewed sense of Gott's arms wrapped around his family and friends in Paradise Valley. Two beige cabin tents rested in his front yard, lit yellow from within by lanterns, a roaring campfire cracking and popping between them, flinging sparks into the night sky. John Hershberger and Ira Shrock, the two new men, stood warming in its glow.

Caleb joined them for a few minutes, showing his palms to the flame while they talked of old times, the weather and the coming spring.

"The soil here must be even better than back home," Hershberger said. An old friend of Caleb's, his long face bore his customary pleasant smile. "Your wheat is as thick as any I've ever seen."

Caleb turned his back to the fire and saw how the moon silvered the tops of his winter wheat and highlighted the white kapps of his two daughters, returning to the house arm in arm.

"*Jah*, it's rich," Caleb said, "and if we rotate crops like always, it'll only get better. We'll fight weeds for a year or two, but not too many rocks." Weeds and rocks weren't really what concerned him, but this was not the time for that discussion. "My girls are headed in. Time for evening prayers," he said, and with a goodnight wave to John and Ira, headed for the house.

During prayer time he couldn't help noticing Miriam's downcast gaze. She looked like she'd been crying. Rachel's freckled face, usually bright and open, was drawn and tight, harboring some dark secret. Something was going on between them, but Caleb only chuckled to himself as he rose to go upstairs. At such times his daughters were a mystery to him. He silently thanked Gott for his wife, whose job it was to unravel the mysteries, the endless parade of troubles and triumphs that came with a houseful of daughters.

⌇

Miriam let her dark hair down and dressed herself for bed. By the time she turned in and put out the lantern Rachel was already asleep, red hair splayed across the pillow and her breathing slow and steady. But Miriam was haunted, charged and quickened by thoughts of Domingo, of his pet name for her.

Cualnezqui.

She loved Domingo, she knew that now. Was it possible his little lie and his blank expression hid the same feelings for her? If so, an inconceivable choice awaited her somewhere in the future. She was a baptized member of the church, and Domingo was not Amish, but Miriam could not help how she felt. Suffering her private torture in the stillness of the night, sleep did not come for a long time. Finally she closed her eyes and uttered a simple prayer, asking for direction. She found a familiar and yet ever-surprising release in handing the problem over to Gott, and fell asleep with the prayer still on her lips.

⌇

In the cave-black hours before the first hint of dawn Miriam's mind swam up from sightless depths, random visions flitting past like bright silver fish as she fought toward the surface of a moonless sea, to the place of crystalline dreams. In an instant she was lifted, whisked through space and time into a startling midday light. Her dress and stark white prayer kapp vanished and she found herself wearing the coarse cotton pants and shirt of a peasant laborer. Dark, heavy hair fell loose about her shoulders, down her back, and windblown strands tickled her face.

Trapped in the timeless space between dream and memory, it seemed she owned no past or future.

She stood on the razor's edge of a sun-washed ridge. On one side the land fell away in a steep slope dotted with drought-stunted oak trees, twisted pines and clusters of prickly pear cactus. On the other side a sheer rocky cliff dropped straight into oblivion, where only a dry wind moaned through the crags.

She knew this place. The ridge overlooked their new home in Paradise Valley.

Mexico.

A great dark stallion appeared in the distance, rising suddenly at the highest point of the ridge. Head held proudly, mane flying like a flag, he surveyed the valley below as if he owned it.

The stallion's head turned and his eyes found Miriam. He took a half step back and tossed his head, a blink of recognition. She held his gaze. Sunlight glinted from steel muscles as he reared up on powerful hind legs and hurled himself toward her. He galloped flat out, tearing along the edge of the cliff, bounding over boulders and fallen trees, racing toward her with an urgency, an intensity she did not understand until she heard a different sound.

It was a small sound, a faint rustling of dry leaves from a thicket of scrub brush in the foreground, between her and the stallion. Staring hard, searching low in the tangled bracken, she spotted a pair of large round eyes—eyes of amber framed in black. The eyes of a predator, focused on her alone. A black jaguar crouched there, coiled and motionless, waiting.

Watching.

Their eyes locked. The great cat tensed, dropping a fraction deeper into his crouch, his decision made. He exploded from the brush as if he had been fired from a cannon, bunched muscles flinging him over rock and snag with astonishing speed, but the stallion was almost upon him. Approaching hoofbeats spun the jaguar about, ears laid back, fangs exposed in an ear-splitting scream, coiling to spring at this new challenge.

Black and sleek and powerful, the jaguar launched himself at the charging horse, and the two beasts locked together. The stallion twisted, reared, bucked, but the big cat clung fast by claw and fang.

Paralyzed with terror, Miriam watched the deadly battle in agonizing slow motion. She saw the whites of the stallion's eyes, the desperation in his struggle. She saw the singular resolve of the savage cat, bent on destruction. She saw a hoof slip over the edge of the rock, pawing for a new grip and finding only empty space.

Slowly, like a felled tree, the stallion tilted and toppled. With his head thrown back and the jaguar still clamped to his neck, he plunged over the edge into the abyss, turning and tumbling, his hooves thrashing as he plummeted out of sight.

She ran screaming, scrambling over rocks, reaching for him as though she could somehow turn back the clock and prevent this from happening, but it was a futile gesture. Hopeless.

He was gone, leaving nothing behind but the moan of the wind in the rocks.

Miriam awoke sitting bolt upright in bed, gasping, damp with sweat despite the cold, memory flooding her mind. The dream burned brightly in that moment, and she understood it completely. She knew what it meant, who it was about. The magnificent free-spirited stallion her dream had conjured was no horse at all, but a man.

Domingo.

The vision burned itself into her consciousness and filled her with dread, for it had been etched in her mind almost from birth that a man who lived by the sword would surely die by the sword. Domingo's own father had perished fighting in the Mexican Revolution, along with his sister's husband. This ringing premonition that Domingo would somehow follow in their footsteps shook her to the core.

She had witnessed a transformation only yesterday on Saltillo Road, the moment when Domingo the hired hand became Domingo the Warrior, his blade pressed against a bandit's throat, his body taut as a fence wire, his eyes cold and hard and merciless, piercing through tangles of long black hair. Domingo the fierce. Domingo the *protector*.

"*He is gentle,*" his sister Kyra had said, "*until someone he loves is threatened.*"

If Domingo's metamorphosis from farmhand to warrior was indeed triggered by the need to protect someone he loved, Miriam needed to know if she was that one. Before he'd left for home—*was it only last night?*—she had emboldened herself and given him every chance to declare his feelings for her, if he had any, but he said nothing. He became, if anything, more aloof than ever, leaving her to wrestle with her own doubts and insecurities. In the end she resigned herself to the belief that he wanted only friendship from her, that he granted her respect because she had taught him to read. He didn't even *see* the woman behind the teacher's veneer, let alone share her feelings.

But that name haunted her. Cualnezqui, he called her. A Nahuatl word, it had been Domingo's pet name for Miriam alone, from the day she and her family arrived. "*Friend,*" he explained when she asked him what it meant, and for an entire year she believed him. But last night, as he was riding away, Rachel told her the truth, and the earth shifted.

Cualnezqui did not mean *friend* at all.

It meant *beautiful one*.

So why did he not speak when she gave him the chance? Had he been teasing her all this time? Was he treating her like a child? The questions consumed her.

Never before had she met such a man. She was smitten and she knew it, though she had always tried to hide it—partly because she was Amish, and partly because she was Miriam. Her dreams and desires were her own, jealously guarded lest they make the rounds of the gossips' tongues and come back in whispers to ridicule, or worse. The church would take a dim view of her feelings for a man who was not Amish. He was not even American, but a half-breed native Mexican.

And then, with a shock, she recalled the brief prayer she'd uttered before falling asleep, asking for a sign.

She had gone to sleep with a plea for help on her lips and awakened to a vivid, pointed dream. Now she was plagued by the nagging fear that perhaps the dream was the answer to the prayer. Could it have been a cryptic warning from Gott himself? Would it somehow be up to *her* to save Domingo?

Knowing she would not go back to sleep, Miriam slipped out of bed and dressed herself in the dark so as not to wake her four sisters sleeping in the same room. The house had grown cold in the night; she went downstairs to stoke the stove.

Chapter 2

When the rooster crowed, Rachel awakened with such excitement that she barely noticed Miriam was already gone from the bed. She sprang from under the covers like a child on Christmas morning and rushed to the window again, just like yesterday, to make sure nothing had changed.

The wagons and buggies and hacks were still parked in a row by the lane. Tents glowed in the yard, their lanterns already lit, while down by the kitchen garden a flurry of sparks leaped from the red embers of a dying campfire as one of the men dropped a fresh log onto it.

Their new neighbors had been here since Friday night and she still hadn't gotten over the excitement, because *Jake* was with them.

She'd waited a whole year for Jake Weaver to come, the last two months without hope because she received word that his father had decided not to bring his family to Mexico. Rachel's own father was the cause of it. Caleb Bender, because it was his duty and it was the truth, had written his friends in Ohio and told them about the bandit troubles. His candid letters had changed Jake's father's mind about moving across the border into such turmoil.

The news that Jake would not be coming had driven a nail through Rachel's heart. Yes, she had barely reached courting age before her family pulled up stakes and moved to Paradise Valley. But she and Jake had known each other all their lives, and in the midst of the storm that the state of Ohio unleashed upon the Amish, the two of them discovered strengths in each other that they had never noticed before.

"I would do a great many things for you," Jake had said, and it was as if a veil lifted and her future unfolded before her eyes with astonishing clarity. They both knew with a calm and unwavering certainty—suddenly, yes, but beyond any childish doubt—that they were meant for each other. That certainty, and their faith, had now been tested by a separation of a thousand miles for an entire year.

But now he was here. At the eleventh hour Jake's father had relented and allowed his son to leave the family farm and come to Paradise Valley as a hireling of John Hershberger.

The eastern sky had only begun to turn purple. A sharp snore came from simpleminded Ada, sleeping in the other bed with her two youngest sisters. Rachel woke them, then rushed to put on yesterday's dress and pin her long red hair under her covering. She wanted to finish her chores quickly and leave plenty of time to change into her Sunday clothes for *gma*. Today there would be church services in the Benders' barn.

And Jake would be there.

She hurried downstairs, past the living room, where her brothers were just beginning to stir from their blankets on the floor, through the kitchen, where Miriam and Mamm were already starting breakfast, and stopped by the back door to put on her coat. She lit a lantern, grabbed her bucket and stool from the back porch and headed for the barn.

Setting her bucket and stool down at the milking corner,

she put a little feed into the manger and went out to rouse the cows. As usual, she found them lying in the grass not far away, waiting. When the cows saw her lantern, they hauled their heavy bodies up and plodded toward the big door, long accustomed to the routine. Her bare feet were freezing from the dew, so she stood for a minute in the impression left by a cow, absorbing the warmth before she followed them inside.

As she went back through the door of the barn someone laid a hand on her shoulder. She gave a little shriek and nearly dropped the lantern as she spun around.

"Good morning," Jake said, smiling sheepishly. "I'm sorry I scared you."

She melted into his strong arms and warmth flooded through her. She said nothing. No words were necessary.

He gave her a too-brief hug and said, "I'll help you with the milking. I'll have to round up John's cows and milk them too, so I'll be needing the space."

She nodded, stifling a giggle. "Miriam will be here in a minute. We wouldn't want her to catch us like this."

Milking was no longer a chore with Jake beside her. Nothing was the same. Her whole world had taken on new and vibrant colors.

⟳

That morning, for the first time since the Shrocks and Hershbergers arrived, the three Amish families gathered for church services in the Benders' barn. Miriam sat on a backless bench alongside her sisters, but part of her was elsewhere. Despite the pure and palpable joy in the air that morning—for they had been reunited and were a community again—Miriam's mind kept wandering, reliving an all too vivid dream.

They sang a few songs from the *Ausbund*, Hershberger said

a long prayer of thanks for traveling mercies and then her dat got up to speak. He fidgeted and shifted uneasily from foot to foot, for Caleb Bender was not sanctioned by the church as a preacher. It was one thing to speak in front of his family on Sunday morning, but a crowd of fifty was very different.

"I was thinking on it this morning at breakfast," her father said, standing before the assembled families, the women seated on one side and the men on the other, all of them dressed in their Sunday best. "I was thinking about how in the beginning, every time Gott made something new He always said it was good. And it goes along like that until after He makes a man. But then comes the first time Gott says something is *not* good. He said it was not good that the man should be alone."

Now he had Miriam's full attention. *Alone*. The word struck a chord in her. It meant almost twenty and unmarried, with no prospects.

Her dat paused, biting his lip, choosing his words carefully.

"Gott meant for Adam to have a wife, a helpmeet," he said slowly. "But I think mebbe there is more to it than that. I believe the thoughts of Gott are truth, whether He thinks them in a small way or a big way."

There was great stillness then as everyone stared at him blankly, not sure what he meant by this. Miriam glanced at the faces of the boys sitting across the aisle. At the mention of a wife, Jake Weaver's attention drifted subtly from Caleb's face to Rachel's. The faintest trace of a smile touched the corners of his eyes before he turned his attention back to her dat.

But then she saw Micah, the strapping big twenty-one-year-old son of Ira Shrock, sitting next to Jake. She couldn't help noticing that he glanced at her too often for it to be accidental.

Micah had been there too, on the wagon with her on the way back from Arteaga when the bandits struck and tried to take her. In her mind it was Domingo who had saved her, taking down the bandit whose pistol was aimed at Micah's back, but Micah had done his part, too. When the second bandit tried to climb over into the wagon to drag her away, it was Micah who stopped him. At the very least, Micah had helped save her life. She was indebted to him.

Caleb cleared his throat. "What I'm trying to say in my clumsy way is that if Gott says it is not good for *the man* to be alone, then it is probably not good too for *people* to be alone. We—my wife and children and me—have been alone in a strange land for a year now . . ."

His thoughts overwhelmed his voice for a moment and he paused to collect himself.

When he looked up again, his eyes found John Hershberger and he said quietly, "I think mebbe Gott meant for us to be with Him *and* with one another. I cannot tell you how full my heart is this morning when I look out and see that we are no longer alone. It is very, very good."

Miriam knew from personal experience that it was definitely not good to be alone. Keeping her eyes on her father, avoiding Micah's glances, she felt a pang of guilt. Domingo was not Amish. It was inevitable; any sort of relationship with him would surely bring the censure of the church, but she couldn't help herself. His voice echoed in her head.

"*Cualnezqui.*"

Beautiful one.

Chapter 3

The youth held a singing at Caleb's that evening, boys and girls facing each other on benches in the barn. There was the usual jockeying for position as boys tried to sit across from a girl whose eye they wanted to catch.

Rachel paid attention. Jake was there with the Hershberger boys and their sister Lovina. As a teenager alone in a strange land, Jake would naturally be treated as one of the family by the Hershbergers. He would be paid, of course, but he wouldn't see a penny of it. John Hershberger would mail Jake's earnings home to his father, as was the custom. Until he was twenty, or married with a home of his own, everything Jake earned would go to his father.

Ira Shrock's children came to the singing, too—his four older sons and two of his daughters. Both of Rachel's brothers were there. Harvey Bender never missed a singing, but now even Aaron came and sat with the other boys, which was unusual. At twenty-two he didn't have to attend, since it was mainly a social function for older teens, and he hadn't been to a singing back home since his twin brother, Amos, died four years ago. But back in the fall his older sister Mary had delivered twins, a boy and a girl, and named the boy Amos, after the lost brother. It was as if Aaron's twin had been reincarnated, and the dark cloud of loss that hung over him vanished like a morning mist. Awakening from his doldrums, Aaron smiled more often and began to mix with the other young men. He talked more and walked a little taller, held his shoulders a little straighter.

Jake Weaver took a seat right across from Rachel, as expected. Though it was something of a thrill for her, by now their courtship was old news to the rest of the girls and didn't cause much of a stir. What *did* pique Rachel's interest was when Micah Shrock shoved Aaron aside so he could sit directly across from Miriam.

At nearly twenty it was getting late for Rachel's older sister, and separated from the large Amish community in Ohio, Miriam's prospects were slim. Even now, with the arrival of two more families, the two older Shrocks were the only Amish boys in the entire country who might remotely be considered a match for her.

Rachel did everything she could, elbowing Miriam and nodding in Micah's direction, but her sister's face was drawn tight and she shook off all of Rachel's hints, steadfastly refusing to make eye contact with Micah. When the singing was over Miriam went straight into the house with the adults, giving him no chance to talk with her alone.

Later, when they were in bed and the rhythmic breathing from the other bed told Rachel the younger girls and Ada were already asleep, she touched Miriam's shoulder in the dark and broached the subject.

"What's wrong with Micah Shrock?" she whispered. No point beating around the bush.

Miriam drew a deep breath and exhaled slowly. "Nothing. Micah's a nice enough boy. I just think he's a little immature."

"Boy? Miriam, he's six-foot-three, and he's the oldest unmarried *boy* in Paradise Valley."

Miriam didn't answer for a second. "That doesn't make him a man. He just seems so . . . I don't know."

"Seems so *what*? Amish?" She let the word hang for a moment before she went on. "I think you only have eyes for Domingo, Miriam. I know he's handsome, and I like him too, but he's not one of us. You're playing with fire."

Miriam's head turned toward her and she raised herself up on an elbow. "Domingo is not interested in me, Rachel. He has never said anything to make me think he sees me as anything but a friend."

"Cualnezqui," Rachel whispered. "Why would he call you *beautiful* if he didn't have feelings for you?"

Miriam hesitated for a long time. "Who knows? Maybe he was teasing, the way you tease a little girl, calling her pretty. Besides, it's a Nahuatl word and he thinks we don't know what it means. I bet after he finds out we're onto his little joke he won't say it anymore. So you can relax, Rachel. He's our friend, and that's probably all he's ever going to be."

"But you like him."

"Everybody likes him. Even Dat is crazy about him, so don't make it sound like it's just me."

"Dat doesn't look at him the way you do. I've seen it, Miriam. You should be careful what you want. Why, Kyra said he's not even a Christian. Kyra's mother raised her to be a good Catholic, but she said their father made a Nahua warrior out of Domingo. He doesn't even go to church."

"Domingo is a good man, and it's not our place to judge outsiders," Miriam whispered. "The condition of his soul is between him and Gott."

"But he *is* an outsider, Miriam. If you married him it would break our mother's heart."

Miriam's voice came across the darkness more like a hiss than a whisper. "So now I'm going to *marry* him, Rachel? First of all it's up to the *man* to choose, not the girl. I told you, Domingo has never once said he wanted to be anything more than a friend. I don't know where you get these crazy ideas!"

Miriam punched her pillow twice and flopped back onto it with a sigh.

Rachel waited a minute to let her calm down and then whispered, "I only wanted to know what was wrong with Micah, that's all. He's a good worker. Strong. For a girl in your position, he seems like a good option."

"A good worker," Miriam echoed. "What you really mean is a good provider—a good *husband*. You might want to consider that I'm not just a girl in my *position*; I'm a human being with thoughts and desires of my own. I barely know Micah, so I don't like to say anything bad about him, but he seems a little pushy if you want to know the truth. Besides, I don't know what we would talk about. As a friend, I don't have anything against him, but if I ever find the man I want to marry—*if*, I say—he'll be a man I can talk to, a man who can think and carry on a conversation about something besides farming."

Conceding defeat, for now, Rachel rolled over to face the other way.

"Good luck," she whispered into her pillow.

⤳

Domingo showed up for work at dawn on Monday morning, and Caleb had him hitch up the surrey. After breakfast Domingo went along while Caleb took Ira and John on a tour of the valley so they could pick out their plots.

"That's a fine-tempered mare," Caleb said to Hershberger as he snapped the reins and his new buggy horse broke into a smooth pace. John Hershberger had brought him a two-year-old standard-bred mare to replace the one taken by bandits last fall. "You chose well, John. You always did have an eye for a horse."

"They had another mare at the sale for a cheaper price," John said, "but it wasn't near as good as this one. All I did was pick the one you would have picked, Caleb. Anyways, it's a lot easier to spend somebody else's money."

Caleb chuckled at John's little joke. He had known John Hershberger all his life and trusted him like a brother.

Ira Shrock, sitting beside Domingo in the back seat, had remained silent up to now, his eyes nervously scanning the horizon as the surrey crossed the main road and headed into unbroken pasture on the other side of the valley. Now he leaned forward and revealed the reason for his nerves.

"Caleb, what are we going to do about those bandits?"

Caleb's eyes went wide and he scanned the horizon himself. "What bandits?"

"The ones who attacked you on the way back from Saltillo. Have you already forgotten?" There was a trace of indignation in his voice, and a fear that he had not shown in front of the women and children. "They threatened us—and they said they would be back. What do we do if they come back, Caleb?"

Domingo chuckled, answering Ira in High German. "Those two won't come back here."

Ira looked around at him in surprise. "Well, they *said* they would. What makes you think they won't?"

Domingo shrugged, glancing at Ira from under the flat brim of his hat. "It was in their eyes. They know I am here, and they are afraid of me now."

"Jah," Ira said, his red face growing redder, "but mebbe this time they bring more of their friends."

Domingo shook his head. "I don't think so, Herr Shrock. If you want to know what these men will do, you have to think like a bandit. They were defeated and had their weapons taken away—by a couple of farmers and a girl. Herr Bender even took one of their horses. They were shamed, and they knew their compadres would have no mercy. Men like that will not go back to camp and tell the truth about what happened. They will make up a grand lie about how they were attacked by an army of fierce warriors, and they were lucky to escape with their lives." Domingo cast a wry smile at Caleb and added, "The last part is true enough—they *are* lucky to be alive."

But Ira was not persuaded. "I still think we have to do something, Caleb—for our wives and children. If men like that come with guns to Paradise Valley we will be at their mercy."

Caleb pondered this for a moment. "Ira, I have lived here for a year already and I have seen many bandits, but most of the time they only want food and water. Those are the only two who ever tried to do us harm, and Domingo is right—they probably will not come back."

The four men climbed down from the surrey in the shadow of the ridge on the opposite side of the valley and walked through the grass, smelling and tasting and seeing for themselves the quality of the soil and the lay of the land. Even in February the midday sun was warm enough, and a gentle breeze ruffled the prairie grasses. A gray hawk cruised high over their heads, riding the upward air current along the face of the ridge.

"This is a mighty fine parcel," John Hershberger said, slinging his coat over his shoulder and gazing back across the valley at Caleb's place. "If the weather truly holds like this, why, we can grow vegetables year-round, just like that salesman said."

Caleb smiled. "Jah, I'm beginning to believe it myself. Winter is nearly over and we only had snow a couple times yet. I'm thinking I'll start planting this week."

"Well I guess we'll find out then, won't we?" Ira said. Eyeing a hummock a quarter mile to the west, he mused, "I like the look of that rise yonder. Good spot for a house and a banked barn, if it only had a tree or two on it. What do you think, neighbor?"

John Hershberger squinted at the place and nodded. "I think we should go and take a look, Ira. The good thing about being first is we get to choose, and we got plenty here to choose from. No need to be hasty."

The sound of hoofbeats turned the three men around. A Mexican cantered across the open field toward them on a tall, heavy-boned black horse with a long mane and untrimmed hair obscuring large hooves.

Ira Shrock tensed, his brow furrowed. "Would that be a bandit, Caleb?"

"*Neh*," Caleb said, a trace of a grin on his face. "Bandits don't dress so good. I know this man. His name is Diego Fuentes, the overseer from Hacienda El Prado. A decent man—or at least he has been kind to us."

Fuentes was dressed in corduroy pants, a hunting jacket with a leather shooting patch on the shoulder, riding boots and a narrow-brimmed city hat. He tipped his hat to the three Amishmen as he dismounted and walked over to them, leading his horse by the reins.

"Buenos días, Señor Bender! I see your new friends have arrived." Fuentes's English was quite good.

Caleb introduced Hershberger and Shrock, and they gave Diego Fuentes a strong, one-pump Amish handshake.

"That's about as stout a horse as I ever seen," Hershberger said. "Friesian?"

"Sí," Fuentes answered, reaching up to rub the jaw of his black stallion affectionately. "They are rare in Mexico. He was a gift from the *hacendado*—smart and docile, and strong as a plow horse."

The four of them walked over the land a little ways, Shrock

and Hershberger checking out potential home sites and talking to Fuentes.

"A question is in my mind yet," Hershberger said. "We're gonna need a lot of timber, and I wondered if mebbe we could take some from the ridge. I know the ridge doesn't belong to us, but Caleb told us you let him cut a little for his roof last year."

Fuentes winced. "That would not be such a good idea now. Two more farms and more to come soon—I am sorry, but I think perhaps it would be too much, señor. The trees on the ridges are not very big anyway, and they are a little sparse."

"It is Señor Fuentes's duty to keep watch over the timber here," Caleb explained. "The local villagers would strip the ridges and use it all for cooking fires if he let them, so he has to set rules. They can take deadfall, but everyone knows the standing timber belongs to the hacienda."

"Sí," Fuentes said. "It is all I can do to keep the hacienda blacksmith supplied. If the local people see gringos cutting timber they'll want to know why they can't do it as well."

Ira Shrock's red face clouded over with concern. "What will we do, then? We can't build houses and barns and fences without timber, and it would cost a lot of money to get it by train from Ohio."

The Mexican's face lit up with an idea. "The hacendado owns a big parcel of land twelve miles from here, up in the mountains to the west. It is very difficult to get to, and none of the local people have the horses to haul heavy loads over those roads, but your draft horses could do it. There is plenty of big timber there, señor. You can take what you need, only you must agree to pay one third of your logs to the hacienda."

Ira and John considered this briefly, then nodded and shook hands with Fuentes.

"That's a fair deal," John said.

Chapter 4

Caleb's boys were busy that week, plowing fields for spring planting while the Shrocks and Hershbergers picked out sites across the valley and started work on their homesteads. Domingo spent the entire week helping Caleb bring in the winter wheat. Miriam drove the wagon for them, watching Domingo work alongside her father, hoping for a chance to talk to him privately. She didn't know what she would say, or even if she would have the nerve to say what she was really thinking. In the end it didn't matter because she never had a moment alone with him.

Until Friday afternoon. The wheat was all in, and after lunch her father stood in the front yard picking his teeth and talking to Domingo about turning the stubble under. When Miriam walked by, he stopped her.

"Miriam, see if Mamm needs anything from the store. I want you and Rachel to take the buggy into town."

She had been so busy she forgot. Once a week Caleb sent a couple of his daughters into town to trade butter and cream for whatever they needed at the mercado in the hacienda village, and pick up the mail at the post office.

"Jah, Dat," Miriam said. She had already turned back toward the barn when Domingo spoke up.

"Herr Bender," he said, "I know it is only a few miles to town, but I don't know if it is wise to send your daughters without someone to protect them."

Caleb pondered this for a minute.

"Jah, mebbe you're right," he said. "It's better to be safe than sorry."

Domingo took the reins, wearing a gun belt around his hips, and Miriam rode up front with him while Rachel sat in the back. It was a fine spring day, full of sunshine, the open fields dotted with clusters of some kind of little purple wildflower, the birds boasting and chasing one another on a cool breeze. Domingo spoke very little, keeping his eyes on the road as the buggy horse paced smoothly along toward the hacienda village. Miriam thought of a thousand ways she might open a dialogue with him, but she couldn't say what she really wanted to say with Rachel right there in the back seat. She sat quietly with her hands in her lap, trying to hide her nerves. She was anxious, partly because she was naturally shy and introverted, and partly because of that gun. Guns always made her skittish, but a handgun was the worst because it was not a hunting weapon. A pistol was mostly for shooting at a man.

When they reached town Domingo jumped down from the surrey and tied the horse to the hitching rail in front of the mercado—the grocery store. Rachel and Miriam climbed down with a block of butter wrapped in paper and a jug of heavy cream that they planned to trade.

"You have Mamm's list?" Miriam asked, checking to make sure her white prayer kapp was still in place after the ride.

"Jah," Rachel said, "but I don't need it, really. She only wants some salt and cloves."

"Oh. Well then, since it's not very much, why don't you take care of the trading and I'll walk down to the post office to get the mail?"

Rachel looked at her a little sideways. "Why don't we just stay together? We've got all afternoon."

Miriam glanced at Domingo, leaning casually against the hitching post, and Rachel's eyes narrowed.

"I see," Rachel muttered. "Well, it's your life, sister." She hooked a finger in the jug of cream and snatched it away from Miriam, then turned on her heel and stalked into the mercado without another word.

The street was crowded with Mexicans in rickety wagons, going and coming, buying and selling. Everyone seemed a little more animated than usual, and Miriam felt it, too. The first hints of spring brought an air of expectation and well-being. Walking beside Domingo, Miriam's mind flitted through all the words she'd been practicing in her head, but none of them sounded good enough when the moment was actually upon her. His hand rested on the butt of the pistol at his hip, his elbow slightly extended, and she even thought once or twice of casually slipping her hand under his arm, but the thought made her blush and she knew she didn't have the nerve. When he glanced at her he almost seemed to smile, but he said nothing. The man could be dreadfully stingy with words.

He waited outside as she went into the post office and collected a little clutch of letters from the man at the counter.

"Letters from home," she said, flipping through them as she rejoined Domingo in the dusty street. "But none for me. They're all for Mamm and Dat, from friends in Ohio."

Domingo grabbed her arm and pulled her to the side as a horse-drawn wagon rumbled by a little too close for comfort.

"Thank you." She smiled up at him while he still held her arm. "I'm glad you came with us today. I feel safe when I'm with you."

He smiled back. "You are welcome, Cualnezqui."

But then he let go of her arm and said nothing else, turning to head up the street. He went a few paces before he turned around and looked back.

Miriam had not moved. Another wagon trundled close by, loaded with hay, but she ignored it. Her frustration welled up, and she knew she was going to say something or burst.

"I know what that word means," she said, in High German. "Cualnezqui."

He turned about and came back to stand in front of her. He seemed to measure her then, looking deep into her eyes, but in his face she saw only compassion. It was not what she was looking for, longing for.

"Someone has told you," he said.

"You told us it meant *friend*, but then we found out from Kyra that it really means *beautiful one*. And you saved it for me alone. Why would you do that?"

He looked away, and then his eyes went to his sandals. He shrugged and said quietly, "Because you are beautiful?"

She studied him for a few seconds, confused, unsure of what to say next. She took a half step closer so that he was forced to look down into her face.

"When a man calls a woman beautiful, it makes her think he is . . . *fond* of her."

A small nod, but he said nothing.

"Domingo, why won't you talk to me?"

He took a deep breath and raised his head, again looking elsewhere, as if he could not bear to look into her eyes.

"Respect," he said softly, then turned away abruptly and started walking up the street, leaving her behind.

She rushed to catch up with him, and when she did she grabbed his elbow without thinking. They stopped again, their feet crunching in the cinders in front of the blacksmith shop as a hammer rang against an anvil in the background.

"Respect?" she said. "Is it respectful to make fun of me, calling me beautiful? Is it respectful to lie to me? There is no respect in words you don't mean."

"But I *did* mean it. You *are* beautiful, and I am very . . . *fond* of you." He shrugged. "But a man does not live only by his feelings. A man must respect another man's fences."

"What is *that* supposed to mean?"

"Look around you. There are beautiful women in the village, but they are married. Everywhere, there are fences. A man who does not respect another man's fences is not an honorable man."

"I am not married."

"No, but you are a *yanqui*, a white woman, and I am Nahua. Your family owns property and I am poor. Then there is your father, and your religion. Fences."

"What has my father to do with it?"

Domingo turned and started walking again, but she clung tightly to his arm and kept up. An old woman in front of the butcher shop stopped to stare at her prayer kapp. Miriam ignored her.

"I have worked on your farm for a year now," Domingo said, "and I have learned enough about the Amish to know that your father would not wish to see his daughter with a half-breed Mexican. I have great respect for your father and I will not betray his trust."

"Then you *are* fond of me, but you hold back because of my father?"

"Jah, and your religion."

"Because I am Amish?"

"Because you are Christian."

"But, Domingo, your own mother is a Christian."

"Jah, and it was never easy for them. Because my mother was a Christian, she saw the world in a different way."

"All right, then tell me. How does a Christian see the world so differently from a Nahua?"

Two little boys chased each other down the street and dodged right between Miriam and Domingo, forcing them apart, but then he held out his arm for her to take it again as they walked.

"In ancient days," he said, "the Nahua earned the favor of the gods by conquering other tribes and offering the lives of their prisoners—their *enemies*—as a sacrifice. Ours is a religion of the strong, and in Mexico it is good to be strong. But the Spaniards brought with them a new religion that tells us we should be kind to our enemies and sacrifice *ourselves*. Their priests tell us we should be content to be poor and enslaved, that we should turn the other cheek, that we should grovel in the dust and bear insult with meekness and gratitude—insult at the hands of the very Spaniards who brought us this religion."

"But the Bible says—"

"*Your* bible. Not mine."

She stared at him then, at the fire in his eyes.

"You are full of anger."

"Three hundred years' worth," he answered.

The truth of this was in the set of his jaw. A history of conflict and oppression lay deep in his bones. He was too close to it. Only an outsider, a yanqui with the pacifist underpinnings of the Amish, could see the whole picture, and she had to try to make him see it. She squeezed his arm and spoke softly.

"Where will it end, Domingo? The Nahua conquer other tribes, the Spaniards conquer the Nahua, the revolutionaries conquer the Spaniards, and one day someone will conquer the revolutionaries. Bloodshed begets only anger, and more bloodshed. Don't you see? Ours is a Gott of love. The only way for men to live in peace is to conquer anger itself, and the only way to do that is through forgiveness—through love. You will not find forgiveness with a gun in your hand. Sooner or later someone must say *enough*. When men find the courage to lay down their weapons and listen to each other, *then* they will find peace."

His expression did not change. "Spoken like a Christian," he said, and it did not have the ring of a compliment. "But this is Mexico. Here a man must fight or die. In the end, I think Mexico will tell us whose god is right, Cualnezqui. Your father would die for what he believes, and I admire him for that, even if I do not understand him. I admire you too, for you are not only beautiful, you are wise and good. But this is a very high fence, Cualnezqui, and you must understand that my feelings are not important. I will respect your father's fences, no matter what I feel."

His reasons were sound and his words well chosen, but they still stung. Maybe it was the pain of rejection, or maybe it was because they were nearing the mercado where Rachel might see them, but Miriam let go of his arm. Warring emotions raged inside of her as she pulled away and withdrew behind the safety of a blank stare. Her lips tightened into a thin line and the words came out flat and colorless.

"Then please stop calling me Cualnezqui. My name is Miriam."

Chapter 5

While Ira and John mapped out their plots and broke ground for houses, their sons started digging a huge irrigation well just like the one Caleb and his sons had dug the year before. Miriam and Rachel spent the next week teaching the boys how to make adobe out of the dirt from the well; the girls had become experts while making all the bricks for their own house and outbuildings. John Hershberger put Jake in charge of the brickmaking crew, and Rachel took singular delight in showing him how it was done.

Miriam watched them together, saw the way Jake looked at her younger sister, the way he listened to her, respected her. The way he *smiled* at her. They were very good together, and it was a little irritating after what had happened with Domingo.

Fortunately, she didn't see Domingo very often. He was only a hired hand, so most of the time he was off somewhere plowing or planting or helping build one of the new houses. Her heart still leaped when she saw him, even at a distance, but her face kept her feelings secret. Domingo probably didn't even know he had torn a hole in her heart. She would wait, and take whatever came. Either Domingo's heart would change or the pain would wear away over time.

Twice a week Miriam taught school for the Amish kids, as well as any of the local Mexican children who wished to attend. Through the winter Domingo had attended her class regularly, pretending to ride herd over his two boisterous nephews while he learned to read along with the children. But when the planting started in late February, he stopped coming to class. What with the building of two new houses across the valley and the planting of oats and wheat and corn and clover, he claimed he didn't have time for school, but Miriam suspected he was avoiding her. In spite of her own discomfort, she fervently hoped he would continue to sharpen his reading skills, if only by reading the copy of *Don Quijote* she had given him at Christmas.

In her spare time Miriam helped Emma plant trees. Levi and Ezra, Miriam's brothers-in-law, had finished both their houses in late fall and now were busy plowing their own fields, turning the new soil again and again to let the sun kill the weeds. Her sister Emma, Levi's wife, grew bigger by the day that spring, her second child due to be born in late summer. Emma kept house for Levi, tended her kitchen garden, cared for little Mose, and spent what little spare time she had putting out trees. The trees were Emma's passion. She missed the forests of home, and when she wrote to ask the newcomers to bring trees they overwhelmed her with saplings and seeds and nuts from Ohio. Every day she and her growing belly could be seen planting oaks in strategic spots around the houses so they would one day provide shade, planting lines of poplars and elms along the driveways and scattering an army of maples and fruit trees along the edge of the woods at the base of the ridge.

Miriam kept very busy that spring, telling herself in dark private moments that Domingo was right about the fences, and it was for the best. But the dream of the stallion and the jaguar came to her again one night, as vividly as the first time, and it haunted her. Try as she might she could not banish him from her heart. She could not stop herself from hearing the whispered word *cualnezqui,* and she could not shake the feeling that the recurring dream was a veiled premonition of things to come, a disturbingly clear vision from Gott himself. All her life her religion had taught her to be careful of what she wanted, but now she was learning that the wanting itself was not always a choice. Most of the time a girl could choose what she would *have,* but she could not always choose what she *wanted.* The wanting simply would not go away. Domingo had captured her heart, and like it or not, she wanted him.

But he made no move toward her. Domingo stopped by at Hershberger's once while she was helping the boys make bricks, and she couldn't keep herself from making eye contact. When he made a little joke she couldn't keep herself from laughing a little louder than the others, and when he made a casual observation about the bricks she was the first to acknowledge his expertise. But he made no move toward her. He was polite and treated her exactly the same way he treated everyone else, but nothing more.

And he no longer called her Cualnezqui.

⟳

The spring had passed and the trees on the ridges had leafed out by the time Ira Shrock looked up and realized they were very late in getting the lumber they needed from up in the mountains.

"We should go soon," he said to John as they were lunching on leftovers on the back of the wagon one afternoon. "We'll be needing lumber to build barns before harvest, and we don't have any laid by yet."

"Jah, that's right." John took a bite of a biscuit loaded with salt pork and gazed up at the mountains as if he could hear the timber calling him. "It'll need to cure for a couple months, at least. Caleb, do you think we could mebbe borrow your wagon and team one day next week?"

Caleb smiled. "Only if you let me drive it. I'm thinkin' we should let some of the girls go, and make a picnic of it. The mountains ought to be beautiful this time of year. It will be a nice outing for all of us."

"You hear that, Ira?" John's long face split into a grin. "It's a mighty stout old man that calls a day of logging a picnic. Caleb, we'd be glad to have you and your boys along, and bring the girls, too. Many hands make light work."

⁓

Miriam had just finished teaching school for the day when Kyra arrived in the oxcart to pick up her two boys. Kyra was helping stack desks against the back wall and straighten up the buggy shed when Rachel ran in, literally skidding through the doorway, giddy with excitement.

"Miriam, we're going on a picnic in the mountains!" she chirped, bouncing with glee, unable to contain her excitement. "Jake's going, and Dat said we could ride together on the hack, so long as we have a chaperone. Just think, Miriam, a whole day together!"

Miriam smiled. Her younger sister hadn't quite gotten used to the new freedoms that came with being seventeen and able to court openly.

"That's nice. So who else is going?"

"Dat said all the men are going except for Levi and Ezra— somebody has to stay here and keep watch. The children are staying behind with their mothers, but the teenagers are going. It'll be great! Oh, I can't wait to tell Jake."

Kyra slid a desk against the wall, and when she straightened up she pushed a wave of black hair out of her flushed face and spoke to Miriam in Spanish.

"*Que pasa?* I didn't get a word of that." Kyra had learned a little English from Miriam, but Rachel's Dutch was beyond her.

Miriam repeated the news in Spanish, and Kyra's eyes lit up. "A picnic! May I come, too? The mountains are beautiful in early summer. The flowers are all in bloom and I can show you which ones to dig up and bring back for the garden."

"Oh, sí!" Rachel beamed, switching to Spanish. "Mamm will be thrilled. I'll check with Dat, but I'm sure it's all right." Rachel bolted out the door as quickly as she had come in, leaving Miriam and Kyra shaking their heads and chuckling.

A week later the men hitched their draft horses to three heavy wagons, loaded up the axes and saws and log chains they would need and set out before dawn. Caleb took the lead wagon with Domingo. Ira Shrock and John Hershberger drove the second, and Micah Shrock sat in the third one, check lines in hand. Miriam was about to climb up onto the back of Caleb's wagon when he pointed and told her to ride with Micah.

She stood there for a minute with her mouth hanging open, stunned. The last thing she wanted right now was to encourage Micah. Her father had never shown the slightest interest in her love life, and now he was playing matchmaker? Micah would think it was *her* idea. Given a choice, she would rather have ridden anywhere else. She started to argue, but Caleb turned his back before she could answer, so she did as she was told. Then, in the semidarkness, she spotted Kyra sitting in the back of Micah's wagon with her two boys and several of the teenagers, so before she climbed aboard she caught Kyra's eye and jerked a thumb toward the front seat. Kyra grinned and shook her head, but when Miriam's eyes widened and her lips narrowed, Kyra relented and climbed up front. Miriam took the outside seat, keeping Kyra between her and Micah.

Rachel, Jake and Lovina brought up the rear in a hack carrying food and cooking utensils for the day. Miriam turned around and looked back at them as the team lurched forward. Even in the half-light she could see the mischievous grin on Lovina Hershberger's face. At least now she knew who had put her father up to it. She pulled her coat tight about her and faced forward, her lips a tight line.

Micah talked the whole way, mostly about himself. He leaned around Kyra, grinning at Miriam, and prattled on about the farm he would one day have for himself in Paradise Valley. Occasionally she gave him a perfunctory nod and said, "I see," but she didn't even attempt to hold up her end of the conversation. Kyra sat between them trying to keep up, once in a while elbowing Miriam and biting back a knowing smile.

There was a chill in the mountain air even after the sun rose above the peaks. As their wagons climbed the narrow switchback trails they found the terrain as rugged and steep as Fuentes had predicted, but the views were spectacular. The deeper they drove into the mountains the taller and denser the forest grew, with snowcapped peaks looming in the blue distance.

Once, as they lumbered along the steep mountainside, Micah pointed out a grizzly on the opposite slope, nearly a mile away. Shambling into a little clearing, the bear raised her head and sniffed the air.

Kyra said something in Spanish, and Micah didn't understand.

"She says the bear has cubs," Miriam translated.

Micah squinted. "Her eyes are better than mine. I see the mother, but where are the cubs?"

Again Miriam translated, and Kyra answered. "Behind

mama, in the trees. See—she smells the air to make sure they are safe."

They watched for a moment, and sure enough, two fat cubs gamboled into the clearing to join their mother.

"How do you know she's not sniffing for us?" Micah asked with a nervous chuckle.

Kyra shook her head. "She won't come near the wagons, but I am happy she is on the other side of the valley. A mama bear with her *niños* can be a dangerous thing."

Micah nodded thoughtfully. "Well, then I hope she stays over there. I got a shotgun under the seat in case I spot an easy deer, but I'm thinking a twelve gauge wouldn't be much use against a bear."

"No," Kyra said. "It would only make her angry."

❧

High in the mountains the air was sharp and rich with the smell of the forest—damp earth and rotting leaves. When they found the place, the boys went into the woods above the road and set to work cutting large pines, stripping the limbs with axes and sawing logs into twenty-foot lengths with two-man crosscut saws. Always conscious of the land itself, they were careful not to clear-cut the plot, choosing trees some distance apart.

Caleb found a place where the logging road swung up against a little ledge. The draft horses dragged the logs down close to the road with chains, and using a system of planks and ropes and cant hooks and pinch bars the boys were able to roll them onto the wagons without too much difficulty. It was heavy work, but gratifying. Before noon they had one of the wagons loaded and tied down.

The girls built a cooking fire down near the wagons, and by lunchtime a large pot of bean soup was simmering over the coals. The men and boys sat shoulder to shoulder on a log and the girls served them, happy to do their part. It was the Amish way; girls were not expected to cut timber, and men did not cook or wash dishes. After everyone had been served the girls took seats on the hack to eat, and when everyone was through eating they gathered the bowls and spoons. A small cauldron of water hung over the fire, warming for the wash.

The boys wandered back up into the woods. The girls set the hot water on the tail of the hack and rounded up dishes while the three fathers sat by the fire to talk for a bit. Domingo, who at twenty-one did not consider himself one of the boys, stayed by the fire with the men. John Hershberger pulled out a pipe and packed it with tobacco from a drawstring pouch. It was an old homemade corncob pipe, worn smooth and brown about the bottom of the bowl, with an elderberry stem. He pulled a kitchen match from his pocket, struck it with a thumbnail, lit his pipe and flicked the spent match into the fire.

"Those boys are sure eager to work," he said, glancing up the hill where the boys had gone.

Ira frowned. "They work hard, all right," he growled, "when they work. But that Micah likes to play too much. I bet he's got them all wrestling yet. That one's like a little boy sometimes— too much energy and not enough sense."

Miriam shot a brief I-told-you-so glance at Rachel when she overheard this from Ira—Micah's own father supporting her feelings about him. The sound of laughter came from the woods above them, but no ringing of axes. Maybe Ira was right.

Ever the peacemaker, Hershberger gazed thoughtfully at the distant peaks and changed the subject.

"It sure is nice up here," he said, drawing on his pipe. "Not like I thought Mexico would be. Beautiful country, and downright peaceful—so far. The only bandits I seen yet are the ones you brought home with you from Arteaga, Caleb. You think mebbe things are settling down a little bit?"

Caleb shrugged. "They come and go. Sometimes we don't see any for a month or two, and then there will be two or three bands in one week."

Domingo grinned at this.

Hershberger squinted over his pipe, smiling. "*Was ist es*, Domingo? What do you know that we don't?"

"Rumors, that's all," Domingo answered, using High German. "They say there is trouble brewing in the west and many have gone there. The Revolution did not solve *all* our problems, Herr Hershberger. In Mexico there is always trouble somewhere—*federales* and mercenaries moving this way or that. Right now they are busy elsewhere. They will be back."

Chapter 6

When they finished washing dishes Miriam and the other girls went up into the woods with shovels and burlap sacks, looking for flowers, herbs and roots. Kyra and her two boys led the way, and Miriam's dog tagged along, scouting the undergrowth for anything worth chasing.

Miriam envied Kyra just a little—her peasant blouse and colorful embroidered skirt. She always wore her hair down, long and wavy, framing dark flashing eyes that were enough to cause envy all by themselves, even without the flower in her hair. Though Miriam was quite content with her modest Amish appearance, she sometimes felt a tiny sting of envy over Kyra's freedom to put her beauty on display. People often said Miriam and Kyra looked like sisters, and it always gave her a little burst of guilty pride.

The slope was steep but the going fairly easy in the deep shade of the high canopy, where tall pines and massive oaks created a kind of cathedral aura and kept the undergrowth down. Still, patches of sunlight dappled the ground here and there, and the forest floor was dotted with all kinds of wildflowers.

Beside a boulder Miriam found a cluster of large blooms with brown and yellow striped petals. She called Kyra over.

"Tiger flowers," Kyra said. "They will do well in your garden, or in a window box."

Miriam dug them up and stuffed them into a sack. It was only the beginning. Kyra found all sorts of different flowers, and she named every one of them. In a little sunlit meadow she found mounds of dahlias, and in the shade along a trail, banks of pink and white impatiens. There were even orchids clinging to the sides of the trees, like red spiky crowns bursting from a nest of green fronds.

Kyra stopped at a small pine with lush green vines wrapped all around its base.

"Moonflower," she said. "These are lovely on a fence in the evening."

"But there are no blooms," Rachel said.

Kyra laughed. "Not now. They come out when the sun goes down. That's why it is called *moon*flower. You'll see. In the evening it comes alive with big white flowers and the fragrance is wonderful. The ancient Nahua used moonflower vines for all sorts of things, even to make rubber balls for *ulama*, a game like football. Some people make a kind of hair tonic from it."

She knew the names of all the plants, and their uses. They spent two hours prying plants from the ground with shovels, bagging ornamentals and native cures for all kinds of ailments from rheumatism to skin rashes. Kyra knew which plants were good for headaches, stomach cramps, beestings, nausea, even a small weedy-looking thing whose roots she said could be boiled to make a tonic for the common cold. Miriam was about to pull up a pretty little green vine when one of Kyra's boys shoved her away and sent her tumbling.

"*No*, teacher," he said, shaking his head, eyes wide.

Miriam looked up in surprise to find Kyra laughing. "Juan is right—you mustn't touch that one. It is like poison ivy, only

50

a hundred times worse." Then, still giggling, she leaned closer and lowered her voice. "Especially for a man. It does things to a man that we must not speak about."

∽

"We need to hurry," Caleb said, tying down the second load. "It gets dark quick in the mountains." The sun was dropping toward the peaks in the west, and he figured there were maybe three hours of daylight left. Ira took a team of draft horses and drew the loaded wagon up out of the way to make room. Caleb took another team and was maneuvering the last wagon into place when John called out to him.

Four Mexicans on horseback plodded slowly around the bend from behind them. They were dressed in layers of coarse cotton with short-waisted jackets in place of the normal peasant's poncho, and they were bristling with guns and bandoliers. Their heads drooped, sleeping in the saddle, and even the horses' heads hung low as they ambled along.

Caleb's heart stopped and the color drained from his face. The lead horse was a big bicolor Appaloosa, the front half liver-colored, the back half white with leopard spots.

El Pantera.

As they neared the last wagon one of the Belgians snuffled. All four of the bandits looked up at once, saw the wagons and the three men sitting on them. Their pace did not change, but they didn't take their eyes off the Amishmen as they approached and slowly scraped by the line of wagons on the narrow road, occasionally glancing up into the woods. There was no sound from the woods at the moment, but anyone could see that this was a logging operation. The bandits would know there were other men up in the forest, but it wasn't the *men* Caleb was worried about.

The Appaloosa stopped next to Caleb's wagon, and El Pantera's gaunt face glared. A jagged scar ran down across one eye, and the iris was milky white. He and the man behind him both wore slouch hats, while the third bandit wore a shapeless felt sombrero. All of them were heavily armed with pistols, bandoliers across their chests and rifles in their saddle scabbards.

"Buenos días," Caleb said, his voice hoarse. He would not forget that face as long as he lived, but he fervently hoped El Pantera did not remember him. They had met once before, a year ago on Saltillo Road. Domingo had later warned him to keep his daughters away from this man, a white slaver with no conscience, a dangerous man.

El Pantera squinted at him. "I know your face, señor. We have met before."

Sitting on the bench of the empty wagon with the check lines still in his hands, Caleb was paralyzed with fear. He could manage only a slight shake of his head. Words failed him.

John and Ira had not moved, frozen in place, wide-eyed, but there was nowhere to run. The best thing was to remain calm and civil.

El Pantera blinked and his eyes narrowed. He shook a crooked finger at Caleb and his face twisted into an evil grin. "I *remember* you. The road to Arteaga! You were the one with the two beautiful daughters. One of them—the young one—I remember she had red hair. Very pretty. I don't suppose you have brought your lovely daughters with you, no?" He sat a little taller in his saddle, craning his neck toward the woods.

Caleb shook his head, trying to mask his revulsion. "No, Señor Aguilar. They are not here." Technically, they weren't. His daughters were up in the woods. It was a lie, but he saw no choice, and he would repent of it later. If he lived.

"Well then, I don't suppose you have anything to eat. We have traveled far and we are hungry."

"We have already eaten, but there is some soup left," Caleb said weakly. "You are welcome to it."

The ringing of axes came from the woods above, and a moment later the rhythmic rasp of a crosscut saw.

"What about your young friend?" El Pantera said, watching the woods where the noises came from. "The son of Ehekatl. Is that one still with you, señor?"

"Sí." Caleb pointed over his shoulder with a thumb. "He is working. But Domingo is no threat to you, and we have nothing you would want."

El Pantera threw back his head and laughed. "Make no mistake, señor, there are very few men who threaten me, and if I want something I will take it. I am not afraid of your little friend. Now where is that soup?"

While the four bandits dismounted and tied their horses to the wagon, Ira and John climbed down and helped Caleb take the half-empty cauldron from the back of the hack and hang it over the coals. The four bandits rifled through the dishes on the back of the wagon for bowls, then helped themselves to the soup without waiting for it to heat up. They ate standing, drinking straight from the bowls as if they were starving. Even as he turned up the bowl, El Pantera's hard eyes watched the three Amishmen constantly.

Caleb was just beginning to think things might turn out all right when disaster struck. Miriam's dog barked, up the hill to the right, away from the sounds of the logging crew. El Pantera glanced in that direction just as the sound of girlish laughter rolled down through the trees. He said nothing, but his eyes crinkled with a lascivious grin as he turned toward Caleb and nodded slowly, the lie discovered. Without taking his eyes from

Caleb, he casually backhanded the chest of the man next to him and gestured toward the woods where the laughter had come from.

The bandit flinched, then dropped his half-full soup bowl on the ground and scurried up the bank into the woods. Horrible, unthinkable pictures flashed through Caleb's mind, but he felt utterly helpless against such men. All he could do was pray.

John Hershberger's hands shook as he removed his hat and held it against his chest. His daughter Lovina was up in the woods with the others.

"Please, sir. We have done you no harm. We have shared our food and fire with you and shown you only kindness. *Please* do not harm our girls. They are chust children."

El Pantera's head tilted, and his grin turned quizzical. "*No hablo Inglés*," he said. "But I know the sound of begging, and it is music to my ears."

Caleb translated for John, his eyes locked on El Pantera as he spoke. "He says he is not moved by your pleas, John. This man has no conscience. Pray that Gott will intervene."

El Pantera chuckled softly as he squatted down to dip another bowl of soup from the cauldron. When he stood up again he looked over his bowl at Caleb and said, rather ominously, "Tell your tall friend we will be good to his daughter, señor. *Very* good."

Caleb refused to repeat this. He shook his head and said nothing.

∽

Domingo balanced himself atop a large downed pine, walking up the trunk and clipping limbs off with an axe, his bandanna tied around his head to keep his long hair out of his face. Despite the chill in the mountain air, he had long since shed his shirt. His chest was slick with sweat, peppered with wood chips, and he wore only the coarse cotton pants of a peasant. Raising his axe high over his head, he snapped it downward in a powerful stroke aimed at the base of a limb, but his foot slipped as he swung and the axhead overshot the limb. The force of the blow cracked the handle. He raised it up to look at it, then called out to Micah.

"I broke my axe," he said in German.

Micah, who was dragging the sheared limbs out of the way, paused and answered, "There's a spare handle in the back of the wagon, and a hammer to set the wedge."

Domingo nodded, jumped nimbly from the tree trunk and ambled down the hill toward the wagons with his cracked axe.

Halfway there, out of the corner of his eye he caught an odd movement through the trees off to his left, and stopped. Dropping into a crouch to see through the brush, what he saw made his heart race. A hundred yards away, a man was moving stealthily up the slope toward where the girls had gone to hunt flowers, and it was not an Amishman. He could see, even at a hundred yards, that this man wore a pistol at his waist and a sombrero on his head. Domingo's heart pounded. The bandit was surely not alone, but whatever was happening down at the wagons would have to wait because this one was heading directly toward the girls. He would have to be dealt with, and quickly. Gripping his cracked axe tightly near the head, Domingo stalked the bandit like a cat, looping around to take him from behind.

He was unarmed but for the axe, so he moved in short silent bursts from cover to cover, the way his father had taught him. The bandit did not look back, didn't know he was being followed.

The girls fell silent. Domingo had heard their laughter in the woods even while he was cutting limbs, but now there was nothing. Kyra was with them, he knew this much. She would see the bandit before the others, and maybe his sister would find a way to hide until he could get to her.

The bandit slowed, his head scanning side to side, searching the undergrowth. Domingo closed on him little by little, but he was still fifty yards back when the bandit stumbled upon the girls.

There were screams and shouts as he dragged one of Kyra's boys out of the bracken. Miriam's dog bristled and snarled, but the bandit brandished a pistol and Miriam held her back. In the noise and confusion Domingo saw his chance. He broke from cover and charged up the slope, shifting his grip on the axe in case he had to throw it to buy a few seconds. His odds were not good, but there was no other way.

He was still twenty yards away when the bandit heard him and turned. The pistol swung around and came to bear. Domingo kept charging, raising the axe to hurl it, but before he let it go there was a loud metallic *whang*! The bandit's sombrero went flying and his head snapped forward. He crumpled, dropping hard to his knees and pitching face-first into the leaves.

Kyra stood over him, breathing hard, her face flushed, the shovel cocked over her shoulder in case she needed to swing it a second time.

"Beware the mama bear with niños," she hissed.

The others were getting to their feet as Domingo knelt over the unconscious bandit and took the revolver from his hand. Underneath the prone body he found another pistol and a knife.

"Is everyone okay?"

Kyra nodded. "Sí. We are unharmed."

Domingo handed the axe to Miriam. "Stay here until I call you. Tie his hands and keep your shovel close." Then he wheeled about and raced downhill toward the wagons.

Chapter 7

El Pantera flung the bowl away and wiped his mouth on a sleeve. "I wonder what is keeping Gomez," he said. "I should know better than to send an old man to do a young man's—"

He didn't finish the sentence because he glanced up and saw Domingo. The native stood on the edge of the woods, twenty feet up the hill, leveling two pistols at the three bandits.

El Pantera spread his arms and smiled as if he were greeting an old friend. "Finally, we meet the son of Ehekatl once again! How have you been, young one?"

The smile remained on his face, but his hands drifted down, coming to rest on gun butts.

"If I were you, Señor Aguilar," Domingo said calmly, "I would take those pistols out very slowly and put them on the ground. All of you."

El Pantera's leering smile faded, and no one said anything for a long moment. His hands did not move. One of his compadres leaned close to him to whisper something, and all three bandits laughed.

El Pantera pointed. "The guns you are holding, young one—they belong to Gomez, no? Perhaps you should know, before you throw away your life, that old Gomez was always deadly with a rifle, but he could not even hit the ground with those pistols. They don't shoot straight."

Domingo shifted uneasily. "Perhaps it is not the weapon, but the man who holds it."

El Pantera shrugged. His hands had still not moved from his hips, and now the other two pulled their coattails back and spread their feet a little farther apart.

"Ah, well. It is a pity you cannot believe me, young one. So like your father, you are. You did not have to die this day, but I can see in your eyes that your mind is made up. Alas, you will get only one shot. You will miss, and then you will die. After you are gone we will take vengeance on your friends, and what will you have bought with your short life, eh?"

Domingo said nothing, his eyes steady and his hands steadier. There was nothing left to be said. The air crackled like the stillness before a storm.

El Pantera's hands wrapped around the butts of his guns and his shoulders tensed, but in that moment the silence was broken by the double click of two shotgun hammers.

All three bandits turned their heads in unison and looked over their shoulders to see Micah standing beside the wagon with a double-barrel shotgun pointed at them.

Micah said nothing, his eyes hard.

Domingo cleared his throat. "That twelve gauge shoots a very wide pattern, *ladrón*. I have seen it bring down three birds with one shot, and there are two barrels. Perhaps you would like to reconsider."

Caleb, Ira and John had been standing by the hack all this time, afraid to move. Now Caleb stepped forward, his hands out, his voice calm.

"Stop this," he said. "No one has been hurt and no damage

has been done. Why must anyone die? We are men. We can talk."

El Pantera looked at Caleb with vague amusement in his eyes. He seemed to relax as his hands moved away from his guns.

"The *viejo* is right," he said to Domingo. "This is a difficult situation. So what will you do now, young one?"

Domingo had not lowered his guns. "My father spoke of you often, Aguilar. He said you seldom give your word, but when you do, you keep it. Is this true?"

El Pantera stroked his stubbly chin. "It seems a foolish question. If a man is a liar, he will say he is not. But your father was right: I do not give my word lightly."

"I have heard there is trouble in Mexico City. Is that where you were going?"

The bandit grinned. "Sí. There is work there, for a man who knows how to fight."

"Then go there. Give me your word you will not harm these people and we will let you pass."

El Pantera glanced once more at Micah and his twelve gauge, rock steady, bracing himself against the wagon wheel.

A casual shrug. "All right."

"Your word, Aguilar."

El Pantera took off his hat and swept his arms wide in a mock bow, though his lips sneered. "You have my word, son of Ehekatl. I swear on your father's grave we will harm no one and we will not look back . . . *this time*. And will you give Gomez a burial befitting an old soldier?"

Domingo chuckled. "I will be happy to do that if you wish, only Gomez is not dead. He just has a little headache." He turned his head and shouted up into the woods, "Kyra! Bring the bandit down here!"

A minute later, the rustling of leaves grew louder as Gomez

stumbled down out of the trees without his sombrero, his hands tied behind him and three young women following close behind with shovel and axe.

The bandits mounted their horses and started down the road with El Pantera bringing up the rear. At the last, he turned the big Appaloosa around and glared at Domingo.

"I will not forget this day, young one. Mark my words—we will meet again, and you will *pay*."

Then he spun about and spurred his horse to catch up. Miriam's German shepherd, still bristling and snarling, gave chase for a hundred yards before she came trotting back with her tongue hanging out. Micah kept the shotgun trained on El Pantera's back until he was completely out of sight.

Miriam stayed back, watching from the edge of the woods until the bandits were gone. She was shocked to see Micah pointing his shotgun at them, but she was utterly stunned by what happened next.

Ira Shrock stalked quickly over to his eldest son, who still held the shotgun cradled in his arms, and slapped him. Hard. Ira's jaw was working, his face beet red, his whole body twitching with rage, and there was fire in his eyes.

"*What did you think you were doing, boy?*" Ira bounced on his toes, his fists clenched as he fired the words at Micah's face. "Why on earth would you even *think* of threatening a man's life like that? Would you really want to spend eternity in *hell?*"

Micah, a head taller, looked down at his red-faced father with a blank expression, his feelings hidden but for a trace of thinly veiled indignation in his eyes.

"They said they would take vengeance on us," he answered quietly.

Ira drew back and slapped him again, harder. "They *said?*

TALK! A heathen's words are mostly *lies*, son! Did you see them harm anyone? Did they ever take their guns out of their holsters? NO! You come mighty close to casting yourself into hell forever when you point a shotgun at a man who didn't do nothing but *eat some of our soup*! Would you become a murderer over a bowl of *soup*?"

Domingo had apparently heard enough. He turned and slipped quietly up into the woods.

Micah had not moved, the shotgun still cradled in his arms. "I could have repented of it later, and they—"

Ira slapped him again. Micah's head swiveled and came back to where it was, only now his mouth was closed tight.

"And what if they *killed* you? Did you think of that, boy? What if they shot you down even as you murdered one or two of them? Would you face Gott with blood on your hands? FOOL!"

Ira railed and fumed for another minute or two while Caleb and John stood some distance away with their arms folded and their backs turned, pretending not to hear. Miriam understood this, too. She did not agree, though it did not escape her notice that she too had declined to speak up. Ira was his father. It was his right, his responsibility, and none of them would interfere. Ever.

When Ira finally ran out of words he stalked off down the road toward the last wagon, presumably to cool himself off. The other boys had come to see what was happening and heard the whole tirade. Now they quietly faded back up into the woods, and Micah remained by the wheel of the lead wagon, staring at the shotgun in his hands, blood trickling from the corner of his mouth.

When she judged that Ira was far enough away Miriam padded softly down the bank and went over to Micah.

"Are you all right?"

A slight nod. He didn't look at her. There was a distinct handprint on his cheek, and the beginning of a bruise.

"Micah."

After a few seconds his head turned and he looked down at her.

"Micah, it's all right. Whatever you meant to do, just ask and it will be forgiven. You're alive. We're *all* alive, thanks to you, and ours is a Gott of mercy."

A thin line of silver appeared in the bottoms of his eyes and he looked away from her again, embarrassed.

Softly she said, "Micah, tell me the truth—tell *yourself* the truth. You would not really have killed those men, would you?"

The pain in his eyes deepened as he looked down at the shotgun in his hands. His thumb moved over the top of the stock to the lever that released the breech, and he pushed it sideways. The shotgun broke in the middle, twin barrels hinging down.

Miriam's mouth opened but she couldn't speak, tears springing to her own eyes as she reached out slowly and brushed a fingertip across the empty barrels where the shells should have been.

She reached up then, with the same finger, and gently turned his chin so that he faced her.

"Micah, you mean to tell me it was never loaded? *The whole time?*"

He nodded grimly.

"Then why didn't you say something to your dat? Why didn't you tell him, Micah? Why did you just stand there mute?"

What she saw in his eyes then was almost too painful to bear, but at last he spoke. In a voice that had been scraped raw by a fierce, proud anger, he said, "It would have done no good. *Nothing* pleases him."

As if to put an exclamation point on his words, he snapped

the shotgun shut. Leaning into the wagon, he shoved it under the seat, then turned away and strode up into the woods with his fists buried deep in his pockets.

She let him go. He needed to be alone, and there was nothing left to say. There were things she did not understand about men and probably never would, but it was a fact that sometimes a man, faced with a pain too great to endure, would simply choose to do nothing. Sometimes he would see no option but to stand there like a mule in a downpour and bear it.

Two hours later the last wagon was loaded and tied down. The shadows grew long, the sun just touching the western peaks. They would have to hurry to get the heavily laden wagons over the worst of the mountain trails before darkness fell.

While the men hitched up the horses, Miriam scrambled on top of the logs with Kyra and her boys, but when she looked back and saw Micah alone on the seat of the last wagon, she climbed down without a word and went to sit beside him.

Sensing that he needed company, if not words, she sat close to him. Neither of them said anything for a long time as he wrestled and cajoled his team of Belgians up and down the mountain ridges. But later, as the sun dipped behind the hills and the clouds turned to simmering coals, she bumped him with a shoulder and said quietly, "Are you okay?"

He nodded. "A couple hours with an axe can cure a lot."

"It's good you can bounce back so easy."

He glanced down at her and smiled a little, then his eyes went back to the road. "It's not so hard if you've had plenty of practice."

"Your father gets like that often?"

A shrug.

"You should have told him the gun wasn't loaded, Micah."

"He would have hit me again, for talking back. Once his hackles are up, he can't hear nothing. I'm never so good as he thinks I *should* be, but I'm never so bad as he thinks I am."

"All the more reason. If you help him see the good in you, maybe he will soften."

But Micah's eyes hardened, his upper lip curving into a sneer as he barked orders and snapped the reins, urging the horses up a little grade.

"Let him think what he will. The son he *thinks* he has is the one he deserves."

Chapter 8

On the long drive home Caleb constantly scanned the lengthening shadows of rocks and trees for signs of an ambush. But they were only shadows, devoid of threat. Perhaps El Pantera was, after all, a man who kept his word. The log-laden wagons encountered no more trouble on the return trip, arriving at the farm well after dark. Exhausted by a long day of hard work and a tense ride home, Caleb slept that night as one dead.

The next morning the men gathered at the saw pit. By the time the sun had climbed enough to take away the night chill the older sons had already shed their coats and sweated through their shirts as they drew the two-man ripsaw rhythmically up and down, up and down, slicing logs into lumber.

As Caleb and John put their shoulders into cant hooks and rolled a fresh log onto the trestle, Ira walked up. He leaned his forearms on the edge of the wagon.

"Caleb, we need to talk," he said. "We got to do something about these bandits before somebody gets killed or, Gott forbid, they do harm to our daughters."

Caleb climbed down from the wagon and John followed, lighting his pipe.

"I'm not sure what we can do," Caleb said. "I'm as fearful of these men as you are, Ira. They are hard men, without conscience, but would you become as they are? In the end I think we must do everything we can to avoid provoking them. We must not become their enemies."

There were gray circles under Ira's eyes. He had not slept well, and even now his red face was clouded with worry. "That kind of thinking may be fine for most of these vermin, Caleb, but this El Pantera fills me with dread. What kind of country is this, where evil men do as they please without anyone to stop them?"

"I will stop them," Domingo's voice said. He had come up behind Ira and overheard most of the conversation. "I will stop them if I can, but you must understand a few things, Herr Shrock. Most of the people you will meet are ordinary hardworking farmers like you, but there has been a war. Now that it is over, these northern hills are full of Pancho Villa's rabble, men from the border towns who were swindlers and thieves before they were soldiers. El Pantera's men fought with Villa during the Revolution, and it was there that they learned to storm a hacienda, to slaughter and rape and take what they want. It is not easy for some men to unlearn such things."

Ira stared hard at the young native as he took off his hat and poncho and laid them under the wagon seat.

"This is what comes of war," Ira said. "It kills a man's conscience and makes him capable of all manner of abominations. This El Pantera is such a man, and what is to stop him from coming here?"

Domingo pulled his hair back and tied a bandanna around his head. "I have told you, he will not come here, because he was Pancho Villa's man, and Villa has never allowed his men to attack El Prado. As long as Villa lives, El Pantera will not come to Paradise Valley."

John Hershberger drew on his pipe and said thoughtfully, "But there must be others who do not belong to Villa's army. Surely the new government will protect its people from such men."

"Jah, but the federales are spread thin. There are policemen in the cities and towns, but you have come to a far corner of the mountains. Here, we must protect *ourselves.*"

The eyes of Ira and John were full of angst as they watched him unfasten his gun belt and lay it in the wagon on top of his poncho.

"Domingo," Caleb said, "if you were us, what would you do?"

"If I were you I would arm myself and do what is necessary to protect my family." Domingo spoke matter-of-factly, but he could not hide a little smirk—Caleb's young friend knew what the Amish answer would be.

It was John who confirmed it. "We cannot do this."

Ira's face flushed red and he jabbed a finger at Domingo. "We *will* not do this! Better to die once than burn in hell forever."

Domingo cocked his head as if something about Ira puzzled him, but he said nothing.

Caleb sighed. Despite his own misgivings it had become clear that his neighbors would never rest until he made an appeal to the government for help. He laid a calming hand on Ira's shoulder.

"I believe it is our Christian duty to make peace with all men as far as we are able and trust Gott to protect us, but mebbe there is something more we can do. The hacendado once told me about a man in Monterrey, a Señor Montoya, the government official who decides where to send troops. I did not want to appeal to him, but mebbe if it would help you sleep easier, I suppose it would do no harm to write a letter. Perhaps we can persuade him to send a few troops to Paradise Valley."

Domingo shook his head. "It is too easy for a bureaucrat to ignore a letter from a gringo, Herr Bender. He probably will do nothing anyway, but if you want his attention you must go to Monterrey and talk to him yourself."

After a lengthy discussion they decided it was best to present a united front; there was strength in numbers. All three of them would go to Monterrey, along with Domingo.

The trip took a whole week. Driving home, as he came back into Paradise Valley, Caleb could see Mamm from a great distance, watching him from the driveway. Nervous ever since Domingo thwarted the bandit attack on Saltillo Road, she fretted constantly when any of her family was away from home.

Over supper Caleb told everyone what had happened in Monterrey.

"We had to wait two whole days just to get in," he said. "Señor Montoya's office was in a big fancy building with marble floors and tall columns. After two days waiting, he listened to us for five minutes and then told us he could not help us. He waved his arms and said there is trouble everywhere in Mexico, little uprisings here and there because of rumors about the new government shutting down the Catholic churches. The federales at his disposal are all very busy, and he could not be concerned with a handful of yanqui farmers who were not even born in his country. He also said it costs a lot of money to feed soldiers and buy horses for them. After we left Monterrey on the train going back to Arteaga to get the buggy, Domingo told us that this last thing Señor Montoya said was all that really mattered."

Mamm's head tilted. "You mean about the money?"

"Jah. Señor Montoya was hinting that he wanted money for himself. This is how it works with the officials here. If you want something, you have to pay somebody to get it. If you don't want to pay, then get out of the way because there is always someone else who *will* pay."

Mamm's face fell then, first into a puzzled frown, and then into a kind of weary acceptance.

"We don't have that much money, do we?"

Caleb shook his head, and the same weary look came into his eyes.

"No, Mamm," he said quietly. "We don't."

Chapter 9

By mid-July Caleb's corn was in and he needed to make a trip to Saltillo to sell some of it. The new irrigation well across the valley was finished, so John Hershberger went along to buy a windmill. Domingo rode with them for protection, and Caleb took Miriam and Micah along to sell the produce.

"Shame we have to go so far to market," John said as the farm wagon trundled through the low country in midday. "A day there, a day back, and a day in the market—three days is a long time to leave the wife and children alone."

Caleb nodded. "They told us there would be a new rail line from Arteaga to Paradise Valley pretty soon. I still don't see any sign of it, though. Things don't move too quick in Mexico."

After traveling all day they camped outside Arteaga for the night, and early the next morning drove on to Saltillo. Stacking produce on a makeshift plank table in the market, Miriam couldn't help noticing the worry in her father's eyes when he insisted that Micah stay with her while the men went on to the foundry with the wagon.

The market street was crowded as usual. Señora Teresa Tomasina was there, and she remembered Miriam from previous visits. It seemed the toothless old woman was always in the market selling something when Miriam came there.

Again, as she always did, the old woman warned her about the niños. Miriam smiled and nodded respectfully, then explained to Micah about the pickpocket children roaming the streets. She was an old hand by now and had learned to hide her money where little hands could not reach it.

Micah's lip curled into a sneer. "Thieves. I'm starting to think Mexicans are born knowing how to steal. Let them try."

"They're just children," she said. "This country has been at war for a long time. Many of these children have no father to teach them or provide for them. They do whatever they can to survive."

"Well, stealing is not the way. Someone should tell them you can go to hell for it."

"Perhaps someone should teach them a better way."

He eyed her cautiously. "Is that what your school is about? You're going to teach these little thieves a better way?"

"Stealing is what they do—it's not who they are."

He knifed a hand on the table for emphasis and said, "If you steal, you're a thief. That's who you are. And I'm not so sure it's a good idea for Amish children to be in school all day with thieves."

She pondered this for a second and answered calmly, "I was thinking mebbe it would be good for thieves to be in school all day with Amish children. And an Amish teacher."

"Jah, that might be, but it might be that you think too much about the children of the World and not enough about the ones in your own family."

She could see from the look in his eyes that his mind was

made up about the pickpocket niños, so she let it drop. Micah had not lived in Mexico long enough to really know the people. Perhaps in time he would understand.

They sold most of their produce during the day. By late afternoon the crowd had thinned and Micah and Miriam had nothing to do. They leaned on their elbows on their rough plank table, getting drowsier by the minute in the summer sun. Señora Teresa Tomasina sat back in a rickety chair by her produce stand, her head thrown back under a floppy shapeless gardening hat, cooling her brown leather neck with a paper fan. The streets of Saltillo were much warmer than the high plateau of Paradise Valley.

There was a commotion on the far end of the street, and Miriam looked up. She heard wailing and shouting, saw people running. The uproar swelled and spread, rolling toward her like a wave. A young Mexican woman in a long painted skirt ran down the middle of the street, arms waving over her head, black hair flying, screaming something as she ran. Across the street a man stepped out from behind a cart of oranges and suddenly fell to his knees, knocking his sombrero to the ground as he grabbed his head in anguish. Everywhere, people ran this way and that, wailing.

As the young Mexican woman drew nearer, Señora Teresa Tomasina rose from her chair and came to see what the fuss was about. When she finally understood the words the girl was shouting, Señora Tomasina crossed herself, bowed her old head, and began praying to the Virgin Mary.

"Francisco Villa está muerto!" the young woman wailed as she passed. "Some devil has murdered him! Pancho Villa is dead!"

The wave of anguish rolled over them and passed on down the street as peons spilled out of doorways and alleys and ran screaming or fell to their knees in despair.

Miriam told Micah what was happening, and he looked at her in near panic. The city was in turmoil, and they were separated from Caleb and John.

Micah's eyes were full of worry. "What will we do? The streets are overrun, and the whole city must be this way. How will they get to us with the wagon?"

"I don't know, but they will find a way." She stared down the street across the growing tumult. "Jah," she said, nodding calmly, "Domingo is with them. They will find a way."

"Domingo," Micah muttered. "Always Domingo. Sometimes I think you put too much faith in him. He is only a Mexican."

She opened her mouth to answer, but two strong hands gripped her shoulders from behind. She jumped and spun around.

"Domingo!" Miriam cried, her eyes wide. "Where did you come from? Where is Dat?"

"Come with me," he snapped. "Quickly!" He grabbed Miriam's arm and began to drag her the wrong way down the street.

Micah hesitated, standing by the remains of the produce glaring at Domingo. "What about the corn? What about our boards and bricks?"

"Leave it!" Domingo yelled over his shoulder. "Follow me, *now*!"

Micah finally bolted after them, leaving everything behind, elbowing his way through the crowd in the chaotic street until he caught up with them. At the next corner Domingo led them to the right and down an alley to the next street over, where it was not so crowded. Running as fast as they could manage in the chaos, the three of them went barreling around the corner of a leather shop and nearly ran into the back of the wagon. Dat was sitting up front with the reins in his hand, waiting.

Micah wheeled about and caught Miriam by the waist, in one swift motion hoisting her bodily up onto the back of the wagon between two large crates. Domingo ran around to the front and vaulted up into the seat. Caleb had already snapped the reins and called out sharply to the two Belgians that leaned into their heavy load. The wagon heaved forward.

Miriam found a place to sit in the back among a wagonload of steel parts, piles of angle iron and pipe, boxes of bolts and sheets of corrugated tin. Micah settled in next to her and held on while Caleb pushed the horses to a trot, hurrying out of the city with his cargo.

"Why is everyone so fearful?" Micah asked.

"Somebody murdered Pancho Villa," Miriam said.

"Jah, I heard that. But the whole city has gone mad, everyone running wild as if the murderer was chasing them himself. Did it happen in Saltillo?"

"No, I heard someone say he was driving near his hacienda in Parral when someone shot his automobile full of holes."

"Then why is there such turmoil in Saltillo?"

"Because he was *Pancho Villa.* He was a great leader, a man of the people. He was almost a god to them, and now their hope is crushed. There is no telling what they will do when their grief turns to anger. Domingo said we need to be clear of the towns before nightfall."

Micah stared at her then, and his eyes narrowed. He leaned close. "Domingo again," he whispered. "You really like that Mexican, don't you?"

She met his eyes. "Everyone likes him—except Schulman. Domingo is our friend."

"That's not what I meant. That day when we were logging and he pointed his guns at those bandits, standing there all sweaty, without his shirt, wearing that rag around his head like an Indian, I saw the way you looked at him, Miriam."

Her jaw tightened. Crossing her arms, she broke eye contact

to stare at her father's back. "The look you saw in my face was fear. I was afraid they were going to kill him. They would have, if not for you. I haven't forgotten that, either."

Micah would say no more, but it was clear from his bristling silence that he was not satisfied with her answer.

Domingo found a safe harbor for the night in a little hollow of the foothills between Arteaga and the first mountain pass. They made camp, and Miriam cooked dinner over a campfire. Afterward, the men sat around the fire talking while she cleaned up and washed dishes at the back of the wagon. She was drying the last of the dishes by lantern light when Micah came up behind her, touched her shoulder and spoke quietly.

"I'm sorry about what I said in the wagon, Miriam—about you and Domingo." He was holding his hat in his hands, turning it slowly by the brim, looking down at it. "I'm not so good at knowing how to talk to a girl, that's all."

This, she understood. Sometimes the best of men didn't know how to speak to a woman.

"It's all right." But she didn't look at him. She finished drying a bowl and packed it into the box at her feet. He didn't go away. Clearly, there was something else he wanted to say.

"A question is in my mind," he said. "Why am I here?"

"What do you mean?"

"I mean, why was I asked to come along on this trip? Hershberger has sons of his own, and he has Jake, too. He could have brought one of them to Saltillo, but he didn't—he asked me to come instead." Micah was still turning that hat in his hands, staring at it, when he mumbled, "I guess I was hoping John invited me because you asked him to, that's all."

Miriam straightened up and looked at him. A lantern hissed softly on the tail of the wagon, casting dark shadows in the lines of his face.

"It wasn't me, Micah. And I doubt that it was John, either. You're right, he would have brought one of his own unless . . ."

Miriam cast a sideways glance at the three men sitting around the fire. Domingo's hands worked the air, telling an animated story, while Caleb whittled on a stick and John sat smoking his pipe.

"Unless what?"

"Unless my dat asked him to bring you along." She hadn't thought about it until now, but it was the only explanation.

"Your father? Why would he do that?"

A little smile crept onto her face. "It can only be that he's worried about his nineteen-year-old daughter becoming an old maid schoolteacher. I never knew my dat to play matchmaker before. But wait . . ." She shook a finger, remembering. "He *did* tell me to ride with you the day we went logging."

Micah's shoulders sagged and a sadness came into his eyes. "I thought you rode with me because you wanted to," he muttered.

"Oh, I *did*—when we were coming home. But my dat told me to ride with you that morning, when we were heading out."

Micah's face softened and his lips moved silently, working over the words he wanted to say before he said them.

"Well, I'm glad for that. It was mighty fine having you beside me all the way home. Miriam, I know I'm not the smartest man in the world but I'm strong and hardworking and honest and . . . and I like you an awful lot." He looked her in the eyes, hesitating. "I want to tell you that I liked you from the first time I saw you. You're pretty, and it makes me feel good when I'm with you. I'd like to call on you if it's all right."

Miriam had seen brief glimpses of his humble side before, but rarely. In the company of other boys he was dominating, yet she had already seen that he was a different person when no one else was around. She almost glanced over at the fire again, at Domingo, but she caught herself. Her heart still quickened when she saw the native working shirtless in the sun with a bandanna around his head, or heard his laughter from the fields, or saw the graceful way he mounted his horse. There was a rare and irresistible power in him, tinged with wildness, and she was certain he had feelings for her as well. But he was an outsider, and in the end that path could only lead to shame and disgrace and separation from her family. Anyway, he'd had his chance. That day in town she'd given him every opportunity to speak his feelings, but he'd refused.

Now here was Micah. The only suitable Amish boy in the entire country wanted to court her, and her dat was on his side. She trusted her dat, trusted his judgment. If he thought enough of Micah to push him on his daughter, then maybe she should give the boy a chance.

She nodded. "All right. You may call on me."

Micah's face broke into a wide grin and he leaned forward impulsively as if he meant to kiss her, but she pulled back, glancing at her father sitting right there no more than forty feet away.

Micah settled his hat back on his head, following her glance to the three men by the fire, nodding slowly. She could not tell if he was staring at her father or Domingo.

"I will win you," he said. "No matter what it takes, I will win you." With a casual ease he hoisted the heavy food box onto the wagon for her before he strode back over to the campfire with a smile on his face and a new bounce in his step.

Chapter 10

A few days later, Miriam and her sisters joined the older women for a quilting bee in the Benders' living room. Ira's and John's wives were there, along with Lovina Hershberger. Emma, Miriam's married sister, was getting very large, her time drawing near as the summer warmed. While Emma stitched, her baby Mose crawled around on the floor. As the light from the windows faded from blue to purple Emma got up to light the lanterns and asked, "Where are the boys?"

Mamm looked up. "Oh, Harvey's in the tack room yet, mending harness, and Aaron went down to Ezra's to visit with the twins."

Miriam smiled. "One of them, anyway. Aaron can't make it through the day without seeing his nephew."

"Does my heart good, the way he dotes on that child," Mamm said. "I can't believe your dat let him give Little Amos a harmonica, though. His tiny hands couldn't even hold on to it."

They all fell silent for a moment, remembering. Aaron's twin brother, Amos, had kept a harmonica for years, playing it in secret, or so he thought. Everyone knew, and cherished the memory.

Hunched over the edge of the quilt frame, Lovina said absently, "Dat got a letter today saying Freeman Coblentz's are coming down in the spring, and a lot more people next summer. Hannah Coblentz said there might even be a preacher in the summer crowd."

Esther Shrock, Ira's wife, looked up from her stitching and her eyes widened. "Really? A minister? That's wonderful news!"

"Jah, now we can have baptisms," Lovina's mother said.

Lovina cast a mischievous sideways glance at Rachel and added, "And weddings, too."

"Shush," Rachel said, blushing, pretending to concentrate on her work.

But it was too late. The older women peppered her with questions, and Lovina primed the pump at every turn. Rachel managed to dodge most of their questions—after all, a couple's talk of marriage was a very private matter—but her face turned as red as her hair, and Miriam knew she and Jake had been talking about it.

Then Lovina turned the same mischievous smile on Miriam. "And Rachel might not be the *only* one thinking about a wedding."

All hands stopped, and all eyes turned to Miriam.

"Oh?" Mamm said, her needle pausing halfway through a square of fabric. "Miriam, is there something we don't know?"

Lovina mouthed the words silently, *Miriam and Micah.*

Miriam's eyes narrowed and she glared, but Lovina wouldn't let up.

"She rode with Micah when we went logging that day."

"There was nowhere else to sit," Miriam countered.

"The road was rough, too. I guess that's why you had to sit close and hold onto his arm, then. Oh, and she rode home from Saltillo with him in the back of Dat's wagon the other day, too." Her eyes danced, watching Miriam squirm.

Miriam could have cheerfully strangled Lovina in that awkward moment, with Micah's mother sitting at the table.

"Is this true?" Esther Shrock asked. There was an unmistakable twinkle in her eye. "Are you and Micah courting, Miriam?"

She hesitated for a long awkward moment, thinking. Over the last few days, since she'd agreed to let Micah call on her, a host of conflicting emotions had assailed her. It wouldn't do for anyone to see the pictures flashing through her head, or hear the voices—Domingo and his talk of fences, the rage in Ira's face as he slapped his son and the pain in Micah's eyes. Miriam really didn't want to discuss any of these things in front of Esther Shrock. Privately she knew her infatuation with Domingo was not quite dead and buried, nor was she entirely sure how she felt about Micah, even now. It might have only been pity that made her decide to let him court her.

But everyone at the table was staring, waiting for an answer.

She looked up at Esther Shrock and heard herself saying, "Jah. Micah and I are courting."

They meant well, she knew that. The way they carried on—Esther Shrock and Mamm beaming, exchanging knowing glances as if they could already see themselves as in-laws. It was a great compliment in its way. Miriam expected it, and yet they seemed a little *too* happy at the news of her courting. In the end their exuberance was very nearly insulting, as if they were saying, We thought you would *never* find a man.

⟨⟩

Later, when the house was quiet and dark and everyone else had gone to sleep, Miriam rolled over in bed, leaned up on an elbow and whispered, "Rachel, are you awake?"

"No. I'm sound asleep."

Miriam could hear the grin in her voice. Rachel was enjoy-ing this, too.

"Did you see the way that little vixen put me on the spot?"

She felt the little quiver in the bed, Rachel giggling silently. After a moment the giggling stopped and Rachel said, "There's nothing to be ashamed about, Mir. I *like* Micah. He's a good man, and you saw how he faced down those bandits. He's very brave. He'll be good for you."

"Maybe," Miriam conceded, but a question nagged her as she laid her head back down on her pillow. *He might be good for me, but will he be good to me?* She felt as if part of him was kept hidden, and most of the time he seemed almost haughty. The things he was proudest of—his brute strength and fierce competitiveness—worried her. Too often a boy ended up being just like his father, and after what she'd seen at the logging camp that was a troubling thought.

In the middle of the night the dream came to her again. Once again she awoke in a sweat, Domingo's face filling her mind.

"This is unfair," she whispered through her hands, sitting up in bed. "But it will pass. Surely it will pass."

⁓

On a Saturday afternoon at the very end of July Emma went to water the trees she had planted. As the sun sank in the west and a golden light slanted across ripening fields she put a barrel in the back of the hack, pumped it full from the well and made her weekly rounds.

Half finished with the trees along her father's long driveway, she straightened up, a bucket in one hand and the other pressed against the small of her back, straining against the counterweight of her swollen belly. *Soon now*, she thought, *Levi's second child will come into the world.*

She handed the empty bucket up to Ada, who dipped it into the barrel and handed it back. Emma smiled at her sister, but Ada only rolled her bottom lip into her mouth and chewed on it. At twenty-eight she was the oldest of Caleb's daughters, but she had the mind of a child. In need of continuity and familiarity, Ada mourned the loss of her Ohio home more deeply than the others, but she'd been doing better lately, visited less frequently by frightful bouts of depression and hysteria. It helped to keep her busy, and Ada was always glad to do her part when she could, which meant whenever the task was simple enough for a child. Emma sometimes wondered what demons swooped like dusky bats through her older sister's mind in the dark hours, but Ada seldom spoke, and when she did it was usually only mimicry of something she'd heard Mamm say.

Emma had bent over to pour water on a little poplar sprig when she heard hoofbeats—Domingo, heading home for the day. He slowed and stopped, hopped down and tied the horse to the back of the hack.

She admired his horse. "Star is looking like her old self these days. You've been kind to her."

"I would be a fool not to. She is a fine animal," Domingo said, stroking his horse's face. "A great gift."

His head tilted and an eyebrow went up as he appraised Emma's ballooning waistline. "Emma, you should not be doing such work. That baby is coming any time now."

He reached out, beckoning with his fingers, and she handed over the bucket. The first time he bent down to pour from it his hat fell off. He picked up the flat-brimmed hat and sailed it up to Ada, who fumbled it against her chest, dropped it into the water barrel, then fished it out half full and jammed it on her own head, dousing her white kapp and clapping her hands with childlike glee as water ran down her face.

Emma walked beside Domingo as he hauled water and Ada filled the bucket, his hat cocked absurdly on her head.

"These trees will change the face of Paradise Valley," Emma said wistfully. "Someday this will be a beautiful shady lane. I can just see it."

Domingo smiled, carrying water, saying nothing until Micah's courting buggy passed by them, trotting briskly along.

Micah waved as he passed, Miriam sitting primly beside him with her hands folded in her lap. She barely acknowledged Emma and Domingo before her eyes went back to the front, expressionless.

Emma glanced from Miriam to Domingo and knew instantly that something had happened between them, though she couldn't begin to guess what it was. It could be that Miriam was only behaving this way because of Micah, who was known to be a little jealous. Emma made a mental note to ask Miriam later.

But then Domingo said the strangest thing.

"I don't understand your God."

Emma blinked. Her head tilted. "What brought that up?"

"Micah." Domingo stopped and faced her, bucket dangling. "Earlier this summer, when Micah pulled the shotgun on those bandits at the logging camp, he saved my life and his father beat him for it. Ira's God was angry with Micah for doing something that saved us all."

Emma's eyes wandered, slightly embarrassed. "Jah, I heard about that. Ira can be hard sometimes, but he is still Micah's father."

Bending down, pouring water gently so as not to wash out the roots, Domingo said, "The Amish God is a mystery to me."

Emma shrugged. "Sometimes He is a mystery to me too, but Gott is Gott."

Domingo shook his head. "At least the Spaniards' God is

useful to them. He keeps the peons calm. But I don't understand the Amish God at all. The Amish don't conquer anybody, and their God tells them not to fight back when they are attacked. What kind of God is that?"

Emma thought for a moment before she answered. "Gott does not serve us; we serve Him. We are His children."

Domingo's eyes held suspicion. "If you are His children, why does He let bad men attack you? Why can't you fight back?"

"Because it is a sin to kill. It is in the nature of men to fight, to steal, even to kill, but with Gott's help we may overcome our nature. The fight is not out there, Domingo, it is in here." She tapped her chest. "We work to conquer *ourselves*."

He handed the bucket up to Ada. "But this makes no sense. Isn't your God the same as the Spaniards' God? The men who ruled our country for so long came with a sword in one hand and a cross in the other. The Spanish God has no quarrel with killing."

"That is not Gott you are seeing, Domingo, it is men. There have always been men who used religion for their own ends, to wield power over other people for selfish reasons. Maybe such men only *pretend* to know Gott."

Domingo laughed, a brief sardonic chuckle. "Where is the man who does *not* pretend?"

But he had not thought it out. Emma knew the answer— *Domingo's* answer— to this question.

"Dat," she said. "There is no pretense in my father."

Domingo's features softened, and the sneer faded from his face.

"Your father is a puzzle to me. I have never known a man like him."

Ada grunted, leaning over the water barrel and glaring impatiently at Domingo.

"Sorry," he said, handing Ada the bucket. A sad smile came into his eyes then, and Emma couldn't tell if it was confusion or resignation.

A hawk screamed, wheeling overhead. Gazing up at it Domingo said, "Pacifist or not, you are a dangerous woman, Emma. If a man wanted to find this God—your father's God—where would he find Him?"

"His footprints are everywhere," she said, "but only if you know how to see them. Can you read?"

"Sí, I read very well these days, thanks to your sisters. Miriam gave me a book to practice my reading. A big thick book about Don Quijote. I have read it twice now—much faster the second time."

"Do you have a Bible?"

"No."

"Does your sister Kyra have a Bible?"

"Sí."

She shrugged. "Read it. Start anywhere. If you look for Gott, He will find you."

"Maybe I will," he said, casting an odd glance at Micah's buggy as it disappeared behind the tin-roofed adobe home of Ira Shrock a half mile away. "But only because it makes no sense."

He hefted his bucket and went back to watering the saplings. When he turned around again, Emma had dropped to her knees in the driveway, her head pitched forward and both hands wrapped around her belly.

She looked up at him, her face red, one part grimace and one part grin. "I think you were right, Domingo. This baby is coming *soon*."

Chapter 11

When Caleb got everyone together for church services in the Benders' front yard the next morning the women were all abuzz with the news of Emma's new baby. It was a difficult delivery, but his Rachel was there. Somehow, as always, Rachel knew what to do. Late Saturday night a beautiful red-faced baby girl had come squalling and kicking into the lantern-lit bedroom at Levi and Emma's house. They named her Clara. Mother and daughter both made it through the delivery well and healthy, and by sunrise the only thing left to do was give thanks.

Caleb was perhaps a little more thankful than most. Of all his daughters Emma had always been the closest to his own heart, and it seemed that she struggled mightily with pregnancy. He had said nothing, though he had worried constantly and breathed a great sigh of relief when it was over.

But the arrival of Baby Clara laid another brick on the weight of angst that lately clouded his mind. He tried to ignore it, tried to trust Gott, but the problem would not go away. What would happen if *real* evil came to Paradise Valley now? Not just the little bands of hungry vagrants he most often saw, but men who meant real harm. What would happen to his children, to his *grandchildren*, if El Pantera's men descended upon them?

Caleb had never felt so vulnerable in his life. That Sunday, while so many gave thanks in the sunlight, he offered up a silent, fervent prayer from the darkest corner of his heart.

Please keep my girls from harm.

So far, prayer had been enough.

Micah came to the youth singing that night and afterward slipped away to be alone with Miriam for a time. When he'd first started courting her she'd expected him to press himself upon her, but he didn't. He was gentle with her, holding her fingertips in his and gazing into her eyes in the moonlight behind the barn. She saw a gentleness in him sometimes. It was in the way he played with the little ones that very afternoon, rolling in the grass like a big bear, letting them think they had conquered him.

But she could read his eyes, for he was not a complicated man, and in him she saw a great desire held in check by a fragile patience. Perhaps she saw too much, for she also saw his pride. He was proud of his gentleness and patience, as if they were tools that he would use to pry open her shell.

He was trying to win her.

On a Saturday in October, Micah and Miriam decided to take a picnic basket and hike up to the top of the ridge with Jake and Rachel. It was a lovely mild, sunny day with a light breeze, cool enough at the crest of the ridge to wear a shawl. Rachel and Jake had wandered off into the trees to be alone for a bit, leaving Miriam and Micah sitting on the picnic blanket near the ridgetop where the cliffs fell away into oblivion.

They had run out of things to talk about, as they often did, and Miriam sat hugging her knees, staring out across the low hills to the north, listening to the chattering of the birds in the brush. She barely noticed when Micah took off his hat. But then he leaned over, put an arm around her and kissed her. He had kissed her before, but never like this. It caught her by surprise, though she must have smiled because he watched for her reaction and then gave her another kiss, longer and more intense than the last one.

She had grown used to Micah. She felt comfortable and safe with him, and when they talked it was pleasant, but only pleasant. When he kissed her it was nice, but only nice. Miriam understood that she had always expected too much of Micah, and perhaps even of life itself, yet she was patient too, and thought that perhaps over time she might peel back the lay-ers of this uncomplicated man and find something to cherish. Something to love.

But as he went to kiss her a third time she pulled away and rose to her feet. Her hand came up to cover her lips, her fingers quivering.

"What is it?" he asked, still sitting. His head turned, scanning the tree line. "Are Rachel and Jake coming back?"

She shook her head, not saying anything because she couldn't.

It was this place.

The realization had come upon her like a cold wave, filling her with dread. This was the place of her dream—the exact spot. It had been two months since the vision last came to her in the night, and she had almost forgotten. Now the images came flooding back: the rocky ridge sloping into the ragged tree line on one side where the Bender farm quilted the valley far below, and on the other side dropping steeply away into nothingness. In the distance stood the treeless, boulder-strewn ridgetop, which looked exactly like the place in her dream where she had seen the great dark horse rearing up, charging. A gust of wind moaned through the crags and a chill went through her.

Micah rose and put his arms about her shoulders, watching her face. "What's wrong, Mir? Are you okay? You look like you've seen a ghost."

She could not answer him. Even if she could have found the words to describe it, she still would not speak of her dream to Micah.

The scream of a horse echoed through her mind and she looked down at herself, at her clothes. Her hand rose slowly, trembling fingers reaching, touching her prayer kapp to make sure it was still in place.

Micah clung to her, holding her in his arms until her mind quieted and she came back to herself. She looked up at him as if seeing him for the first time.

"I'm sorry," she said. "It's just . . . it was a very queer feeling I had." She couldn't bring herself to tell him. Not about this. "An odd premonition, I guess. It was nothing. I'm okay now."

He squeezed her a little tighter and she nestled into his arms.

"You're safe with me, Mir. I promise, I will let no harm come to you. You'll always be safe as long as I am with you."

He meant it, and she really did feel safe with him, at least to a degree. But in her heart, and in her dreams, there were dark places and evil men far beyond Micah's ken.

∞

When the field corn was ready at the end of October they held a husking bee. It was Micah's idea. Back home in Ohio a husking bee would have been a grand rollicking social occasion for the Amish youth—usually only boys and girls of dating age.

After the corn had all been shocked and left to dry for a time, eighteen or twenty of the young people would get together in the late afternoon and couples would compete against one another to see who could shuck the most corn. At least that was the *grown-up* reason for the husking bee. The teenagers liked it because they could spend time together as couples.

But that was in Ohio, where they had a large community. In Paradise Valley there were only a handful of teenagers and hardly enough couples to make a pretense of a real husking bee, so they let the kids join in, and even some married couples. Levi and Emma were there, and Ezra and Mary.

The shocks were all lined up in rows in the field, like odd-shaped shoulder-high hats. Miriam and Micah chose a row, went to the first shock and faced each other across it, pulling ears from the dry stalks, slicing them open with a corn husker strapped to their palm, peeling away the shucks, tossing the bare ears into a pile between the shocks and spreading the husks at their feet. As they worked their way down the shock, they would kneel on the spent husks to keep their knees out of the damp earth.

Everyone worked quickly. It was what passed for competition among the Amish, work made into a game, but Micah took it seriously. His hands flew—slicing, ripping, tossing and breaking off another ear even before the last one hit the ground, his face twisted in concentration as he worked at a fever pitch.

Facing him on her knees, Miriam said, "Go easy, Micah. It's supposed to be fun. Give the young ones a chance."

His hands didn't slow down as he glanced worriedly at Jake and Rachel, two rows over. "It's not the young ones I'm worried about," he said. "Jake and Rachel are already a shock ahead. That boy is *fast*."

She laid a hand on his forearm. "That's okay. It's the number of ears, not the number of shocks that counts. Anyways, you wouldn't have to win at *everything*, would you?"

He paused for a second, his head tilted in a puzzled stare. "What else would you have me do? Miriam, you're the *reason* I want to be the best at everything."

He snatched another ear and ripped it open, a trickle of sweat crawling down his forehead as his eyes concentrated and his hands flew.

She watched him for a second and said calmly, "You're always trying to impress me, Micah. Maybe you should relax a little."

A quick, nervous glance. "I'm always trying to *win* you, Mir. I just want to be the best."

"That's what I mean. Winning isn't everything, and best doesn't always mean strongest or fastest."

He smiled at that. "Spoken like a woman," he said, but his hands did not slow down.

Chapter 12

Caleb was alone in his field when the bandits came. It was early November, on a Saturday after the chores were done, which was a good thing because most of the young people had gone to the store in the hacienda village.

They came down out of the western mountains, a dozen horses taking their time, moving at a canter, cutting directly across Levi's fields toward Caleb's house. Perhaps it was the way they casually ignored the road and trampled a man's crops, or perhaps the way they held themselves proudly in their saddles, but something about them told Caleb these were El Pantera's men.

Shouting as he ran, he herded Mamm and Ada from the kitchen garden into the house, told them to bar the door, and then walked out into his field to face the bandits.

All the blood seemed to drain out of him in that moment, as even from a distance he could make out the horse in the front of the pack—a big bicolor Appaloosa.

El Pantera.

As they drew closer he also recognized the little weasel who had stolen the horse from Emma's buggy a year ago, who tried to kidnap Miriam on the way back from Saltillo in February, and whose stolen horse came home with Caleb after Domingo and Micah thwarted the kidnapping attempt. The weasel had promised to return. Now he had come for his revenge, and brought El Pantera with him.

Caleb made his stand in a fresh-plowed field just beyond the kitchen garden, watching them come. He braced himself, unbuttoning his work coat and spreading his feet, keeping his hands away from his body so they would see that he was not armed. No matter what he did, he knew there was a fair chance El Pantera would just shoot him like a dog, but he would not hide from them. If they wanted his life they would at least have to look him in the eye when they took it. There was nothing more he could do, so as they closed on him he said a silent prayer asking for deliverance.

The horses kept on coming, still cantering directly at him without changing pace as if they didn't see him, but he saw the grin on the weasel's face. In the last moments Caleb could even hear the laughter.

He dodged to the left at the last second to avoid being run down by the Appaloosa, but El Pantera's boot swung out and clipped him on the side of the head. Reeling, he bounced off another horse's hip, spun around, got kicked in the back of the head by the weasel and went down hard. He was only vaguely aware of the hooves pounding around him as the last of them passed by. He saw nothing at that point, but he heard raucous laughter and the weasel's voice fading away.

"Buenos días, Señor Horse Thief! I told you I would return!"

When he regained his senses a few minutes later, Caleb raised his head from the soft earth and looked toward the house. The front door was broken and hanging by one hinge, but the bandits' horses were gathered in front of the barn.

Hatless, he managed to get to his feet and stumble up to the house. Martha and Ada crouched by the stove, huddled together. Ada was wailing, wild-eyed, as Mamm stroked her back. A nod from his wife told Caleb they were okay. If he'd been thinking straight he would have stayed there with them, but in his addled state he went back out the door and staggered up toward the barn.

Standing in his barn lot dazed and confused, Caleb watched helplessly as the armed men plundered his barn. The girls had taken his good buggy horses to town, but the bandits strung up a fine standard-bred colt and two mules, turning the rest of the animals out. El Pantera himself shot a cow that wandered into his path, and with his pistol still in his hand, he turned and grinned at Caleb.

"Where are the pretty girls, gringo? In your casa I found only an old woman and a loco fat girl—no use to me at all."

Boots scuffled in the second level of the barn, and El Pantera shouted up to his men, a few of whom had climbed up to throw down sacks of oats.

Caleb's fear quickly turned to rage, and his anger made him do a foolish thing. He stalked right up to the barn and stood in the wide entrance as they were mounting their horses and leading away a team of mules loaded with sacks of his grain.

Raising a fist, he yelled at El Pantera, "What gives you the right to do this? Who do you think you are?"

But the bandit only laughed and spurred his horse. Caleb tried to dodge out of the way, but he couldn't move quickly enough, and this time the big Appaloosa caught him flush. He was knocked off his feet and skidded to a stop on his face in the hoof-churned mud of the barn lot as the bandits galloped past him, laughing and whooping, waving their hats and firing their guns into the air. Horses flashed over him, and it was only by a miracle that he was not trampled.

Barely conscious, he felt the snort of a horse near his head. Large hooves stamped and pawed the ground around him as he lay waiting for the gunshot that would end it all. But it never came.

El Pantera's raspy voice came from somewhere above, and there was a casual sneer in it. "I think I will let you live this day, Señor Bender, but only because you are such a good provider. We will be back."

Hooves pounded as El Pantera raced away to catch up with his men, and then there was silence.

When Caleb finally managed to struggle to his feet he took inventory of himself. Half blind with a headache, his chest hurt when he breathed and his knees shouted with pain, but he had not been shot and his arms and legs seemed to work. More important, the bandits had not harmed his wife and daughter. They had taken nothing that couldn't be replaced.

Hobbling past the house as quickly as he could, Caleb leaned a palm against the windmill and watched the bandits ride into the distance. He stayed there, motionless, waiting to make sure they turned north around the end of the ridge—*away* from the hacienda village—because in that moment his only thought was to see that his girls were safe. He had not yet begun to deal with his own rage and fear, the awful sense of utter helplessness and violation.

But things could have gone much worse.

Once he was positive the bandits were leaving the valley he wiped the mud from his clothes and went to the house to see about his wife and daughter, then went back out to the barn for a block and tackle so he could hang up the dead cow and bleed it out. No sense wasting good beef.

⟲

The next day, a Sunday, everyone was there when an automobile drove down the road and turned in at Caleb's driveway. It was a shiny new convertible driven by none other than the hacendado, Don Louis Alejandro Hidalgo, with his overseer Diego Fuentes riding in the passenger seat. Caleb rarely saw Hidalgo because he traveled abroad most of the time or stayed at his villa in Mexico City, but he sometimes spent a few weeks at the hacienda around planting time and harvest.

Most of the women were in the house fussing over Emma and her new baby girl. All of the men and boys stopped whatever they were doing and stared at the automobile when it pulled up in front of the house. None of them had ever seen one in Paradise Valley. It seemed out of place, a visitor from another world, another time.

When the introductions were done and the two Mexicans had run the long gauntlet of Amishmen who lined up to shake hands, the boys went off to get up a baseball game and a clutch of men wandered up toward the barn to talk. Caleb led them that way without meaning to. He had it in the back of his mind that the owner of the hacienda had come to inquire about yesterday's bandit raid, and the barn would help him recall the details. Hidalgo stepped carefully after they went through the gate into the barn lot, working interesting little feats of stride and balance to keep from soiling his fancy shoes or getting manure on his expensive suit.

"Señor Bender, I was very sorry to hear about what happened here yesterday," he said as they passed from hard sunlight to the cool shadows inside the barn. "Was anyone hurt?"

Caleb's hand went involuntarily to his ribs, one or two of which he suspected might have been cracked. He couldn't take a deep breath without a stab of pain.

"No. Thank Gott no one was hurt. Only my wife and eldest

daughter were home, and the bandits didn't harm them. They killed one of my cows, though." Even now, his wife and the other women were preparing a feast of steaks for the whole Amish community. The beef would not last long.

"Of course there was no way for me to know," Hidalgo said. "But if I had known what was happening, I assure you these *bandidos* would have paid with their lives."

It was common knowledge that he kept a force of twenty well-trained mercenaries to protect the hacienda.

"Thank you, Don Hidalgo, but I would not want anyone to die—certainly not over a couple of mules and a few sacks of grain. We have neighbors who will help us recover from the loss. In the end I am only glad that most of my daughters were in your village when the bandits came."

Levi and Ezra nodded at this. The Amish would take care of their own. But Caleb had seen the fire in Levi's eyes and knew that his son-in-law had an axe to grind.

Levi glared at Hidalgo. "What kind of country is this, where bad men are allowed to roam free and take whatever they want? Is there no law? Would we chust have to wait and let them kill us all?"

"My men are at your disposal," Hidalgo explained patiently, "but you are miles from the hacienda, so we do not know what is happening until it is too late. When you see trouble coming you should send a rider immediately and then barricade yourselves in the house and defend your home until my men can get here."

"We can hide in our houses," Caleb said, "but we will not use guns against men. We are a peaceful people."

Hidalgo took off his white fedora and wiped his brow with a silk handkerchief, staring into an empty stall for a moment. When he spoke again, Caleb could hear frustration in his voice. "Señor Bender, things have changed. When you came to

Paradise Valley we had little to fear from Pancho Villa's men. Now that he is dead, there are no guarantees. I cannot promise you that *hordes* of bandits will not sweep down upon us. It is different than before." He waved his hat in the general direction of the hacienda. "Always before, my little garrison at the hacienda was an adequate deterrent against the rabble that passed through your valley, but now I cannot say. Again, I would advise you and your people to arm yourselves. I cannot promise to be able to defend you against what may come."

Caleb shook his head slowly and repeated, "We will not take up arms against our fellow man."

"Then I don't see how I can help you if you will not defend yourselves. Perhaps you could appeal to the government for help, send someone to talk to the official I told you about in Monterrey—see if he will send troops to Paradise Valley."

"We have already done this," Caleb said, his own patience wearing a bit thin. "Señor Montoya would not help us. He said his troops were badly needed in other places and he could not be bothered with a handful of gringo farmers."

Hidalgo sighed and gave a tired shrug. "This does not surprise me. Did you offer him money?"

Caleb's eyebrows went up and he flinched, surprised by the open talk of a bribe. Was he the only one who thought it unethical?

"We don't have the kind of money it would take to buy troops."

Hidalgo and Fuentes both huffed at this, almost laughing, but not quite. Hidalgo stared at Caleb for a long moment.

"Señor Bender, if you will not defend yourself, and you cannot pay people to do it for you, then may God help you."

Caleb stared back and nodded slowly. "Gott has brought us *this* far."

Chapter 13

There was very little discussion at the Bender farm about whether or not they would have another community feast on the day after Christmas. It was a foregone conclusion. The first one, the year before, had been such a resounding success that in most of their minds it already seemed an established tradition. This year's gathering would be twice as big. The Shrocks and Hershbergers were all there, plus the German farmer Ernst Schulman and his wife, Domingo and his sister Kyra, and all the kids from Miriam's school plus their families. Even the weather cooperated, with a light breeze and temperatures in the sixties. Men and boys who had lived in Paradise Valley for less than a year kept taking their hats off and grinning up at the bluebird sky in utter disbelief, marveling at a place where a Christmas feast could be held outdoors in shirtsleeves.

Before the feast, a kind of segregation existed. The Amish boys stood shoulder to shoulder with their backs against the wall of the barn while the older men talked in the open bays of the buggy shed, gazing out over fields and pastures, stroking their beards and gesturing with work-roughened hands. The women rushed around getting food to all the tables lined up in the yard, and the Mexican families mostly stood off to themselves whispering to each other, gaping at the sheer volume of food.

During the meal another kind of segregation existed; there were tables for men and tables for women. Babies and toddlers sat on their mothers' laps, with one notable exception—Aaron hijacked Little Amos from his mother, and kept him.

It was a rare thing to see an Amishman holding a baby at mealtime, but no one seemed to mind—least of all Mary, who was busy enough with Little Amos's twin sister. The twins were able to walk now and growing like weeds.

Miriam was helping clear away the tables after everyone had eaten, and amid the hustle and bustle Micah and Levi Mullet, Miriam's brother-in-law, wandered over to her.

"Look at that," he said. "Levi and me were just talking about Aaron and that nephew of his."

She could see Aaron walking alone down into the stubbled remains of the cornfield, carrying Little Amos in the crook of one arm.

"Jah," she said, smiling. "Does the heart good to see Aaron's spirits lifted like that. I didn't think he'd ever get over his brother."

"Well," Levi said, "that wasn't what we were talking about exactly. It's about that thing in his hand."

Then she saw it. Aaron was holding the harmonica, and as he walked he leaned his head down close to Little Amos and blew softly into it.

"I can't believe your dat allows that," Micah muttered. "We don't hold with musical instruments, and your dat knows it."

His eyes were hard, his face drawn.

"Maybe so," she said, "but every time I see Aaron with it, I'm reminded of Amos, and how much we loved him. I think that child—and that harmonica—mean more to my brother than any of us can imagine. I can't help feeling it would be a sin to take that away from him."

"But it's just not right," Levi hissed. "It was wrong when Amos did it, and it's wrong now. It's against the *ordnung*."

Miriam turned around and fixed Levi with a burning glare. How could one who had been forgiven so much still be unwilling to forgive such a small thing? Surely Levi knew—surely Emma had told him that her *sisters* knew of their deception. None of them spoke of it outright, but they could count, and the sisters knew that Levi and Emma's first child was born barely six months after their wedding.

"Lots of things are against the ordnung," she said coldly, "but sometimes we love the person so much it's just better to look the other way. Forgive and forget."

Apparently the hint found its mark because Levi's eyes narrowed and his mouth drew into a tight line. He wisely chose not to respond.

Micah's head tilted in confusion. He had not been there and did not know of Levi and Emma's deception. He opened his mouth to say something, but Miriam picked up a stack of plates and walked away, toward the house. Micah wasn't acting like himself, and she was fairly sure he was only trying to make an impression on Levi. It didn't matter. Micah would understand or he wouldn't, but either way, this was not a debate she wanted to air in public.

When she came back out of the house Micah and Levi had gone up toward the barn and the horseshoe pits, while over by the end of the tables stood a mixed group of Amish and Mexicans, talking and cutting up. In their midst she spotted Domingo in his cotton work clothes and striped poncho, grinning. There were two little boys clinging to his legs, standing on his feet while he stomped around pretending to try and shake them off. The air rang with their laughter, and the two boys looked up at him with hero worship in their eyes.

She stopped in her tracks without meaning to, caught by the sight of Domingo with the children. Something in it pierced her.

When she realized she was staring she shook herself and turned away quickly, hurrying to her work.

"It will pass," she muttered to herself as she gathered a handful of glasses from the table. "It will."

That evening, after the guests had all left, the young people held a singing at the Bender house. Later, Micah took Miriam's hand and slipped away with her to the buggy shed.

"We've been courting for a little while now," he said. He seemed different this night, quiet and nervous. The self-righteous façade he'd worn for Levi had vanished, gone and forgotten. He seemed far less self-assured when no one else was around.

She nodded. "Five months now."

"They say a minister is coming in the summer."

"Jah," she said, unable to make out his face in the shadows. "That's good news. We'll have baptisms again."

He was quiet for a second. "And weddings," he finally whispered, shifting his feet.

She smiled. "Jah, that too. I've been thinking about it a lot lately."

"Really?"

"Rachel won't talk about it, but I have a sneaky suspicion she and Jake are already thinking of marriage. They will both be eighteen soon and Jake is very mature for his age. I think—"

"Miriam, I wasn't talking about Jake and Rachel."

A jolt went through her. "No?"

"No. Mir, I know we haven't been courting all that long but we're not getting any younger, and I was wondering if maybe in the fall, after the harvest, maybe you and me could uh . . . Do you think you might be willing to be my wife?"

Miriam knew this was coming, yet it still caught her off guard. She was glad for the darkness. Try as she might, she knew she could not keep the angst and reluctance from reaching her face, though even the darkness couldn't make up for the awkward silence that hung between them.

"You don't have to give me an answer right away," he said, rushing his words. "Harvest is a long ways off yet, so there's plenty of time."

Still, she could think of nothing to say. Emotions boiled to the surface, choosing sides and warring against one another.

"Miriam, I love you." He had blurted it out rather clumsily, as if he'd only just thought of it. "I love you very much and I promise I will make a fine husband to you. You'll never want for anything so long as I draw breath."

He meant it, and his sincerity left her with a pang of guilt. Perhaps it wasn't his fault that the things he did to impress her fell short. Maybe it was her. It mattered less to Miriam that he could outwrestle anyone in the valley or lift a half-grown heifer off the ground by himself than that he would chastise Aaron over a harmonica. She wanted a man who understood her, who could see through her, who would listen to her and talk to her about the things that really mattered, a man who could dream with her—a man who thought she was more beautiful than a sunset.

But he was right about one thing. She wasn't getting any younger.

She took his hands in hers and spoke gently from the darkness. "Micah, you're right—there's plenty of time. It's just that this is a really important decision and I . . . I'll need time to think about it. Could you wait a little while for an answer?"

His shadow swayed slightly, looking away, pondering. "How long?"

She did her best to sound positive, almost cheerful. "I don't know. A week?"

He nodded. His voice came out soft, a little deflated. "Okay. A week."

Discipline. Miriam mouthed the word over and over to herself.

The blue rectangle of moonlight had crept three feet across the floor since she first went to bed. Rachel lay next to her, sound asleep, her breathing deep and regular, but Miriam's mind would not rest.

She tried hard to think only about Micah but she couldn't keep flashes of Domingo from intruding—those dark eyes shining with laughter, his shoulder muscles rippling in the sun when he chopped corn, his dark hair flying in the wind when he raced the painted pony bareback, the fire in his eyes when he took down the armed bandit who tried to kidnap her. He was *beautiful*, but he was also a man of depth and principle. Teaching him to read, she'd found him a quick learner, intelligent and inquisitive. She could still see him tossing his nephew into the air—the laughter, the trust, the love, the shock that went through her like an arrow when her mind framed the moment and cast it into the future, seeing a father with his son.

But Domingo is forbidden, she thought. *And Micah is the only Amish boy of the right age in all of Mexico. It is discipline I need now, and discipline I shall have. I should not care so much for Domingo. I am wrong even to let myself think of him. Micah loves me. He wants* me to be his wife, and he is a good man—an Amishman who would be devastated if I said no to him. My family likes him and wants me to marry him. My mother would be crushed if I turned to an outsider, and I would be banned.

Family is everything.

Time is all I need. In time there is forgetting. Time heals all.

Time and discipline.

I will do what is right.

I will do what I must.

Cualnezqui.

⁓

It didn't take a week; it only took two sleepless nights. On the third day, after the singing on Sunday night, in the darkness out behind the buggy shed, Miriam gave Micah his answer.

"Jah," she said. "In the fall, I will marry you."

He swept her off her feet, swung her around three times and gave her a hearty kiss before he put her back down. Afterward, they went back to the house straight-faced, as if nothing had happened. It would remain a closely guarded secret between a man and his betrothed. It was tradition.

⁓

Miriam and Micah only saw each other once or twice a week that winter. The cold season was neither as long nor as deep as it had been back in Ohio, so there was always work to do. The Shrock homestead was far from finished, and Micah's father kept him busy turning fields and building fences. The men made two more trips into the mountains for timber that winter. Ira Shrock and his strong sons worked every day until after dark, ambitiously fencing in more than a hundred acres of pasture for the raising of beef cattle.

Because Domingo worked for her father, Miriam saw him every day, though she tried not to. He remained polite and distant, almost cool toward her, but once in a while he turned away from her a little too quickly and she could have sworn she saw the glimmer of regret in his dark eyes.

In March of that year the Coblentz family arrived with three big wagonloads of farm equipment and household goods, and everyone pitched in to help them get a foothold in the valley.

In spite of all the busyness, there was love in the air that spring. The oldest Coblentz daughter, a blond-haired blue-eyed girl named Cora, was unattached. Aaron went up to Saltillo with Caleb to bring the Coblentzes to Paradise Valley, and on the return trip Cora sat next to him all the way home. By the time their little wagon train pulled into the Benders' driveway Aaron was smitten. Before the wagons were even unloaded he asked Cora if he could court her, and she said yes. Startled by his great good fortune, Aaron smiled for a week.

Miriam's younger brother Harvey began courting Lovina Hershberger that spring as well, so it seemed that despite the odds all the courting-age teenagers in the valley were suddenly paired off.

The Coblentzes brought nine children with them, most of whom were school age, and Miriam's school grew. The Paradise Valley settlement felt like a viable community now, and it thrived in other ways, too. Miriam's older sister Mary bore another son that spring, and Emma's belly swelled with her third child in as many years.

Life was good.

Chapter 14

The spring flew past in a flurry of work and busyness, the days growing long and the corn growing tall. Before they knew it high summer was upon them and it was time for the much-anticipated large group to arrive from Ohio.

In mid-July five families came down together with all their kids and dogs and horses and chickens and furniture, and overnight the settlement doubled in size. There were supposed to have been six families, but the minister had not come with them as planned. The next day the eldest of the new arrivals, a man named Roman J. Miller, addressed the whole crowd after church services to dispel rumors and make sure everyone understood what had happened.

Miller was a tall thin man with a long black beard and a deep booming voice. He stood up in front of them and said, "As you all know, Ervin Kuhns, an ordained minister, was supposed to come with us, along with his whole family, but he got left back. His uncle Abe got kicked in the head by a horse and laid there two weeks, but he didn't pass yet, so Ervin and his family stayed behind to wait. Now, they're still gonna come, but I'm thinking they'll be along a couple weeks later than the rest of us, that's all."

⌒

Emma's third child came into the world later that summer, a healthy boy with a head full of wavy hair. Mamm was down with her back pain when the baby came, so Miriam went with Rachel to Emma's house to help with sterilizing, boiling and ironing. Delivering babies had never been one of Miriam's strengths. Rachel, on the other hand, despite being young and single, was fast building a reputation as a natural and instinctive midwife. She seemed to have a sixth sense. The birthing went smoothly, a first for Emma. Her two earlier pregnancies had been troublesome. Her first baby was born prematurely, and she almost lost the second one early on.

On a bright summer afternoon, while all the men were in the fields, Emma lay holding her new son as her two sisters cleaned up the room. Her honey-colored hair spread over the pillow and her blue eyes shined with pride as she gazed on the tightly wrapped son sleeping on her breast.

"I thought he would never go to sleep," she said. "This one has a mind of his own. Levi wants to call him Will, and now that I see how he is, I'm thinking it's the right name for him."

Miriam tied the corners of a sheet around the soiled laundry and dropped the bundle next to the door, then came and sat in a kitchen chair next to Emma's bed. Rachel lowered herself onto the foot of the bed, folding her hands in her lap.

"You two can go home now," Emma said. "Really, I'll be fine, and Levi will be in soon."

Miriam shook her head. "We'll stay by you. You have *three* babies in this house now." Mose, Emma's firstborn, was not quite two years old. "You're going to need us for a day or two."

Rachel nodded, and made no sign of leaving.

Emma stared at Rachel for a moment and said, "Child, what's

wrong? I know you're tired, but you haven't said three words all day and that's not like you at all. Is there something troubling you?"

Rachel looked down at the hands folded in her lap and answered quietly, "Jake and I are thinking about getting married in the fall, after the minister comes."

Miriam's eyes widened. "Rachel, it doesn't surprise me that you and Jake will be married, but I *am* surprised you would come right out and tell us. Your wedding plans are supposed to be secret."

"Pfff. How is it a secret with us? Everybody knows already that Jake and I will be married one day. It's just maybe a little earlier than they thought."

"Jah, you're only a child yet," Emma said.

"I'm eighteen, Emma."

"No! Oh, how quickly the years pass! My little sister . . . *eighteen years old*. But Mir's right, girl—why are you telling us this now? You must have a reason."

"Emma, you and me have always told each other everything, and Miriam needs to know anyway because I want her to be one of my *navahuckers*." This was no great surprise either, but Miriam smiled warmly and reached out to take her little sister's hand.

"But there's another thing," Rachel said. "Emma, I told you this because . . . well, because I want to ask you about something else. Something secret that no one ever talks about. I don't know if I did right."

The worried look in Rachel's eyes spread to both her sisters. Emma spoke first.

"What is it, child? What have you done?"

"I . . . I told Jake there would be no bed courtship."

"I see."

A little silence fell, and Miriam knew the darkness in Emma's face was not disapproval—it was remorse. Emma had kept it secret that she was with child when she and Levi married, but her sisters knew. Though it was done quietly and never discussed, bed courtship was unquestioned in Ohio. It was a matter of practicality in a place where the winters were brutally cold. On a Saturday night, a boy might have to drive an open buggy ten or fifteen miles home in single-digit temperatures, only to drive back the next morning for church. The houses were uninsulated, and beds were at a premium with so many children. Bed courtship began as a practical way for a courting couple to keep warm, but for some it opened the door to temptation.

"I know it was normal back home, but I don't think it's necessary here because the farms are close together and it's not so cold," Rachel said, rushing her words defensively. Then she lowered her eyes and added, "But mostly, I was afraid."

"Because of me?" Emma asked gently.

Rachel nodded.

"Now I understand. Is that what you said to him—that it was because of what happened to me?"

"Oh, *no!*" Rachel's fingers came to her lips. "I wouldn't speak about that to anyone, Emma. I told him the bed would be too crowded because there were already two of us in it."

Miriam slapped her shoulder, laughing quietly. "You didn't really say that."

"I did! There's not enough beds as it is. Do you want to sleep on the floor with the scorpions?" This was only half jest. Miriam had found a scorpion in the kitchen just yesterday—one of the pale, lethal kind.

"No, I don't," Miriam agreed. "What did he say?"

Rachel chuckled. "He just smiled and said okay. Jake has a way of looking right into me, and he understands. I felt bad, then, because I'm not sure it ever even crossed his mind."

"You're a lucky girl," Emma said. "But I have to ask you, does Jake know about . . . what happened to me?"

Rachel shrugged. "I don't know. He has never said, but Jake is no fool. Could be he's just too polite to talk about it. Anyway, he loves you just like we do, and he would never speak ill of you."

Emma stared at her younger sister for a moment and then said, "That's good, too. You are wise beyond your years, Rachel. Gott has blessed you, and I'm glad you've found such a man as Jake. He'll make a good husband."

Emma's eyes turned to Miriam, and there was a knowing in them. Miriam had remained awfully quiet. "Well, what about you and Micah?"

Miriam blushed, shaking her head demurely. It was a deeply embarrassing question that only Emma would dare to ask, but it was also true that only Emma would get an answer.

"No."

"If he asks, what will you tell him?"

Miriam squirmed, scratching her head, avoiding Emma's steady gaze. Then she looked up, grinned sheepishly and said, "I'll just tell him the bed is too crowded already."

Chapter 15

The following Saturday afternoon Micah and Miriam doubled up with Jake and Rachel in the surrey and went to the hacienda village. Long before they reached the village they heard singing, and as they drew closer they could see a crowd gathered by the cattle pens on the outskirts of town. Big, bright red and white letters arced like a comet across the side of a large paneled wagon, advertising *Dr. Lothar's Traveling Medicine Show, Prestidigitator and Hypnotist*. The sign was apparently all it took to hypnotize Micah. He forgot all about going to the dry goods store and steered the buggy toward the cattle pens.

Dr. Lothar was a skinny little man with a great big voice. He wore a pinstriped three-piece suit that somehow managed to look threadbare and elegant at the same time, and a bowler hat cocked a little too sideways. There was a stage built onto the back of his wagon, and as Miriam, Micah, Rachel and Jake walked up Dr. Lothar was parading back and forth, doing card tricks and telling jokes in bad Spanish with a German accent. He invited a Mexican boy up onto his small stage and made him pick a card, pulled the card from behind the boy's ear, then pulled a coin from behind the other ear. Next, he drew a live dove out of a bandanna he borrowed from the boy.

The crowd was hooked, and so was Micah. He couldn't take his eyes off Dr. Lothar as he finished his magic routine, sent the smiling child offstage with a piece of hard candy and launched into a florid speech on the countless virtues of Dr. Lothar's Amber Nectar, a patent medicine in a stoppered bottle that he held up to show the crowd.

Caleb Bender had long ago taught his daughters that men worth listening to didn't need to shout, and real miracles were never sold for money, so Miriam ignored Dr. Lothar and looked around to see who else was there. Scattered through the crowd she spotted half the young Amish in Paradise Valley, most of whom were hanging on Lothar's every word. She caught a glimpse of Kyra and her two boys, and she figured Domingo must be around someplace as well.

Dr. Lothar claimed his Amber Nectar, made from an ancient recipe whose secret a thousand Aztec warriors had died to preserve, would cure everything from hiccups to measles, make rheumatism vanish like the morning dew, grow hair on bald heads and make gnarled old women feel like the sultry señoritas they remembered from their golden youth. Why, he couldn't prove it, for it had happened in a cattle town far away from here in the distant land of Wyoming, but Lothar swore he had once seen this very same potion bring a dead cat back to life.

By the time the huckster finished his speech Micah was already elbowing his way toward the back of the wagon, where Dr. Lothar's lovely assistant pulled bottles of Amber Nectar from a box and offered them for sale.

"What is Micah doing?" Aaron had come up behind them with his girlfriend, Cora, who smiled and said hello. Aaron's

116

hat dangled from her hands. He wasn't wearing it because he was carrying Little Amos on his shoulders.

"I think Micah went to buy a bottle of that stuff," Miriam said. "His dat let him have a crop of his own this year, so he's got a little money." Changing the subject, she reached up to touch fingers with Little Amos. "I see you have your helper with you today, Aaron. He's growing like ivy."

Aaron's big hands held the child's bare feet so he couldn't fall, and Amos seemed perfectly at ease riding high on his uncle's shoulders. At nineteen months old he was already wearing Amish pants, suspenders and a flat-brimmed hat, his downy hair cut into the customary bowl shape. Little Amos smiled at Miriam, then raised his harmonica to his lips and blew a note, which set him to giggling.

"Jah, and he's learning to play, too," Aaron said, grinning. "Mary lets me borrow him sometimes, and I thought mebbe he'd like to see the show."

Micah came rushing back and handed Miriam a shiny bottle of Dr. Lothar's Amber Nectar. "This stuff is good for what ails you," he said proudly.

Miriam smiled and thanked him for the gift. She couldn't help feeling a little embarrassed that Micah could be so gullible, though she managed to keep a straight face.

But Aaron, good-natured as he was, couldn't leave well enough alone. "You know, Micah, I was talking to Domingo just a minute ago—he's around here someplace—and he told me not to buy that medicine they're selling. He said it's mostly *mescal*, whatever that is."

Jake chuckled. "Mescal is a kind of poor man's liquor the local people make from cactus juice." Then, when Rachel shot him a questioning glance, his face darkened and he quickly added, "I've never tried it, though."

"Jah, well," Micah said, a little indignantly, "Domingo doesn't know everything." He said this to Aaron, studiously avoiding Miriam's glance.

"Hey, Micah," Jake said, standing on tiptoe to see over the crowd, "did you see the monkey?"

"What monkey?" Micah took a long look over his shoulder. Another wagon was parked near the back of Lothar's. Larger by half, this one had a big mural of zoo animals on the side.

"They got a cage with a monkey, over in the cattle pen," Jake said, and Miriam recognized a mischievous gleam in his eye. "It costs ten pesos to get in the cage, but if you can pin the monkey you win a *hundred* pesos."

Sure enough, Miriam could see just the edge of an iron cage in the cattle pen, partially obscured by the animal wagon. There were people gathered around it.

Micah's eyes narrowed. "How big is this monkey?"

"Oh, he's just a little thing," Jake said. "About knee high."

Miriam saw trouble coming. This was almost like gambling—not the sort of thing most Amishmen would even consider—but Micah harbored a measure of pride when it came to wrestling. He wandered off toward the cattle pen without another word. He might be able to *handle* trouble better than Miriam, but she could see it coming from a lot further away.

She tried to call him back, but a little mariachi band had cranked up on the stage in front of Dr. Lothar's wagon, just four Mexicans in gilded sombreros and matching silver-studded outfits—a guitar, trumpet, fiddle and squeeze-box. They drowned her out, and Micah never looked back. She ran after him, dodging through the crowd.

By the time she caught up with him, Micah had made it all the way into the cattle pen and was listening with rapt attention while Dr. Lothar shouted the praises of "this wondrous ape." The black iron cage was about fifteen feet square by eight feet high, and in the middle of the space sat a chimpanzee. He wasn't moving or anything, just sitting calmly in the dust of the cattle pen with his arms draped over his knees, staring straight ahead as if he was bored. Miriam looked around and saw that the others had followed her to see what would happen. She grabbed Micah's arm and dragged him off to the side, where no one would hear.

"Micah, don't do this! It's foolish."

"Och, how hard can it be, Mir? Why, you heard Jake—it's just a little monkey. He don't weigh no more than fifty pounds. All I have to do is put him on his back—"

"No! These people are cheaters, liars. It's a trick, Micah. They'll take your money and you might even get hurt. Don't do this!"

He took her shoulders, smiled a patient, fatherly smile and explained. "Miriam, a hundred pesos will buy a few acres of land. My *own land*, Miriam, and a house won't cost hardly anything with all the neighbors we have now. We'll have a good start on our own farm!"

She wanted to reason with him, to talk him out of it, but she had learned to read the look in his eyes. He glanced down at the green medicine bottle she held in her hands, and right then she knew it was hopeless. Aaron had injured his pride when he said Micah's "miracle elixir" was nothing but mescal. Worse, Aaron said it was Domingo who told him this. Worse still, he said it in front of Miriam. Now Micah was looking for a way to salvage his pride, and he really couldn't conceive of losing a wrestling match to such a small monkey. It was a lost cause. She already knew there was no way he would be talked out of it.

She took a deep breath and nodded curtly. "All right, then. You go wrestle that monkey."

Aaron, Cora, Rachel and Jake gathered around Miriam and stood next to the cage to watch while Micah paid his ten pesos, rolled up his sleeves, and left his hat with Dr. Lothar.

Miriam leaned close to Jake and whispered, "I'm a little angry with you just now. You put him up to this, and don't you pretend for one minute that you didn't do it on purpose."

The mischievous grin crept back onto Jake's face. "What? It's just a little monkey, Mir. What can go wrong?"

"Plenty. If it's so easy, why didn't you go in there yourself?"

A shrug. "I don't have ten pesos." This much was true, but he still had that mischievous gleam in his eye. "Anyways, Micah's bigger than me."

A crowd had gathered by the time Lothar opened the cage door and, with a sweeping bow, ushered Micah into the cage.

Micah circled the monkey in a half crouch, slowly, arms away from his body, looking for an opening.

The monkey didn't move. He paid no attention as the big Amishman eased around behind him, but when Micah was about to make his rush the chimp stood up, turned to face him and backed away a couple of steps. They stared at each other, Micah in his crouch and the monkey standing on all fours, leaning on his knuckles in the loose dirt of the cattle pen.

Micah's eyes narrowed, and a little smile curled the corners of his lips.

Jake leaned close to Miriam and whispered, "I know what he's thinking. All he has to do is put the monkey on his back, so he's going to rush him and try to sweep his legs."

Jake was right. This was exactly what Micah tried to do, but apparently the chimp had seen it before. The instant Micah started to move forward the monkey charged. He leaped through the air and landed on Micah's chest, wrapping his hairy legs around his waist before he could react.

Micah tried to sling the monkey off, but those powerful hands grabbed his shoulders and began to shake him. In a blinding flurry, the chimp shook Micah so hard his arms flopped like a rag doll and his head danced madly on his shoulders.

Micah managed to stay on his feet but he lost his balance and stumbled backward into the bars. The chimp clung to him, shaking harder than ever, and Micah's head crashed into the bars. He staggered sideways and his head played the bars of the cage like a xylophone.

Micah grabbed fistfuls of hair on the monkey's sides and pitched forward, trying to hold the beast in place long enough to fall on top of him and pin his back to the dirt, but he wasn't quick enough. The chimp leaped clear and landed on his feet. Micah hit the ground face-first and a little cloud of dust rolled out from around him.

The monkey circled him, loping on all fours, watching.

The crowd of Mexicans laughed and shouted, but Miriam couldn't tell whether they were cheering for Micah or the ape.

Micah drew himself up onto his elbows and shook his head. The monkey kept circling, even when Micah got to his knees. The attack didn't come until he rose to his feet. Still dazed, Micah had no chance to fend off the lightning charge of the ape. Before he knew it the monkey's legs had locked around his waist again, his arms were flopping, the back of his head clanging against the bars.

As he neared the corner of the cage Micah tried a desperate spin move, but once again the monkey was too quick. Micah hit the ground face-first, his arms empty. After a moment he raised his head and peeked around to see where the little demon had gone.

The chimp had leaped onto the bars and scrambled up to the ceiling, where he swung casually by one hand, watching Micah spit dirt.

Micah dragged himself up to a crawling position. The monkey dropped nimbly to the ground and circled him again, loping on his knuckles, watching.

Micah looked up—not at the chimp, but at Miriam. It was only the briefest glance, and then he hung his head. Beaten.

The crowd fell silent. A few even walked away, unable to watch anymore.

The big Amishman didn't raise his head again, nor did he try to get to his feet, because he had already seen what the ape would do if he stood up. He would not get up again. Crawling toward the cage door on hands and knees, he motioned for Dr. Lothar to let him out. He'd had enough.

In that moment Miriam's heart broke. Her fingers came up to cover her lips and she could not keep the tears from her eyes. Even though Micah had brought this on himself, in the end she knew he didn't really do it to win a hundred pesos. He did it to win *her*.

What broke her heart was that he had failed.

Chapter 16

Miriam's school started on the same morning that her father left for Arteaga to pick up Ervin Kuhns, the minister, and his family.

Right after breakfast the new kids showed up for their first day of school. The five new families had formed a tent village across the valley between the Shrock and Hershberger farms, and sixteen new kids walked across the valley that morning, lunch pails in hand.

Miriam and Rachel cleared the breakfast table as quickly as possible, then hauled it out the door to the buggy shed and came back for chairs. Kyra showed up with her two boys to help.

As if things weren't chaotic enough, Ada sat in the middle of the living room floor the whole time, rocking and wailing. Ada had been doing better lately; she hadn't gone into one of her crying fits in months. This was an unexpected setback.

A half-dozen new kids came through the front door and Miriam directed traffic, shuttling the children around Ada, through the kitchen and out the back door toward the buggy shed. Ada, apparently feeling ignored, wailed louder and started banging her head on the floor. Flummoxed by all this madness,

Miriam stood in the kitchen pressing her palms against her temples and trying to figure out what to do next.

"Mamm, isn't there anything we can do to quiet Ada?" she asked. "What's wrong with her anyway?"

Mamm was leaning at the kitchen counter, washing dishes in a galvanized washtub. She looked over her shoulder and said absently, "She has a sore throat. I'll see after her. You just go on with your school."

Ada must have heard her mother, because she grabbed her throat with both hands and launched into a racking cough. When the cough died down she moaned and screamed louder than ever. Mary came in the back door, bringing her boys up from next door for school. She was carrying her newborn in one arm and Little Amos in the other. Amos's twin, Amanda, trailed along behind, sucking her thumb and holding on to her mother's skirts. Amos clung to his mother's neck and didn't even raise his head.

Kyra came right behind her, looking for more chairs for the school in the buggy shed. She lifted a kitchen chair and started toward the back door, but stopped when Ada let out a particularly loud howl. Still holding the kitchen chair in front of her, she asked Miriam in Spanish, "Is something wrong with Ada?"

"Sí," Miriam said. "Her throat hurts and she has a fever."

"I think she's coming down with a cold, that's all," Mamm said. "I'll mix up some lemon and honey as soon as I'm done washing up."

Kyra set the chair down and a look of concern came into her eyes. She tugged at Miriam's sleeve. "Light the lantern and let me look at her."

Miriam put a kitchen match to the lantern, turned it up and followed Kyra into the living room.

Kneeling in front of Ada, Kyra tried to get her attention,

but the big woman ignored her and rocked even harder, bumping her forehead on the floor, moaning. Kyra took Ada's face in her hands and held her still. Looking into her eyes she said, "Aaaaaah," and yawned wide to show Ada what she wanted.

Ada snuffled a couple times, but she finally complied.

"Aaaaaaah."

Miriam held the lantern close. As Kyra peered down Ada's throat, her eyes grew big and the worried look turned to fear. She closed Ada's mouth, patted her gently on the cheek and said, "Gracias."

Mary, who had watched all this closely, said, "Something must be going around. Little Amos isn't himself either, and he says his throat hurts."

Rising quickly, Kyra went to the kitchen, motioning for Miriam to bring the lantern. Gently, she turned Little Amos about in his mother's arm so that he faced her, pried open his mouth and used a wooden spoon handle as a tongue depressor. Miriam held the light close.

Little Amos squirmed and cried, wrenching his face free of Kyra's grasp, but not before she got a good look.

"I was afraid of this . . ." she whispered, her voice trembling. "This is no cold. It is the *strangler*."

Miriam shrugged and shook her head, confused. "The strangler?"

"Sí. I talked to one of the women in the traveling show in the village last weekend. She said they had just come from Nuevo Laredo, where there were rumors of an outbreak on the American side. I didn't want to say anything because I did not think it would come here. I prayed it was not true."

"But what is it? What are you talking about?"

"The woman said the gringo name for it, but I cannot say it. It was dip . . . dip . . ."

Miriam's eyes widened. "Diphtheria?"

Kyra nodded. "Sí. Diphtheria. That was the word."

Their Spanish eluded Mamm, but she heard the word *diphtheria*. Her fingers bit into her prayer kapp and she moaned loudly, plunking heavily into the chair Kyra had left in the middle of the kitchen.

"Are you sure?" Miriam asked.

"Sí, I have seen it before. There was an outbreak near Agua Nueva last year and one of my little cousins died." She wiggled a finger at her throat. "The strangler leaves a gray coating in the throat, like leather. Both of them have it."

Miriam took a deep breath and tried to think. Her first duty was to her mother, so she knelt in front of Mamm and translated what Kyra had told her.

Mamm covered her face and began to wail, rocking back and forth in the chair, just like Ada. "Oh, what will we *do?*"

Miriam looked to Rachel. "Go get Aaron," she said quietly. "He's in the barn." In Caleb's absence, Aaron was the man of the house. As Rachel went out the door, Miriam turned to Kyra as calmly as she could, her hands clasped in front of her. She had no knowledge of diphtheria—only that it was very bad.

"What will happen now?" she asked, in Spanish.

"The fever will get worse and the throat will swell. Sometimes there are sores on the skin."

Kyra averted her eyes then, and Miriam knew there was more. Something she did not want to say.

"And then?"

Tears formed in Kyra's dark eyes. "The throat swells shut and cuts off the wind. It is a terrible death."

Miriam took a deep breath and fought for control, for her mother's sake.

"They will die?"

Kyra nodded slowly and dabbed at her eyes with a handkerchief. "Perhaps Ada will live, but the little one . . . It is much worse for children."

Miriam steeled herself, summoning strength she wasn't sure she possessed. *Think.*

Aaron stormed through the back door and rushed to Miriam's side with Rachel right behind him. He reached out without a word and took Little Amos from his mother.

"Rachel said something is wrong with Little Amos," he said. The boy wrapped his arms around his uncle's neck and laid his head on a shoulder. Aaron touched a rough hand to the forehead and a deep worry lined his face. "He's feverish. What is it?"

"Diphtheria," Miriam said. "Little Amos and Ada both have it."

Aaron's face blanched ash gray and his eyes widened in terror, but within seconds something came over him. It was a subtle thing, but suddenly he looked very much like his father—that iron resolve.

He spoke to Kyra in Spanish. "What must we do?"

Mamm wailed again. Without looking, Aaron reached back to squeeze her shoulder, and she quieted.

"*Think*, Kyra. Tell us what we should do." His calm tone commanded focus.

Kyra took a deep breath and blew it out. "First, you must close the school, Miriam. Send the children home quickly. The disease is very contagious. Everyone should stay in their own house for a time and not move about. Boil water, wash everything, then iron it. Do not share dishes. Don't drink from the dipper at the well. Mary should leave Little Amos here, since the strangler is already in this house and there are no other little ones here. Your mother can care for him. Mary must keep her other children away."

"But what can we do for *this one?*" Aaron asked, "How do we make him better? Surely there is a home remedy you or some of the other local women know about. There must be *something!*"

He was almost shouting. His eyes had grown hard and fierce, and everyone in the room fell silent because they knew why. He was thinking of the other Amos, his own twin brother whom he had loved more than life itself, who died of the Spanish flu. Aaron would not live through that again. He would move heaven and earth first.

Kyra shook her head and averted her eyes, unable to face his intense glare. "Not here. In the city there are doctors with medicine, an antitoxin that might save them, but by the time you get them to Mexico City or Monterrey it will be too late."

"Another place then. There must be medicine someplace closer. *Think, Kyra.*"

Suddenly Kyra's face lifted, a ray of hope. "My cousin! Agua Nueva! There was an outbreak only last year, and there is a doctor in Agua Nueva. He has seen the strangler before, so perhaps he still has medicine!"

Aaron nodded firmly. "Agua Nueva is only thirty miles over the mountains to the west. We can be there before dark. Rachel, you'll go with me to take care of them while I drive. Pack food and water, some blankets and whatever we need for Little Amos while I go and hitch our fastest horse to the surrey. I will drive that horse to death if I must."

Ten minutes later a long trail of dust hung over the road in the west end of Paradise Valley. Aaron leaned forward in the driver's seat, his wide-brimmed hat shoved low over his eyes as he white-knuckled the reins, shouting, willing his best horse up into the mountains at a hard trot. Rachel sat in the back holding a coughing, sweating child on her lap and keeping an arm around Ada, who leaned against her and moaned constantly from a fire in her throat that she did not understand.

Over and over Rachel muttered the only prayer she could think to pray.

"Please, Gott, help us. *Please.*"

Chapter 17

I n midafternoon the surrey rolled down from the heights above Agua Nueva, hurried across the railroad tracks and turned onto the main street of the ramshackle mountain town. A few poncho-clad peasants stopped and stared, and two mangy dogs harried the exhausted buggy horse right up until Aaron pulled back the reins and stopped in front of the train station.

Rachel leaned out and shouted at a portly woman on the boardwalk. The old woman wore a colorful scarf on her head and carried a canvas bag in her hand. Her other hand was on the door, about to enter the station, but she stopped when Rachel called to her.

"*Por favor*, señora, tell me where we can find a doctor. We have a sick child."

The woman pointed. "Two streets down," she said. "Past the blacksmith shop."

"Gracias," Aaron shouted over his shoulder, already rolling. When he found the place he didn't even tie the horse, but jumped down, grabbed Little Amos and helped Ada down out of the surrey.

"See to the horse," he said to Rachel without looking back, almost dragging Ada up across the boardwalk, where he banged on the doctor's door.

The horse was badly lathered, drooling foam around his mouth and panting heavily. Rachel took the reins and eased him around to the stables behind the blacksmith shop. The smith showed her to a stall, where she gave that fine animal food and water and rubbed him down before she left. It was about then that she noticed her own throat was getting sore.

Rachel let herself in through the front door and nosed around until she found them in a back room. Ada and Little Amos lay on separate cots on opposite sides of the room with a little dresser against the wall between them—the only furniture. Afternoon light slanted through a window on one side, and there were two unlit lanterns hanging overhead. The place was clean but spare. To Rachel, Dr. Gutierrez looked to be no older than Aaron, a slight man dressed in khaki, his shirttail hanging out. Standing over Ada, the doctor raised a hypodermic and gave it a thump with his middle finger.

"You must be Rachel," he said without looking. "Your brother told me you would let yourself in."

Aaron stood flat against the wall by the door, waiting, staying out of the way.

"I'm afraid your friend was right, Señorita Bender, it is diphtheria. It is good you brought them so quickly, but it may already be too late."

The doctor had already undone the shoulder of Ada's dress, but when he leaned over with the needle, she realized what was about to happen and went all wild-eyed, screaming and crabbing away from him until she overbalanced the cot and crashed to the floor in the corner.

Aaron calmly lifted the cot out of the way and knelt over her. He spoke to her with a lowered voice, the way he would have calmed a spooked horse, and she quieted. Gently but firmly he wrapped her in a hug that hid her face and trapped her arms while leaving her shoulder exposed for the doctor. The prick of the needle sent her into another fit of kicking and screaming, but Aaron had her now. When the doctor backed away, finished, Aaron kept holding her, talking in soothing tones until she finally calmed down, then righted the cot and helped her back into it. Only after he had returned to his post by the door did Aaron reach up and rub the little parentheses of blood seeping through the shoulder of his shirt where Ada had bitten him.

Little Amos did not fight when Gutierrez injected his behind, though he began crying softly. As soon as the doctor moved away Aaron sat down on the cot and picked up the child. Amos wrapped his arms around his uncle's neck and laid his head on the same shoulder Ada had bitten.

Rachel had missed most of the conversation, and she wanted to be sure about the antitoxin. "Doctor, was that the medicine my friend Kyra told us about? Will it cure them?"

Gutierrez's head bobbed side to side, ambivalent. "Sí, señorita, it is the antitoxin. But you must understand, this is not a cure."

"But Kyra said . . ."

Gutierrez shook his head. "No. To put it simply, diphtheria cells make poison and put it into the blood. The antitoxin will counteract the poison, and sometimes it is the difference between life and death, but the disease will run its course. This boy was already very sick and the swelling may not have reached its peak. The disease is not done with him yet, señorita. He will have to fight it off in his own strength."

"No," Aaron said quietly. "He will fight it off in the strength of Gott."

To Rachel, this was unsettling news. It seemed the end was still not clear.

"Will they live?" she squeaked. Aaron flinched, so bluntly had she voiced his fear.

The young doctor shrugged weakly. "I don't know. This one, she is a grown woman and I think she will make it. But the boy . . . it is too soon to tell. We will know in the morning. I suppose your brother is right—his life is in God's hands."

Aaron was rubbing at his shoulder as Gutierrez talked, and the doctor noticed.

"Is that blood on your shirt, señor?"

Aaron nodded.

"Your sister bit you?"

"Sí, but it is nothing."

"Nothing? Señor, diphtheria is very contagious. When your throat begins to swell, then you will not think it is nothing. Do either of you have a sore throat?"

Rachel coughed, nodded. "I do," she said.

The doctor prepared antitoxin for both of them. "If it is given early enough, sometimes the effects of the disease are milder," he said.

"Well then," Aaron said, "is there any way you could come to Paradise Valley and give it to the rest of our people?"

"How many?"

"I don't know . . . over a hundred in our settlement alone. More than that at El Prado."

The doctor shook his head. "I don't have that much antitoxin, but I know a doctor in Saltillo who does. There is a telegraph office in the train station. As soon as I can I will wire him and inform him of the outbreak. I'm sure he will send someone to your valley."

Squeezing Rachel's arm to administer the shot, Gutierrez said to her, "You are a strong one, señorita, and we caught the disease very early. Perhaps it will not be too bad."

Then he asked Aaron if they had a place to stay. "If you don't, I can offer you a cot in the other room, but you will have to give it up if a patient needs it."

"I will stay here," Aaron said. His eyes pointed to the pine plank floor next to Little Amos's bed.

"But, señor, you are welcome—"

"I will stay here."

Ada squirmed on the narrow cot. Her eyes, white with terror, were glued to Rachel's face. She was whimpering still, but under the circumstances she was doing better than Rachel expected.

"I will stay here, too," Rachel said.

The doctor nodded slowly, smiling a little. "I see. Well then, we will try to make you comfortable. My wife and I live upstairs. She will bring you something to eat at dinnertime, but it may not be much. I am only a poor country doctor; most of my patients pay with chickens and corn."

"You heal this boy, Doctor," Aaron said, "and I will find a way to pay whatever you ask."

⤳

Rachel slept fitfully that night on the pallet the doctor's wife made for her on the floor beside Ada's bed. In the middle of the night she awoke to the sound of thrashing, and then a voice in the darkness.

"What's wrong?" Aaron shouted, and she knew by the desperation in his voice that he was talking to Little Amos.

"Rachel, light the lantern, quick!"

Scrambling in the pitch-black for the matches, she managed to find a lantern and light it. Aaron was sitting on the cot holding Little Amos, who was flailing about with his arms and kicking his little feet. His mouth was open as if he wanted to scream, but no sound came out.

"He's burning up," Aaron said.

She held the lantern close. "His lips are blue," she said. "He can't breathe."

"Get the doctor!"

Rachel's curly red hair hung loose about her shoulders but she was fully dressed; she'd been sleeping in her clothes. She lit the other lantern and ran to the stairs. In less than a minute she came back, trailed by the young doctor. His hair was tousled and he was just now fastening a pair of pants under his nightshirt. He knelt by the cot and put a stethoscope to Amos's chest while Aaron held him. The child's chest heaved and his arms and legs tightened with it, fighting with all his strength to draw breath through his swollen throat. Even in the last few minutes they had seen his struggles growing weaker.

"His throat is closing," the doctor said.

Aaron leaned toward him, fire in his eyes. *Do something.*

"*Lo siento*, Señor Bender, but there is nothing more I can do." There was grief in his eyes, and his hands shook as his face sank into them.

Aaron reached out and laid a hand on the young doctor's shoulder. His voice came out soft and full of compassion.

"*Please*, Doctor. You must know *something*. There has to be a way."

Gutierrez raised his face. He looked away for a moment and his eyes narrowed in thought.

"There is one thing," he said. "It is possible to cut a hole in the throat, only I have never done it before."

Aaron shrugged. "But you know how it is done?"

"I think so, but I have never even *seen* it done, and it is dangerous because the child is so small and I would have to sedate him."

Aaron studied his face. "Will he die if you don't do it?"

The doctor stared at Little Amos for a moment and the grief returned to his eyes. He nodded.

"He will not see the dawn."

"Then do it," Aaron said. "No matter the outcome, I will thank you for trying."

Gutierrez rose to his feet, the decision made. "Señor Bender, I think perhaps your resolve is more contagious than diphtheria. How much does he weigh?"

"About thirty pounds," Aaron said.

It didn't take long. Gutierrez went away for a minute and came back with a tray covered by a white cotton cloth on which lay a scalpel, scissors, glass tubes and bandages he would need, carefully lined up. Rachel held the tray while he gave Little Amos a shot to put him to sleep and then held his own breath for fear the boy's strained, fragile breathing would stop.

A minute later he swabbed iodine on the little cleft at the top of the breastbone and made a cut with the scalpel. Amos lay flat on the cot, his breath now coming in hard spasms. Aaron knelt on the other side of the cot, holding the child's head and knees firmly, his lips moving in silent prayer.

The doctor parted the flesh and found the trachea, then without hesitation made a small incision. The boy's chest heaved and there was a little suction sound as he drew air and blood through the hole. Quickly, Dr. Gutierrez plucked a glass tube from his tray and inserted it into the hole.

In mere seconds the child's breathing leveled out, his chest rising and falling normally. The rasping disappeared, air now bypassing his constricted throat. Soon the blue began to fade from his lips and some of the color came back into his cheeks. The doctor drew a great quaking breath of his own and sat back on his haunches wiping sweat from his brow with the sleeve of his nightshirt.

"It is *working*," he whispered, wide-eyed, as if it was a complete surprise to him. As if it was a miracle. Then he shook himself out of his reverie and set about taping the tube in place and bandaging around it.

Aaron had not moved. His stoic expression had not changed. He said nothing, and Rachel was careful not to stare at the tears tracking his cheeks.

She glanced over her shoulder at Ada. At bedtime the doctor had given her something for pain, which apparently knocked her out. By Gott's grace she had slept through the whole ordeal, and until now Rachel hadn't even noticed the snoring.

By the next evening the swelling in Little Amos's neck had gone down and his fever had abated. The day after that, Gutierrez tested his throat by placing a finger over the end of the tube. Amos breathed normally, through mouth and nose. This was a great relief, considering that Aaron and Rachel had been taking turns holding him round the clock to prevent him from pulling the irritating tube out of his own throat. The doctor sedated him one more time, removed the tube and stitched up the hole.

By Monday morning Ada was feeling much better, Rachel's symptoms had nearly disappeared and the incision on Little Amos's throat was healing nicely with no sign of infection. Dr. Gutierrez reluctantly acquiesced when Aaron insisted it was time to go home.

Aaron paid the blacksmith, hitched the horse and brought the surrey around, then went inside to settle up.

"How much do we owe you?" he asked, bouncing Little Amos in his arms.

The doctor chuckled. "I have only been a doctor for a year,

Señor Bender, and I have not yet learned how much to charge. Most of the time it doesn't matter because the people I treat have no money anyway. Just do what they do—pay me whatever you can, whenever you can. Whatever you think it is worth."

"I can't do that," Aaron said with a proud glance at his nephew. "I won't ever have that much."

Chapter 18

They sang as they bumped along the rocky road at the crest of the long ridge coming back from Agua Nueva. The sun shone brightly, the high mountain air was cool and clear and their faithful buggy horse was sound, well rested and eager to work after three days in the stable. Aaron and Rachel were too jubilant to contain themselves, so they sang old hymns to pass the time. Little Amos occasionally blew an off-key note on his harmonica, and it made Aaron laugh every time. Even Ada felt well enough to sing along with them. It had always seemed strange to Rachel that Ada could sing better than she could talk, but then again it didn't require nearly as much thought. A song came with its own memory, and the words were always the same. Ada loved anything that was always the same.

They were about halfway home, still riding the ridgetop above the tree line, when Aaron heard something, stopped singing and leaned out to look behind them. When he turned back around the smile had gone from his face, replaced by terror.

"Bandits," he said. He snapped the reins and hurried the horse, but it was a futile gesture. Within a minute a dozen bandits swarmed past both sides of the buggy. One of them swept in close and grabbed the reins by the horse's neck and hauled back. The horse's head turned sharply and he pulled up, slowing to a stop.

The others turned and trotted back toward them, led by that unmistakable Appaloosa. El Pantera dismounted in front of them and ambled casually back to the buggy.

Rachel cringed. Maybe it was the white eye with the jagged scar angling down across it, the hollow grin or the patently false air of civility, but something about this man reminded her of a coiled snake, ready to strike without warning. He made the hair stand up on the back of her neck. Two of his men stood holding the bridle of the buggy horse while several others dismounted and sauntered over to stand behind their leader. Half of them remained in their saddles, leaning to get a better look. At *her*.

El Pantera stopped a few feet away from the buggy and touched a finger to his slouch hat.

"Buenos días, amigos! My friends and I heard singing and we wondered who these pilgrims were who traveled our road so happily on this fine bright day." He was smiling as gaily as if he were about to break into song himself. "What is your name, señor?"

"*Me llamo* Aaron Bender."

"Bender! The name is familiar to me. I know your father. You are friends with young Domingo, no?"

Aaron nodded, reluctantly. "Sí. Domingo is our friend."

The smile faded from El Pantera's lips. "You should choose your friends more carefully, Señor Aaron Bender."

Rachel was sitting directly behind her brother and she could see his breathing quicken. She shifted Little Amos off her lap and eased him down between herself and Ada to make him a little less visible, but the movement caught the bandit leader's eye. He craned his neck and peered into the back of the surrey.

"What is this? We have a niño? Oh, he is a *fine*-looking boy!"

El Pantera took a half step toward the buggy and Aaron tensed.

"Leave the boy be," Aaron said evenly. "He is not well. The strangler is on him."

El Pantera's eyebrows rose and he recoiled a step. His men murmured among themselves.

But Little Amos knew nothing of bandits and paid them no attention at all. He raised his harmonica to his lips and blew a note, then burst into laughter. Rachel snatched the instrument from his hand and shoved it into his coat pocket.

El Pantera shook a finger at Aaron, grinning. "I think you try to trick me, Señor Aaron Bender. Anyone can see this boy is not dying, and if he were, you would not have been singing so happily, would you?" He turned to his men, palms up. "Why does everyone lie to us and treat us as if we are outlaws? We are not such bad men. Come, let me see the niño."

He held his hands out and took a step forward, reaching toward Little Amos.

It happened so quickly no one could have seen it coming, let alone prevented it. Aaron planted a hand and vaulted out of his seat, landing on his feet between El Pantera and the buggy.

There was a quick flurry of movement, like a snake striking, and then El Pantera jumped back. Only then did Rachel see the knife in the bandit's hand, and the blood on the blade.

Aaron's face was a frozen mask of surprise as his head tilted and he slowly looked down at his hands, clamped on his belly. Blood oozed from between his fingers.

The world seemed to hold its breath for a split second, and then Rachel screamed.

Aaron raised his bewildered face to plead with El Pantera. "Please, señor—please don't hurt the . . ." The words tailed off as the big Amishman slumped to his knees, pitched over onto his side and drew himself into a ball, squirming in the dust, his breathing growing fast and shallow.

Rachel's whole world swirled and tilted. Sheer horror flooded her mind, and reason fled.

El Pantera looked up at her and spread his hands in apparent apology, grinning sheepishly, waving the knife absently.

"I did not mean to do that, señorita. It was only my hand, you see? My hand did it all by himself. Señor Aaron Bender should not have jumped at me like that."

Empty, meaningless words, but as he said them there was a rustling noise and she heard a low guttural moan that swelled quickly into a bone-chilling, inhuman wail. The buggy tilted as Ada leaped out the other side. She tumbled when she hit the ground, and as she rolled over, Rachel saw that she was clutching something tightly in her arms. A tiny hand flew up in front of Ada's face. Little Amos!

Rolling over and scrambling awkwardly to her feet, Ada ran blindly with her head down and her arms wrapped around the child—straight toward the mounted bandits.

Two of them drew their guns, but El Pantera shouted, "*Loca!* The girl is crazy! Let her go!"

She lumbered between their horses, wild-eyed and oblivious. Laughing and whooping, the mounted bandits raised their pistols into the air and fired, yelling, "Run, crazy woman, RUN!"

Rachel watched in horror as Ada tripped over a rock and fell again, her dress and heavy cotton underskirt flying up, thick white legs cartwheeling through the air. But she clutched Little Amos tight against her, protecting him as she rolled. She stumbled to her feet and staggered on, wailing and swaying.

Rachel started to jump out and chase after her sister, but an iron hand gripped her wrist and snatched her backward. El Pantera dragged her screaming out of the buggy, and her feet bounced on the coiled body of her brother. Aaron didn't move or cry out. He lay very still.

Too still.

She fought and twisted, trying to wrench herself free from the bandit so she could see about her brother, but El Pantera was too strong. In the struggle he ripped her prayer kapp from her head. All the pins came out and her hair went every which way. El Pantera grabbed fistfuls of red hair and dragged her over the rocks, laughing.

"Be careful with this one," he said, leering at her as he flung her down in front of his men. "She is a rare one—young and spirited, with hair like *flames*! She will bring a pretty penny!"

They bound her hands with twine and tossed her into the saddle with one of the bandits—a wiry, hawk-faced little man who stank terribly. He looked familiar. Another of them took the buggy horse out of the traces and tied a rope to his neck while El Pantera shouted orders for some of his men to throw the gringo's body in the buggy and roll it off the road, into the trees where it would not be seen.

Quaking with shock and terror, Rachel desperately scanned the road to the east for Ada, but she was nowhere in sight. Gone, and Little Amos with her. Rachel dared not even think what their fate would be, lost in the middle of the mountains with no one to help them. No one even knew they were here.

She wept uncontrollably. The bandit in the saddle behind her told her to shut up, then smacked the side of her head roughly, but she could not stop crying. She simply had to endure the blows until he tired of it and stopped hitting her.

With his arms tight around her there was no way to get away from him. He leaned against her, rubbed his hands over her body, pressed his lips into her hair and whispered, "I would have had your dark-eyed sister once, if it had not been for your little friend Domingo. But that's okay, for tonight I will have *you*, and I think you are probably a sweeter berry even than your sister. I will make you *mine*, pretty señorita."

It was then that she remembered the weasel. That voice. She had been there two years ago, with Emma in the surrey, when the weasel and his friends forced them to trade a broken-down pinto for their best buggy horse. The mere thought of him made her physically ill, and the smell nearly made her retch. She wondered if he'd had a bath since the last time she saw him. Watching helplessly through a flood of tears, she saw three bandits hoist Aaron's limp body into the back of the surrey and push it down the hill. The buggy got away from them, gained speed, bounced twice over the uneven ground, crashed hard into a twisted pine at the edge of the woods and tipped over in a tangle of weeds and vines. Strolling casually back up the hill, the three of them mimed the crash with hand gestures, chortling.

Then, suddenly, it was over. Everyone mounted their horses and trotted away, following El Pantera down a logging trail deep into the pine and oak forest to the north.

It hit Rachel like a flash flood. Her entire world had been swept away in the space of five minutes—captured and bound like a slave, carried off by the worst kind of men to a fate she dared not even contemplate, her brother stabbed, her sister and nephew lost in the wild mountains—and there was nothing she could do about it except pray.

Her first and most fervent prayer was for Aaron, Ada and Little Amos. The second one was for Jake. Bouncing along on horseback with the arms of the weasel around her, she whispered, "Please, Gott, don't let Jake come after me. Don't let these monsters get their hands on him. Please just let me die instead."

Chapter 19

Fear came upon Ada like a fog.

In Agua Nueva her terror of the room in the strange place and the dreadful hurt in her throat overwhelmed her sometimes, forcing her to close her eyes and try to rock the fog away, the comfort of rhythm her last resort, the only comfort she could find. The strangeness surrounded her, nipping at her like a mean dog so that sometimes she had to bang her head to keep it from getting inside. At least Rachel was there. Rachel was real and good, part of home—not as good as Mamm, but still good.

Ada hadn't understood why they had to go to the strange place to begin with, or if they would ever go home again, but she could read faces and she knew Rachel and Aaron. When they left the strange place and started singing it meant they were going home. Back to Mamm. Back to normal.

The songs they sang in the buggy made her feel safe too, for they were carved deeply on her mind. The words had always been there. The songs knew her and loved her the way her bed did. They made her happy, chasing away the memory of the strange place and the hurt in her throat. Everything was so nice until the strange men stormed by on their horses and the buggy stopped.

When the horses came and the buggy stopped, the fog crawled back in. Her tongue swelled up to push against her eyes and she couldn't see very well. When the bad man came up to the buggy the thrumming came with him, a deep soft hum swelling and ebbing in her head until it drowned out voices so she couldn't hear them anymore. The fog closed in.

Aaron scared her, jumping down like that, and then the bad man did something to him, and Rachel screamed. Madness, meanness, terror, fighting, all of it jangled together, and then she saw Aaron's hands.

Blood! Blood! Blood!

When Aaron fell down bleeding, holding his stomach, the low humming rose to a piercing scream like a train whistle. Her eyes shook and her ears throbbed. She had to run away. *Right this minute, Ada Bender!*

She didn't know she had grabbed Little Amos. He was just there in her arms as she went tumbling across the rocks hurting her elbows. But she felt him then, knew him, clung to him.

A piece of home, small enough to carry, her arms whispered. *Run away!*

Suddenly her feet found the earth under her and she was upright again. Her legs pumped and ran, all by themselves. Horses came out of the fog, big horses with big teeth and sharp hooves, and then the ugly faces of strange men, laughing, jeering. But she couldn't see very far and there was no turning in her legs. Bending over to hide from them, she plunged between the horses and by some miracle left them in the fog. *Run away!*

Then came the noise of lightning, over and over, and bad men shouting words she couldn't understand. Her knees tried to hide from the noise and she went down again. She barely saw the hard ground coming, but some part of her heard Little Amos crying, felt him clinging. If she fell on him he would be hurt and she would be in trouble, like the time she fell on baby Barbara, so she turned enough to make the ground hurt her shoulder instead.

The sleeve of her dress ripped and one of her elbows screamed at her, but as soon as she stopped rolling her frightened legs raised her up again and she ran. She ran, wailing, because it was the only thing she knew. *Run away!*

The fog thickened and the pounding in her ears drowned out all sound. All she could see was the two wagon ruts in front of her, and she stayed between them because there was order in them, boundaries, and she needed them. It seemed she ran for hours before she collapsed, spent and gasping, unable even to wail anymore. She could go no farther. The fog, the fear, the screaming in her ears, all of it caught up with her and grew until it overwhelmed her. Any second now the evil would catch her from behind and swallow her.

She curled herself into a ball, still clinging to Little Amos, until the fog began to swirl and howl. As the din folded itself about her she felt herself falling, spinning into the vortex.

⟳

Nothingness. Silence but for the whisper of the wind.

Oblivion yielded to a growing, swelling tumult of fear until out of a tornado of white noise came the distant sound of a baby crying. Swimming up out of mottled darkness, Ada opened her eyes in bright sunlight to find Little Amos kneeling beside her, crying, slapping her shoulder and face, shouting.

"*Wachen,* Auntie!" *Wake up!* The baby's cheeks were red and his eyes swollen, his hat missing. Tears covered his face and a string of snot hung from his chin.

Sitting up, rubbing her eyes, Ada tried to remember, but the slate was clean.

"Mamm?" she cried, her voice high and brittle, but Mamm was nowhere to be seen. Looking around, she saw that she was in a barren rocky place that dropped off on both sides to a line of trees and shadows. Nothing was familiar except the wagon ruts running past on both sides. Fear gripped her and she began to moan and rock.

"MAMM!" Louder this time, and high-pitched, almost a scream. Her voice echoed back from the canyon, mocking her. Barrenness, emptiness. She rocked harder. Her eyes filled and a keening welled up from the back of her throat. A little wind blew frizzy hair into her eyes, and she reached up to rearrange her kapp, but it was gone.

"RAAACHELLLL!" A warbling scream.

Only the wind answered.

The pounding began, and the low hum. Fog threatened the edges of her vision. She moaned louder and rocked harder, all the way down, tapping her head against the rock, but a small voice broke through.

"*Durstig,* Auntie." *I'm thirsty.*

Little Amos knelt beside her, pleading. So helpless. He looked to her, to *Ada,* for water.

She blinked and forgot to rock. She wiped her eyes and the fog seemed to subside for a moment.

Ada had always been, and still was, a child.

No one had *ever* looked to *her* for help.

In that moment, something clicked. Deep inside, perhaps in the blood of her father, some tiny awareness awakened, and for the first time in her life she felt burdened by someone weaker, more helpless than herself. This little one wanted his mamm— needed her even more than Ada needed hers.

She lifted Little Amos onto her lap, took up the hem of her dress and wiped his face clean the way she'd seen his mother do. Then she hugged him and snuggled her face into his warm neck. Words of her own would not come, but she made a habit of memorizing the words of others, especially the things they repeated in moments of crisis.

"Shhhh, little one," she cooed. "Gott knows. Shhhh."

Quietly he complained again of thirst, but there was no water. "Shhhh," she said, and rocked him. They sat that way for a long time, until this new arrangement of things settled on her heart and made itself comfortable. For the first time in her life there was something only she could do for someone that only she could help, and in her simple mind this small knowledge shaped itself into a mission.

Find this boy's mamm. Find Mary.

Ada had no idea how to go about it or where to begin, but the darkness of her innate pessimism told her that Mary would not come to her. She must move. She knew at least that much.

Gathering the child to her, she staggered to her feet and looked around.

The tracks. She recognized wagon tracks, for she had seen them all her life. They were familiar, and familiar was good. She would follow the ruts as long as they lasted, but which way? Directions were all the same to her, the comings and goings of sun and moon a mystery. Wagon ruts led both ways from where she stood, and there was no way to know which way pointed to home.

But when Rachel had been so upset riding to Agua Nueva in the surrey with Ada's head on her shoulder she had repeated words over and over as if there was magic in them. Somehow the words had made Rachel feel better, so Ada repeated them now.

"Please Gott help us please."

Nothing happened. She stood silent for a good five minutes, the wind blowing her frizzy hair about, lashing her face and the red face of Little Amos, but in the end the road still looked the same in both directions. The words themselves might have made her feel better, but nothing really happened. Gott did not show her the way. Worse, a coyote began to yip and howl, and the eerie sound filled her with dread. She had heard the stories when they thought she wasn't listening. Coyotes were evil, like very mean dogs. Sometimes they would steal babies and *eat* them.

Clutching Little Amos tight against her, Ada's fear grew, clouding her vision and pounding on the doors of her mind. She turned her back to the yipping coyotes and *ran*.

Heavy and unaccustomed to running, she lumbered awkwardly, stumbling often. The thirty-pound child in her arms weighed her down so that she staggered and weaved even more than usual because she couldn't wave her arms for balance. In a few short minutes, panting for breath, her heart thumping like a drum, she slowed to a walk.

But walking, or something, kept the fog from closing in. She would not stop again. Lumbering on, she clung to three simple thoughts: *Keep going, follow the ruts, find Mary.* She made it into a kind of song and repeated it to herself. She was still afraid— terrified, in fact—but she held off the fog and stumbled forward as one possessed, a woman with a purpose greater than herself.

The fog was there. It was always there, but it did not close in. The fog feared this new Ada.

The road seemed endless, the scenery unchanging. She didn't know if it would ever change, for she had no concept of time or distance. Home, for all Ada knew, might lay as far away as heaven, in some other direction.

Every so often when she missed a step she would fall down, but always she protected the child. Her arms ached, her knees throbbed, her elbows were skinned and bleeding and protesting, yet she refused to listen to any of them. At least for now, Ada had no room for Ada.

Keep moving, follow the ruts, find Mary.

Her feet blistered, then the blisters burst and bled. She refused to stop because she was afraid she might not remember to start again.

Something had happened to the night. Bandits must have stolen the darkness, because she had walked for so long that surely the darkness should have come, and yet the sun still shined.

Limping now, hobbling on ruined feet and swollen knees, with blood congealing on a half-dozen ugly bruises, she plodded stubbornly on for an eternity, past dinnertime and Christmas and Rachel's birthday, until it came upon her all at once that she was getting cold.

Her shadow had disappeared. The sky had changed from deep blue to dim purple, and still the road ahead looked no different than the road behind.

Keep moving, follow the ruts, find Mary.

Little Amos fussed and cried a little. His voice cracked with a drying throat, but he had given up asking for water. Just before full dark he began saying he was hungry and cold.

When it grew too dark to see the wagon ruts Ada walked a little farther and then stopped, afraid of stepping on a snake. Snakes were mean and evil, worse than coyotes. Now she, too, began to shiver from the cold, so she lay on her side on the bare rock and pulled Little Amos up inside her coat. They warmed each other, and before long the shivering decreased. Completely spent, both mentally and physically, Ada melted into the rock and went away.

Chapter 20

Caleb returned home that Monday afternoon. He dropped off Domingo in San Rafael and trundled into Paradise Valley a day late, without the preacher. He half expected to meet one of his sons or John Hershberger on the road home, coming out to check on him, but he made it all the way back to the valley without seeing a familiar face.

As soon as he rounded the end of the ridge and caught sight of home he was filled with a deep sense of foreboding. His people had long awaited the arrival of an ordained minister. It would be cause for major celebration, since no Amish settlement was complete, or even entirely functional, without one. Under normal circumstances they would have posted one of the boys at the ridgetop to watch for his wagon. They would have spotted him ten miles away, and by the time his wagon reached home there would have been a crowd waiting to greet their new preacher. Even if the lookout reported that Caleb was alone, the whole settlement would have gathered to find out why. But no one turned out. He saw smoke rising from a few cooking fires at the Amish farms, but despite good weather there didn't seem to be anybody out and about. Very disturbing.

Finally, after he turned in and made it halfway up his driveway his wife and children straggled out of the house to greet him. Even from a distance he could see Martha wringing her hands, and the dark look on all their faces filled him with dread. Something was terribly wrong.

He stopped short of the house, and Mamm hurried up to him as he climbed down.

"Diphtheria," she said, fighting back tears. "Many of the children have taken ill."

It knocked the wind out of him for a minute. This was worse than anything he could have imagined. "We must get a doctor," he finally said.

Mamm shook her head. "One is already here. He came from Saltillo late Saturday in a fancy automobile and stayed up all night giving everyone shots. He's over with the newcomers just now, at the camp. Already one of the new children died."

"Who? Which one?"

"Little Enoch Byler. He was three. We buried him yesterday." She lowered her head, struggling to speak. "There will be more."

Caleb removed his hat, hung his head and was silent for a few seconds. When he raised his head again he said, "I guess this explains why no one is asking about the minister." Important as the preacher was, his absence paled in comparison to a diphtheria epidemic.

"But wait," Caleb said, "the doctor got here on Saturday? Why, I left on Friday and nobody was sick yet. How did a doctor get here so fast?"

"The doctor in Agua Nueva wired him when Aaron got there. He asked him to bring medicine to Paradise Valley."

"Why was Aaron in Agua Nueva?"

Mamm dabbed at her eyes and struggled for control. "Because the first ones to get sick were Ada and Little Amos. Kyra saw the sickness on them two hours after you left. She didn't think Little Amos would live. The poor child was very sick—it's worse for the little ones. Aaron and Rachel took him to Agua Nueva in the surrey. And Ada, too."

The color drained from Caleb's face. "So, are they all right? Where are they now?"

Mamm snuffled, fighting a sob. "They haven't come back yet. We've heard nothing. We only know they were with the doctor in Agua Nueva on Friday, and he had medicine. The doctor who came here said that if everything went right they might be home yesterday."

Caleb nodded, staring down the road to the west. "If they don't get back tonight, I'll go looking for them in the morning. Could be they're broke down someplace in the mountains."

Miriam was standing next to her mother, listening. "Where *is* the minister?" she asked.

Caleb sighed. "Ervin Kuhns and his family didn't ever come to the train station in Arteaga. Me and Domingo waited for them all day Saturday, thinking mebbe they just missed the train and took another one later, but they never showed up. We went back on Sunday, but they still didn't come yet. In the afternoon, finally some passengers from Nuevo Laredo told us the border was closed and no Americans were allowed to cross just now. They didn't know why, but when I talked to the stationmaster he said sometimes they close the border to keep a disease out."

Miriam nodded slowly. "There was a medicine show in the hacienda village last weekend, and one of the women told Kyra they just came from the States. Maybe the medicine show people were the ones who brought it here. So what will Ervin do?"

"I don't know," Caleb said. "They might wait in Laredo for the border to open up again, but I don't think so—not if they don't know how long it will be. If it was me, I'd get on a northbound train and go back home. Anyways, Ervin's got his own wagon. If they do make it to Arteaga, he can get here without our help. It just won't be as easy."

Mamm kept staring down the road to the west as if she could will the surrey to appear out of the mountains with Aaron, Rachel, Ada, and Little Amos in it.

"I'm mighty worried about my children, Dat. I hope they're all right."

Caleb put an arm around her shoulder. "Don't fret, Mamm. I'm not worried a bit so long as Aaron is with them. They'll be fine."

A dark sense of foreboding gripped his heart like a cold fist, but he hid his dread behind a reassuring smile. It was his job. Mamm looked to him for hope.

⟡

Rachel clung to the horse's mane, leaning forward as much as she could, doing anything to put some space between her and the weasel who shared the saddle with her. Her hands tied, his arms around her holding the reins, there was no way to avoid him, no way to keep his hands from groping. Every time she straightened up he put his face next to her ear and whispered his dark desires. His breath was foul, his body odor worse.

"*Mi pequeña fresa madura,*" he kept calling her. *My little ripe strawberry.*

Just let me die, she prayed. *Please, Gott, just take me home.*

They rode for hours on the narrow trail without stopping, up and down rocky ridges, through mountain passes and along babbling bottomland creeks, working their way ever northward. In the evening, before the light completely failed, they finally stopped in a little mountainside meadow and made camp. The weasel dragged her from the saddle and threw her down, turning his back on her while he tended to his weary horse. No one seemed concerned that she might run. They were in the middle of the wild mountains and there was no place she could go.

One of the men had shot a young deer with his rifle an hour before they stopped. Now El Pantera slung the field-dressed carcass on the ground in front of Rachel, untied her hands and pulled a hunting knife from a sheath at his back—the knife with the rosewood handle, the one that felled her brother. She was sitting cross-legged on the ground when he threw the knife so that it stuck firmly and quivered an inch from her knee.

He leaned close with that evil grin and said, "The knife is for skinning the deer, señorita. If you get other ideas, I will use it to skin *you*. Now get to work. My men are hungry."

She picked up the bit of rope they'd used to bind her hands and used it to tie her hair back out of the way while she skinned the deer. One of the bandits built a fire, and an hour later the deer hung spitted on a green sapling, roasting over the fire.

They had built the fire between two downed logs, and after they had tended and tied all their horses they came one by one and sat on the logs warming themselves in the glow of the fire. Darkness had fallen, and two rows of faces leered at Rachel, laughing raucously at their own rude remarks as El Pantera made her come and sit beside him on the log.

They passed around a canteen, and when El Pantera had drunk his fill he handed it to Rachel. She didn't want to drink after these animals but her throat was parched and she didn't know when she would be offered water again. Their eyes were on her as she wiped it clean with her sleeve and turned it up.

She got a big mouthful and almost swallowed before the pain hit. Fire exploded in her throat and she pitched forward instantly, spitting, gagging, coughing uncontrollably. Some of the bandits laughed so hard they fell backward off the log.

Pounding on her back, El Pantera grinned widely and said, "Our little strawberry doesn't like mescal. I suppose it is an acquired taste."

Later, after they had eaten most of the venison and some of them had begun to yawn, they wandered off to get their bedrolls from the piles of gear and saddles by their horses. El Pantera went away for a minute but he returned shortly with a set of wrist irons dangling from his hand. He held them up to show her—two iron cuffs shaped like Ds, with a short length of chain between them.

"Such a pretty girl," he said. "I want you to have these bracelets. My gift to you."

He threw a horse blanket down next to a skinny pine not far from the fire, made her sit on the blanket and wrap her arms around the tree. He put her hands in the cuffs, took a little T-shaped tool from his pocket, inserted it into the barrel of the D and gave it several turns until the latch clicked.

Squatting beside her, gazing into the simmering fire, he tucked the tool into his vest pocket and said, "We would not want you to wander off and get eaten by wolves in the night, señorita. I think you will be warm enough here. Sleep well. I have big plans for you."

His ominous words haunted her for a long time after he walked away, for she had heard rumors about El Pantera and the kind of business he engaged in. She tried very hard not to think about it, to concentrate on finding a way to get comfortable lying on a horse blanket with her arms wrapped around a tree. Her life was over—she had already accepted that—but the endless possibilities of horror and torture that awaited her frail human form before she would be allowed to die plagued her thoughts for a long time. Again, she prayed for death, for release. Eventually she cried herself to sleep.

She jolted awake, but she couldn't move. Someone was straddling her, holding her down, and his hand was clamped over her mouth so she couldn't scream. The fire had died to embers and in the darkness she couldn't see his face, but she knew the smell of his putrid mescal-tinged breath.

"Make a sound, *mi pequeña fresa madura*," the weasel whispered, "and it will be your last, do you understand?"

Wide-eyed with terror, she barely had the presence of mind to nod. She understood, and she did not doubt for a second that the weasel would do as he said.

His hand moved away, but in the next instant he stuffed her mouth full of a filthy rag and tied a bandanna tightly around it so she couldn't scream even if she wanted to. She would have. She would have screamed loud enough to shake boulders loose from the mountains and then welcomed his knife, but all she could manage was a muffled moan.

Rough hands grabbed her ankles, flipped her onto her back and yanked so that her arms stretched tight against the handcuffs. She could only make out the dimmest silhouette in the paltry light cast by the dying embers of the fire, but it was enough.

She raised a leg and kicked hard. Her foot found his chest and drove him backward, but in the next instant he bounced back and punched her in the jaw, his foul breath brushing her face with dire threats.

Dazed now, and helpless, she turned away from the weasel and stared at the dying campfire. The patch of simmering coals pulsed a dim red. In the moonless night it was the only thing Rachel could see, so she fixed her gaze on it, hoping to find a way to remove her mind from what was about to happen.

But the coals moved. Against the blackness, as if by magic, a burning ember the size of a man's fist floated slowly up out of the ashes and hovered all by itself, three feet above the ground. The coals crumbled, the campfire drew breath and a little flame sprang up.

Startled by the sudden brightness, the weasel turned his head to look, and as he did the ember arced through the air like the end of a baseball bat and caught him flush on the jaw. Sparks flew. The weasel flipped over and landed on his back, partially on top of her. The flames of the campfire leaped higher, and in their light she saw El Pantera standing over them both, holding a thick branch like a spear, the pointed, smoldering tip a foot away from the weasel's face.

El Pantera's eyes sparkled in the freshening firelight, and his lips curled as he hissed, "Would you ruin my prize, Ramirez?"

The weasel tried to crab backward, to put some distance between himself and the glowing spear, but El Pantera planted a foot in his middle and held him down. Rachel found it hard to breathe with the bandit on top of her and her mouth plugged. She shifted a little and somehow managed to fill her lungs.

Rubbing a still-smoking jaw, the weasel's voice came out high-pitched and quivering, pleading for his life.

"I would have done her no harm, my captain. I only wanted—"

The burning branch inched closer and cut off his words. He squirmed in terror.

El Pantera seethed, his white eye glowing in the firelight. "Do you know what your moment of fun would do to the price of this girl when she is sold? *Do you?*"

The weasel's head vibrated, a quick and fearful no.

"I thought not. You nearly cost me a lot of money, Ramirez. You are a short-sighted fool, and if you cost me money, *fool*, it will cost you your life. Are you prepared to die for this girl?"

The smoldering spear inched closer as he spoke, and even Rachel shrank from the mental picture of what might be about to happen to the weasel. The terror in his eyes told her he saw the same picture.

"No, my captain." It was a hoarse whisper.

El Pantera wavered, then casually tossed the branch into the fire. With one hand he reached down and grabbed the smaller man by the collar and flung him into the darkness. The weasel hit the ground with a grunt and rolled, then skittered off toward the trees like a wounded spider.

El Pantera knelt down and untied the bandanna, pulled the rag from her mouth.

"Are you . . . unharmed?"

She nodded. "Sí."

"Get some sleep," he said, then rose and walked away.

She waited several minutes, afraid to move, afraid to breathe, afraid some new horror might descend upon her. Finally, when all was quiet, she rolled over and scooted up to the scrubby pine sapling to relieve the pressure of the handcuffs. Her hands were numb. Curling herself into a ball at the base of the tree, she pulled her hair about her face and tried to make herself small. She fervently wished she could just disappear.

Thoughts of home flooded her mind. She saw Jake's smiling eyes and prayed again that he would not come after her. He would never fight these men; he would only try to reason with them, and then they would kill him. Her mother's face came to her, praying, agonizing, perhaps never knowing what had become of her daughter.

Rachel wept softly in the darkness and prayed for Aaron, that by some miracle he might live. Then she wept and prayed for someone to find Ada and Little Amos before it was too late. When the red streaks of dawn stretched over the mountaintops she cried and begged for a swift end to deliver her from the coming evil, and for Gott to give her poor mother a measure of peace.

Chapter 21

Ada awoke with a chill. Pitch-black. Clouds covered the moon and she couldn't see her own hands. Something had awakened her, but she didn't know what it was. At night the fog came in a dark red tide, creeping in from the edges of her eyes and bringing the hum with it. She wrapped her arms around herself and started to rock. Something was not right. Her memory worked well enough, or so it seemed. Spurred by throbbing knees and a hundred dire pains from torn feet to skinned elbows, her plight showed itself to her right away. She knew she was lost, and she remembered why. But something else was wrong, and it refused to be coaxed to the front of her mind.

The air was perfectly still, as if the world held its breath. Total silence, total blackness. The unknown surrounded her. She began to rock harder until a little squeak of a sound came to her, faint and distant.

She stopped rocking and listened. There it was again, like a baby crying, far away. It was only then that she realized her arms were wrapped tight about her and there was no child in them.

Little Amos!

The cry came again, piercing the red hum.

To her right, somewhere. She turned her head, listening, and when it came again she knew the direction. Pushing herself to her feet she forgot to be afraid—until she found that she couldn't walk. There was no ground, no sky, no rocks or trees, no stars. Only black space, the whole world a yawning pit of unknown, waiting to swallow her, to throw her off a cliff. Ada tried to take a step, but she couldn't make her foot go down without knowing what lay beneath it. Holding her arms out in front of her, she tried sliding her feet so they stayed in contact with the earth, though her head felt vulnerable. Her eyes widened, yet there was only blackness and she didn't know what demons might dive at her like bats. Afraid to stay and afraid to go, she stood still until the red hum swelled and she began to hyperventilate.

Again she heard the baby's cry, fainter this time but still in the same direction. From the distance behind her, she heard the yip of a coyote and a chill ran down her spine. Coyotes steal babies and *eat* them.

She couldn't let that happen. Slowly, groping with splayed fingers, she knelt down until she found the ground. Lowering herself onto her hands and knees, she began to crawl. It was easier with her hands because she could feel her way. Crawling, she ignored the complaints of her battered knees and inched her way toward the sound. The going was slow and painful, but she would not stop. The coyote yipped again, and was answered by another, closer. Still, she did not stop.

She might have crawled for hours, she didn't know, but his cries kept getting louder until finally she was near enough to hear Little Amos whimpering right there in front of her. She reached out, expecting to touch his warm little body, but her hand landed on nothing. He was right there—*somewhere*. She could hear him breathing, yet her hand landed on thin air. She drew her hand back and slid it forward from her knee, keeping contact with the rock. Her fingers found the edge of a little drop-off. Lying flat on her belly, she reached down into the blackness beyond the lip. Her hand, groping, touched the cloth of his coat and her fist closed about it.

Hoisting Little Amos over the lip of the rock, she gathered him to her breast and wrapped her coat around him, rocking, moaning.

He smelled. Ada knew what that was—she'd smelled it often enough through a lifetime of babies, but her mother always fixed it. Mamm always knew what to do.

But Mamm was not here. Mamm was far away, and she was probably asleep. Still, Ada had seen it enough times to memorize it, so she decided to fix it herself, even if she couldn't see. First, she took off his coat and spread it out like a blanket. When she went to smooth out the coat, her hand found a lump and fished in his pocket to see what it was.

The harmonica. She stuck it in the pocket of her dress and laid Amos down on his back. In total darkness her hands pulled his suspenders down, took off his pants. She folded the diaper and used it to wipe him, the way she had seen her mother do a million times.

The coyote yipped again. *Much* closer. Another one answered from a different direction. Ada dropped the diaper and snatched up the baby. The clouds parted and a half-moon began to cast a dim light over the rocky landscape. Swaying and moaning, hugging the child, now she could see shapes moving in the dark, hear the clicking of toenails against rock.

There were more than two, and they were circling her.

She was surrounded. There was nowhere to run.

One of them stopped, a faint patch of blackness only slightly darker than the bare rock around it. She would not have known it was there at all if she hadn't seen it moving. The silhouette narrowed, turning, creeping straight toward her.

Ada whimpered and closed her eyes, dreading what was about to come. She squeezed Little Amos tight.

"Shhhh, little one. Gott knows."

Because of Little Amos her own fears remained in check and she didn't go away from herself. It was because of him that she thought of the harmonica. The harmonica was happy, and it loved him. It would ease his fears until the last. She pulled it from her pocket, put it to her lips, and blew.

There was a sudden flurry as a coyote scrambled. He had been right in front of her, only a step or two away, and she heard toenails skittering on rock as the dark shape beat a quick retreat. She blew again, louder. The shadow withdrew further, turned broadside to her, and stood watching from a distance.

Little Amos giggled and tried to take the harmonica. Snatching it from him, Ada blew it again. Honking. She had no idea how to make a tune on the instrument, nor did she care. She merely put it to her mouth and blew as hard as she could, over and over.

Every time the coyotes started to circle, closing in on her, she blew the harmonica. For a long time it worked and they stayed away, but then they seemed to grow accustomed to it. They learned that the noise did them no harm and they began to ignore it, once again trotting steadily in an ever-closing circle. They wanted Little Amos.

Again, her hope faded. She could see them now, approaching cautiously, haltingly, sniffing, and the red fog nearly closed off her sight. One of the coyotes dashed in and danced away with the dirty diaper, and then two others merged with his shadow and fought over it. The three growled at each other, tugged and ripped at the diaper until finally one of them slung it to the side. Abandoning it, they turned back toward Ada.

But beyond the coyotes, she caught a glimpse of a larger

shadow, rushing as silent as an owl in flight, low across the rock behind the coyotes. The quiet was shattered by a coyote yelp that merged with a chilling scream, the beginning of a great snarling, snapping racket. The coyotes darted away from her, silhouettes dashing toward the fight.

They were all gone. All of them. She knew they weren't far away, for her head rattled with the clamor of a furious battle just a stone's throw from where she sat, but at least for the moment they were not watching *her*.

Clutching Little Amos, she pushed herself to her feet and moved away, tiptoeing at first, then running. There was nothing to follow. She had forgotten the wagon tracks and would not have seen them anyway in the dark. She just ran.

And ran.

When she was out of breath, she slowed to a walk, panting, listening for the coyotes. She could no longer hear them. Afraid to sit down and rest for fear the coyotes would come again, she kept staggering forward.

Keep moving, her inner voice repeated. *Find Mary.*

She felt she had walked far enough to be back in Ohio. Her breath returned, but her arms ached from carrying Little Amos, and they began to droop. Just when she thought she could go no farther, she heard that scream again, echoing from canyon walls. It was far behind her now, yet the sound still curdled her spine and put the spurs to her. On legs driven by terror, looking back over her shoulder, she ran headlong into something that did not yield.

It knocked her backward and she fell heavily. When she rolled over and sat up, gathering the crying child against her, she looked up to see a Mexican standing in front of her. In the pale moonlight he was no more than a blackness, an uncertain silhouette like the coyotes, but she could make out the shape of a sombrero on his head. One hand was on his hip, the other pointed to her right.

She blinked and stared, shushing the baby.

The Mexican didn't move. As her eyes adjusted she saw him a little better and thought maybe it was not a man after all. Slowly, holding Little Amos, she rose and crept closer to the Mexican. An arm's length away, she began to think maybe he was a tree.

Her shaking, probing hand found the rough surface of a shattered pine with a broken flap of bark lying across the top that in the dark, in silhouette, might look a little like a sombrero. The arms were all that was left of the tree's dry, broken limbs. Hitching Little Amos higher on her shoulder, she started to go around the tree, but her toe caught on a rock and kicked it loose.

The rock bounced once . . . and disappeared. Silence, as if it had vanished. Leaning over, holding on to the limb for support, she saw that the dead tree clung to the very edge of a sheer cliff. She couldn't see the bottom, but she could tell it was a long way down.

Ada backed away and sat heavily on the ground, staring, trembling.

This tree was her friend. She didn't question it, or even think about it. She simply accepted that the tree had kept her from running over the cliff. If she had run off the cliff, Little Amos would have gotten hurt and she would be in trouble. The tree had stopped her. He had saved her from trouble because he chose to, because he wanted to. He was her friend.

"Thank you," she mumbled, because her mother had taught her to say it.

When she tried to gather up Little Amos to walk some more she found her arms too tired and achy to hold him. She couldn't even lift him. Lying on her side, she drew him into her coat, for his skin felt cold. Ada had no idea where his coat and pants had gone, but now the child was wearing only a shirt, and his legs were freezing.

Little Amos wouldn't stop shivering, even inside her coat. When Ada was cold her mamm always wrapped her in a blanket. She needed a blanket for Little Amos.

In a rare blinding flash of inspiration she sat up and started tearing the skirt from her dress. Underneath it she still wore a heavy cotton slip, so she could tear off the skirt without having to "run around naked." She'd never quite understood why, but Mamm didn't like it when she ran around naked. The dress was old, the seam frayed, so her skirt tore off easily. Sitting spraddle-legged on the rock, she laid Amos in the middle of the cloth, bound it around him several times and then drew him up against her, inside her coat again.

But her arms gave out quickly, exhausted from hours of carrying the thirty-pound child. She laid him down in her lap and let her weary arms fall limp at her sides. He seemed content, though he still shivered a little. But as he lay there, she noticed the pointed corners of the dark torn cloth against the white cotton of her slip, and it was as if they called to her.

She had seen native women carry their babies in bundles like this without using their hands. They tied the corners of a blanket together and hung the bundle around their necks.

She tried it. She fought with the loose corners for a long time, trying to figure out how to make a knot like the native women, but she couldn't do it. When she had given up and sat slumped over with her eyes closed, puffing in frustration, her hands returned to the cloth all by themselves. She had forgotten what her hands knew. Long ago her hands had learned to tie her shoes, but only if she didn't think about it. She kept her eyes closed tight, thinking only of shoes, and when she opened them again, the cloth was knotted.

She stuck her head through the hole and tested the knot with her neck.

It held.

Slowly, for she was bone-weary and hurting in every joint and pore, she stumbled to her feet, groaning. Little Amos hung nicely against her belly. Fastening her coat around him as best she could, she grinned proudly at the little round face peeking out at her.

It was his face that reminded Ada of her mission. Though her memory was porous and most things eventually fell through the holes, looking at Little Amos summoned one last clear purpose.

Find Mary.

But there was a sheer cliff in front of her. She couldn't go any farther; she must turn one way or the other. But which way led to Mary? Ada had no idea where she was, let alone which direction she needed to go.

Lost and confused, she stared blankly at the gnarled, broken tree for a minute before her mind once again conjured a sombrero on his head, arms at his sides, and she remembered that the tree was her friend. His arm had been pointing to the right the whole time, waiting patiently for her to notice.

Smiling broadly, she blew her friend a twisted note on the harmonica, then waved goodbye and staggered off to the right.

Downhill.

Chapter 22

Caleb slept fitfully that night, tossing and turning while snatches of dark, ominous dreams nipped at the edges of his sleep. He awoke an hour earlier than usual, but there would be extra chores in the absence of Aaron and Rachel, so he dressed himself and went out.

When the chores were done, the family gathered for breakfast, and there with them was the doctor. An expatriated American by the name of Leonard Gant, he'd been bunking in Caleb's basement for the last couple of nights while he tended the diphtheria victims in Paradise Valley. Dr. Gant was about Caleb's age, a gray-haired, sophisticated gentleman who wore a three-piece suit and tie to the breakfast table. He had run his own practice in Saltillo for twenty years and was fluent in Spanish, but the Benders relished the opportunity to speak English for a change.

"I'll be heading back home in a day or two," the doctor said over bacon and eggs. "I've administered antitoxin to everyone at risk in your Amish colony, but some of the younger ones are still in danger. Today will tell the tale, I think. Caleb, your wife tells me your children haven't returned from Agua Nueva. Any news?"

Caleb shook his head, took a sip of coffee. "No, and I'm thinking they should have got back by now. Chust as soon as I'm done eating, I'm going to look for them."

Even with a guest, the table seemed empty and quiet in the absence of Aaron, Rachel, and Ada. Especially Ada. She was always there. In all her years, unless she was laid up sick, Caleb couldn't remember a single breakfast without her.

"I'm sure they're fine," Gant said. "Dr. Gutierrez probably just wanted to hold them for a day or two to make sure the toddler was on the mend."

The sky was streaked with pink, the sun just beginning to peek over the eastern horizon. There was a nip in the air, and blue shadows still clung to the bottomland when Caleb and Harvey hitched the Belgians to the farm wagon and drove around front. Domingo cantered up from the east on Star, and for some reason Jake Weaver was trotting up Caleb's driveway on one of Hershberger's saddle horses.

They converged in the front yard at the head of the driveway. Caleb hauled back on the reins, bringing his team of Belgians to a shuddering halt.

"Good morning," Jake said, leaning on his pommel. "I heard you were going out to look for Aaron and Rachel this morning and I wondered if I could go along. John said it was okay with him."

"Harvey's going with me—and Domingo," Caleb said. His dark-eyed younger son, on the bench beside him, tipped his hat to Jake. "I don't know as we'll need help."

Jake nodded. He would never argue with a man old enough to be his father, but Caleb couldn't miss the crestfallen look, or the way Jake slumped a little in the saddle. The boy was worried about Rachel.

"But then," Caleb said, scratching his beard, "I'm thinking another pair of eyes couldn't hurt anything."

"What is that?" Domingo was standing tall in his stirrups, peering down the road to the west into the shadows at the base of the mountains.

"Where?" Caleb stared, but in the pearly light, with a thin morning mist hanging over the road, his fifty-year-old eyes could see nothing.

Jake craned his neck, staring hard while his horse pranced nervously. "Domingo's right. There's something lying in the road. Maybe somebody's burro lost a bag of beans."

Caleb thought he could see a lump in the road, but it was nearly a mile away. He wasn't sure he really saw anything until the lump rose up and began to move. To Caleb's eyes it was only a blurry black and white speck, but as soon as it began to walk he recognized that peculiar swaying gait.

Ada!

Snapping the reins and shouting his draft horses into action, he swung hard right, ignoring the driveway and angling across a ripe field of oats at a reckless gallop. Two horses passed by the wagon on either side, Domingo and Jake racing ahead.

By the time Caleb got there they had already dismounted and were walking alongside Ada, gripping her upper arms and trying to get her to stop. Caleb jumped down from the wagon and ran to his daughter.

Ada's kapp was missing and the skirt of her dress torn off. Her frizzy uncut hair shot wild over her shoulders, down her back, in her face. Filthy and bruised, scratched and bleeding in a dozen places, she was taking short little baby steps on swollen feet, limping badly. Her eyes stared without seeing and she babbled incoherently.

Caleb had to block her path just to get her to stop walking, and even then she didn't seem to recognize him. When she pushed against him it struck him that the odd bulge under her coat felt a lot like the flesh and bone of a toddler, and his heart leaped.

But when he started to undo the hooks she grabbed his wrists, squeezing with a strength he didn't know she possessed, and pushed him back. Her chin jutted and her eyes flared, the familiar angry expression he'd seen occasionally when Ada didn't get her way. As soon as he backed off, she shouldered past him, hobbling, limping.

"Help me," he said, and the three of them tried to steer her to the back of the wagon. But as soon as they put their hands on her and started to exert a little force she let out a bloodcurdling wail and flailed with her arms until they backed away.

She plunked down heavily in the middle of the road and rocked back and forth, clutching her secret bundle. The baby hadn't made a sound, hadn't moved. That stillness, combined with Ada's bizarre behavior, filled Caleb with the darkest dread.

It must have upset Jake, too. He stared at her for a moment, shaking his head. "Something terrible has happened," he said. Then his eyes grew wide. "Rachel!" Without another word he slung himself up into the saddle and tore off down the road toward the mountains at a wild gallop.

"Domingo, stop him!" Caleb shouted, pointing.

Domingo leaped on his horse and took off after Jake.

Caleb knelt in the road next to Ada, trying to reason with her, but she paid him no attention. Her bottom lip stuck out and she stared straight ahead, bleary-eyed, on the verge of collapse.

The chugging of an automobile motor approached, then died. A few seconds later Dr. Gant knelt next to Caleb.

The old doctor examined Ada briefly, lifting her eyelids, gently checking her pulse. But when his hands went near the hooks and eyes of her coat she shook him off, leaned lower over the bulge and crossed her arms on top of it.

"She may not even know you're here," the doctor said.

"Oh yes," Caleb said, his eyes flashing wide as he rubbed his wrist. "She knows. We need to see about the child, but she won't let anyone near him. She goes into a tantrum. What can we do, Doctor?"

"I can give her a sedative."

He went back to the car for his other bag, and as he was rummaging through it a buggy pulled up. Mary and Ezra jumped down. Mary ran, breathless, her mouth open, stark terror in her eyes, shouldering her father aside as she knelt in front of Ada.

She gripped her sister's round face with both hands, forcing Ada's vacant eyes to focus on her.

"Ada?"

Ada had been rocking steadily and moaning, a low keening from the back of her throat, but when her eyes fixed on Mary she blinked and the moaning abruptly stopped. Her face tilted down. Black fingernails on grimy, blood-streaked fingers worked slowly at the hooks of her coat.

They all watched in awed silence as Ada opened her coat, slipped the knotted cloth over her head, carefully lifted the heavy bundle and held it out to Mary.

Utterly speechless, Mary's shaking hands peeled back the black cloth to reveal a face. She clutched her son to her breast and bent low over him, weeping.

Ada reached into her pocket, raised a fist to her mouth, blew a curiously loud note on the harmonica, then held it out to Mary. But Mary's head was down, her face pressed against her child. Ezra reached down to take the harmonica, but Ada snatched it back and glared at him. As soon as Ezra retreated she offered it again, and a little hand came out of the bundle to take the harmonica from her.

They didn't have much trouble with Ada after that. The men got her into the doctor's open-top Nash, and the whole caravan turned around and went back to Caleb's house.

Dr. Gant said that Ada and the baby were both badly dehydrated, and Ada vindicated his diagnosis by drinking a quart of water without stopping. He checked her out as thoroughly as he could, and then the women drew buckets of water and took her upstairs to set about cleaning her up while the doctor tended to Little Amos.

The front door opened. Domingo came in, followed by Jake, hat in hand. The young man's eyes were hard, his mouth open and his breathing sharp, like a man fresh from a fight.

Caleb went to him, laid a hand gently on his shoulder and spoke quietly to him, in Dutch. "I know how you feel, son, and we *will* do something. But first we must learn all we can from Ada and then we must act *together*. The last thing we want to do right now is go running off in different directions. That would only make things worse. Do you understand?"

Jake's eyes dropped away and he nodded. His breathing slowed.

In a little while Miriam came downstairs to the living room, where the men were waiting.

"Is your sister all right?" Caleb asked.

"Jah. There's more strength in her than we know, Dat. Mamm worries me more than Ada. She's gone to pieces."

He nodded. "High-strung, your mamm is. I will speak to her and try to ease her mind. Could Ada tell you anything about what happened to Aaron and Rachel?" He braced himself for the worst.

Miriam's shoulders slumped, and she couldn't look at her father as she spoke. "We couldn't get much out of her. She kept saying *bad* over and over, and sometimes she would drag a finger down across one eye, like this."

Like the scar on El Pantera's face. Caleb swallowed hard. "What else? Did she say anything else at all?"

A small nod. There were tears in Miriam's eyes. "She said *Aaron* and she said *blood*. Then she got so upset it was no use talking to her."

Jake had crept close, listening. "What about Rachel?" he asked, his eyes focused and intense.

Miriam sighed deeply and shook her head. "I tried, but she either didn't know or couldn't remember. I think she told me all she knows."

Chapter 23

Caleb's heart was in his throat as he and Harvey set out in the wagon while Jake and Domingo scouted ahead on horseback. Dr. Gant offered to go with them, but Caleb declined. There were sick children who needed him more.

Three hours later, high up on the barren ridge halfway to Agua Nueva, Caleb spotted Domingo and Jake up ahead, kneeling on the ground. Rushing to the site, Caleb set the brake and climbed down from the wagon.

Domingo rose to meet him. "Something happened here. There is blood."

Unprepared for the sight of so much blood, dried brown on the barren rock—the blood of one of his children—Caleb's knees almost buckled and his voice quavered.

"Tell me what happened. Where are Rachel and Aaron?"

"Find the buggy and it will tell us something," Domingo said, his eyes roaming the crest of the ridge. "Bandits will steal a horse, but they would have no use for the surrey. It has to be here somewhere."

Harvey spotted the wrecked surrey right away, down the hill at the edge of the trees. He ran down to it and shouted back up to the others, "Aaron is here!"

Aaron lay trapped between the seats in the crumpled surrey.

Together they righted the buggy and pried him out of it. His normally ruddy skin was pale yellow and cold to the touch. When they stretched him out he uttered a muffled groan. His chest rose and fell slowly under a shirt soaked with blood.

Caleb leaned over him, pressing a finger under his jaw, feeling for a pulse. Fast and shallow. "Aaron," he whispered.

No answer.

"I don't know how he's still alive," Caleb said, pulling aside the soaked shirt. "He's lost so much blood. He's been stabbed—it's a knife wound, not a gunshot." Caleb almost choked on the words, imagining the horrifying scene.

Harvey gave up his own shirt to make a bandage, then they struggled up the hill with Aaron as gently as they could and laid him in the back of the wagon. Harvey brought a buggy robe from the wagon box, and he and Jake tucked it around Aaron while Domingo left them to their work and went to scout around on horseback.

"What do we do now?" Harvey asked.

Caleb took off his hat, wiped his brow on his coat sleeve. "We got to get him home as quick as we can. I can't do nothing for him here."

"Agua Nueva is about as close as home, and there's a good doctor there," Jake said.

"There's a better one at home," Caleb said, rising, standing in the back of the wagon. "Harvey, you keep him still and I'll try to drive smooth."

Hoofbeats announced Domingo's return. He trotted up to the wagon and stayed in his saddle.

"Did you see any sign of Rachel?" Jake asked, his voice quavering with fear.

Domingo held out a prayer kapp. "I found this down the hill a little ways."

"Ada's kapp was missing," Caleb said. "It could be hers."

Jake held the kapp up to his face, pinched a long hair from inside it and held it up to catch the sunlight.

"Red," he said. "Rachel. So what happened to her?"

"I'm not sure," Domingo answered. "I circled this whole place twice and didn't see any other traces. There's an old trail about a quarter mile back where I found the tracks of ten or twelve horses in a soft place, going north. Bandits."

But as Domingo talked he kept glancing at Caleb. He was holding back. There was something else he wasn't saying.

Caleb spoke up. "Tell us what you think, Domingo. All of it. We are all men here."

With a reluctant glance at Jake, Domingo said, "Rachel would never have left her brother's side or let Ada go wandering off by herself unless she was dead or captured."

Caleb nodded.

"If she was dead, I would have found her."

"So they have taken her."

"There is no other explanation."

Jake was incredulous. "Why would they take her captive?"

Domingo shrugged. "To sell."

"To *sell*? What does that mean?"

"As a slave," Domingo said. "There are rich men who will pay a lot of money for a young girl. Surely I don't have to explain—"

"No," Jake said, breathing deeply, his eyes wide and his fists clenching and unclenching. "You've told us enough." He untied his horse from the wagon, hooked a foot in a stirrup, and swung up into the saddle.

"I'm going after her."

The look in the boy's eye told Caleb there was no point in arguing with him. But now he faced an impossible choice. Should he try to save his son or pursue his daughter?

Domingo, waiting patiently in his saddle, stared at Jake and held out a hand, palm down. Both of them remained where they were and waited for Caleb to speak.

"I don't know what to do," Caleb finally said, his eyes pleading. "I want to go after Rachel. But the bandits already have a head start, and Aaron is barely alive. He will surely die if we don't get him to a doctor quickly."

"Señor Bender," Domingo said softly, "we have only two saddle horses." He waved casually toward Jake. "You will not stop this lovesick fool from going after Rachel, and it would be suicide for him to follow bandits into those mountains without me. There is no choice for you to make. You and Harvey must take Aaron home. Jake and I will go and find your daughter."

The young man's judgment was sound, his words wise. Caleb nodded slowly. "Be careful," he said. "And bring my Rachel home."

⤳

It was chilly in the heights, even in summer. Jake buttoned his denim work coat and turned up his collar, but the thought of his Rachel in the hands of those bandits left him shivering anyway. A whirlwind of horrors haunted his imagination as he followed Domingo up and down narrow mountain trails. If they couldn't find Rachel and bring her back, he was pretty sure he'd never be warm again.

Domingo trotted along at an even pace through forest and creek, up and down and around steep mountainsides on the meandering trail, moving ever northward.

"Can't we go any faster?" Jake asked for the tenth time. Alone with Domingo he spoke German, because Domingo's German was much better than his own Spanish.

Domingo shrugged, his shoulders hidden under a striped

poncho. "Jah, we can go faster, but then the horses will have to stop and rest. We must pace ourselves."

His flat-brimmed hat snugged tight on his head, Domingo's eyes constantly scanned the ridges and trees up ahead and on both sides. Most of the time he refused to talk, and it took a while for Jake to realize that he wasn't being unfriendly, he was just listening.

"Are you sure we can find them?"

Domingo gave him a sideways glance, almost a smirk. "I am not the tracker my father was, but I think I can follow the tracks of a dozen horses through the soft dirt of the woods. Anyway, I think I know where they are going, or at least I know the area."

"Really?" This was a surprise to Jake. "You know these men?"

Domingo nodded. "In this part of Mexico there is only one man who kidnaps girls to sell. El Pantera."

"The one who came to the logging camp last summer? Who robbed Herr Bender in the fall?"

"The same."

Domingo followed the bandit trail down to where the tracks disappeared into a creek. He didn't hesitate but pushed Star right into the middle of the shallow creek. They began sloshing upstream.

Jake drew alongside. "How do you know El Pantera?"

"My father knew him. They fought together in the Revolution." Domingo answered without looking up, his eyes scanning the banks for the spot where the bandits left the creek.

"And you know where he lives?"

"I know *of* it. They say he has a little ranch in a remote place called Diablo Canyon, far to the north in the mountains west of Arteaga. My father said it was well hidden, and well guarded. El Pantera keeps a small army there—twenty or thirty men."

This was grim news to Jake. "Twenty or thirty," he muttered. "How can you fight so many?"

Domingo chuckled. "I can't. I have only a rifle, and you will not fight at all. Our only hope is to get in and out without them knowing we are there, and to do this we must be *quiet*."

Jake saw the sideways glance full of doubts about his ability to be quiet, but he still had a lot of questions. From now on he would talk more softly.

"How far is this place?" he whispered.

Domingo shrugged. "A long day's ride, probably."

Jake slumped in his saddle, his heart sinking. "Then they are already there."

"Maybe not. They might have stopped someplace for the night. El Pantera is in no hurry."

"How do you know this?"

"The tracks are close together. Their horses are walking, not even trotting. Anyway, El Pantera knows no one would be foolish enough to come after him in these mountains without an army. Even an army failed, once."

Suddenly he pointed to a bare spot on the bank. "*There* it is."

Domingo spurred his horse and trotted up the bank onto dry ground, picking up the trail of the bandits where they left the creek, moving steadily northward.

Rachel was numb, all emotion wrung out of her during the night. She clung to the saddle listlessly, her face expressionless. At least she was alone. No one's hands groped her today, for as soon as the weasel cinched the girth on his saddle that morning El Pantera put Rachel on his horse alone and made the weasel ride bareback on the stolen standard bred. The weasel sulked, humiliated while the others harassed him mercilessly with their callous jokes. He didn't answer them, but the hounded look in his eye let them know that sooner or later someone would pay.

The bandits moved through the woods and creeks at an unconcerned pace, their horses ambling along. El Pantera was supremely confident, fearing no one in his corner of the mountains.

Before noon Rachel could make out a rocky bluff through the trees up ahead, rising high above the trail on the left. A quarter mile from the bluff they reached a clearing, where El Pantera stopped the column and waved his hat over his head.

A lone rifleman stepped out from behind the rocks on top of the bluff, returning the signal with his sombrero. El Pantera spurred the Appaloosa and they pressed on.

A few minutes later the column of horses rounded a sloping field of sandstone boulders at the base of the bluff, heading downhill and to the left into a steep-sided canyon. Sheer walls of rock towered a hundred feet high on three sides. On the floor of the canyon Rachel could make out a little clutch of adobe buildings—a house off to one side, and beyond it a long structure that looked like a bunkhouse. Behind the bunkhouse lay a two-acre garden patch, looking wilted and unkempt, the cornstalks yellowing. A rail fence stretched all the way across the back end of the little box canyon, making use of the walls to form a natural corral. A large all-wood barn stood in the center of the fence, and next to it a wire pigpen where two sizable hogs lay in the strip of shade cast by the barn. The house was partly shaded from the midday sun by a huge old oak tree, but apart from that only a few spindly pines and cottonwoods stood isolated on an otherwise rocky landscape. To Rachel's eyes it was a red and desolate place. What was left of her heart sank, and she wondered how much worse things could possibly get.

The horses picked up the pace a little as they neared home, cantering toward the barn.

∼

Caleb worked his team of Belgians with a delicate finesse, steering them over the gentlest ground he could find on the long rocky ridge. Harvey lay beside his wounded older brother in the back, holding him as steady as possible. Caleb glanced back often, each time praying he wouldn't see the hope gone out of Harvey's bright face. At nineteen, Harvey was his youngest son. They'd lost Aaron's twin brother, Amos, in the flu epidemic of 1918, and if Aaron didn't make it Harvey would be the *only* living son. The thought was almost more than Caleb could bear. He prayed for mercy and strength and drove his horses on, his shoulders tight, his forearms tense.

Three hours later, as the wagon crept down the last of the narrow switchbacks at the base of the ridge and crawled out into the flatland of Paradise Valley, with home in sight, Harvey called to him.

When Caleb looked back and saw urgency in Harvey's young face, he hauled back on the reins and stopped.

"I think he wakes," Harvey said. "He tried to talk."

Caleb scrambled into the back of the wagon and lay propped on his elbows at Aaron's side, their faces inches apart.

"Aaron."

The eyes didn't open, but his head turned toward Caleb's voice and his lips parted. He made no sound and yet there was no mistaking what his tongue said.

Dat.

Caleb gripped his shoulders and squeezed. "Son, you *hang on*. We're almost home. There's a doctor in the valley and he can fix you. You're gonna be all right."

Aaron winced weakly and his face moved from side to side slowly, feebly. Caleb wanted to believe the wince was only pain, but deep down he knew his son too well. It was surrender. He couldn't fight anymore. Aaron had the heart of a plow horse, but the slack skin and ashen complexion did not lie. Aaron had fought his way to the surface, using his last ounce of strength to communicate one last time.

It was enough to break a father's heart.

Aaron's mouth moved, but his breath was so faint that no sound came out. Caleb laid his wide hat aside and leaned close, placing his ear against his son's lips.

"What is it, son? Are you trying to say something?"

The lips moved again, and this time a single word brushed against Caleb's ear so lightly that at first he wasn't sure he'd heard it right.

"Amos."

He pulled back and stared. *Amos.* Had death drawn so near that he was seeing his twin brother on the other side? But then Aaron's eyes opened for a moment. When Caleb looked into them he saw tears, and behind the tears a desperate need, a burning question. Wounded as deeply as Aaron was, with such great loss of blood, Caleb knew an ordinary human should never have survived the night. More than once on the long drive home he had wondered what was keeping his son alive—what lay beneath this inner pool of strength, this mountain of resolve?

Now he knew.

Caleb nodded, tried to smile. "He's fine, son." His voice broke, but he got the words out. "Little Amos is at home with his mother. Ada brought him back to us safe and sound. He's fine."

Aaron closed his eyes, and an unmistakable satisfaction crinkled the corners. He drew a deep breath, let it out like a sigh, and never drew another.

Chapter 24

The afternoon sun slanted sharply through the trees as Jake and Domingo came across the place where the bandits had camped the night before. Domingo knelt down by the cold campfire between the two logs and pressed his hand into the ashes. Rising, he wiped his hand on his pants.

"The coals underneath are still warm. They camped here last night and headed north again this morning. They would not have stopped if they were close to home. I'm thinking Diablo Canyon is another three hours' walk."

Jake was leaning forward in his saddle, watching. His head tilted. "So what do we do now? Do we keep going?"

Domingo looked up at the sky. "Only as long as the light holds. I can't track them in the dark, and this close to Diablo Canyon we don't dare light a torch. From here on we must move slowly and be very careful."

Jake shifted uneasily in his saddle. "I don't mean to complain, Domingo, but I would feel mighty bad if something happened to Rachel because we took too long being cautious."

Domingo gave him a look. "And what good will it do Rachel if we get ourselves caught? I have said from the start that our only hope lies in El Pantera not knowing we are here. Now that we're getting closer it's more important than ever to be invisible."

"I'm not afraid of him."

Domingo chuckled, swinging back up onto his horse. "Only because you do not know him. I am not afraid to die, but I do not love the idea of dying for nothing. There will be lookouts posted on the heights, watching."

⁓

Miriam was worried about her mother. A son and daughter missing, possibly hurt or killed, and diphtheria terrorizing the valley, leaving one of the newcomers' little ones dead already and several more in danger—with Caleb gone, it was just too much for Mamm. Her hands shook constantly, and she sat at the kitchen table dabbing at her eyes with a crumpled handkerchief all day, ignoring her work, weeping quietly.

Late in the afternoon, when she finally got a break, Miriam wandered out to the buggy shed to check on her school supplies and to have a moment to herself. She kept paper, chalk, pencils and erasers in a cedar box on a high shelf, but the school had been empty for a week and there were rats about.

Everything was fine, though she noticed as she trailed her fingertips over a tabletop in the half-light that the place needed a good dusting. The deafening silence made her miss the kids even more.

The door hinge squeaked and a soft footstep crunched the dirt. Micah's silhouette filled the doorframe.

"I thought I might find you here," he said as he took her in his arms. "We got a lot of troubles just now, don't we, Mir?"

She laid her head against his chest. "Jah, I'm really worried about Rachel and Aaron. Thank Gott Ada found her way home with Little Amos."

"I heard about that. It's a miracle, her being crazy and all. I don't know how she ever—"

"My sister is not crazy, Micah, she's just slow. She can't help it."

His head backed away and he stared down his nose at her. "I didn't mean nothing by it, Mir. I just meant—"

"I know what you meant, and you're right about it being a miracle, but what Ada did would be a heroic thing even for me, and I'm not *crazy*." Although there *were* moments when she doubted her own sanity. She pulled apart from him then, and turned her back.

Micah was silent for a minute, then said, "I heard Ervin Kuhns never showed up at the train station when your dat went to get him. Is this true?" He was quick to change the subject whenever he'd stuck his foot in his mouth.

She nodded, her back still turned to him. "Jah, it's true."

"Maybe he's just late and he'll show up on his own in a day or two," Micah said, and laid a hand gently on her shoulder. "We'll be needing him later in the fall, Mir."

Miriam shook her head. "Dat didn't think so. They closed the border. Dat said that Ervin probably just went back home."

Distracted, Micah took his hand from her shoulder and wandered a few steps toward the other end of the shed, where Dr. Gant's car was parked.

"That doctor's sure got a fancy automobile," he said. "I can't believe your dat let him leave it in the buggy shed, though."

Streaks of afternoon light slanted in from the cracks around the bay doors and dappled the doctor's Nash convertible. The cloth top was folded down.

"We get rain this time of year, and Dr. Gant is our guest. Dat didn't think it was right to leave his car outside."

"Well, I guess it doesn't matter since there's no school

now. Oh, that reminds me. Who will teach school after we get married?"

Miriam turned around and looked straight at him. "I will," she said.

He put on a beneficent smile as he closed the gap between them and took her shoulders in his hands. "No wife of mine is *ever* gonna have to work a job, I promise you that."

She leaned back, staring at him in the shadows. "I don't *have* to teach school, Micah, and I don't get paid for it. It's not a *job*; it's something I want to do because the children need me, and I'm good at it."

Shaking herself out of his hands, she stalked past him, through the open door and down toward the house without looking back.

Movement in the distance caught her eye—a wagon coming slowly down the road from the west, drawn by a familiar team of horses, with a familiar figure holding the reins.

Dat!

She broke into a run, shouting as she burst through the back door of the house, "Dat and Harvey are home! They're coming up the drive!"

Miriam never broke stride but ran straight on through the house, out the front door and down across the yard to meet the wagon. Her two youngest sisters poured out behind her, and she heard their footsteps following, anticipating a glad reunion. But as she neared the wagon she saw her father's face, and Harvey's.

Despair was the only word for what she saw in their faces, and it was clear they had both been weeping. Only once before in her life had she seen her father weep, and now the memory filled her with despair because she knew what it meant. Her steps slowed and her hands came up to cover her mouth even as her eyes found what she already knew they would find in the back of the wagon—a long, low shape, shrouded entirely in a buggy robe and perfectly still.

Leah and Barbara caught up with her, and as Caleb brought the wagon to a halt the three of them stopped short, a last desperate effort to stave off the unthinkable for at least a few more seconds. Mamm burst between them crying, "No, no, no . . ." and ran right around to the back of the wagon. Breathless, wide-eyed, she reached out hesitantly and peeled back the buggy robe to reveal Aaron's booted feet. She collapsed to her knees before Caleb and her daughters could reach her.

When they caught up to her the whole family huddled around Mamm in the dirt behind the wagon, and the wailing began in earnest.

⟲

The sun had gone down and the light faded to dusky gray when Domingo stopped his horse and held up a hand. His eyes scanned the landscape up ahead, peering through the treetops. Jake eased up next to him, curious.

"What is it?"

"You see that high bluff up ahead on the left? There is a man up there with a rifle."

Jake squinted. "Really? I see no one."

"He's gone now, but I saw him move between those two rocks. He didn't act like he saw us. El Pantera's ranch must be close—maybe just beyond that bluff."

"So what do we do now?"

"Hide," Domingo answered, climbing down and leading Star into denser cover, uphill and behind them. "We can't get any closer until after dark."

Jake followed him up into the rocks on the mountainside. They found a place not far away, completely out of sight from either the trail or the bluff, where wild grasses had grown up around the edge of a little spring. They tied the horses and let them graze.

Domingo gathered a handful of some kind of berries, and while they waited in the twilight they found a spot to rest.

Leaning back against a rock with his arms crossed behind his head, staring at a purpling sky, a question came to Jake for the first time.

"Domingo, why are you here?"

Domingo gave a derisive snort. "To keep you from killing yourself. Without me, you would have wandered in the mountains until you starved. Even if you were lucky enough to trail them to Diablo Canyon you would have blundered in and gotten yourself shot, and Rachel would be lost forever."

Jake refused to be put off by his unkind remarks, chiefly because they were true. "But, Domingo, even I know this is a fool's errand. It makes sense for me because it's Rachel, but I can't help wondering why a man like you would risk his life for someone else's girl."

Domingo pondered this for a moment, plucking a blade of grass from the ground and chewing the end of it.

"She is Caleb's daughter," he finally said, "and I have great admiration for the man. He looks on me like a son, and I have come to love his family. Caleb treats other people with respect, and puts them above himself. This is how he lives. I still do not understand why, but I know that if things were different Caleb Bender would not hesitate to risk his life for *me*." He shrugged. "So I am here."

Jake nodded slowly. There was more to Domingo than he'd thought. "I'm *glad* you're here. You're right—I wouldn't have a chance without you. I'm not even sure there's a chance *with* you. Only Gott can get us out of this mess."

Chapter 25

Two hours later they set out on foot toward the bottom of the bluff, quietly, keeping to the shadows. They stopped once while Domingo debated about whether to circle around and silence the lookout on the bluff, but in the end he decided it was too risky. If the guard got off a single shot, the others would be warned and there would be no chance of escape. He moved ahead slowly, staying under the trees.

Working their way over boulders and rocks, hugging the bottom of the sheer cliff to avoid the eyes on top, they rounded the bluff and got their first glimpse of Diablo Canyon, past the bluff and down to the left.

Some of the bandits had built a huge fire in front of a long bunkhouse, and by the light of the fire Domingo and Jake could see the lay of the place. The house and bunkhouse sat opposite them on the other side of the canyon, and in the weak light of a half-moon they could just make out the barn and corral, deeper into the canyon to the left.

"We have a chance," Domingo whispered. "Rachel is in the barn, and if we are careful we can get to it without being seen."

"How do you know she's in the barn?" Jake asked. Domingo's reasoning constantly baffled him, though he was seldom wrong.

"She is too valuable to tie her outside for the coyotes, and there are only three main buildings. The outhouse and smokehouse are too small, and the woodshed is falling down, so Rachel is either in the house, the bunkhouse, or the barn. I know that El Pantera has a woman, and his woman will never allow a pretty young girl to stay in the house. If he put her in the bunkhouse with thirty men she would not last the night." A shrug. "Unless she is dead, she has to be in the barn."

Jake nodded. "So how do we get to the barn?"

"*We* don't. You will wait here and watch. I will stay under the canyon wall where the lookout can't see me until I can get behind the corral fence and follow it to the barn. Watch for me to come around the back side of the barn—with Rachel, I hope. When you see us come out, I want you to get back to the horses, *quietly*. Bring them down to the trail and wait for us. We will need to get away quickly."

"I want to go with you. Rachel is my girl."

Domingo patted his shoulder. "I know this, but your clumsy gringo feet would get us caught, so *listen*—you must do exactly as I say. There will be a guard at the barn, and I will have to take him down. If you hear a shot, or if you see me come out on horseback, run. Don't wait for me, just run back to the horses as fast as you can and get away from here. Do you understand?"

Jake nodded. "Be careful, amigo."

Domingo disappeared into the shadows, leaving Jake to wonder if maybe he should have brought along the rifle, just for consolation.

A half hour passed and nothing changed. The men around the campfire came and went, laughed and sang and gambled and squabbled, but none of them made a move toward the barn.

And then, suddenly, Jake sensed movement in the corral. His eyes had grown accustomed to the dark. He held a hand up to block the glare of the distant campfire, and in the moonlight he could make out forty or fifty horses shifting like a tide in the corral, the whole herd trotting toward the far end in the shadow of the canyon wall.

Something had made them nervous. Jake couldn't see him at that distance, but he knew it could only be Domingo, creeping along behind the fence toward the barn.

He held his breath, watching so intently that he was completely unaware of anything behind him until he heard a little noise like metal scraping against leather. It was a faint sound, and very brief, like a pistol being drawn from a holster. And it was very close.

He froze. He lay perfectly still on the rock, waiting, hoping he was mistaken.

But then someone whispered into his ear.

"Did you really think it would be so easy, gringo?"

Jake didn't look around to see who it was. It didn't really matter—his job was to watch out for Domingo. He yelled as loud as he could.

"DOMINGO! IT'S A TRAP! RUN!"

He expected to be shot any second, but all he heard was laughter. There were *two* men behind him—he could hear them both laughing.

One of the bandits cupped his hands around his mouth and shouted even louder than Jake, "Sí, Domingo! It is a TRAP! Run, Domingo, RUN!"

The two bandits cackled at themselves, and in the dark distance Jake saw a figure rise up from behind the fence.

Domingo. He had almost made it to the barn.

Two shadows appeared from behind the barn, two more

rushed around from the front, and two others rose up from the field behind Domingo. All six dark figures converged on him and a short, furious fight ensued. No shots were fired, but a minute later Jake could make out a small gang of men dragging a limp body up the rocky road toward the campfire.

He rolled over slowly and sat up. One of his captors held a revolver, the other a shotgun.

"If you have a weapon, gringo, you would be wise to hand it to me. Slowly. My amigo, his shotgun has a very light trigger and he is always a little nervous."

"I have no weapons."

Again they laughed. "What were you going to do, throw rocks?"

"Maybe the gringo was going to shout insults at us," the other one said, and then doubled over, chortling at his own joke.

"Come, get to your feet, boy. Ochoa will be here with your horses in a minute. Oh, sí, we know where you hid your horses. Our sentries have been watching you all evening. We thought you two young fools would *never* make your move."

There were at least twenty bandits sitting around the campfire in front of the bunkhouse on makeshift benches and short sections of logs, smoking hand-rolled cigarettes and swigging from whiskey bottles and pottery jugs. The bandoliers were gone, and most of the pistols, but the men looked as fierce as ever. El Pantera himself rose from his seat near the fire and set his jug on the ground as the horses trotted into the firelight and his men tossed Jake roughly to the ground in front of him.

Domingo lay at the far end of the circle holding his ribs, one eye swollen nearly shut, bleeding from his mouth, his hat missing. He rose up onto an elbow and looked at Jake. In place of his usual blank defiance there was a note of apology in the native's face, of sorrow. More than anything else, the look in Domingo's eyes struck fear into Jake's heart. If Domingo was defeated, all hope was lost. They were going to die.

"Put their horses in the barn," El Pantera said. "I will look them over in the morning and decide. As for this one"—he nudged Jake with his foot—"he is young and healthy. What do you think, my compadres? Perhaps we should liven our fiesta with a little sport?"

A cheer went up and half the men jumped to their feet, shouting, "Fight! Fight! Fight!"

El Pantera knelt down and helped Jake to his feet—gently, smiling as if he were a friend. He slapped the dust from Jake's shirt and squeezed a shoulder, then turned to his men with a look of exaggerated fear.

"I don't know. He is a strong young buck . . . perhaps I should let someone else try him first. I am afraid he will *hurt* me."

Raucous laughter and more cheers. "Fight! Fight! Fight!"

He turned back to Jake and shrugged. "What can I do? My men have been with me in the field for a month and they have fought very hard. They are good men, and I have promised them a grand fiesta. Now they want their entertainment and I cannot deny them."

A large knife appeared from behind his back and he held it in front of Jake's face. Firelight glinted from the steel. His men cheered, chanting him on.

"What do you say, young buck? You and me, *mano a mano!*"

Jake didn't answer.

El Pantera held his free hand out to one of his men, wiggled his fingers. The ragged bandit grinned, drew a knife from a sheath at his belt and handed it, butt first, to his leader. El Pantera lifted Jake's hand, wrapped his fingers around the handle, and stepped back.

"I will make you a deal," the bandit said. "If you win, my men will let you and the girl go free, no?" He looked to his men, who grinned broadly and laughed, nodding agreement. These were men who had fought alongside El Pantera often, in close combat. They knew how this would end.

Jake stared, holding the blade loosely at his side. When the clamor died he said calmly, "I don't fight," and tossed the knife into the dirt at its owner's feet.

El Pantera blinked. His brow furrowed and his head tilted. "You don't *fight?*" He squinted, his mouth slightly open. Quick as a snake, his fist slashed through the air and struck Jake flush in the jaw.

Jake staggered, but didn't go down. Holding his arms down at his sides, refusing even to rub his aching jaw, he straightened up and stared.

El Pantera turned to his men, eyes wide with mock surprise. "He doesn't fight!"

More raucous laughter as El Pantera looked Jake up and down— his farmer's clothes, the flat wide-brimmed hat, the bowl-cut hair.

"I *see*," he said. "You are from Señor *Bender's* tribe! I have heard rumors that your people don't believe in fighting, but I thought this could not be true. Is it?"

Another nod.

The bandit leader stroked his chin, thinking. "I wonder, do you believe in *dying?*" The tip of his knife came up slowly and pressed against Jake's belly. "This knife has already met one of your kin. Tell me, young buck, if I am about to do the same to you, will you fight *then?*"

Jake shook his head. "It is a sin to kill. It is against Gott's law."

El Pantera chuckled, shaking his head as he lowered the knife.

"*Ayeee.* You people are *loco.*" He turned away and paced beyond the fire, stopping at the other end of the little circle made by his men. He stared down at Domingo. Holding his ribs, Domingo hobbled to his feet and stared back, defiant.

Standing nose to nose with Domingo, El Pantera said, "Tell me, young buck—what would you do if I was about to slit your *friend's* throat while you watch? Would you fight then?"

El Pantera raised the knife and casually laid the razor edge under Domingo's jaw. Domingo didn't flinch, his hands hanging at his sides. The bandit turned and leered at Jake, his white eye reflecting the red of the fire.

Dead quiet hung over them until one of the men hissed, "Do it! *Kill* the traitor, my *capitán.*"

"Silence!" El Pantera shouted. The smile disappeared from his face and he glared at Jake, waiting for an answer.

Jake's breathing quickened, but he was not looking at the bandit leader. With deep sorrow he looked Domingo in the eye and said quietly, "I fear hell more than I fear you, El Pantera. If you choose to murder this man in cold blood, it is between you and Gott. I will not throw away my own soul."

El Pantera considered this for a second and his eyes grew fierce. He shoved Domingo down and stalked back toward Jake.

"*But this makes no sense!*" he raged, waving his arms, the knife still flashing in his hand. "Look around you! I am king of this place! Why would a young man think he can come into my camp and steal a girl, a girl who belongs to *me,* without a fight?"

Then he froze, peering deep into Jake's eyes as the answer came to him. He crept closer so that their faces were mere inches apart, and a knowing grin turned up the corners of his lips.

"Aaaahhh, *now* I see. A young man would only do this if he was *not* thinking. A young man would only do this if he was in *love* with the girl! Tell us the truth, gringo. This girl, she is your lover, no?"

Jake swallowed hard, but said nothing. It was answer enough—the bandit read his eyes.

"Rodrigo!" he shouted. "Bring the girl!"

One of the older bandits trotted away toward the barn. A few minutes later he came back dragging Rachel by an arm. He flung her down next to the fire, and she looked up at Jake, her eyes red with weeping.

She shook her head slowly, mouthing the word *no*.

His heart melted when he saw the terrible sorrow in her eyes, for he knew his Rachel did not fear for her own life. He nodded to her, slightly, his heart grieving already over the life they would never share, and hoping his own glance conveyed as much as hers. Even now, she was the finest sight in all the world.

Chapter 26

El Pantera paced back and forth between them.

"Do you see my problem, young buck?" He spread his hands and collected devoted gazes from his men. "We are having a fiesta! My men are weary, and like any benevolent leader I want to entertain my troops.

"Now, I have had a taste of tequila and I am in the mood for a fight, but if you will deprive my men of their sport, then I think the next best thing is to offer them this little red-haired girl as a reward and let them amuse themselves. For me this would be a shame because my men, they are rough, and they will ruin her. She is a great prize and I would lose a lot of money, but what else can I do? I have already promised and I cannot disappoint them. I am a man of my word, young buck."

Their eyes locked and El Pantera waited for his answer, the only sound the crumbling of a spent log in the campfire. Sparks danced upward, and one last desperate gamble came to Jake's mind. There was still a small chance.

"I will fight you," he said at last. "But not with a knife. I will wrestle with you."

The men laughed uproariously at this, slapping their knees and pounding each other's backs.

Grinning, El Pantera held up a hand to silence the laughter.

"Wrestle?" He raised his knife between them in a clenched fist. "To die on an enemy's blade is an honorable end, a warrior's death. You would rather have your neck twisted like a chicken? I do not understand you at all, gringo."

He stared a moment longer in silence. When Jake didn't answer, the bandit shrugged, tossed the knife away and took off his jacket, still shaking his head in disbelief. "But if this is your choice I suppose I must honor the wishes of a guest."

Jake reluctantly tossed his hat aside and took off his work coat, the gravity of the situation only beginning to sink in. His chances against this seasoned warrior were extremely slim. He would most likely lose—and die. But a slim chance was better than none, and El Pantera had given his word in front of his men that he would let Rachel go if Jake won.

The bandits made a great happy fuss as they moved back to make room, tipping the short log sections they'd been sitting on and rolling them out of the way while El Pantera dropped his gun belt and stripped off his shirt. A scattering of glossy scars pocked his lean frame, the residue of many battles.

Jake declined to take off his shirt with Rachel watching, but he removed his suspenders. No sense giving El Pantera one more thing to grip.

The bandits closed about them in a ring, shouting and cursing, cheering on their leader. Jake and El Pantera circled each other in a crouch, feinting and testing, looking for an opening until suddenly the bandit rushed him and they locked arms.

El Pantera tried to sweep his legs right away, but Jake was ready. He kept his feet back, wide apart, so as the bandit tried to sweep he took advantage of the split second when the taller man was off-balance. He surged forward and both of them toppled to the ground with Jake on top.

But he couldn't hold El Pantera, who was lean and strong, with ropy muscles as hard as iron. In a wild, unexpected flurry of twisting and writhing and jolting elbow shots, the bandit escaped his grasp and crabbed away.

They both jumped up and circled each other again, the hoots and shouts of El Pantera's cheering section more raucous than ever. They went at each other for ten minutes, neither of them able to get a clenching hold on the other, but then Jake began to notice that the older man was panting. He pressed, keeping the pressure on, never giving El Pantera a chance to catch his breath, and finally found an opening.

He noticed that every time he charged, El Pantera tried to hook him with his left arm and take him down.

Jake charged again, but this time he blocked the left with a forearm, ducked under it, and before the bandit knew what was happening Jake's arm was locked around his neck from behind. El Pantera fought like a wildcat, clawing at Jake's forearm, hooking his legs, flailing with his elbows, but Jake had him. He would not let go.

They toppled over, Jake landing on his back in the dust with El Pantera on top of him. The bandit flung himself from side to side, twisting, squirming, trying to turn over or find some leverage so he could get that crushing arm off of his throat, but Jake had him and would not let up.

Suddenly El Pantera's hand ceased clawing at Jake's forearm and flopped into the dust beside him. His whole body went limp. Assuming the bandit had lost consciousness, Jake released the pressure on his neck, shoved El Pantera aside and rolled away from the limp body.

He crawled a few feet and stopped to catch his breath, still on hands and knees, his heart already swelling with joy and pride. By some miracle he had *won*, and now he would claim his prize.

There was a strange murmur among the bandits as Jake drew himself up onto his knees, but he didn't realize what was happening until a boot crashed into the side of his head. He spun around and hit the ground, dazed.

El Pantera leaned over him, his grinning face swirling among bright spots of light.

"Perhaps next time you will not be so quick to believe your victim has gone to sleep. Ahh, but then there will be no next time for you, young buck."

Jake tried to roll away and get to his feet, but before he could get up El Pantera's bony fist smashed into his ear. This was not wrestling, and Jake knew nothing of boxing, but they were in El Pantera's camp and the rules, apparently, were flexible. A rousing cheer went up from the other bandits as Jake staggered to his feet and stumbled backward, reeling before a hail of blows to his face, and went down again. This time the bandit pounced on him, straddling his chest and locking his long fingers around Jake's throat.

Jake bucked and fought with all his remaining strength, trying to pry the bandit's hands from his throat, but there was no escape. El Pantera's iron claws held, and his thumbs pressed hard into Jake's windpipe. The cheer began to fade into the distance as Jake's vision narrowed so that he saw only the bandit's grinning face.

He had lost. As the world began to slip away his last thought was of Rachel, and how he had failed her.

But then, amid angry shouts from the bandits, the hands released their hold as El Pantera was violently wrenched from his chest. Jake rolled onto his side, coughing, gasping, and opened his eyes. El Pantera lay on the ground with Domingo on top of him, pummeling his face for the few seconds it took for the others to close in and drag him off their leader. A half dozen of them threw Domingo to the ground and attacked him, all of them at once.

El Pantera sat up, wiping blood from his mouth. Domingo lay six feet away, facedown, unconscious, with a bandit's pistol pointed at the back of his head. The bandit, a toothless old man in a straw sombrero, held a tenuous finger on the trigger and looked to El Pantera for approval.

But El Pantera shook his head, raised a hand. "No, Miguel, save that one. If you shoot him now he won't even feel it. I want to take my time with him. Before I am finished he will beg for a bullet, but it will not come."

Getting slowly to his feet, El Pantera limped over and picked up a bottle, bit the cork out of it and took a long pull. When it came back down, he wiped his mouth with the back of a sweaty hand and waved roughly at the prisoners.

"Take the three of them and chain them in the barn. Tomorrow, after the *jefe* comes for the girl, we will take our time with the other two." He glared at Jake as he said this, and the look in his eye sent chills down Jake's spine.

Rachel lay curled up in the dirt, weeping into her hands. One of the bandits grabbed her arm, yanked her to her feet and shoved her toward the barn. Another very large man lifted Domingo like a rag doll and slung him over a shoulder while two others prodded Jake toward the barn with their rifles. Rachel broke away from her captor and threw herself at Jake.

He wrapped his arms around her and felt her warmth, a touch of heaven in the middle of hell. She looked up at him, her eyes full of questions.

"How did you find me?" she whispered, in Dutch, so the guards wouldn't understand.

The two Mexicans behind him cursed and jabbed Jake with their rifles, but he only held her tighter and kept walking.

"Ada," he said. "She made it all the way home—with Little Amos."

"Oh, thank Gott! Did you find Aaron?"

A guard clouted his ear with a fist, but he clung to Rachel, shielding her.

"Jah, and he was still alive when I last saw him, but just barely."

She buried her face against his chest and wept.

The guard punched him in the back of the head, shouting, but then the one carrying the lantern intervened and said, "Let the two young lovers have their little moment. They don't know what is coming tomorrow. A moment of bliss will only make their torture worse." All the guards laughed, as if this was a cheerful thought. They kept on prodding Jake with their rifles, but at least they let Rachel walk with him to the barn.

She looked up at him, her eyes full of tears, and cried, "Jake, why? Why did you come to this awful place?"

He tried his best to smile with his swollen face, refusing to let even a hint of regret tinge his voice. "Rachel, how could I not come for you? How could I live with myself if I didn't try?"

"But now they will take your life!" she wailed.

He pressed her head to his chest and whispered into her ear, "You are my life."

Once inside, one of them grabbed Rachel by the hair and snatched her away. She screamed, reaching out to Jake, and he fought to get to her, but two others took his arms and dragged him to a stall on the opposite side of the barn.

As the bandit flung Rachel into her stall, he could hear her sobbing, even above the rattle of the chains.

The big man dumped Domingo's limp body in the same stall with Jake, then turned around and left. Domingo never even twitched.

Two bandits remained in the stall with a lantern. One of them knelt down with a pair of irons, pulled out a little T-shaped key and fastened the irons onto Domingo's wrists.

A log chain snaked through the dirt and straw of the stall, its ends padlocked to the corner posts. The bandit snapped a padlock through a link in the middle of the log chain, securing Domingo's shackles to it.

Tightening the screws on Jake's handcuffs, the other one said, "There is enough slack in the chain so you can reach the water bucket, gringo." He nodded toward a grimy oak bucket against the wall. "We wouldn't want you to die of thirst—El Pantera knows much more interesting ways to die. Someone will bring food later, if there is anything left after the hogs are fed."

Both bandits laughed at this, but the younger one, lifting his lantern and looking around the stall, said, "Miguel, where is the other lock?"

The toothless old bandit shrugged. *"No sé."* I don't know. "Maybe Pablo took it with him. He's an idiot."

The younger one railed, "There were six locks in here only a few days ago! What do these morons *do* with them? How can you expect me to put this gringo on the chain without a lock?"

"No sé!" Miguel repeated with raised eyebrows and an exaggerated shrug. "I work the garden. I don't know nothing about no chains—*you're* the jailer."

Both of them were weaving and slurring a bit. The mescal had been flowing all night, and it made Jake think maybe there was one slim chance left. Maybe they didn't know. It was worth a try.

"Um, *excúsame,*" he said, and both bandits stared at him as if they didn't know he could talk.

"Do you have a key to *that* lock?" he asked, pointing to the padlock that held the end of the log chain around the corner post.

"Sí," the younger one said, holding up a key ring full of keys.

"Well then, why don't you just pass the chain through my arms and lock it back to the post? It will be easier for me to move around the stall, and you won't need another lock."

Jake held his breath, afraid the two bandits would know what he was up to, but they just looked at each other, shrugged and went to unlock the chain from the corner post. After they passed the long chain through Jake's arms they padlocked it back to the post, picked up their lantern and left him in the dark.

Chapter 27

Jake smiled, hardly daring to believe his captors were really that gullible. But he would do nothing yet—best to wait a while and let things die down.

"Rachel!" he called.

"Jake?" came the answer from the darkness.

"Are you all right? Have they hurt you?"

There was an awkward pause that worried him.

"No, I am unharmed," she finally said. "Jake?"

"Jah?"

"I love you."

Those words, from Rachel, even from the darkness in the middle of hell, warmed him. But they also broke his heart.

"I love you too, Rachel. Try to rest."

He would say nothing of the trick he had up his sleeve for fear the guard might hear him, even though there was little chance of the guard understanding Pennsylvania Dutch.

He knew a trick, a way to get off the chain, but despite the overwhelming urge to free himself and go to Rachel's side, instinct told him to talk to Domingo first. The native had not moved, and Jake was afraid he might even be dead. A little moonlight angled through the cracks of the barn, enough so that Jake could see his friend lying motionless in the dirt where they had dropped him. Jake brought the water bucket and knelt beside him. Untying the bandanna from around Domingo's neck, Jake wet it, squeezed it out and wiped the native's face with it. There was a gash on the side of his head where someone in the melee had pistol-whipped him, and a cut on his chin, probably from a boot.

After a while, as Jake swabbed the wounds on Domingo's face, he started to come around. He squinted through swollen eyes, trying to focus in the dark stall.

"Jake?"

"Jah. I am here."

"Where are we?"

"In the barn, chained in a stall. I guess they use it like a holding pen for the girls they kidnap."

Domingo groaned. "Is Rachel all right?"

"Jah. She's in a stall on the other side. I saw them put her in there. She's on a chain, like us."

Domingo's hand lifted the log chain, held it to his face. "Too heavy," he muttered, dropping it. "We will never be able to break this."

"We don't have to. They locked your handcuffs straight to the chain, but not mine. They only passed the chain through my arms. I can get loose."

Domingo blinked, raised his head and stared.

"How?"

Jake smiled, remembering. "When they made us go to public school, Rachel and I got to be friends with an Englisher boy named Anthony. He called himself The Great Antonio. He did little magic tricks for a hobby, and sometimes he would show me how he did them. Look . . ."

214

Jake took a loop of the long chain and poked the links up through the iron cuff against the flat of his wrist. When the loop was big enough he passed his hand through it and then pulled the loop back out.

"See? Simple," he said, holding up his hands. He was still wearing the handcuffs, but the chain was no longer between his arms. "I can't believe they fell for it."

"That's a good trick," Domingo said, laying his head back down and closing his eyes, "but it won't do *me* any good. Or Rachel."

This was true. Domingo's handcuffs were padlocked directly to the chain. Jake had no answer for that.

"Can you put it back on?" Domingo asked. He winced, and laid his arm over his eyes.

"Jah, sure. Same way. But I want to go see about Rachel first."

"No. It's too risky," Domingo muttered from behind his arm. "We have an advantage—they don't know you can get free. There will be a guard with a lantern right outside the barn door, and if he hears you and comes in we lose our advantage. We will only get one chance, so we must make it count. Do you have a plan?"

Jake shrugged. "I don't know where I am or how to get home. Even if I did, I don't know how to get you and Rachel free. But I did have a plan. My plan was to wake you up and ask you what I should do."

Another groan. "My head is killing me."

He lay still for a long time, and Jake thought he had gone to sleep until he grunted, "We have to take a guard, get his key. There is no other way."

"But you have no weapons."

"Then we will take him with our hands. I can't do it alone— you will have to help me, Jake."

Jake sighed. "I don't think I can do that."

Domingo moved his arm from his eyes and stared at him in the striped moonlight. "Then you will die, and I will die, and Rachel will be sold into slavery."

The harsh reality of his words struck Jake like a slap to the face, but he didn't answer.

The arm went back over Domingo's eyes. "There is time. Our best chance is later. They have just returned from battle and they are celebrating. Let them drink their fill. I have to rest now, try to clear my head." His words were a little slurred.

But Domingo was right, and Jake knew it. Reluctantly he put himself back on the chain and stretched out in the stall to wait. A minute later he turned to Domingo and asked, "How will we get the guard to come close?"

There was no answer. Domingo's breathing was slow and regular, asleep. Or unconscious.

Even from the barn he could hear that the party in the bunkhouse had picked up steam. Someone had broken out a guitar and a squeeze-box, and thirty half-drunk bandits were singing. *Singing.*

The unfairness of it all washed through Jake like a wave, alone in the darkness, in chains. None of them had asked for this, neither he nor Domingo, and certainly not Rachel, but all of them faced an unthinkable fate now, all because of these low men and their greed. As he lay there listening to their drunken singing he couldn't stop thinking about Rachel's dismal future. He grieved over it. An uncommon anger festered in him, and grew.

Caleb tended to Aaron personally. He laid him out on a makeshift table in the living room, washed him, dressed him in his Sunday clothes, laced his boots on his feet and combed his hair. He draped a blanket over Aaron's legs, covering him up to the chest and folding the cold hands placidly on top of it.

It was the hardest thing he had ever done, and it took something out of him that he knew would not be replaced. He aged five years in a single afternoon, and when he finally stood back and gazed upon the slack gray face of his son, ready for the grave, his own mountainous resolve failed him. He sank to his knees and wept.

He didn't even look up when he felt Harvey's hand soft on his shoulder. Shaking his head, Caleb whispered, "It's not right. A man should not have to bury his child."

But it was a momentary self-indulgence. From upstairs he heard the cries of his wife, consoled by a bevy of daughters, yet inconsolable. Martha's bloodcurdling wail made him flinch the first few times, explosive grief building pressure and erupting. Then the wailing would cease for a time and he would hear nothing, though he knew what lay between the screams, and the silence filled him with an even deeper dread. Something in her had broken. Between the outbursts of wailing Martha would whimper quietly, her eyes roaming, searching, until she sought the nearest face and asked, "Where's my Rachel?"

One of them, usually Miriam, would sit beside Mamm, put an arm around her and patiently explain for the tenth time that Rachel had been taken by bandits, and that Jake and Domingo had gone to fetch her back. This was all they knew, for Caleb had spared them the details. A fresh horror would creep into Mamm's face and she would shrink into herself, babbling softly for a time, whimpering, unable to get her mind around so much catastrophe all at once—so much loss and uncertainty. So much fear. Her daughters would sit holding her, rubbing her back and shoulders, begging her to lie down and try to sleep, but she made no sign that she heard them.

After ten minutes of frightening incoherence she would suddenly remember poor Aaron lying dead downstairs, and the cycle would begin anew with a heartrending wail.

The wailing Caleb could take. What he couldn't bear was that question, repeated without fail every ten or fifteen minutes, and the unsettling fact that Mamm's broken mind simply wouldn't accept the answer.

"Where's my Rachel?"

The whole valley was full of wailing and mourning. A few people stopped in to offer condolences and grieve with the family, but many stayed away because of the quarantine. John Hershberger came by to tell Caleb he and his sons would build a box and have it ready by tomorrow afternoon.

They were all there in the evening: Emma and Mary with their husbands and babies, Ada, Miriam, Leah, Barbara and Harvey. Everyone but Rachel. Mamm didn't last long downstairs because she couldn't look at Aaron without wailing, and Emma was finally forced to herd her back upstairs just to get her calmed down. Even as she labored up the steps Caleb heard Mamm's tired voice, raspy and exhausted, asking Emma, "Where's my Rachel?"

The Benders treated grief the way they would have treated any insurmountable task—they divided it among themselves and shared it.

Long after dark, when the room had fallen silent but for the guttering and hissing of two kerosene lanterns, Dr. Gant came in.

"They told me about Aaron," he said, glancing at the body. "Caleb, I can't tell you how sorry I am. It must be a terrible blow. I wish I could have come sooner, but I've been so busy."

Rising from his chair, Caleb shook the doctor's hand. "It's all right. Your work is with the living."

Gant hung up his hat and sat down in a kitchen chair beside

the rest of them without saying a word for a minute or two. There were dark circles under his eyes and he moved slowly, worn down by long hours and great responsibility. After a while he leaned forward, put his elbows on his knees and his face in his hands, fingers tousling his full head of gray hair.

"I watched three children die today," he said through his hands. "The Yoder baby this morning, and a twelve-year-old boy this afternoon—William Yutzy. The little Coblentz girl passed just an hour ago. I did all I could, but it wasn't enough."

An anguished moan went up from the girls, and the women wept anew. The Yoders were a young couple whose oldest child was just beginning school. The lost infant was their youngest. Caleb didn't know the Yutzy boy because they were from Geauga County and had only been in the valley a few days. But he knew little Suzie Coblentz well. She was a pretty little thing and only four years old. The day, somehow, grew even bleaker.

"But we've turned the corner now," Gant said wearily. "The others are all improving, and I don't think any more will die."

Mamm's wail pierced them from upstairs. Dr. Gant pulled himself upright and stared at the ceiling over his head.

"Is she all right?" he asked.

Caleb sighed deeply without looking up. He shook his head. "She's been like that all afternoon. I'm scared she's losing her mind."

"I can give her something," Gant said quietly.

This was not done, normally. Medicine was to be avoided when possible, especially when it was only for comfort. Caleb sat staring at his callused fingertips for a long time, pondering his own part in dragging his family to Mexico, questioning his own wisdom and goodness, beaten down by doubt and guilt.

"All right," he finally said.

Chapter 28

R achel bolted awake in the middle of the night, frightened. Her chains rattled as she sat up, staring, trying to make sense of the shadows in the barn. Something had awakened her and filled her with dread, but she had no idea what it was.

The moon had gone down and the barn was deathly quiet. The only light came from the lantern of the guard outside the barn door, shining through the cracks. She strained her eyes, peering through the slats of the stall toward the door. Nothing moved, but something was not right. Maybe it was only some strange sound that had stirred her—a rat, perhaps—but she couldn't be sure.

She gave up and started to lie back down when suddenly it struck her again. It wasn't a sound, or a sight. Her nose caught a faint whiff, and she knew.

That smell was familiar, and it chilled her to the bone. Crabbing backward, dragging her chains, she stared at the dark wall just inside her stall, eight feet away. There was nothing in front of her but pure blackness, yet now it seemed that part of the blackness shifted and grew.

The straw crunched, right next to her. A sinister whisper came to her on a wave of foul breath.

"Did you miss me, mi pequeña fresa?"

And then a low chuckle.

A panic-stricken scream welled up and almost burst out, but a callused hand clamped itself over her mouth and pushed her down, hard, into the straw.

Kneeling next to her, the weasel whispered into her ear, as close as a lover. "Everyone is sleeping, my sweet strawberry. The midnight sentry was very tired and happy to let me take the watch for him. Now we are going to finish what we started last night, no? Do not scream, señorita. I will not harm you—if I did, that pompous windbag would hunt me down and kill me. But I swear to you, if you make a sound I will put my knife to your little boyfriend. *Entiende?*"

She nodded. He lifted his filthy hand from her mouth and stepped back, to the far corner of the stall. "Excuse me for a moment, mi fresa," he said, chuckling darkly. "Don't go away."

In the blackness she could see nothing, but she heard him dropping things in the dirt—heavy things, like knives and a gun belt. Lastly, there was a softer rustling that must have been his coat.

She knew there was no way she could stop what was about to happen, so she removed herself from it. Even when he came back and lay alongside her she refused to cry out, no matter what, because of Jake.

But why did Jake have to come? She wept for him even now, amid the terror.

He moved against her, and in the dead silence she could hear the rustling of the weasel's clothes, the clink of his belt buckle, the nervous breathing—and the stench was palpable.

A hand clamped over her mouth again, and foul breath

blew hot on her face. The time was near. In desperation she carried herself far away and saw herself riding with Jake in the wagon, in Salt Creek Township. The sun shined and a warm breeze kissed her face. She could see Jake's smile, his kind eyes.

But she was snatched back to the present by the tiny clink of a chain and a gurgling grunt. The grimy hand jerked away from her face, and boots kicked furiously at her legs. The weasel rose up and away from her for no apparent reason, but she could still hear him kicking, flailing. It made no sense.

It suddenly dawned on her that they were not alone! The thrashing noises she was hearing were the sounds of a deadly scuffle.

Rachel sat up and tried to see. Something was happening over against the wall—black shadows writhing in the dark. Legs flailed, boots crashed hard into wood, and she heard a fierce grunting like a man straining against a heavy load, animal rage vented through gritted teeth.

The kicking and thrashing gradually stopped, but the grunting didn't.

She gathered herself and crawled backward at first, putting herself as far away as possible, for she did not know, could not fathom what fearful thing had just happened right in front of her. But as her pulse began to slow and reason flooded back into her petrified mind, she knew that two men had just fought, and the ensuing silence could only mean one of them had been rendered unconscious. Or dead. It occurred to her as a minute passed, and then two, that if the weasel had won the fight she would already know it. All she could hear was heavy breathing, straining, grunting. And yet the struggle seemed to be over. No one moved.

Light. She needed light. She had to see for herself. Groping to the bottom of the deep pocket of her dress, she felt three kitchen matches. Taking one out, she began to crawl toward the sound, dragging her chain. She still did not know who, or what, was in front of her, so she stopped a few feet short of the grunting and struck the match with her thumbnail.

The light flared, and in it she saw a sight so grotesque that she leaped back in horror, dropping the match. The light winked out, returning her world to a blackness deeper and more terrifying than before.

But the image had been burned into her mind: the weasel lying on his side, staring straight ahead with bulging, unseeing eyes, his lips blue, his tongue protruding, a thin dark chain pulled hard into his windpipe, one arm lying limp in the dirt and the other still clenched at his throat. A pair of strong hands gripped the handcuff chain on either side of his neck, shaking with brute force, even now. And from over the weasel's shoulder another face glared at her, also unseeing, though very much alive. Veins stood out, and the face grimaced with an unthinking rage.

Jake's face.

Rachel crawled to him, reached for him in the dark, found his head with her hands. Jake's whole body quivered, still pulling with all his might against the chain.

"Jake."

She gripped harder, instinctively turning his face toward her despite the complete darkness.

"Jake! It's me, Rachel! Jake! Let go!"

Slowly, his arms began to relax. The chain clinked.

"You can let go now, Jake. It's over."

She felt him come to himself. His arms went limp, his head turned, and then, with a little surprised wail of grief, he snatched his handcuff chain over the bandit's head as if it had burned him and lurched backward, crabbing away from the weasel's body and out of Rachel's grasp.

She heard footsteps, running away. Jake flashed through the strips of lantern light from the door and stumbled headlong into the stall gate on the other side of the barn. The hinge squeaked as he threw the gate wide and staggered into the stall, moaning.

Those eyes. The clenched teeth. The *rage*. She had barely recognized him. Fearing for Jake's sanity, she knew she had to do something quickly, before he took a notion to run screaming outside and wake up the rest of the bandits. It took all of her willpower to make herself do it, but she reached out to the weasel and felt through his shirt pockets for a handcuff key.

Nothing.

She moved down his body, found his pants pocket in the pitch-dark and searched until she found the little T-shaped tool with a tip like a tiny gun barrel. Her hands shaking, she fitted it into the handcuff and turned it, quickly.

The key tightened down and wouldn't turn any more.

The other way. She cranked it the other way, five, six, seven turns, and then she heard the click. The cuff fell away from her wrist.

She had the presence of mind to drop the key into her dress pocket as she ran across the barn. Probing with her hands like a blind person, cuffs dangling from one wrist, she groped her way into the stall and followed the sound of moaning until she tripped over Domingo and landed on top of Jake, huddled in a corner.

She put her arms about him, pulled him close and kissed his face.

"Shhhh. It's all right, Jake. Everything is all right. It's all right . . ."

A stirring, behind her.

"Rachel?"

Domingo. His voice was weak and raspy.

"Jah, it's me," she whispered. "Jake strangled the guard. I have the key."

"Give it to me." Already, Domingo sounded more focused. Pulling the handcuff key from her pocket, she groped in the dark until she found Domingo's hand and put the key in it.

"Should I go get the lantern from outside?" she asked.

"No." Chains rattled as Domingo dropped his handcuffs in the dirt. "As long as the lookout on the ridge can see the lantern burning he will think everything is okay. Leave it."

Holding Jake, consoling him, trying to bring him back to his senses, she heard Domingo crawl over to the wall where the water bucket sat. She heard water sloshing over the sides of the bucket when he dunked his whole head in it. Domingo sat up and leaned back against the wall, where she could just make out his silhouette. He shook the water from his hair, tied the bandanna around it, and dropped his head into his hands.

"Are you all right?" Rachel asked.

"Jah, I will be," he said. "Give me a minute. What hour is it?"

"I don't know. Two . . . three, maybe."

Domingo sat motionless for a few minutes, breathing, collecting himself.

"Get Jake's cuffs off," he finally muttered, handing her the key. "Star is in one of these stalls with Jake's horse, and the saddles are probably on the rail, but we'll need another. The buggy horse they stole, will it come to you?"

"I think so. He knows me well."

"Then get him in here. Quietly. I'll go and get the guard's weapons."

Domingo used the slats of the wall to pull himself to his feet, then staggered out of the stall clutching his ribs.

"Jake," she said, gripping his face. "Jake, I need you to help me. *Please*, Jake."

He nodded, finally. "All right. What would you have me do?" His voice sounded washed out, forlorn.

She got him up, took his cuffs off and dragged him to the stall at the back of the barn where the horses waited.

"Saddle these two," she said. "I'll get the other one."

Rachel was helping Jake tighten the last strap when Domingo came and shoved a rifle into Star's saddle scabbard. Wearing the weasel's gun belt, a bandolier of bullets on top of his poncho, a bandanna tied around his head and black hair hanging down his back, Domingo looked like one of the bandits. After Jake finished with the saddle he just stood there staring at his hands, despair and confusion written on his face.

"I will open the big cattle gate," Domingo mumbled, rubbing his forehead. "We'll drive the herd out with us as we go."

"Why?" Rachel asked. "I thought we had to sneak out quietly."

"No matter how quiet we are the guards on the bluff will see us, and their rifles will wake the others. This way we can create confusion and slow them down. The bandits will have to get their horses back before they can come after us. If we are lucky the herd will hide our tracks and make it harder for them to follow us. What's wrong with Jake?"

Rachel hesitated, staring at her boyfriend. She was afraid to say it out loud because of what it might do to Jake, but Domingo deserved to know the truth.

"He fears for his soul," she said softly as she reached up and rubbed Jake's arm. "He killed a man."

Jake said nothing, but he swayed and his knees started to buckle.

Domingo caught him, held him upright. He locked his arms around Jake's shoulders and looked him in the eye.

"Is that what's wrong with you? You thought you killed that guard?" Domingo grinned and forced a laugh. "No, Jake, he is not dead; he's just out cold."

Jake blinked, stared. "He's not dead?"

"No! You can't kill these bandits—they're tough as coyotes. I checked his pulse. His heart beats like a racehorse."

"Are you sure?"

"Jah, I'm sure. He will wake up in the morning with a headache, that's all. He probably won't even remember what happened."

Rachel shot Domingo a little sideways glance. She wouldn't interfere, but she knew what she had seen.

"I'm going to see for myself," Jake said, turning.

Domingo grabbed his arm and pulled him back. "There is no time to waste. We must go. *Now*."

The corral was wide but not deep, framed as it was by the box end of the canyon. All three of them were good riders, so they had no trouble getting behind the herd and driving them through the open gate. When they had cleared the gate Domingo shouted and whooped, firing a pistol over the horses' heads and driving them into a frenzy.

The panicked horses raised a dust cloud as they thundered past the bunkhouse and then the main house, scattering the embers of last night's campfire and trampling the edge of the cornfield. It was pure bedlam. Jake and Rachel took the flanks while Domingo brought up the rear, riding hard and lying low in the saddle as bandits scrambled from the bunkhouse in their nightshirts, shouting, firing blindly with their pistols. But it was dark and most of the bandits were drunk. A couple of bullets ripped the air over Rachel's head, rifle fire from the lookouts on the bluff, but nothing came close.

Once they had gone half a mile or so downhill from the ranch Domingo eased up the pace. But the three of them held their spread and did their best to keep the entire herd ahead of them.

The steep-sided canyon gradually gave way to boulder-strewn slopes, and hours later, as the sun rose red over the jagged peaks in front of them they pushed the herd down through a twisting valley of cactus and sage. Halfway to Arteaga they came across a stream where they stopped to drink.

Domingo got off his horse and dropped to his knees by a little willow at the edge of the stream. Lying flat on his belly, he sunk his head in the cold water, then lay back on the bank, one arm over his eyes. Before he mounted his horse he took the knife he'd salvaged from the weasel, peeled a few strips of bark from a willow branch, chewed on one of them and stuffed the others into his pocket.

Chapter 29

Caleb didn't sleep much that night, but whatever potion Dr. Gant had given Mamm must have been powerful because she went to sleep and never stirred the rest of the night. No longer able to take the smallest thing for granted, he laid a gentle hand on her back a dozen times during the night, to make sure she was breathing. An hour before daylight he rose, dressed himself, and went downstairs.

Aaron was still there, still dead. It was not a dream. And even with Mamm sound asleep, the echo of a question lingered in the air.

Where is my Rachel?

Leah and Barbara had already stoked the stove and were cooking breakfast. Miriam, Ada, and Harvey had gone out to do their chores.

"Mamm's still sleeping," he said to the girls as he took his coat down from the hook by the back door. "Leave her be. She'll wake when she's had enough."

Hollow and drained, he went through the motions of doing chores, but Aaron was all around him. If Aaron were alive, *he* would be the one feeding the livestock right now.

After breakfast Dr. Gant drove over to San Rafael for the day, worried about an outbreak among the villagers. After the doctor left, Caleb walked alone across the valley to Hershberger's farm, taking his time because he needed to be alone with Gott. There were a lot of questions he needed answered.

In the distance he saw men digging with shovels at the base of the opposite slope. Little Enoch Byler had been buried there while he was gone, in the shade of a cottonwood tree. Now the site would become the burial place for the whole Amish community. They were digging three smaller holes and one big one.

He found John working in the doorway of his barn with his sons, fitting planks together for Aaron's coffin. The sight drove another nail into Caleb's heart, but he swallowed the pain and soldiered on because it was all he knew to do. Two smaller coffins were already done and sitting on sawhorses off to one side. John's teenage son was fitting hinges to the lid of one of them while the sound of hammering came from inside the barn.

John paused when Caleb walked up, and gave him a solemn nod for a greeting. No words were exchanged, or needed. Caleb took off his coat, rolled up his sleeves, grabbed a planer and set himself to work smoothing raw planks.

⟢

The sun shined brightly that afternoon, a warm breeze ruffling the wheat. To Caleb, such fine weather seemed almost cruel.

They held all four funerals at once, on the second level of the Shrocks' new banked barn, because it was closest to the burial site. Since there was no preacher, John Hershberger got up, read from the Bible and said a few words. A couple of other men read and spoke, but not the fathers. It would have been too hard on them. Caleb sat through the whole thing thunderstruck, still unable to fathom a world without his son in it. There was singing and prayer, and though he was there for a long time, it all went by in a blur. Too soon, the time came to file past for one last look into the faces lined up side by side in four boxes in the middle of the crowd—two small, one medium, one large. Even on such a day there were no loud cries, no wailing, for it was the Amish way to endure such things stoically. Shy Cora Coblentz paused by Aaron's coffin for a long moment, touching fingertips to the back of a pale hand, her delicate hopes shattered.

Then came Mary, holding Amos. Little Amos leaned out, smiling, trying to reach his uncle one last time, and Mary let him touch the cold face before she pulled him back. Caleb was standing close enough to hear her whisper, "Remember him, child. Uncle Aaron loved you so."

Then came the closing of the lids, the turning of the screws, and four boxes were lifted by strong hands to be carried up the hill. Men's voices sang as Caleb stood beside his distraught wife at the foot of the hole and watched the dirt whumping onto the wooden box containing the earthly remains of his son.

Dr. Gant was there, on the edge of the crowd, and Domingo's sister Kyra in a black dress and veil. Miriam sought her out and took her, arm in arm, to stand with the family.

When it was all over and the crowd dispersed, Kyra took the chance to grab Harvey's arm and drag him off to the side, by the corner of the house. Miriam had only been able to give her the scantest information about what happened in the mountains, and where Domingo had gone.

Miriam listened in, interpreting for both of them when Harvey's spotty Spanish failed him.

"Who were these bandits?" Kyra asked, peeling back her veil. "And how many?"

Harvey shook his head, uncertain. "Domingo said he thought it was El Pantera and ten or twelve of his men."

Kyra gripped his shoulders, staring into his eyes. "*Where* in the mountains? How far?"

Harvey shrugged. "I don't think he knew for sure. He said something about a place way up north, somewhere to the west of Arteaga. That's all I know."

"He didn't say anything else? Nothing?"

"No, that's all he said, but . . ."

"But what?"

"It's just . . . I saw something in Domingo's face I never saw before." Harvey's dark eyes roamed away from her and his voice dropped so that she could barely hear him. "It was only for a moment, when he looked at me, but I saw it in his eyes. Kyra, he was scared. Domingo was very afraid."

∞

By midmorning Domingo had let what was left of the herd go and angled off to the right, following a trail toward a mountain pass.

"This is a hard road," he said. "And crooked. It comes out at the logging place."

Jake's horse ambled along next to his. "How far are we from Arteaga?"

A shrug. "Twelve, maybe fifteen miles."

"Well then, wouldn't it be easier to just ride on into Arteaga and take the lowland road south from there?"

Domingo shook his head. "The easy road is not always best. As soon as they round up a few horses El Pantera will come after us, and if he catches us out in the open things will go very badly. We will have a much better chance in the mountain passes."

They pressed on all day, narrow trails cresting cold rocky

peaks and then winding down through dense green forests that closed about them like jungle while all kinds of wild birds called to them from the trees. Rain fell on them twice during the day, but it didn't last long. At least there were plenty of little springs and streams—a good thing, since they carried no canteens. They also carried no food. They had to make do with nuts and berries picked from the brush in passing. Domingo would not allow them to stop for more than a minute or two.

By late afternoon Rachel noticed that Domingo was slumping forward, his head hanging low, hair obscuring his face. He looked to be sleeping in the saddle—very unusual for Domingo. The trail was well marked, and Jake had taken the lead for the last hour or so. Domingo was beginning to lag behind. Rachel dropped back to check on him.

As his horse pulled alongside hers, she touched his arm and he instantly perked up.

"Are you okay?"

"Sí, I am all right," he said, though his speech was sluggish, his voice soft and tired.

"You don't look all right. Domingo, maybe we should stop for the night, someplace where we can find food. I'm starving."

To her surprise, he considered this for a moment. "I don't know if I can ride through another night, or the horses either. But if we stop, and they catch up to us, we will never see the sunrise."

"El Pantera won't ride through the night," Rachel said. "He will camp."

He looked sharply at her, his brow furrowed. "How do you know this?"

"They camped night before last, on the way to Diablo Canyon. Some of his men didn't know I understood Spanish and they talked where I could hear. They didn't want to camp.

They wanted to go on, but the Appaloosa is night-blind and El Pantera won't travel in the dark because he is too proud to be led around by the nose."

"This explains much," Domingo said, nodding, and he seemed to relax a little. "Maybe it will be all right, then. A couple of old *campesinos* have a ranch at the bottom of this valley, friends of my father. We can stop there and rest. I think maybe we have no choice, but I hope you are right about El Pantera's horse."

She smiled, laid a reassuring hand on his arm. "Gott is with us," she said, "or we would not have gotten *this* far."

The trail was wider near the bottom and less steep, so while Jake scouted ahead Rachel kept her horse alongside Domingo, afraid he might pass out and fall from the saddle without them knowing. Instinct told her to keep him talking.

"Domingo."

He raised up a little and squinted as if he were having a hard time seeing her.

"Domingo, back at the barn . . . that guard was dead."

He smiled weakly as his eyes went back to the trail ahead. "Jah. Dead as an anvil."

"Then why did you lie to Jake?"

"Because he was useless. He couldn't think about anything else, and we needed him. What difference does it make?"

"It was a lie. It is a sin to lie."

Domingo didn't bother answering.

"Sooner or later we will have to tell him the truth," she finally said.

"Why?"

Rachel's eyebrows went up in surprise. How could anyone not understand?

"Because he is guilty of a great sin, and if he doesn't know it he can't repent. His soul must be clean before Gott."

Domingo stared, and a little anger flared in his eyes. "Jake saved you from being raped by that animal. He saved your life—and mine, too. He saved his own life, and the lives of all the other innocent people that weasel would have killed someday. How many sins did he *prevent* when he killed that worthless—"

"Every man is Gott's creation," she said, interrupting him.

Domingo fell silent for a moment. Finally he asked her a question, very softly. "Rachel, do you think he *meant* to kill the guard?"

She didn't have to think long before answering. "No. Never."

"Neither do I. I know Jake, and he is no killer. It was a mistake. In the dark, he just didn't know when to quit, and El Pantera made him afraid of quitting too soon, that's all. If what I've read is true your God will not punish Jake for such a mistake. All I did was take away the guilt that Jake put on himself. A small, kind lie."

She turned in her saddle, brushing wild red hair back from her face. "You've read the Book? The Bible?"

A shrug. "Some of it. It makes a little more sense to me now. Or at least your people make more sense. I always thought your religion was the refuge of a coward—but your father is no coward, and neither is Jake. So I read the Book. There were things I could not understand, and I still do not completely agree, but at least now I understand a little."

They came out of the trees into a meadow, a green strip of bottomland with a creek running through it. Jake was already there, sitting on his horse at one end of the meadow, talking to a bent old man in a ragged straw sombrero. Behind them lay a small ramshackle farm: a scattering of buildings, a corral bounded by a split-rail fence, and a garden patch hemmed in by a thick hedge of prickly pear cactus. Four or five goats and two burros with washboard ribs watched them over the fence of the corral. A dozen brown chickens strutted about pecking for insects, and a thin line of smoke came from a stovepipe on one of the outbuildings.

As they got closer the old man spotted Domingo and his leather face broke into a wide toothless grin.

Slowly, Domingo swung down from his horse and greeted the man with a hug. They talked for a few minutes like old friends, but in a harsh language, different from Spanish.

"I couldn't understand much of what he tried to tell me," Jake said, still mounted on his horse. "My Spanish and his Spanish are like two different languages."

Domingo laughed. "You're right. Señor Navarro and his wife are Nahua. They speak Spanish only a little better than you, and it is colored with Nahuatl. But he says his wife has a pot of beans cooking in the summer kitchen, and she will make dinner for us."

Señora Navarro fed the fugitives tortillas and beans spiced with some kind of peppers that were almost too hot for Rachel and Jake. Then she tended Domingo's wounds and made him drink a strange yellow concoction that seemed to put life back into him. They spent an hour talking around the table in the Navarros' little thatch-roofed hovel, and then she made up pallets for them all.

It was the first time Rachel had felt safe since leaving home nearly a week ago. She lay down on the straw pallet and fell quickly into a deep and dreamless sleep.

Chapter 30

She awakened at the first crowing of a rooster in the dark predawn hours and found the old woman already cooking tortillas. Señora Navarro told her in broken Spanish that Jake was out fetching water and Domingo was in the corral saddling the horses, anxious to get under way.

They left the Navarro ranch in the pink and gray hour of dawn with a bellyful of tortillas and beans that, under the circumstances, seemed like a feast.

Two hours later, when the sun had climbed high into a bright blue sky, they had already cleared the next mountaintop and started down into another of the endless valleys when they heard the distant echo of gunfire. A lot of it.

Domingo stopped his horse and gazed back up the slope. "That came from behind us," he said. "The Navarros."

Jake's horse pawed the ground impatiently. "El Pantera?"

"Sí. Who else could it be? They will know we spent the night at the farm, and we are not very far in front of them."

Horrified, Rachel's eyes filled with tears. "Would the bandits really shoot those old people? Just for helping us?"

Domingo shook his head. "No. El Pantera knows the

Navarros, and there are things even he will not do. He would not kill a couple of old campesinos, especially if they are Nahua, but he would slaughter their goats and chickens so that next time they will think twice about aiding his enemies. Those who help us will pay a high price. Remember this."

He spurred his horse down through the forest, picking up the pace, his eyes focused on the trail ahead. Domingo had been more like himself this morning, leading Rachel to believe there must be something to the old woman's home remedies, only now he seemed more intense, more worried than ever. She caught up with him as they trotted around rocks and trees.

"Domingo, are they going to catch up with us?"

"I don't know. But their horses are used to these passes and ours are not. They can push those ponies very hard when they want to, and we are still a long way from home. We must hurry."

❧

Domingo kept up the pace all day, driving as hard as he dared, stopping only to let the horses water when they crossed a stream. Jake and Rachel ate while they rode, gnawing on strips of dried smoke-cured meat Señora Navarro had given them. Rachel was pretty sure it was goat jerky. Jake must have known what she was thinking because once, after wrenching a bite from the end of a tough strip, he glanced back at Rachel, raised his eyebrows and said, "Not baa-a-a-ad."

At least he seemed to have recovered his sense of humor.

The mountainous terrain was even steeper and rougher than the trail the bandits had taken on their way to Diablo Canyon. Every time they broke into the open above the tree line Domingo would stop for a minute and look back over the valley they had just traversed. Twice during the day he spotted the bandits, still following. The second time, a look of outright alarm spread across his face. It was late in the afternoon, the sun dropping toward the western peaks.

"They are close," Domingo said, shading his eyes. "There are six of them, and the Appaloosa is leading."

Yanking his horse around and galloping up the slope, he shouted, "Hurry! We must get to El Ojo or we are all lost."

He pushed his horse to a hard gallop for nearly a mile, until they broke into the open above the tree line where they saw a solid wall of limestone cliffs dominating the crest. All three horses were lathered and gasping when he finally slowed down at the base of the cliffs. Only then did Rachel see the offset in the cliffs that marked the entrance of a narrow pass, a crack in the limestone. The yellow walls of the crevice were jagged and pocked, carved in steep terraces like pictures Rachel had seen of the Grand Canyon, and the path through the bottom wound back and forth so she couldn't see very far ahead. There were places where it was so narrow that two horses could not run abreast of each other. Domingo rode on ahead while Jake and Rachel followed through the deep shadows of the pass for nearly a quarter mile, until they came out the other side to find a steep boulder-strewn mountainside dropping away in front of them.

When they came out into the light, Domingo had already swung down from his horse and pulled a rifle from the saddle scabbard.

"What are you doing?" they both asked at once.

Domingo reached into his saddlebag for a length of heavy twine and tied one end of it to his rifle barrel. His hands jerked the knot down with a feverish haste.

"There is not much time. You should go." His eyes pointed to a trail sloping off to the left toward the tree line.

"But what are *you* going to do?" Jake asked.

"I will hold them here. You get her home, Jake. Stay on

this trail, bear left at the fork, and you will come to the logging camp. You know your way from there." He slashed the twine with his knife and tied the other end to the butt of his rifle to make a sling.

"Why can't we just keep running? If we ride hard—"

"It's too late, Jake! We cannot outrun them—El Pantera is almost upon us. This is your only hope." Domingo slung the rifle across his back and draped a bandolier over a shoulder.

"Then I'm staying, too," Jake said flatly.

"And do what? This is not going to be a wrestling match. Men are going to *die*."

"If you stay here, *you* will die," Rachel said, her voice quavering.

Domingo's eyes were fierce and he spoke quickly. "It is a hard truth, Rachel, but sometimes men must fight to protect those they love. I don't know if I will be able to stop them, but I can hold them for a while. If they make it through the pass you will have to get to Hacienda El Prado or you will die."

"But—"

"Take my horse," he said, handing Jake the reins. "I won't be needing it anymore." Then he turned to Rachel. "Please tell my mother and my sister that I am thinking of them, and ask your father to look after them." He looked away for a second, hesitating. "Also, I want you to give Cualnezqui a message for me. Tell her . . . tell her maybe I was wrong. I don't know." He reached up and gripped Rachel's wrist, his dark eyes full of regret, searching for words. "I do know this—*there is no greater love*. Now *go!*"

He turned his back on them and bolted toward the limestone cliffs, leaping from rock to rock in sandaled feet.

Stunned, Rachel sat motionless, watching him until he disappeared into the crevice. Disconsolate, yet too shocked for tears, she turned her horse about and began picking her way down the rocky trail along with Jake.

Minutes later, as they reached the tree line they heard the echo of rifle fire from the pass behind them, and the smaller pop of pistols. Jake spurred his tired horse and they trotted as quickly as they could down through the softer ground of the forested slope, even as the sounds of a furious battle rattled the mountaintops. By the time they reached the bottom of the valley the shooting had stopped, and an eerie silence fell.

All the way up the next slope Rachel kept looking back over her shoulder hoping to see Domingo emerge, and at the same time deathly afraid she would see that bicolored Appaloosa charging out of the shadows of the crack in the mountains.

Neither happened. There was only an ominous silence, and the moan of the wind through the rocks.

◌

Perhaps it was because of Aaron, or because everyone looked up to Caleb Bender, or maybe they were all prompted by the same Spirit to seek company—devastated parents leaning on one another—but whatever the cause, all the Amish in Paradise Valley gravitated to the Bender home that afternoon. Word spread of the impromptu gathering, and they came by buggy and wagon and on foot, filling the house to overflowing, spilling out the doorways and up the stairs, all of them dressed in their Sunday best.

They brought food and broke bread together. They sang the old familiar songs from the Ausbund, then Caleb read portions of the Psalms, words of hope and strength and deliverance, and one by one the men prayed for Rachel and Jake. They prayed for the faith and strength to be grateful for what the Lord gives and not question what the Lord takes away. Blessed be the name of the Lord. One of them even prayed for El Pantera, that Gott would either change his heart or stay his hand. No task was too large for their Gott.

It was all a great comfort to Miriam, partly because of the words, the reminders of who they were, but mostly the songs, the voices, the supplications, the hearts strung together as one in common faith. They were a community, a family. They rejoiced and suffered, laughed and cried, lived and died as one. They all felt it. In such a moment, each and every one of them took comfort in knowing they were not alone.

They were loved.

Miriam and her sisters hovered close to their mother, and she seemed to take comfort in the gathering. While it lasted Mamm did seem a little better, a little quieter. The daughters of Caleb Bender closed ranks around her. Together they would endure whatever came. Together they were strong.

Miriam did notice a curious thing that evening, a glaring omission. Domingo's name was never mentioned—not even once. It was as if he didn't exist.

But there *were* prayers said for him. A series of long, fervent, heartfelt pleas went up on Domingo's behalf, though Miriam was the only one who knew it.

Nobody wanted to leave when darkness fell. Instead, they gravitated into little groups to stand around and talk. It was late by the time the last of them left. Leah and Barbara helped Miriam straighten up the kitchen and then they drifted upstairs to bed, leaving her alone with Micah.

Miriam picked up the lantern and walked him out the back door to where his courting buggy was tied.

A muffled wail came from upstairs and Miriam glanced over her shoulder.

"Is she going to be okay?" Micah asked.

Miriam shook her head. "I don't know. If Rachel doesn't come home soon I'm afraid Mamm will lose her mind. I pray to Gott Jake can bring her back. I would just die if anything happened to Rachel."

Micah nodded. "So would Jake. That's what worries me. He's a stout boy, but what can he do against a dozen bandits with guns? I'm afraid he might just get himself killed."

"There is hope yet," Miriam said. "Domingo is with him."

Micah gave a little snort and turned to stare at her. "That's what you think, Mir? A good strong Amish boy can do nothing, but that *Mexican* can?"

She stared back. "That's not what I said."

"It's what you *meant*. You think Domingo can do *anything*. You think he's some kind of hero."

"I didn't mean to make you angry," she said quietly. "I only meant that it's good Jake has somebody with him who knows his way in the mountains, that's all. Even with two of them it seems impossible."

Micah didn't say anything for a minute, but then he softened. He slipped an arm around her shoulders and said, "Jah, it's bad, Mir, but all things are possible with Gott. He is greater than any Mexican."

She'd heard enough. Too tired to bother with him anymore, Miriam said good-night, gave Micah a rather perfunctory peck on the cheek and went back inside, utterly exhausted. Harvey and Dr. Gant were asleep in the basement, her sisters and parents gone to bed upstairs. Pausing momentarily in the living room, Miriam closed her eyes and basked in the silence. Even now, after all the grief and loss, she felt completely at peace here in her father's home. There was no sound at all, save the reassuring *clip-clop* of Micah's buggy horse rounding the house and heading down the driveway.

But then the buggy stopped. There was a muffled shout as Micah's horse pulled up short, and a few seconds later she could hear him turning around and coming back. Perhaps he'd just forgotten something. Miriam started for the back door, but she froze when she heard the sound of other horses, several of them, moving at a quick trot around the house toward the back. No one would come to visit at this hour unless something terrible had happened, but bad news always came by way of a single rider, and she could hear at least three horses.

Bandits! That would explain why Micah had cried out and turned around. She flew to the steps and shouted a warning up to her father, then ran to the front door. Maybe Micah could at least delay them long enough for her to bar the doors. Panic-stricken, she jammed the plank into the brackets and raced for the back door, but too late.

The door burst open just as Miriam reached the kitchen. She skidded to a stop, clutching her heart, for in the doorway stood a breathless, freckle-faced young woman with wild red hair spilling about her shoulders.

Rachel!

There was a split second when the two of them just stared at each other, hardly daring to believe this moment was real, and then Rachel broke down, rushing into her sister's arms. There was a tumult of footsteps on the stairs, shouts of panic turning to screams of recognition and then unbridled joy as the whole family stormed the kitchen.

Peering over Miriam's shoulder, Rachel saw her brother and sisters part to make a path as her mother hurried across the room in a nightgown, her hair loose and untended. Mamm's face contorted and her eyes brimmed with tears as Miriam stepped aside and she wrapped Rachel in a fierce, hungry hug.

Mamm clung to her, weeping openly while the others crowded around to wait their turns. Dat stood there patiently in his nightshirt, the ring of gray hair pointing at odd angles around his bald head. His face held a mixed message. Rachel saw his joy at her return, but it was tempered by a deep and unmistakable sorrow. Looking into his eyes, Rachel mouthed a one-word question.

"Aaron?"

His head moved slightly, side to side, then tilted down, breaking eye contact. So it was as she feared.

Her brother was gone.

Rachel wept with her mother, tears of grief mingling with tears of joy.

Chapter 31

By the time Micah and Jake finished putting away the horses and came inside everyone had gone and dressed themselves and come back. Miriam and her sisters put together a meal for Rachel and Jake while everyone else gathered around the kitchen table.

The pain and sorrow of the last week ebbed, and a tide of joy overtook them.

Even Mamm smiled. For the first time since Aaron's death, Mamm talked a little and made sense. Part of her personality returned. She still wept softly now and then, but she seemed to have pulled back from the brink of insanity.

"So tell us what happened," Miriam said, sitting across the table from Rachel. "We want to know everything."

"It was horrible. Awful." Rachel's face darkened even as she cut off a chunk of steak and stuffed it into her mouth. Slowly, she filled in the gaps in what Miriam already knew, describing how El Pantera and his men stopped the buggy, and what happened to Aaron.

Mamm broke down again at that point. Rachel shot Miriam a worried glance and pressed on, describing how Ada grabbed Little Amos and ran away with him.

"There were twelve bandits—some of them we've seen before. They tied my hands and put me on a horse with one of them."

She told how they camped that night and reached Diablo Canyon the next day. Once or twice Miriam saw something in Rachel's eyes that said she wasn't telling all she knew, but that was okay. The two of them would talk privately later, and there would be no secrets between them then. Miriam understood well enough that there were some things best left unsaid in front of Mamm.

"I thought things were as dark as they could get," Rachel said, "lying there in chains in a stall in El Pantera's barn, waiting to be sold like a slave. But then they caught Jake and it got darker still."

Caleb stared at Jake. "They *caught* you?"

"Jah," Jake said. "And Domingo, too. They were waiting for us, knew we were there the whole time."

"They brought Jake down to the campfire where the bandits were having a fiesta," Rachel said, "and made him fight El Pantera."

The girls all gasped. Micah leaned on the table, eyeing Jake.

Jake raised a hand, shook his head. "I just wrestled him, that's all."

Micah's eyebrows went up. "You *wrestled* El Pantera?"

Jake shrugged, talked around a mouthful of potatoes. "Jah. Would have beat him too, if he hadn't cheated."

Rachel then told how all three of them had been chained in the barn, how Jake got loose and knocked out the guard.

Watching her sister closely, Miriam knew she was hiding something here too, because Rachel was careful not to even look at her.

"We got away in the middle of the night," Rachel said quickly, "and took all their horses with us so they couldn't follow—at least not for a good long while."

She told of the old farm couple who had helped them, and how, the next morning, they heard El Pantera and his men slaughtering the goats and chickens.

Caleb shook his head at that. "Such a waste. Do these men have no shame?"

"No, Dat, they don't," Rachel said. "And there are worse things."

Things about which, Miriam noted, Rachel didn't elaborate.

Miriam could stand it no longer. Up to now Domingo had been a large part of the tale, but he was not here now, at the table with the rest of them. Had he gone on to his house without even stopping?

"Where *is* Domingo?" she asked bluntly. From the corner of her eye she saw Micah turn and stare at her, but she dared not look at him.

A new grief came into Rachel's eyes and she shook her head slowly. "Miriam, I'm so sorry, but I fear we have lost Domingo."

Fighting back tears, Rachel told the story of how they had come to the narrow place called El Ojo, where Domingo made his stand. She paused for a moment, then said softly, "We never heard or saw anything after that, from the bandits *or* Domingo. He stopped them in the pass, but it cost him his life. He sacrificed himself so we could get away."

Miriam struggled to control her breathing. Micah was sitting right there beside her, watching her face. Slowly, she pushed her chair back, rose to her feet, smoothed her dress, and walked stiffly to the back door. She didn't dare turn around.

As she put her hand on the doorknob she said quietly, "Someone has to go and tell Kyra." Then she picked up a lantern from the counter and went out, closing the door softly behind her.

Images clashed and swirled in her mind, and she saw flashes of the barren rocks, the great horse coming to save her, the jaguar—*el pantera*—the battle, the falling.

The emptiness and the moan of the wind in the rocks.

Domingo was lost. It hadn't been her after all, but Rachel he had died to save. He lived by the sword, and now her premonition had come true and he had died by the sword. She'd seen it all in her dream, and said nothing. And if she did nothing to prevent it what right did she now have to feel as if someone had ripped the very heart from her chest? She couldn't breathe.

The gatepost of the barn lot swerved into her path and she clutched at it before she collapsed, sinking to her knees, clinging to the post, the lantern sagging to the ground as she sobbed. A little sound came from behind her—the back door opening, closing.

"*Please*, Gott," she whispered between sobs, "please, please don't let that be Micah."

Soft hands gripped her shoulders. Thin arms wrapped about her and Rachel's voice whispered into her ear, "I'm so sorry, Miriam."

As soon as Miriam could bring her voice under control she glanced back at the house with red eyes and whispered, "I'm surprised Micah didn't—"

"I stopped him," Rachel said. "I told him to wait, to give us sisters a chance to talk."

Miriam touched shaking fingertips to Rachel's cheek. "You're very thoughtful."

Rachel shook her head. "Not really. It's just that Domingo said something right before he left us, and I didn't want to repeat it in there, in front of everybody."

In front of Micah.

Miriam sniffed, trying to draw her mind back from the abyss. "What did he say?"

"He gave me a message, just for you. I don't know what he meant, but he said I should tell Cualnezqui that maybe he was wrong. And then he said, 'I know this one thing is true—there

252

is no greater love.'" Rachel's head tilted then, her eyes puzzled. "Did he mean love for *you*?"

It made no sense to Miriam either, yet the words sounded familiar. She thought they might be from the Bible, but how would Domingo know them?

"Rachel, did Domingo ever say anything about the Bible? About reading it?"

Rachel thought for a moment, and brightened. "Jah, he did, when we were on the trail, running from the bandits. He said he still didn't understand, but he'd read some of it."

Miriam nodded slowly, staring into the lantern, and the rest of the words came to her out of the light.

"I remember now," she said. "It was Jesus who said those words. 'Greater love hath no man than this, that a man lay down his life for his friends.' "

She wept, holding Rachel, the friend for whom Domingo had laid down his life. They stayed there for a few moments, two sisters clinging to each other by a gatepost, a small circle of light in a world of darkness, and then Miriam pulled away, wiped her eyes and helped Rachel to her feet.

She heard the back door open as she was asking Rachel to help her saddle a horse. Micah called out to her.

They waited for him, and when Micah came into the light he laid a gentle hand on Miriam's shoulder.

"A horse?" he asked. "Where are you going so late?"

"Kyra's," she said, palming tears from her face.

"Would you have to go to Kyra's house tonight? It's nearly midnight, Mir. You should wait and go in the morning."

Miriam looked up at him and calmly replied, "They are Domingo's family, Micah—his sister, his mother, his nephews. He bought Rachel's freedom with his life. Do we not owe it to him to respect his family and treat them as our own?"

Micah sighed wearily. He had no answer for this.

"All right, then I'll drive you there. You shouldn't be running all over the country in the middle of the night by yourself."

As the crow flies the village of San Rafael was only a few miles away, but the ridge lay in between. It took more than a half hour by road. A midnight drive on a pleasant night under a sea of stars would normally have been a romantic outing for a man and his betrothed, but a palpable tension hung between them.

Halfway there, after a long silence, Micah said, "I still don't see why you couldn't wait till morning to talk to Kyra."

"Kyra is my friend," Miriam said, her hands in her lap, her eyes elsewhere. She would say no more.

The village was dark and quiet. A few skinny dogs bristled and barked as the courting buggy passed through the dirt streets. There were very few lights in the windows of the adobe huts at this hour of the night. Miriam guided him to Kyra's house at the back of the village, bordering on the bean fields.

"How is it you know where Domingo's house is?" Micah asked, the note of suspicion unmistakable.

"We always come here in the fall to help with the bean harvest. Here, it's this one."

It was only a little two-room adobe house with a thatched roof, but Kyra's hand was evident. Vines covered a shade trellis over the front door, and dense beds of flowers and herbs crowded up against the house.

Miriam knocked, and a minute later Kyra's voice came from inside. "*Quién es?*"

"Miriam." She offered no explanation. Kyra knew she would never come in the middle of the night without good reason.

A bar slid away. The door opened and Kyra stood there, beautiful even now, in the glow of an oil lamp hastily lit. Her raven hair was tousled from sleep, hanging in her face and cascading down over the Aztec blanket she'd used to cover herself.

"What has happened?" she asked, clearly alarmed as she stepped aside and ushered them into the front room.

"It's Domingo," Miriam said, and the fear in Kyra's eyes deepened.

"Oh no." Shaking her head, Kyra took a deep breath and a slender hand came up to her throat.

Miriam nodded gravely. "Rachel came home tonight. Jake and Domingo found her and got her away, but the bandits came after them. El Pantera's men caught up with them, and Domingo stayed behind to hold them off at a place called El Ojo. There was a battle, and Domingo did not walk away from it. I'm so sorry, Kyra."

Kyra's eyes filled with tears. She swallowed hard, but she did not break down.

"I must tell our mother," she whispered, sighing with dread. Striking a match, she lit another oil lamp and set it in the center of a rickety square table. Miriam and Micah pulled out a couple of old kitchen chairs and sat at the table waiting while Kyra went to wake her mother.

The room was spare, a large fireplace at their backs with a cooking rack over it, an oak cabinet next to it, and pots hanging from pegs on the walls. There was a cot against the far wall, neatly made, with pine boxes shoved underneath it. Domingo's bed. In the corner sat a little table, covered with a white linen cloth, bearing a hand-carved crucifix and a handful of stubby candles.

A moment after Kyra's light disappeared into the back room the muffled murmurings of mother and daughter suddenly swelled into anguished cries of grief. Kyra's mother wept loud and long. After a while Kyra came out without her lamp and closed the door softly behind her.

Chapter 32

"M*i madre* will dress herself and come out shortly," Kyra said, joining them at the table. "The boys are away, helping my uncle for a few days. It's good they are not here now because I need to know exactly what happened. Miriam, you must tell me every detail. It is very important."

The whole conversation was in Spanish, for Kyra knew only a few words of English. Micah's eyes wandered about the room as he crossed his arms and sat back, uncomprehending.

"We don't know what happened in the pass," Miriam said, "because only Domingo was there. But the night before, he was severely beaten—twice, according to Rachel and Jake. He was not himself even *before* he turned back to hold the pass."

"Even hurt, Domingo is formidable," Kyra said. "Do not underestimate him. How many were there?"

"Rachel said six, including El Pantera."

Kyra shuddered at the name, but she took a deep breath and asked, "Did anyone come through the pass after Domingo went in?"

Miriam shook her head. "Jake said no one got through, and Domingo never came out either."

"Then we still don't know for sure if he's dead or alive," Kyra said.

The door from the back room opened and Kyra's mother joined them, her eyes puffy and red. A short, stocky woman with the leathered face of one who'd spent ample time in the fields, she wore a plain black dress and a black lace scarf over her graying hair.

"Por favor, continue," she said as she pulled out a chair. She said nothing else, clearly fighting for control, holding a handkerchief over her mouth and moving it only occasionally to dab at her eyes.

"Again," Kyra said. "From the beginning. I want to know any detail you can remember. Any little thing might be of use to me."

Kyra's eyes said she recognized the name Diablo Canyon as Miriam recounted Rachel's story. Kyra's late husband must have talked about it. By the time Miriam finished everyone was crying, except for Micah. He remained stoic, his arms crossed on his chest, understanding almost none of what was said.

"There is one more thing," Miriam said, staring at her hands, pausing to get her voice under control. "Domingo told Rachel to tell you he was thinking of you at the last, and he requested that my father look after you. My father is a man of honor, and he loved Domingo. You will be part of our family from now on. You will never go hungry."

A grim silence hung over the room for several minutes until Kyra's mother rose from her seat and made her way over to the table in the corner. She struck a match and lit the stubby candles, then knelt down, clasped her hands in front of her face and prayed to the hand-carved crucifix.

Kyra rose slowly. "I need to change clothes. I must go and look for Domingo."

Miriam blinked. "Now?"

Kyra nodded, met her gaze. "Sí. The sooner the better. I will not leave him to the coyotes and the buzzards. Miriam, I am deeply grateful to you for coming here tonight. It must have been very hard for you."

Miriam shook her head, tried to smile. "The least I could do," she said.

Kyra went into the back room and closed the door. Micah got up, yawned and stretched.

"Well? Can we go home now?"

Miriam stood up, but her eyes never left that bedroom door. "I should go help her get ready. Kyra needs me just now."

Micah rolled his eyes, but said nothing.

"She is my friend," Miriam said, and went to the back room without another word.

The bedroom was small, containing only three pieces of furniture: a double bed with a straw mattress where Kyra and her mother slept, a dark ancient chifforobe at the other end, and a dresser. The dresser seemed strangely out of place, for while the other furniture was heavy and crudely made, the dresser was dainty and beautiful, with elegantly curved legs. It held three finely crafted drawers with brass pulls and fancy inlaid designs, all highly polished—a very expensive piece of furniture.

Standing in front of the little dresser with one of the drawers pulled out, Kyra saw Miriam staring at it and explained.

"My father brought this home on the back of a hack, covered with a piece of canvas," she said. "He took it from a hacienda that was about to be burned. It is the only beautiful thing we have ever owned." She looked up at Miriam and added, "The only thing the Revolution ever gave us in exchange for my father's life."

She pulled a shirt from the drawer and held it up by the

shoulders—a man's shirt made from the rough, heavy cotton that all the poorer Mexicans wore. Stained and dingy and frayed from long use, it might have once been white.

"My mother keeps what's left of my father's things in here. It's like a shrine."

Kyra laid out the shirt on the bed behind her, pulled out a pair of pants that looked just as rough and laid them with the shirt. Then she began to undress.

"You're going to wear your father's clothes?" Miriam asked.

"Sí. If I am going into the mountains alone, I have a better chance if I look like a man—at least from a distance."

"You're really going to do this? Alone?"

Kyra met her eyes, unflinching. "Domingo is my brother, and we do not even know if he is dead or alive."

"You know how to find El Ojo?"

"Sí, I know the place," she said, stepping into a pair of pants. "The full name is El Ojo de la Aguja." The Eye of the Needle. "We went that way many times when I was a child."

Kyra pulled the stained shirt over her head, slid her hands under her hair and flipped it out, then began twisting and binding all that luxurious hair on top of her head.

In that moment, as Kyra stood there dressed in her father's clothes, the sight suddenly triggered a shock in Miriam, an earthquake tremor of déjà vu.

The dream.

These were the very clothes she had seen in the dream, except that in the dream she'd been wearing them herself. She had nearly forgotten that part because it made no sense. Up to this moment the clothes meant nothing, an anomaly, an afterthought hastily drawn in the shadowy corner of a surreal painting. But Kyra looked enough like her to be her sister, and the sight of her in those rags had jarred Miriam's memory. Her mind flashed startlingly clear images of the desperate fight, the fall, the empty moaning wind and herself . . . clad in the rags of a peasant laborer.

When the moment passed and her senses returned, Miriam found herself leaning heavily on the dresser, her knees too weak to hold her.

The drawer was still open.

There were more clothes in it.

Kyra touched her shoulder. "Are you all right? Your face is as white as your kapp."

Miriam nodded numbly. "Sí. It will pass." Staring into the drawer, she now knew what she had to do.

After a deep calming breath, she lifted a dingy shirt and a pair of pants from the drawer and tossed them on the bed. As Miriam took off her kapp and began removing the straight pins that held her dress together, Kyra suddenly realized what was happening. Her mouth flew open in shock and she grabbed Miriam's shoulder.

"No, Miriam, you cannot do this!"

"You're going to need help. You know you can't do it alone."

"Miriam, no! It's too dangerous, and you'll get in trouble with your people. I cannot let you do it."

Miriam looked calmly into her friend's eyes. "I cannot do otherwise. My people will have to forgive me."

"But *why?*" Kyra's eyes pleaded.

Miriam shook her head, broke eye contact. "Do you believe in dreams?"

A shrug. "Everyone dreams."

"Do you believe they can tell you something, that sometimes the voice of Gott is in a dream?"

"Oh, sí! It is in the Bible."

"Then later, when this is all over, ask me about the dream.

But not now. Right now I could not bear it. How long will it take us?"

"What?"

"El Ojo. How far is it?"

Kyra stared at her for a moment and her shoulders slumped a little, resigned.

"A day there, a day back. Three days at most, if all goes well. Miriam, you're loco. I wish with all my heart that you would not do this . . . and yet I am glad. You are a true friend."

Ten minutes later the two women emerged from the back room with their hair tied up under ragged straw sombreros, wearing heavy ponchos with faded stripes over the clothes of common laborers. There were sandals on their feet.

Micah's mouth fell open in utter shock and disbelief. He shook his head, raised an arm and pointed toward the back room.

"You go in there and change back. *Right now*, Mir! This is an abomination!"

Kyra's mother glanced up from her kneeling place in the corner, but she said nothing.

Miriam went up to Micah and placed a hand gently on his chest. He looked her up and down and recoiled as if she were diseased, his face twisted in disgust.

She lowered the hand, but met his eyes. "The clothes are a necessary evil, Micah. I'm going with Kyra, to help her. We know too well that there are bad men in those hills, and if they see two women traveling alone they will teach us the *true* meaning of abomination."

His head shook, almost involuntarily it seemed. "You cannot do this, Miriam. I forbid it!"

"You *forbid?*"

He blinked. "Jah, I forbid you. If you do this thing, you will not be my wife, Miriam. I have spoken."

There was a noise behind her. Miriam looked over her shoulder and saw Kyra down on her hands and knees pulling a long box out from under Domingo's cot.

She turned back to Micah. His breath hissed between his teeth in bursts as if he were in a wrestling match, his jaw muscles flexing and his eyes blazing. It had never occurred to Miriam to openly defy him but it was he who had issued the ultimatum, and there was too much of Caleb Bender's blood in her veins to even think of abandoning what was right just to please Micah.

"I'm sorry," she said. "Domingo died saving my sister. I cannot let *his* sister go up into those mountains alone. You can forbid me, Micah, but you can't stop me. If you will not have me now, then so be it."

She turned away before he had time to answer, and went to help Kyra with the pine box. Kyra laid the hinged lid back to reveal weapons—the remains of the pistol belts, knives, and bandoliers that Domingo had taken from the bandits. There was also an old Henry repeating rifle. Kyra strapped a gun belt around her thin waist and handed Miriam a bandolier. Standing, she turned to Micah with the rifle propped on her shoulder and said, in broken English, "How I look?"

Miriam knew that Kyra's intention was not to confront or offend. The plain fact was that she didn't speak Dutch and hadn't understood a word of what passed between Micah and Miriam.

But Micah didn't answer; he just snatched his hat from the table, jammed it on his head and stomped out the front door.

Miriam ran after him, calling to him from the open door. "Micah, wait! We're riding back to the house with you. We'll be needing horses."

It was an icy ride home, the three of them crammed side by side on the single bench of the courting buggy. Micah's jaw was clenched, his eyes stone. He never uttered a word the whole way, but he took out all his frustrations on the horse. There was nothing Miriam could do, though she understood. Any Old Order Amishman would be mortally embarrassed at the mere thought of being seen with a girl who was wearing pants, let alone the whole outfit of a Mexican laborer. On top of that, Kyra sat beside them dressed exactly the same, only with a bandolier across her chest and a rifle on her lap. Halfway home, Micah reached behind the seat without a word, shook out a blanket and threw it over them both.

By the time they arrived back at the Bender farm the house was dark and dead quiet, everyone asleep. Miriam and Kyra lit a lantern in the barn and grimly went about saddling two fresh horses while Micah watched, his arms crossed on his chest, his jaw working.

"We'll need food, and some blankets," Miriam said as Kyra saddled a young mare.

"We will need rope, too," Kyra said. Her voice dropped when she added, "For binding the body to the horse."

"There's plenty in the tack room. You go and get the rope while I gather what we need from the house."

Kyra headed for the tack room, and as Miriam passed Micah in the doorway of the barn she stopped and said, "Micah, you may as well go on home now. There's no more to do here. In the morning, tell my mother where we've gone. It won't do any good, but tell her not to worry."

He glared, his arms still crossed. "Miriam, do not do this thing . . . please."

Any other time Miriam might have taken that last word as merely a polite afterthought, but now, as she looked into Micah's eyes in the lantern light, she saw through his innate pride and stubbornness. His voice, though hard, was tinged with regret, and she suddenly realized there was no going back. He had painted himself into a corner. His pride would never allow him to back down once he'd issued an ultimatum, so now he was practically begging her to change her mind. It was the only way he could keep both his pride *and* his girl.

She knew better than to touch him, but she moved a little closer. Tilting her sombrero to look up into his eyes, she said, "I'm truly sorry, Micah. I wish we could have come to an understanding, but in this matter I simply have no choice. I must go. I hope someday you can find it in your heart to forgive me."

Hanging her head, she walked away, the lantern swinging at her side, taking the light with her and leaving Micah standing in the dark. When she came back out with an armload of bread and blankets his buggy was gone.

Chapter 33

Two miles up the trail, as their horses began to climb the first of the hills in the pale moonlight, Miriam dabbed her eyes with the back of a wrist, and Kyra noticed.

"Are you crying?" Kyra drew her horse up close and reached out to her friend. "What's wrong?"

Miriam sighed, sniffed. "It's Micah. I fear I have hurt him in a way that cannot be healed."

Kyra's head backed away, tilted. "How?"

"I humiliated him. Shamed him."

"But how could this be? Was it something you said to him?"

Miriam explained, in Spanish for her friend, what had passed between her and Micah.

Kyra stared. "You mean you humiliated him because you refused to obey him? That is *nothing*, Miriam! He will get over that. It is hard the first time, a little easier the second, and by the hundredth time it is nothing. Trust me, I was married to a proud man myself."

"I only wish it was that simple," Miriam said. "An Amishman expects obedience from his wife, but I am not his wife yet. What shamed him was the clothes, the guns."

Kyra looked at the sky and shook her head in frustration. "Clothes. Are you serious? I guess I will never understand gringos."

"It's not gringos you don't understand, Kyra, it's the Amish. Our beliefs are our law and our bond, our agreement with each other and with Gott. The way Micah saw it, when I laid aside my dress and kapp I was laying aside everything I am, everything I believe . . . everything *Amish*. He had a right to speak out against it. He is Amish."

Kyra said nothing for a long time, thinking. When she finally spoke, her eyes stayed focused straight ahead and there was a hint of quiet anger in her voice.

"I may not understand the Amish," she said, "but I know men. You are wrong about Micah, and you are better off without the coward."

"Kyra, Micah is no coward. We have both seen him do very brave things."

"You give him too much credit, I think."

Now it was Miriam who didn't understand. "What do you mean?"

"You really don't see it?"

"No. See what?"

Kyra leaned close, gripped her forearm. "Miriam, why did we put these clothes on in the first place?"

Miriam shrugged. "To look like men."

"Because?"

"Because the trail is not safe for women."

"Sí. And Micah *knows* this. Your brother died and your sister was kidnapped on these perilous roads. If Micah truly loves you his concern should be for *you*, not the Amish law. No matter how angry he is, a man, if he *is* a man, would never let his love go into the mountains unescorted in the middle of the night. I don't care what kind of clothes we are wearing, he should have insisted on coming with us."

"Oh my," she whispered, as the truth of Kyra's words sank in. Blinded by Micah's anger, she hadn't even thought of it in those terms.

"Sooner or later he will see this himself," Kyra said. "But it will be too late. Face it, Miriam—it is over. Even if you crawl back to him now, he will never forgive you because he can never forgive himself."

Miriam nodded slowly. "Kyra, I'm afraid you're right. He will *never* forgive me."

Her friend's voice came softly, reluctantly out of the darkness. "Do you want to turn back? I will understand."

"No." There was no hesitation, no thought required. "I'm going. Micah will have to wait."

ᐇ

Rachel slept late the next morning. When she finally sat up, rubbing her eyes, she was alarmed to find the room already bathed in sunlight. Miriam was gone, her side of the bed cold. Ada, Leah and Barbara were gone too, probably about their morning chores. Slightly ashamed, even though her family clearly meant for her to catch up on her sleep, Rachel sprang from the bed, dressed quickly, and ran downstairs.

Mamm was in the kitchen, sitting at the table while Barbara put the finishing touches on a big breakfast. Mamm was still not quite herself, but she brightened when she saw Rachel.

"Where's Miriam?" Rachel asked, without preamble.

"I have not seen her this morning," Mamm said, her voice still tired and drawn. "I thought she was out doing chores with Dat and Leah."

Rachel went out the back door and half ran up to the barn, where she found Leah milking cows by herself.

"Where's Miriam? Have you seen her?"

Leah looked around the cow's hind legs, her shoulders working, the steady *rip rip rip* of milk into the pail never wavering.

"No, and I'm a little put out with her. I've had to do everything myself this morning, with only Ada to help. Where did she go?"

Rachel was gazing out the back door of the barn, scanning the pasture for Miriam's shape, looking over the fields for a white kapp somewhere among the corn. There was no sign of her.

"Last night she went to Kyra's house in San Rafael," Rachel said. "She should have been back long before now, but it was late when she left so maybe she decided to stay the night. That must be it. Kyra was probably very upset about Domingo, and Miriam decided to keep her company."

Still staring out over the pasture and the fields, Rachel saw nothing, and yet something was not right. Something bothered her, but she couldn't quite figure out what it was.

Miriam spent the night at Kyra's—it was the only explanation. Rachel grabbed a bucket and stool and went to work.

"Sorry about being so late," she said. "Why didn't you wake me?"

Leah smiled around the swishing tail of her cow. "After what you've been through? Sister, I'm so glad to have you back I would have let you sleep all day."

They were eating breakfast when Micah showed up. He tied his buggy horse to the barn lot fence, knocked twice on the back door and let himself in.

"Good morning," Caleb said. "Have you had breakfast?"

Micah shook his head stiffly, standing just inside the back door with his hat in his hands as if he was afraid to move deeper into the kitchen.

"No. I mean, no thank you, I've already had breakfast. I, uh, I came to give you a message from Miriam. I'm sorry I couldn't get here earlier, but"—he waved a hand toward the other side of the valley—"I had chores."

Then he paused and fidgeted, peeking out the back window as if there were something to look at.

"Well, what is it?" Caleb asked. "Rachel said Miriam spent the night at Kyra's. Is that what you were going to tell us?"

"Well, no," he said, and his gaze went to the floor. "I mean, no, she didn't spend the night at Kyra's. I brought her back here last night. Late. After you'uns were asleep."

Mamm sat upright in alarm.

"Then, where is she?" Caleb asked. "She's not *here*."

"No, she's not. That's what she wanted me to tell you. She went with Kyra."

Rachel's hand flew up to cover her mouth. Now she knew what had bothered her about the pasture—there were horses missing.

"I took Miriam to Kyra's last night and she told them what happened to Domingo," Micah said, his eyes still downcast. "Kyra was very shook up, and her mother too. She said she was going after Domingo, to bring his body back home and give him a proper burial. They left last night. Kyra said they would be back in three days—if there's no trouble."

Rachel cringed, knowing better than anyone the perils of the mountains. *Not Miriam. Not now.* She didn't even want to think about what would happen if Miriam and Kyra ran into bandits in the hills, alone.

Mamm's face twisted in angst, and her mouth worked without words. Her fork clattered unnoticed onto her plate. Shaking hands covered her mouth and she drew a breath for a scream that didn't come.

Micah shook his head and his voice dropped. "I don't know what got into her. She went back in the bedroom to help Kyra, and when they came out both of them were dressed like Mexican men, like peons or bandits or something. They took guns and then they came here to get horses. Must have been three or four hours before daylight when they left here on horseback, headed up into the mountains. Caleb, I *told* Miriam not to go. I *begged* her not to go, but she wouldn't listen to me."

Horrified, Rachel watched her mother sinking back into despair.

The sorrow in Micah's face slowly gave way to the self-absorbed anger of a petulant child. "She's lost her wits," he said through gritted teeth. "Running off in the middle of the night dressed like a Mexican. Dressed like a *man*! Why, I think she's gone loco over that Domingo. Her mind ain't right."

Rachel could take no more. She was about to challenge him herself, but her dat pushed his chair back and stood up straight to face Micah.

"You brought her back here?" Caleb asked in a steady voice, though Rachel could see fire in his eyes.

"Jah, I brought them both in the buggy, but not because I wanted to."

"So you were here when they left?"

"No, I didn't stay to see them off, if that's what you mean. I wanted no part of it."

"But you were here, and you knew what she was about to do." Raising an arm, Caleb pointed a finger in the direction of the mountains and his voice went up a notch. "And you *let her go*?"

"I couldn't stop her, Caleb! I forbid her, but she wouldn't listen. She was *crazy*, I tell you!"

Crazy. Rachel had *seen* crazy recently, and Miriam wasn't even close.

Caleb leaned a little closer, his eyes boring in on Micah. "So you admit that the girl you're about to *marry* went off into those mountains in the middle of the night, and *you* didn't go with her?"

Rachel thought her dat might have overstepped his bounds just a little—Miriam's engagement was a secret. But then Micah asked for it.

Micah's face flashed deep red and his eyes narrowed. He blustered and fumed and opened his mouth to answer, but he couldn't find the words. His hands flailed about and he stomped out the door, slamming it behind him. Rachel thought she heard a garbled shout of rage when he was halfway to his buggy, but nothing she could understand.

Mamm stared into space, her eyes pooling. Just as she had gotten one daughter back, another was lost, and Mamm was thrown right back into the abyss.

It broke Rachel's heart.

Chapter 34

Kyra kept them away from the main road during the night, following a narrow winding path that clung to the edge of the mountains in the deep shadows of the forest.

"It is an old trail," Kyra said, "a footpath of the native peoples for centuries before the Spaniards came. No one uses it much anymore, so I think we will be safer here."

The trail was too narrow for wagons, and in some places so steep that they had to dismount and lead their horses up the treacherous slope. The dawn broke clear, but during the morning the clouds gathered and by noon they had merged into a solid overcast of lumpy gray flannel. A chill wind began to blow.

Sometime in the afternoon they emerged above the tree line. Ahead lay a vast field of yellowish-white rocks sloping up to the base of a limestone cliff that formed the spine of a long razorback ridge.

"This is the place," Kyra said. "You cannot see it from here, but there is a crack in those cliffs. El Ojo—the Eye of the Needle."

Miriam's heart was as overcast as the sky, and as their horses.

picked their way up the slope among the rocks every step filled her with a greater sense of dread. When they reached the crevice in the face of the cliffs they stopped and listened for a moment. Miriam shivered, chilled to the bone partly by the cold wind moaning through the Eye of the Needle and partly, no doubt, from fear of what they were about to find. A gaggle of buzzards circled overhead, watching, waiting.

Kyra glanced up at the buzzards, took a deep breath and spurred her horse slowly forward, into the pass. A hundred yards in, at the narrowest point, they found the bicolored Appaloosa. He lay on his side, shot through the chest, his saddle still in place. His head was turned at an unnatural angle and one leg was raised, jammed hard against the opposite wall. His eyes were still wide, his tongue hanging out, swelling. It was a gruesome sight.

Their horses stamped and whinnied, nervous. Kyra dismounted and led both horses back to a bush growing in a little cut and tied them there.

"We will have to go in on foot," she said. "You can wait here if you wish, Miriam. I don't know what lies beyond."

Miriam shook her head. "The last thing I want right now is to be alone."

They walked back to the Appaloosa, where Kyra knelt and went through the saddlebags.

"There's nothing here," Kyra said. "The saddlebags are empty and the rifle is gone. I think El Pantera did not die with his horse, but I wonder why they left the saddle."

"I couldn't begin to guess," Miriam said.

They stepped over the Appaloosa and continued. Farther in they found another dead horse beside a large bloodstain that didn't come from the horse. But there were no human remains.

"The second horse is facing in the other direction," Kyra

pointed out. "This one tried to get away when the shooting started."

She pressed on, Miriam following. Several times Kyra stooped to examine tracks in the rocky soil—both hoofprints and boot tracks. In two other places she found large dark spots in the ground, still damp with blood.

"My brother put up quite a fight," she said, rising, staring. From here they could see the other end of the pass, where it opened out into sky. Miriam followed Kyra all the way through to the end. They stood gazing over the bald approach on the north slope. There was nothing else to see.

Kyra's eyes narrowed, searching the ground. "Rachel said there were six of them?"

"Sí. Jake said that, too."

"Two of them were killed or badly wounded, probably more, but there are no bodies." She pointed to the tracks leading away to the north. "Only four horses left here, and if they took their own dead and wounded there would be no room for Domingo."

"Maybe he took one of their horses and went after them."

Kyra shook her head. "Domingo was too smart for that. He would never chase them into open country where they would have the advantage. If he managed to get a horse he would have come straight home."

Kyra turned around, and Miriam saw the hope fade from her eyes as she watched the buzzards circling the other end of the pass.

"He is here," Kyra said. "We just have to find him."

They made their way slowly back through the pass, searching the ground for any kind of clue. They found more blood, but no bodies. When at last they came back to the Appaloosa Kyra stopped and looked up. The buzzards were circling directly overhead in a darkening sliver of sky.

"I know where he is," she said calmly. "I don't know why I didn't think of it already. Many times I heard my father talking to Domingo about the ways of war. One of the things my father said over and over was, 'Never defend when you can attack, but if you must defend, take the high ground. Always the high ground.' "

Her eyes traced the terraced walls of the pass, limestone pocked with holes and crevices that would make climbing easy.

"This way," she said, stepping over the Appaloosa. "It is no accident the Appaloosa fell in the narrowest place. This would have been Domingo's first shot, and it had to come from up there."

It was Miriam who spotted it—a tiny tag of red, barely visible at the edge of a rock ledge about twenty feet up. She would not have seen it at all if the wind hadn't lifted a little corner of the cloth right where she was looking. Domingo's bandanna was red.

Kyra found handholds in the rock face and scaled it with astonishing agility. As she raised her head up over the ledge, she froze.

"He is here," she said.

There was no light in her voice when she said it, and Miriam, waiting alone at the base of the cliff, dropped to her knees. There was even a tinge of guilt in Miriam then, as it came to her that the weight of grief descending upon her in that moment was every bit as heavy as when her own brother died. Until now she had not understood just how deeply Domingo had affected her.

Kyra hoisted herself up over the ledge and out of sight. Miriam laid her forehead against the cool stone and wept in silence, dreading what lay ahead. Now there would be a body, lifeless and cold, a tangible end to an unspoken hope.

Instead there came a shrill cry, echoing from the walls of the narrow pass.

"*He is alive!*"

A moment later Kyra's head reappeared at the edge of the shelf, her eyes wide.

"Miriam, he lives! He is badly hurt, and unconscious, but his heart still beats. Bring the rope and one of the horses." Without waiting for an answer, Kyra's head disappeared, and Miriam ran, her heart pounding, to fetch the horse.

She coiled the rope and tried to sling it up to Kyra. It took her five tries, but she finally managed to do it.

Ten minutes later Kyra stuck her head out again.

"I tied him the best I could and passed the rope around the bottom of a little stump," she said. "I hope it holds. Now tie the other end to the saddle."

Kyra used her own body to shield Domingo from the jagged rocks as Miriam eased slack into the rope, lowering Domingo over the edge. He looked dead. His head lolled back, limp. His arms and legs dangled. The rope groaned and twisted, and as he slowly rotated toward her Miriam could see blood matting his hair and covering half his face. One of his legs was bent at a bizarre angle above the knee.

Kyra scrambled down in time to wrap her arms about him and gently guide his body to the ground, shielding the back of his head.

When the rope went slack Miriam hastily untied it from the saddle and ran to Kyra's side. She nearly passed out when she got a close-up look at him. There was blood everywhere, dried on his face and hands, darkening the front of his torn poncho.

Kyra lifted both of his eyelids with her thumbs and winced, shaking her head. "I don't know how he did that to his leg, but that's not the worst of it. There's a knife slash across his chest, a bullet hole through the flesh of his left arm, and a nasty gash on the back of his head. His eyes don't look right."

Miriam stared. "What can we do?"

"Nothing, here, and I don't think he would survive the trip home."

"Can we get him to a doctor?"

Kyra shook her head. "Agua Nueva is even farther—he would never make it. But we can't stay here. It isn't safe."

Thunder rumbled around her words.

"And it's going to rain," she added, glancing skyward. "We need to find shelter, and soon. Once, when I was a child, we camped at an old abandoned silver mine not too far away. We can take him there."

Miriam took a goat skin flask and dribbled a little water between Domingo's lips while Kyra rode down to the woods and came back shortly with two long, slender poles—green saplings she had cut down and trimmed with nothing but a hunting knife and a rock.

Kyra's resourcefulness never ceased to amaze her. The first thing she did was split off a couple of splints from the thick ends of the poles. Miriam had to clamp herself onto Domingo's head and chest, trying to hold him while Kyra locked an arm around his ankle and heaved against the broken leg with all her might.

Domingo moaned and his back arched, but even the pain of setting his leg didn't wake him. Once Kyra was satisfied with the angle of the leg she lashed the splints securely in place with rope.

"I'm afraid this is all we can do for now," she said, glancing up at the threatening clouds. "We need to get moving."

She showed Miriam how to roll the poles into opposite sides of a blanket to make a travois, and then she secured the thick ends of the poles to her saddle, leaving the flexible tips to drag behind and absorb the shock of the rocky path. They laid Domingo on the travois as gently as possible, tied him in place with rope, and started down the trail to the west under a low and ominous sky.

Miriam brought up the rear, her heart in her throat as she watched Domingo bounce along behind Kyra's horse on his makeshift bed. As she rode, she prayed. It didn't take a doctor to see that he was near death, but he *wasn't* dead, and Rachel's miraculous return had taught her that any hope, no matter how faint, was infinitely better than no hope at all.

Chapter 35

News of Rachel's return spread quickly that morning, and buggies traveled back and forth all day as the neighbors came to see her. But the joy over Rachel and Jake was tempered by the news that Miriam had gone off into the mountains with Kyra to look for Domingo's body—a whole new worry.

Jake Weaver was hailed as a hero, but circumspectly, lest they fill the young man's head with pride. Late in the afternoon, when most of the day's work was done, Hershberger granted the young hero a couple hours of daylight to go visit Rachel.

Near dusk, the two of them walked out past the barn lot, up the face of the ridge a ways and sat together on a rock outcropping where they could look out over the valley. Dark gray clouds had crept in during the afternoon, and the freshening breeze brought the clean scent of rain. Distant thunder rumbled in the west. Rachel gazed toward the mountains, where the usual brilliant copper sunset had been blotted out by a sea of clouds.

"Miriam is out there," she said quietly. "I worry about her. What if the bandits are still there?"

Jake shook his head. "After the battle in the pass, I bet the bandits are at home licking their wounds. Anyways, Kyra is with her." He took his hat off, roughed his hair and let the breeze blow through it. Finally he said, "What do you think they will find?"

Rachel shrugged, her eyes forlorn. "I can only hope Domingo is alive, but the way he talked when he turned back . . . I'm so afraid. Domingo believed he was going to die. It was in his words, and in his eyes."

"I saw it, too," Jake said. "But maybe Domingo was wrong."

"He is usually right. I can only hope Gott will provide a way."

"Micah is pretty upset about Miriam," Jake said.

"He should be."

"Did you know they were engaged?"

"Jah. She told me."

There was sadness in Jake's eyes. "I didn't know until Micah told me, just a little while ago. Last night, when he tried to stop her from going, he told Miriam she could not be his wife if she went off with Kyra."

Rachel blinked. "So *that's* why he acted so strange."

"Jah. He didn't really think she would do it, and when she did he had to stand by his word, so now their engagement is off. Micah didn't want that to happen. He loves Miriam."

Rachel's face hardened. "If he loves her, then he should have gone with her."

"If it had been you I would have tried to stop you."

"Jah, but if I had gone anyway you would have gone with me, wouldn't you?"

Jake nodded without hesitation. "If it's important to you it's important to me, Rachel. But Micah doesn't know Domingo like we do, and I think he's jealous. He thinks Miriam likes Domingo."

Rachel was silent for a moment, staring off into the dark distance at a hack coming down the main road.

"She does," she said quietly. "Miriam would kill me for telling you, but it's the truth. I think she's in love with him."

"No . . ."

"Jah, it's true. Miriam never meant to fall so hard, it just happened. At first I was angry with her, but then I remembered it was the same for me. I never really had any choice. You captured my heart, Jake Weaver."

From the look on his face she was fairly sure he would have kissed her right then if they hadn't been in plain sight from the kitchen window.

"That's a shame," he said, then added hastily, "I don't mean you, I mean Miriam—you know, in love with Domingo. It makes me very sad for her because nothing can ever come of it since Domingo is not Amish. He's not even American."

"Miriam knows that. It doesn't make the feelings go away, but she knows. That's why she chose to accept Micah—to keep from breaking Mamm's heart." Rachel chuckled, lowering her head sheepishly. "There was a time, when I first got word your family was not coming to Paradise Valley, I made plans to go back to Ohio by myself. Miriam was the one who stopped me."

"You would have done that? For me?"

"Jah, I would have. But Miriam said my family needed me and I shouldn't abandon them. Family is everything, she said, and she was right."

Jake smiled a little smile and, without looking, reached over and patted her hand. "She's right, and one day soon I hope to have a family of my own."

Rachel blushed, but she said nothing. Confident of Jake's love, she had never once doubted it, nor doubted their future together, whether a minister came to Paradise Valley or not. But in another part of her mind a problem festered. It was a bigger problem even than a wedding, with direr consequences, and yet it was one she had not been able to bring herself to share with Jake.

He was a murderer.

Jake had killed a man, and his soul was in imminent peril of hell if anything should happen to him. What made matters infinitely worse was that he didn't even *know* he was in danger. And it was her fault. She and Domingo had lied to him, so Jake went on blissfully believing he had not killed the bandit that night in her stall.

Clearly he would have to repent of his sin, but that wasn't the problem. Jake would be remorseful. In his heart, he was no murderer. But never in all her life had Rachel ever even heard of an Amishman killing a man except by pure accident. There simply was no precedent for such a thing in an Amish community because it had never happened before. If she told Jake the truth now, she was certain he would be forced to travel back to Ohio, where a bishop would decide his fate. And when he got to Ohio, what would his father say?

Like Caleb Bender, Jake's father was a man of principle. Jonas Weaver would *never* allow his son to return to Paradise Valley. Ever.

Jake could be separated from her forever.

Rachel sighed. Maybe she could wait it out. Eventually the day would come when Jake would be old enough to make his own decisions and go where he wanted. Anyway, it wasn't like he *meant* to kill the weasel; he was only trying to keep him from harming her.

But it was a lie, and she had learned from watching Emma that a sin covered by a lie was a burdensome thing to carry. She knew in her heart that somehow it would come back to haunt them both. And what of his soul? If she guarded her secret in order to keep Jake for herself on this earth, she might very well be depriving him of an eternity in heaven. In her heart she knew—sooner or later she would have to tell him.

But not today.

Kyra picked her path carefully and moved slowly, jostling Domingo's travois as little as possible on the rough, rocky mountain trails. By the time they reached their destination it was too dark for Miriam to tell much about the little valley, other than it was a narrow strip of fertile bottomland at the base of a sheer limestone cliff. A clear brook ran through a sandy wash close under the cliff face, and she could hear it gurgling over rocks and under snags of deadwood piled up by flash floods.

The entrance to the abandoned silver mine was a little ways up a steep forested slope on the side of the valley opposite the cliffs, a black rectangular hole mostly obscured by thick brush and scrawny, twisted trees.

They untied the travois and lowered it to the ground. Kyra picked up a fist-sized rock to pound the back of her hunting knife, and while Miriam gathered firewood she cut the poles of the travois down to make a litter.

"The miners carved out a living space for themselves about fifty feet inside the mine," Kyra said. "There's a crevice in the top that draws the smoke, so we can build a small fire for light and cooking."

Thunder rumbled overhead, and Miriam started toward the entrance with an armload of dry firewood.

Kyra stopped her. "I wouldn't go in there yet," she said, pulling a candle from her saddlebag. "Let me go in first and see what creatures are there."

With a candle in one hand and a heavy stick in the other, Kyra disappeared into the entrance and came back in a few minutes dragging a dead rattlesnake. When she held it up by the tail, its crushed head hung to the ground.

"Dinner," she said, and Miriam shuddered. "They look for a cool place in the summer."

Fifteen minutes later they had tied the horses, brought the saddles into the mine and built a small fire in the square chamber fifty feet down the timber-shored shaft. Just as Kyra said, the smoke drifted up and out of sight through a crevice. After they swept out the spider webs and rats' nests they brought in Domingo's litter and laid him far enough from the fire to keep sparks away from his blanket.

Outside, the deluge began.

Listening to the pounding rain as she casually skinned the rattlesnake by the fire, Kyra glanced up the shaft and said, "Our timing was perfect."

Miriam nodded. "Gott's timing." By candlelight she watched Domingo, the slow rise and fall of his chest, the gray pallor in his bloody face. He was shivering, so she got the other blanket and covered him.

"We should clean his wounds properly now that we have a fire," Kyra said, standing on the snake's head while she peeled off the skin. "There's a little cooking pot in my saddlebag. Why don't you catch some rainwater and put it on the fire to boil?"

By the time Miriam came back with a potful of rainwater Kyra had spitted part of the snake and had it roasting over the small fire.

"I don't think I can eat that," Miriam said.

Kyra was leaning over Domingo, feeling his forehead with a wrist. Without looking up, she said, "You've never been really hungry, have you? We only have one day's food left, and if Domingo lives we won't be able to move him for a while. I think I will have to teach you some new things."

She was right, and Miriam felt a pang of shame for worrying about what she would eat while Domingo lay near death.

"Is he going to be all right?" she asked.

Kyra looked up, shrugged. "I will do everything I can, but

in the end his life is in God's hands." Then she smiled wearily and added, "In the end, *all* our lives are in God's hands."

They had brought a few ears of sweet corn, and Kyra laid two of them in the coals to cook, still in the shuck. Even roasted snake wasn't so bad once Miriam got over the idea of it, and as long as she was careful not to look at the carcass. Sort of a cross between fish and rabbit.

By the time they finished eating, the water was boiling in the little pot. Kyra tore a square cloth from Domingo's shirt and dropped it in. It took an hour to clean his wounds, and when they were done he didn't look much better than when they started.

"In the morning I'll go out and gather some medicines," Kyra said. "If he lives through the night, maybe tomorrow will be better. We'll clean the wounds again and sew them up."

Miriam's head tilted. "With what? We brought no needle or thread."

"Watch and learn," Kyra answered, with a slightly condescending smile. "Everything we need is already here." She felt Domingo's forehead again, then his hands and feet. Her brow furrowed. "He is freezing, and we have only two blankets. You and I will have to keep him warm tonight."

"How?" Miriam asked.

"There is plenty of heat in us, so long as we share it. We will lay against him, like dogs."

Miriam gasped. Her eyes widened and her hand flew up to cover her lips, shocked at the very suggestion.

"Oh, I could *never* do that," she said, her face flushing. "It wouldn't be . . . I just couldn't *ever*—"

"Miriam. He's unconscious. He won't know. Look, I'll leave the bottom blanket over him and we'll lie on top of it, so you won't really be touching him at all. You snuggle up to one side, I snuggle up to the other, and we'll pull the second blanket on top of us. That way all three of us can share two blankets and Domingo can stay warm in the night."

Miriam gave her a sideways look.

"He's freezing, Miriam. We must keep him warm."

Warily she said, "Later, when he wakes, you won't tell him?"

"Not a word, I promise." Kyra's eyes danced, enjoying Miriam's discomfort a little too much. "It's the only way, Miriam. It must be done."

She nodded, her mouth a thin line. The very idea was mortifying to her, but she had to concede the necessity of it. Slowly, nervously, she lay down against his side and put her arm across his chest.

"I will never be able to sleep a wink," she muttered as Kyra put out the candle and lay down against Domingo's other side.

Miriam could feel the rise and fall of his chest, the rhythm of his heart. In the beginning it made her very nervous, but then a strange thing happened. Lying close to him, with firelight flickering dimly from the rock walls, listening to his slow, even breathing, her nerves began to dissipate.

I suppose I can get used to anything, she thought at first, but in a little while she began to realize that she felt safe and warm, and holding Domingo seemed strangely natural. A while longer and she became so completely relaxed that she fell sound asleep.

Chapter 36

D r. Gant came home early that evening and announced that he was heading back to Saltillo in the morning. He hung up his hat and collapsed, exhausted, into a chair. His shoulders sagged.

"We lost two children in San Rafael," he said wearily, "and an old man, but I think the worst is over. I treated everybody I could until the antitoxin ran out, burned a lot of infected bedding and trained them to boil and sterilize. There haven't been any new cases in three days. I think we've stopped the spread."

"You sound like you think you failed," Caleb said. He was building a fire in the stove because the evening was chilly and Mamm couldn't get warm. She sat huddled in a rocker near the stove, crying softly.

Gant sighed deeply, put his elbows on his knees and buried his face in his hands. "It's hard for a doctor to watch children die," he said through his hands.

"It's hard for anybody to watch children die," Caleb answered, his voice thick with emotion as he closed the iron door and latched it. Flames flickered through the grill. "But how many would have perished if you hadn't come? I don't think we can ever repay you."

Gant waved him off without looking up. He had toiled day and night, almost single-handedly stemming the tide of disease, and yet he was haunted only by his failures. His limitations. Caleb gave his shoulder a gentle squeeze as he passed, thinking that it was rare indeed to find such a man wearing a three-piece suit and driving a fancy car.

"Oh, Miriam," Mamm whimpered.

Gant looked up, stared at her. "I'm worried about her, Caleb. I wish there was something I could do."

"Me too," Caleb said, lowering himself into a chair near Mamm, then reaching over and tucking the blanket about her legs. "Mebbe she'll be all right. I don't know."

"I have a friend in Saltillo," Gant said. "A psychiatrist. I might be able to talk him into prescribing something for her if you like."

Caleb only shook his head. "No. We'll take care of her. I think she'll be all right once Miriam gets back."

The girls were cleaning up the kitchen, and when a knock came at the back door Barbara opened it. Micah shuffled in, hat in hand.

Caleb rose and greeted him with a stiff handshake, offered him a chair.

Micah shook his head, remained standing. "I just came to see if you heard anything yet," he said. He acted subdued, apologetic, all trace of pride gone.

Mamm stared at him with red, puffy eyes, and whimpered, "Have you seen Miriam?"

Caleb sighed, sitting back down. "In the morning I will go and look for them. I would have gone already but for . . ." He nodded slightly in his wife's direction. She was oblivious. "Rachel, do you remember how to find this Needle's Eye?"

"It's on the same trail as the logging place," Rachel said, drying a plate. "Just a lot farther north."

"Let *me* go," Micah said, and there was a note of pleading in his voice. "Caleb, your wife is not well. Wouldn't it be better if you could stay here and take care of her? You been through so much already. Let me go look for Miriam."

Caleb considered this for a second. The boy was full of remorse, and it was a remorse that Caleb felt he deserved, but he was hoping to make amends. Micah was trying to do the right thing, and Caleb would not stand in his way.

"How would you find them?"

"Jake Weaver was there," Micah said, twisting his hat in his hands. "I talked to him this afternoon. He says he will guide me to the place."

Caleb nodded grimly, glancing at Mamm. "All right, then. You find my Miriam and bring her home."

⌒

Miriam awoke to the crackling of a bright fire. Draped over Domingo's inert form, she flinched and recoiled away from him, terribly embarrassed, before she remembered what had happened and where she was. Sitting up, she glanced around the little rock chamber and saw that Kyra was gone. She must have already been out and come back once because the fire had been stoked.

Domingo hadn't even twitched during the night. Gently she felt his forehead—neither too hot nor too cold. Good. Pressing a finger under his jaw, she found his pulse. Weak, but regular. She tucked the top blanket close around him, then rose and looked up through the shaft toward the entrance.

Daylight. She felt guilty for having slept so late. Her first impulse was to go out and look for Kyra, but she thought better of it. Kyra probably left her behind on purpose. Someone needed to stay by Domingo in case he awoke while Kyra was out getting breakfast.

Miriam put on her sandals, draped her poncho over her shoulders and walked gingerly up the beamed shaft to the entrance, yesterday's rattlesnake still fresh in her mind.

In the morning light, the valley in front of her was lovely. The night's rain had brought out a lush green in the narrow vale, and the sun lit the limestone cliffs on the other side a brilliant white. The cliffs were alive with brightly colored birds, though they were too far away to tell what kind of birds. Apparently the place was a nesting grounds because there were hundreds of them, coming and going from little black holes in the face of the cliff. Two hawks patrolled high overhead, facing into the wind and hovering motionless as kites, waiting for a chance to strike.

There was movement among the weeds and cactus down in the bottom. For a split second Miriam's heart froze when she saw a Mexican elbowing his way through the brush, a gun belt around his waist, a goatskin hung over a shoulder and a large bundle dangling from his hand. But it was only Kyra. The bundle in her hand was her poncho, folded over and used as a bag. Even now it was hard to get used to seeing a beautiful woman like Kyra in a man's clothes.

A few minutes later Kyra dropped her bundles by the fire and knelt over Domingo.

"How is he?" she asked.

Miriam shrugged. "No better, but no worse."

"'No worse' is good enough for now," Kyra said. "I went to the creek to fill the goatskin. We will need a lot of water. On the way back I found some other things we will need as well."

While Miriam put a pot of water in the coals to boil, Kyra spread out her poncho. To Miriam's eyes it looked like a useless pile of garden clippings—nothing but weeds, roots, and leaves. But not to Kyra. She seemed to know a use for everything.

The first thing she did was dice a handful of some kind of

green herb directly into the pot of water heating up, muttering something about it keeping down infection. While she was doing this she picked up a foot-long stem with dark purple flower petals all over it, plucked some of the petals and ate them.

"Try some of these," she said. "They will stave off the hunger. I'm sorry I didn't get anything else to eat yet, but I was in a hurry to take care of Domingo. His wounds need to be properly cleaned and bandaged."

Miriam tried the flower petals. Not particularly tasty—a little sharp on the tongue—but Kyra was right. It would do until something better came along.

The next thing Kyra did seemed downright strange until she explained it. She picked up a leathery, blade-shaped leaf as long as her arm with a fine point on the tip. Putting the needlelike tip in her front teeth, Kyra winced as she bit down and snapped it off. Then, still holding the little point in her mouth, she drew the blade away from her and extracted a few long, fine fibers.

"See? Needle and thread." She dropped it into the boiling pot, picked up another one and repeated the process. "*Maguey*," she explained. "There are many different kinds, and you have to be careful not to get the wrong one. Some of them are irritating to the skin."

"Maguey . . . Isn't that what they call the big ones, taller than a man's head? They look like a green fountain spewing out of the ground."

"Sí, that is maguey. Some people call it agave. One of the most useful plants in all of Mexico. The flower petals you're eating are from a maguey. When the petals are gone we can roast the stalk over the fire and chew it to get the sugar, like sugar cane."

She had Miriam take a clean shirt from the saddlebag and cut it up for rags and bandages. The rags went into the boiling pot.

When everything was ready they stripped off Domingo's shirt and peeled away yesterday's makeshift bandages. The bullet wound through his arm cleaned up easily enough, though the exit wound in the back took a bit of sewing.

"He is lucky it missed the bone," Kyra said.

The deep knife slash across his chest looked a lot angrier. Kyra cleaned it thoroughly, then sewed it up as best she could and treated it with some kind of salve she pressed out of a thick leaf before finally wrapping a clean bandage around it.

The head wound started bleeding again when they unwrapped it. Kyra put a little white root on a flat rock and pounded it into a pulp with the butt of her knife, wrapped it in a bit of rag and dropped it into the boiling pot. A few minutes later she fished it out, let it cool then wiped the wound with it.

"That should stop the bleeding," she said. While she waited for the coagulant to take effect she sharpened her knife on a stone and plunged the blade into the boiling water to sterilize it.

"I didn't know you were a doctor," Miriam said.

Kyra smiled. "I'm not. But there *are* no doctors where we live, and most of us could not pay one anyway, so we learn how to doctor ourselves. As I said before, everything we need is already here."

Working by candlelight, she honed her knife, shaved around the gash in the back of Domingo's head, cleaned it thoroughly, put a couple of stitches in it and wrapped a fresh bandage around it. When she was done they rolled up what was left of the shirt to cushion the back of his head. Kyra lifted the front of the bandage and looked at his eyes.

"His eyes still don't look right," she said, "but there's nothing more I can do. Now we will just have to wait. I will take the horses down to the creek and tie them where they can graze, and then I will find something for us to eat. You keep watch over him. If he stirs, you should try to get some water into him."

Kyra was gone for an hour, but when she came back she brought a couple of mountain quail. The birds were darker plumed than what Miriam was used to, but still recognizable as quail.

"How on earth did you get quail?" Miriam asked.

"I heard them calling yesterday from the edge of the pine woods, so I set snares by the thick brush this morning. I was surprised to catch them so quickly, but I guess they don't see enough people to be wary."

Before long Miriam had the quail cleaned and spitted, roasting over the fire. Kyra had also brought some wild onions and something that looked like salad greens.

"I never would have believed that such bounty grew in this wild place," Miriam said. "I was afraid we would starve."

Kyra shrugged, wiping her mouth on a sleeve. "Where there is water, there is food. You just have to know how to find what God has provided. There are rabbits here, too. Tonight I will make a stew. Oh, and I brought you something special. You will like this."

She reached over among her growing pile of green things and fished out a large leaf that had been folded to make a little purse, the top tied with twine. Miriam untied the twine and peered down into it.

"White slime," she said. "Thank you."

Kyra laughed out loud. "It is soap, silly. I will stay with Domingo while you go over to the creek and take a bath. It will make you feel better."

"But where did you get soap?"

A shrug. "From a soap tree."

Miriam raised an eyebrow. "A soap tree?"

"Sí. It's a kind of yucca. The soap is in the base and the roots. It's good for your hair too—much kinder than the lye soap your mother makes."

It almost brought a tear to Miriam's eye. It was the little things she missed the most when she was away from home. Her wants were not complicated, but today was Saturday, and tonight the whole family would be taking warm baths. She was beginning to think Kyra was not only a doctor but also a mind reader.

Miriam found a secluded notch in the creek where the bank was high and the water deep enough to bathe. The water ran cold and blue and crystal clear. Kyra's soap worked as advertised. Miriam took her time washing her hair, listening to birds calling as they flew in and out of their holes carrying what looked like pine nuts. They were lovely birds, large and mostly green, their heads and shoulders adorned with a maroon color that caught the sunlight in a surreal way. They looked like some kind of parrot, though she had never seen one in the wild.

When she got back to the cave Kyra was sitting cross-legged on the floor weaving a basket with fibers she had stripped from the leaves of the soap tree.

"The rabbit stew will be ready soon," Kyra said.

"It smells wonderful."

Kyra shrugged. "It will do. I used what I could find—the rabbit, some wild onions, roots and herbs, a couple of peppers and diced *nopales*. I'm afraid we will have to share the pot, but at least we have spoons." She held up two crude wooden spoons she had carved from a length of soft pine. Kyra's hands were never idle.

"How is Domingo?" Miriam asked, kneeling beside him with a candle.

"He has not moved," Kyra said, and as she paused to gaze at him the grief and worry welled up in her face. "If he does not awaken soon I fear he never will."

"I have prayed a thousand times," Miriam said. "I am afraid Gott will grow tired of me."

"Pray a thousand more," Kyra answered softly.

Chapter 37

Micah and Jake left well before dawn, hoping to find Miriam and get her back before midnight. Caleb sat up with his wife well beyond bedtime, keeping a lantern lit in the living room.

It was Mamm who first heard the hoofbeats. She looked, then jumped up and bolted out the front door into the pitch-dark. Caleb grabbed the lantern and ran after her.

He found her standing in the front yard whimpering, bouncing on her toes. Raising the lantern, he put an arm around his wife to calm her, but when Jake and Micah trotted into the light his heart sank. They were alone. Micah climbed down wearily and held onto the reins as he came to Caleb and Martha, removing his hat.

"We could not find them," he said. "I was hoping we would meet Miriam on the road between, but when we reached the pass we still didn't see nothing."

"You didn't find *anything!*" Caleb asked, bracing Mamm for fear she would collapse.

Micah shook his head. "No. The buzzards were feasting on two dead horses, but they were not ours. One of them was the Appaloosa we saw at the logging camp."

Caleb's head tilted. "Liver and white, front and back?"

"Jah, that one."

El Pantera's horse. Domingo must have shot it.

"But we found nothing else," Micah said, his face full of despair. "The rain last night must have washed out the tracks."

Mamm started to cry. "Bandits, bandits, bandits . . ." Her voice trailed off and she wept into her handkerchief.

Caleb held her tight and spoke reassuringly into her ear. "We don't know that, Martha. We don't know anything. All this means is we don't *know* where they are right now. Let's not make too much of it. They are in Gott's hands, and He has proved His kindness to us already. We must trust Gott, Mamm. And don't forget, Kyra is with her."

He gave her shoulders a confirming squeeze and started to turn her back toward the house. Pausing, he looked back at Micah and said, "Thank you, boys, for trying to find her. You must be very tired. You should go home and sleep. In the morning we will meet for church and we will pray for them."

When they went into the house and closed the door Micah was still standing out there holding his reins, lost in darkness.

❧

On Sunday morning, just after sunrise, a ghostly pale column of light filtered down into the mine from the square entrance fifty feet away, outlining the beamed ribs of the shaft in shades of blue. Miriam sat cross-legged in the rock chamber beside a small fire, tending a squirrel Kyra had picked off at first light. A drop of grease fell from the browning meat and the embers hissed and flared.

Kyra had gone to the creek to fill the goatskin. When she brought the squirrel that morning she'd also brought back a sprig from a moonflower vine. There were six blooms on it, big and round and eerily white against the darkness, still open, for they had not seen the sun. No part of the moonflower was edible, and Kyra said the seeds were poison, but she hung the vine on the wall of the rock chamber. "To brighten up the place," she said.

And it did. The ghostly blooms in the pale firelight brought a smile to Miriam's face as she sat combing through her hair with her fingers. Kyra was right about the soap, too. Her hair had never felt so soft and shiny and pretty. Rising, she pinched a flower from the vine and set it in her hair over her ear the way she'd seen Kyra do. *If only Rachel could see me now*, she thought, and it brought a smile to her face.

A groan came from the darkness on the other side of the chamber and Miriam's head turned, squirrel and moonflower instantly forgotten. She grabbed a candle, held its tip in the fire until the wick caught, then shielded the flame with her hand as she rushed to kneel over Domingo.

His lips moved silently and his head rolled from side to side, tilting back a little, trying to see out from under the bandage. Carefully she lifted the rag clear of his eyes, folding it onto his forehead. He clenched his eyes shut at first, but in a moment he adjusted to the candlelight and opened them halfway.

"Domingo," she whispered.

His head turned slowly and he held her gaze. He blinked, confusion furrowing his brow, staring as if he didn't recognize her. His eyes traced the dark hair cascading over her shoulders, lingered on her face and the blue-white moonflower in the flickering candlelight.

Miriam held perfectly still, anxious, watching.

A hand rose slowly, weakly, from his chest and reached out toward her, probing. His fingertips brushed her cheek as his fingers pulled back the curtain of hair. The confusion never left his eyes, but his hand gently caressed her face before collapsing, spent, to his chest. The tenderness of the gesture made her blush.

Heavy eyelids gave up the fight, and as his eyes closed a single word formed in the faint whisper of his exhalation.

"*Dulcinea.*"

Miriam leaned closer, listening, but Domingo said nothing else. His breathing became deep and regular as he lapsed back into sleep.

There was a noise of sandaled feet coming down the shaft—Kyra returning. When Miriam turned to look, the moonflower fell from her hair and she felt a pang of guilt, suddenly ashamed of her vanity in such a moment. She picked up the flower and tossed it quickly into the fire. Kyra bustled in, and when she saw Miriam with her candle hovering over Domingo she dropped the goatskin and rushed to her brother's side.

"He was awake just now," Miriam said. "He turned his head and looked at me."

Kyra squealed, the news filling her face with light. "Did he say anything?"

"Only one word. I think it was someone's name—Dulcinea." She glanced sideways at Kyra, her face darkening, a touch of something alarmingly close to jealousy pinching her heart. "Is this someone you know, this Dulcinea? A friend, perhaps?"

Kyra shrugged. "No. I know no one by that name. He must be out of his head, but at least he speaks. This is good. He is getting better, no?"

"Sí. He is delirious—that must be it." Miriam's eyes turned back to Domingo, but her hand drifted up almost unconsciously so that her fingertips touched the place on her cheek.

An hour later he awoke again, and this time he was more coherent.

"Water." It was a hoarse whisper, his tongue searching, click‑ing against the roof of a dry mouth.

Kyra brought the goatskin and poured a little between his lips while Miriam held the candle.

"More," he whispered.

"How is your head?" Miriam asked as Kyra gave him another sip.

"Hurts," he rasped, clutching at the goatskin. "More."

"Easy on the water." Kyra spoke gruffly, but her eyes betrayed her true feelings. She could not deny her brother.

"Where else do you hurt?" Miriam asked.

"Arm, chest, hip, leg," he said, finally pushing away the goatskin. He tried to raise his head to look down at his broken leg, but he winced and gave it up at once. "My leg hurts all the way to my chin."

"Your leg was badly broken, bruised from hip to knee, and your head is wounded. I set the leg and splinted it, but you should not move. Rest," Kyra said.

He moaned. "How long have I been out?"

"Three days. We were very worried."

"I'm hungry."

Kyra smiled. "That's a good sign. There is a little rabbit stew left from last night. I'll warm it for you. *Lie still!*"

Later, after Domingo had eaten the remains of the rabbit stew and drank half of their water, he looked around and said, "This place is a tomb."

"You need sunlight," Kyra said. "Miriam, let's get him outside."

Miriam and Kyra picked up his litter and struggled up the shaft with him, placing him carefully on the shady slope just outside the entrance, up against the timbers.

"Prop my head so I can see," he said.

Miriam went back in for the blankets, rolling them to make a pillow and raise his head so he could look out over the valley.

Shielding his eyes with a hand, Domingo squinted. Cotton-ball clouds drifted over limestone cliffs, brilliant white in the morning sun, busy with the comings and goings of the birds.

"El Paso de los Pericos," he muttered. "Gracias, Kyra. You were wise to bring me here."

Kyra smiled. "It will be a place of healing."

"Parrot Pass," Miriam mused. "I *thought* the birds looked like parrots."

"Sí," he said. "They are called *cotorras serranas*. They nest in the cliffs in the summer. Beautiful birds. If you can catch one of the young ones, you can make a pet of it and teach it to talk."

Miriam chuckled. "I don't think my father would allow any sort of pet that didn't earn its keep, but you're right, they are beautiful. I've never seen such birds."

"Well," Kyra said, pushing herself to her feet and adjusting the straw sombrero on her head, "we have another mouth to feed. Now that he is awake there are some things he should eat. Miriam, if you need me, just yell. I should be able to hear you from anywhere in the valley."

She propped the old Henry rifle on her shoulder and sauntered down through the trees into the sunlight.

"She's amazing," Miriam said quietly, once Kyra had gone.

Domingo nodded. "There is more to my sister than just a pretty woman."

But even these words came from a darkness, a somberness that seemed to go deeper than his injuries. Kyra was right—he needed light.

"There is more to you as well," she said. "You saved my

sister's life, Domingo. Rachel and Jake made it back home safe and sound, thanks to you."

"And Aaron?"

Her gaze dropped away from him and she choked back tears. "No . . ." It was all she could manage.

He nodded grimly. "I was afraid of that. But I'm glad to hear about Rachel and Jake. Things are not as bad as they might have been. I am pleased."

He did not *look* pleased. The darkness hovered around him, a palpable melancholy. He sighed deeply and closed his eyes.

"What's wrong, Domingo? Is it the pain?"

He shrugged. "Wounds and broken bones will mend, day by day. I can bear pain . . . of the physical kind."

He said nothing else, but Miriam's mind lingered on his strange words.

"Are you suffering another kind of pain? Something *not* physical?"

He didn't answer, or open his eyes.

After a moment she reached out and placed a hand gently on his arm. "You can talk to me, Domingo. You can trust me. What is it?"

He sighed deeply and exhaled, "You would not understand."

"I can try."

His eyes opened, hard and unforgiving. "Have you ever killed a man?"

So that was it. The battle in the pass. She lowered her eyes.

He lay back and draped an arm over his face.

"So, the fight at the Needle's Eye . . . you took a man's life?" She asked it very gently.

"It was not what I expected."

"This was the first time?"

A nod.

This caught her by surprise. Domingo always seemed so at ease with violence and death that Miriam had never thought to ask him such a question. She just assumed. That day when the bandits tried to kidnap her on Saltillo Road and Domingo pinned one of them to the ground with a knife to his throat, what she saw in his eyes then was not doubt or remorse but murderous rage. She could still hear her father's words as he tried to stay Domingo's hand.

"It is a great sin to kill a man."

And she could hear Domingo's seething answer.

"Not in my *religion."*

He lay still, his face hidden, but he breathed through his mouth, too deeply, swimming in troubled waters. He was human after all.

"You are right," she said softly. "This, I would not understand. I have felt the heft of many sins, but I pray that I may never know the weight of that one."

She ached for him, and with him, but he was in a place she had never visited, nor wished to, and there was nothing she could say to him now that would change anything. All she could do was listen, grant him a sympathetic ear and perhaps help him find some small measure of peace.

"Domingo," she whispered.

In a moment he whispered back, "Sí."

"Tell me about it. Talk to me about what happened in the Eye of the Needle. Sometimes it helps to talk."

Chapter 38

Domingo didn't move, didn't speak for so long that she thought perhaps he had not heard her, but finally his voice came, raspy and low.

"Before they got there I climbed as fast as I could, to a high ledge. It was my best chance. On the ground, they would have ridden over me.

"Six bandits came through the pass, one by one. When I killed El Pantera's horse in the narrow place there was shouting, confusion. I shot the man behind him and then another horse. When that one fell, the rider's leg was pinned. I killed him, too. The rest took to the rocks, and there was a lot of shooting. My arm was wounded, but I kept fighting until my guns were empty.

"After El Pantera's horse fell, I saw no more of him until I sat up to reload the rifle. He was standing on the ledge behind me with his gun drawn. When he saw that I was empty he laughed—a filthy laugh, full of malice. He put away the gun and pounced on me with his knife, slashed my chest before I could catch his hand."

Domingo's voice was steady, but he kept his eyes covered with his arm.

"I was weak from the bullet hole in my arm. El Pantera could have killed me easily, but he did not strike to kill, only to wound. He pinned me down and whispered into my face that I would die slowly, that he would take his time and cut me up like a chicken. He said I would suffer for what I did to his horse."

Domingo paused then, taking several deep breaths as he relived a horror.

"He tried to cut my shoulders so I wouldn't be able to use my arms. I had a grip on his knife hand, but I was weak. I could not stop him. When I saw there was no other way I held on to him and rolled off the ledge. We fell a long ways. I remember nothing else."

"But we found you on a ledge," Miriam said. "You didn't fall to the ground."

His arm lifted from his face and he stared at her. "Then I must have caught on a lower ledge. So *that* is why they did not finish me. El Pantera must have missed the ledge or bounced off it. He would have been hurt from the fall too, and the others were wounded. Maybe they could not reach me."

He lay back then, staring at the sky through the treetops, his breathing deep and troubled.

"This was in my dream," Miriam said, suddenly remembering, her eyes wide with surprise.

"What dream?"

She told him of the vivid dream that had come to her more than once, of the stallion on the ridge, the jaguar, the desperate battle.

The fall.

"In the dream I was wearing the clothes of a Mexican peasant," she said. "The clothes of a man. This was the reason I came with Kyra to look for you."

He listened without expression, but when he glanced at

her clothes a pained look came into his eyes and he nodded. "Dreams can be cruel."

It was a mere whisper. He offered no explanation for this curious remark but sank back into solitude, the darkness closing around him. Casting about in her mind for a way to grant him some kind of peace, Miriam remembered the message he had sent to her through Rachel—the words he thought would be his last.

"Domingo, you laid down your life for your friends. It's true, what you said—there is no greater love."

"Noble words."

"A noble intention, no matter the outcome. What you did was *heroic*. You saved the lives of two people."

His head turned and his eyes burned into her. "I *took* the lives of two people."

"You don't know that for certain. We found no bodies."

"I was there. I know what I saw."

"Even so, they were bandits. They were trying to kill you."

Wincing, he raised up on an elbow and his eyes grew fierce. "Sí, they were bandits. But they were also revolutionaries who fought alongside my father for a cause he believed in. They were not just bandits; they were men. I *knew* these men—the two I killed. Morales came to our house sometimes, when my father was alive. His wife's name is Maria, and his son was born with twisted legs—pushes himself around on a little cart with wooden wheels." He paused, breathing heavily, his eyes intense. "I shot that boy's father through the heart. The other one's name was Carlos, and he was younger even than me. Carlos was the one whose horse pinned him. He was screaming, trying to free his leg, looking up at me. I could see panic in the whites of his eyes right before I shot him."

Miriam recoiled in shock and horror. She had not seen the bodies, but suddenly it all became too real.

"It is a hard thing to look into the eyes of a man you *know* and pull the trigger, Miriam. Their faces, their voices, haunt my dreams. Carlos and Morales will not be going home to their families anymore."

He fell back then, spent, and the two of them looked everywhere but at each other for a long time.

After a while she could not take the silence any longer. She spoke very quietly.

"I am Amish," she said, "and we believe that to kill a human being at any time, for any reason, is a great sin. But you are not Amish, so I will not judge you. Anyway, I have always understood outsiders to hold a different view. You were threatened. El Pantera and his men would have killed you if they could—and Rachel and Jake, too. Does not the law excuse a man who only defends himself?"

"The *law*?" A sardonic chuckle. "Law is the whim of this year's ruler. A man must have his own law. What pains me now is not the law, but what is in my own heart and head."

She nodded thoughtfully. "My father has often said we live by a higher law, but I have also heard *you* say that it was not against your religion to kill."

"My religion did not prepare me for what I would see, what I would feel. Facing the edge of El Pantera's knife, everything I knew was swept away like dust. I only wanted to live, to take another breath, to see the faces of those I love once more."

His chest heaved deeply, and Miriam waited.

"The Nahua gods deserted me. At the last, I saw no choice but to roll off the ledge—and take El Pantera with me. It seemed a kinder death."

"But you didn't die," she said.

He shook his head weakly. "No, but all that has come to me since is pain and grief, with troubling dreams I cannot understand."

The truth of this was in his face. Up to now she had felt out of place in this strange debate, standing on the wrong side of the question—an Amish woman trying to ease the conscience of a killer. Reaching deep inside her own honest heart, she finally saw precisely what it was she really wanted to tell Domingo, and she said a silent prayer.

"Every man is born with a conscience," she said, "and sooner or later his conscience is grieved. Your gods have no answer for that grief?"

His eyes wandered and a sigh escaped from the depths of his despair. "No."

It was a delicate moment. She sensed that the darkness of the last three days had opened Domingo's soul like a moonflower. Too much light and he might close again. Too little and the moment would pass.

"Mine does," she offered, very softly.

He lay silent for a long time, thinking. Lying back with his eyes open, looking up through the trees at the deep blue sky, he said, "I have read enough of Kyra's Bible to know a little about your God, and I have watched your father long enough to know a little more. Yours is a God of peace. He would turn His face from one like me."

"Perhaps you should try talking to Him."

A deep sigh. His eyes wandered. "Why would your God listen to me? Who am I to Him?"

"Domingo," she said gently, "the thing you do not yet understand is that my Gott loves you. He always did. He loved you even as you squeezed the trigger."

⌒⌒

The weather in Parrot Pass was perfect—not too cold, not too hot, plenty of sunshine, and a light breeze blowing all afternoon. Domingo slept most of the day, lying out by the mine entrance, and when he awoke in the afternoon he was feeling a little better. Physically. His leg and hip still troubled him, but some of the pain in his head had abated. His vision remained blurry.

Kyra took the rifle with her in the afternoon and came back with a large, dull gray bird swinging from her hand.

"*Chachalaca*," she said as she tossed the dead bird on the ground. "Mexican pheasant. They are named for the noise they make."

"An ugly bird," Miriam said, lifting the bird by its feet, appraising it. "The pheasants back home are beautiful, colorful."

"But these are just as good to eat," Kyra answered. "A delicacy."

Miriam cleaned the pheasant and gathered wood for a fire. None of them wished to go back into the musty depths of the mine until it was absolutely necessary, and it was plain that the fresh air did Domingo a world of good. His spirits had lifted a little. Kyra brought him a couple of stout green limbs, both of them forked at one end. Hardly a word passed between Domingo and his sister, but he sat up against the timbers, pulled out a knife and began trimming the limbs.

"What are you making?" Miriam asked.

"Crutches," he said. "Maybe tomorrow, maybe the next day, I will be able to move around a little."

"Do you think that is wise?"

He raised an eyebrow, shaving a twig from the branch. "It is not wise to lie still too long. The sooner I can move, the better."

Kyra came out of the mine with the cooking pot in her hand. "That pheasant will take a couple hours to roast. I'm going to the creek for a bath before the sun gets too low," she said, holding up the pot, "and I will bring back some *aguamiel*. You'll be all right?"

"Sí," Domingo said, glancing at the rifle leaning against the timbers.

While he had his knife out, Miriam had him trim a couple of forked sticks for the spit while she built a fire. Using a rock for a hammer, she drove the forked sticks into the ground on opposite sides of the fire. A half hour later the bird was beginning to brown, and smelling wonderful.

When Kyra returned from the creek she brought the cooking pot, half full with a milky white liquid.

"Aguamiel," she explained. "Our first morning here I cut the heart from a maguey—the one whose flowers we ate. The hole fills with sap from the leaves. Taste it."

Miriam dipped a finger in the pot, tasted. "Not bad," she said. "Sweet."

Kyra shot a mischievous glance at her brother. "It will give him strength . . . and perhaps sweeten him a little."

Before she thought, Miriam muttered, "He is sweet enough." Then she blushed and turned away to check the fire, hoping he hadn't heard.

They dined on pheasant and greens that evening, washing it down with the nectar of the maguey and sharing the ripe purple fruit of the nopal for dessert. As the sun dipped behind the white cliffs, the sky faded from turquoise to crimson and the parrots ceased swarming to settle in their holes for the night. Miriam sat contentedly by the fire, poking it occasionally with a stick.

"I could live here forever," she said.

Chapter 39

Under Kyra's constant care Domingo's wounds healed rapidly, though the pain in his head lingered and he saw two of everything. Each morning Kyra and Miriam hauled him out of the mine on his litter so he could spend the day in fresh air and sunshine, yet his mood remained dark and he spoke very little. While his handmade crutches were ready and waiting, Kyra wouldn't let him get up. She said his broken leg needed to knit.

Still, when Miriam woke up early on Wednesday morning he was gone, the litter empty, with Kyra sound asleep on the other side. Alarmed, she woke Kyra and they hurried up to the mine entrance.

"There he is," Kyra said, pointing.

Miriam could just make out a shadowy figure in the gray predawn light, down in the valley, hobbling slowly through the brush on the homemade crutches. Kyra snugged her straw sombrero on her head and started to go after him, but Miriam grabbed her arm and stopped her.

"If he went to the trouble to get up on his crutches and leave without waking us he probably wants to be alone. We should leave him be."

A smile slowly curled Kyra's lips. "Is there something going on that I should know about?"

"Sí, but it is probably not what you think. Your brother grapples with his conscience."

Kyra raised an eyebrow. "His conscience? He has said nothing of this to me." She knelt by the remains of last night's fire and sifted the ashes with a stick. Finding an ember still glowing, she began piling dry twigs over it.

"We talked about it the morning he first woke up," Miriam said. "While you were out gathering medicines. The two men he killed in the pass . . . he knew them. It is the reason for his dark mood."

The little catlike smile crept back onto Kyra's face. As she fanned the embers, a small wisp of smoke began to rise. "It is interesting that he spoke of these things with you, but not with his own sister."

"Men are different," Miriam said. "Sometimes it is hard for them to talk to a sister about deep things."

"Like what?"

"Dreams. I think Gott troubles his dreams."

Now *both* of Kyra's eyebrows went up. "You talked to him about God?"

Miriam nodded. "Only a little."

"I thought it was odd when he borrowed my Bible," Kyra said. A tiny wisp of flame licked at her hands as the twigs ignited. "I could never get him to talk about God. I think he believed it would dishonor the memory of our father."

Miriam's eyes were still on Domingo, a pale figure lurching into the low mist across the valley. She sighed. "We put too much faith in words, I think. Best to wait, and see what happens."

Domingo stayed away all day. When Miriam went to tend the horses that morning she spotted him sitting on a rock by the creek near the upper end of the valley, and she watched him for a moment. But Domingo's eyes missed nothing, even now. If she could see him, he could see her, and if he needed help he would have asked for it. She moved on and left him alone.

Late in the afternoon Kyra was spitting a rabbit to roast over the fire when she turned to Miriam and said, "I'm beginning to worry about Domingo. He has had nothing to eat all day. Shouldn't we go look for him?"

"I'll go," Miriam said, picking up the goatskin and slinging it over a shoulder. "You're busy, and I know where he is."

He had not moved, though he was no longer sitting upright. Lying on his back on a slab of limestone overlooking the creek, when Miriam called out to him he raised his head and looked, then patted the rock with his palm. She climbed up to sit beside him.

"Are you all right?"

He nodded, taking a long pull of water from the goatskin flask without rising. "Much better, now."

He was using Miriam's straw sombrero to cushion his head against the rock.

"I wondered where my hat got to," she said. "I couldn't find it this morning."

"I'm sorry. I thought it was Kyra's." There was a curious smile on his face when he said this—the first time she'd seen him smile since his awakening. He sat up, used a fist to reshape the crushed crown of the sombrero, and placed it gently on her head.

"What have you been doing?" she asked.

"Keeping still. Listening."

Bright green and red parrots swooped about the cliffs. She could hear their cries, and the sound of the creek tumbling over stones. A Mexican jay landed on a cactus nearby and let out a sharp hack. The triple caw of a crow echoed down the valley, and from somewhere in the distance the yipping of a coyote.

"Life is busy here," she said.

"More than you know." He winced, shifting his weight from his injured hip. "I spoke to your God this morning."

He seemed embarrassed, almost apologetic. Picking a pebble from a dimple in the rock, he flipped it into the creek. His eyes remained on the creek as he said, "There has been a great weight on me these last three days. I could not sleep last night, and this morning I could bear it no longer. I came down to the creek thinking today I would either find peace or drown myself."

"Well, you haven't drowned yourself," she said.

"The day is not over yet." But he smiled again. "I didn't know if your God was listening, but I told Him this thing was very hard for me to bear, and if I understand your Bible right, it says the weight can be taken away by this Jesus. So I asked for forgiveness—I think Kyra calls it *absolution*."

She held her breath for a moment. "And have you found peace?"

He took a great deep breath and let it out. "Sí. The weight is gone, but there were no voices, no great sign from the heavens. I wasn't sure. I thought maybe your God is very subtle, or maybe it was only the sunshine and the birds and the music of the stream that lifted my spirits. So only a few minutes ago I decided to put Him to the test. I told Him if He was real and this peace was His doing, He should give me a sign."

Her eyes widened. "It is not good to put Gott to the test. What did you ask of Him?"

"It was only a simple little thing." He reached up and ticked a finger on the edge of her sombrero. "I asked Him to bring me the owner of this hat."

Miriam's mouth hung open, speechless.

He shrugged, smiled sheepishly. "I thought it was Kyra's. Perhaps your God plays tricks, but He is real, and He is here. I know that now."

When they got back to camp Miriam told Kyra the things Domingo had shared with her. They expected a lot of questions from him, but as the evening passed he remained his usual quiet self—except that the dark mood was gone. He seemed content for a change, at peace, though he still kept to himself.

"Don't worry about it," Kyra said, when she had a moment alone with Miriam. "It's just his way. Domingo has his own mind, and he will not be told what to think. If I know my brother he will spend many more hours thinking it through before he will talk about what he has decided."

⁓

The next morning he rose early again and slipped out before the girls were awake. He went back to his rock, alone, and stayed until Miriam came to him in the afternoon with food and water. She couldn't resist asking him, once, if he'd talked to Gott any more.

He shrugged. "Mostly I just listen." Without another word he eased himself gently down off the rock and onto his crutches.

Miriam went with him as he meandered about the little valley, and he showed her his world. They stopped at the maguey Kyra had hollowed out, and she dipped aguamiel from its heart for him to drink.

"They make a kind of beer from this, called *pulque*," he said. "Also tequila. A very useful plant."

It became a routine of sorts. Every morning Domingo would rise early and go to his rock, and every afternoon Miriam would join him for a leisurely stroll. He grew stronger every day. The pain in his head eased a little day by day, but the double vision proved very stubborn.

They walked together at Domingo's hobbling pace and talked of many things. Miriam was constantly amazed at how much there was to learn about the rich variety of life all around her. In a place she had first thought was a barren waste, Domingo unveiled a veritable Garden of Eden and shared it with her.

It was a pleasurable time, a time of laughter and discovery, a golden time when Miriam marveled at the fact that she didn't have a care in the world. She'd spent ten wonderful, carefree days in a deserted valley high up in the mountains of Mexico with nothing but a pot, a rifle and a knife, and not once had she gone hungry or suffered for want of anything. She felt perfectly safe and at ease living off the land with Kyra and Domingo.

＊

By the middle of the second week Miriam and Kyra had grown used to Domingo's routine and did not expect to see him in the mornings, but when Miriam went down to the creek on Thursday morning to move the horses she found him already there, leaning on his crutches and feeding leaves to the mare.

"Where is Kyra?" he asked as Miriam untied the horses.

"Gathering breakfast," she said. "Have you had anything to eat?"

"A little. I found some berries, drank some aguamiel from the maguey. I am fine."

She walked slowly, leading the horses a little ways up the creek to find fresh grazing. Domingo hobbled along beside her on his crutches.

"I am strong enough to travel," he said. "We should leave soon. You have been gone almost two weeks, and your people do not know where you are. They will be worried."

"Sí, I worry constantly about my mother, especially after all that has happened. But it's your head Kyra is worried about."

"The pain is gone from my head and I can see pretty good now."

"Still, I think it's best to wait and let Dr. Kyra tell us when you are well enough to ride."

He shook his head. "I cannot ride a horse with this leg, and my hip still hurts."

"Then we'll have to make another travois. You can ride lying down, but it will mean your head has to take a lot of bouncing."

"I hope no one sees me being dragged home behind my sister's horse," he said. "My amigos would never let me hear the end of it."

She tied the horses in a new spot and left Domingo at the water's edge as she waded out into the creek to fill the goatskin. A question had plagued her since that first morning when Domingo awakened, but up to now she hadn't had the nerve to ask.

"Who is Dulcinea?" she said absently, her back to him as she submerged the big flask in the creek.

He gave out a single brief snort of a chuckle. "Where did you hear that name?"

"*You* said it." She tried her best to seem disinterested—she had no right. But an unexpected pang of jealousy had pierced her when he said the name, and now she wanted very much to know more about this Dulcinea. Who was she? How long had he known her and where did he meet her?

"I said that name? When?"

She glanced over her shoulder at him. His eyes narrowed suspiciously, and he frowned. Disquieting.

"Sí. You said the name. I heard you. It was the first thing you said the morning you woke up in the mine. I thought she must be someone very special to you, since her name was the first word to cross your lips in three days."

The frown remained, and now he would not meet her eyes.

She watched him closely, the jealousy creeping back in. "You don't remember?"

He lowered himself with his crutches and sat gingerly on a

little stretch of sand. Settling back on his elbows, he said hesitantly, "Sí, I remember. It's just . . . I thought it was a dream."

She pulled at the sides of the goatskin, drawing water into it, waiting.

"It is from the book," he said quietly.

"What book?"

"You know, the book you gave me last year at Christmas, when you were teaching me to read. *Don Quijote de la Mancha.* It is a big book, a lot of words. But you were right—I read it twice, and by the time I finished I had learned to read as fast as I can talk."

Straightening up, she corked the flask. Her brow furrowed as she waded out of the creek. "So Dulcinea is someone from this book?"

"Sí. You have not read it?"

"No, I gave it to you. I doubt the church would approve anyway."

She set the goatskin on the sand next to Domingo. Perhaps a little too relieved to discover that this Dulcinea was only a character from a book, now she wondered why it bothered him so. A prickly pear stood at the top of the bank, gourd-shaped fruits lined up ripe and purple on the top edge. Carefully she broke a few of them off with her knife, gathered them in her hat and sat down beside Domingo. Now that her hands had something to do, she pressed him for more.

"Tell me about this Dulcinea," she said as she began carefully shaving the thorns away.

He pulled out his own knife and did the same, fidgeting, reluctant to answer, as if his thoughts embarrassed him. His face turned skyward and he squinted at the wheeling parrots for a minute. When he turned back to her the embarrassment was gone from his eyes, replaced by a steadfast resolve.

Chapter 40

Domingo split open a cactus fruit, pried it apart and bit the ripe heart from it. In a moment he spit out the seeds and said, "Probably it was the cave that made me think of it. In the book, Don Quijote falls asleep in a cave and has fantastic dreams. In one of his dreams he meets the perfect woman, the most beautiful woman in all the world."

He put his palms against the ground and shifted his weight from the sore hip, wincing with the pain.

"Like Don Quijote, while I was asleep in the cave I had many dreams, but none compared with the last one. I did not know where I was or how I came to be there, but it seemed I was in a cave, dim light flickering from the rocks, and there was a woman hovering over me . . ."

She waited, hardly daring to breathe. He would not look at her. His voice had become very soft, very quiet.

"She was my dream woman," he said wistfully. "Dark hair lay in shining waves on her shoulders and hung down around a face lit by golden candlelight. As long as I live, I will never forget that face. It was the face of an angel, a face I would die for. A face I would *live* for."

His hand rose and his fingertips touched his temple, pensively, his eyes shining as if the memory still surprised him. "There was a *moonflower* in her hair."

He sat still for a moment, remembering, and then said, "I am not an educated man, so I do not have the words to describe what I saw, what I felt. I can only tell you she was the most beautiful thing I have ever seen. It was the most beautiful moment of my life."

Now his eyes met hers.

"I didn't know," he said. "I really believed it was a dream."

His hand came up slowly, lifting her hair aside and caressing her cheek with a heartbreaking tenderness, exactly the way he had done before.

"Dulcinea," he whispered, and then he leaned closer and, ever so gently, kissed her lips.

It was more than she could bear. She forced herself away from him and staggered to her feet. Knife and cactus fruit fell to the ground, forgotten, as she stumbled to the edge of the water and knelt down to drink.

"Cualnezqui," he said gently.

She didn't answer, didn't turn around, but his voice came to her again, soft and persistent.

"Surely you know that I have loved you from the first moment I saw you."

Still on her hands and knees, Miriam splashed cold water onto her face and watched the droplets shatter her reflection in the pool. Her voice trembled. "Then why have you waited until now to tell me?"

He was quiet for too long. She hesitated, afraid to turn around for fear the moment would burst like a bubble. Finally he spoke.

"Because until this day I did not know how important it was.

326

I have seen my death, and found life. Everything is changed. Days—*moments*—are precious. The sky is bluer, trees greener, the fruit of the nopal sweeter. To pretend not to care for the only woman I have ever loved, now, seems only foolish."

His words burned the morning air. She pushed herself to her feet and turned to face him.

"Do not toy with me, Domingo. *Fences*, you said. The fences are still there. What of your honor?"

"There is no dishonor in love."

She could not stop her feet from carrying her to his side, where she knelt in the sand and took his hand.

Her eyes were downcast, staring at his hand in hers as she whispered, "Domingo, you captured my heart from the beginning. I never really had a choice. But you were right, and the fences remain."

He studied her face for a moment. "Micah?"

"No. I am free of Micah—he has already said he will not marry me now. But what of my father, my religion?"

"I don't know. I only know I could not hide my feelings from you any longer."

She gazed deeply into his eyes and saw no answer. "Nor will I. But I cannot court you."

He shook his head slowly. "I am not asking you to court me, Cualnezqui. I am asking you to be my wife. I promise to make you very happy."

Stunned speechless, her hands came up to cover her mouth, and tears blurred her sight. Somewhere deep within her a key turned in a secret lock. A door opened and flooded her heart with light.

But a great treasure commands a great price. In the very next instant she counted the cost, and the light dimmed. Despair forced her to ask the question.

"Domingo, how will I be happy if I am banned? I was baptized. If I leave the church now, my family will turn their backs on me. I will *lose* my family."

He lay back on his elbows, staring into the distance. A high sun shattered itself on the rippling stream and sent shards of light flitting silent across the face of the cliffs.

After a while, without moving, he said softly, "You would have me become Amish?"

The thought had occurred to her, but somehow it was not foremost in her mind.

"I would only have you know my Gott," she said. "After that, I would be content to let *Him* tell you who to be." Then it occurred to her that she should at least admit the possibility. "But you *could* be Amish if you chose. My father thinks of you like a son. You would be accepted, and it is a good life. I would not be honest if I said the thought didn't quicken my heart." It was the perfect solution.

His eyes watched the sky, and a sad smile crept onto his face.

"Look at those buzzards," he said.

She shaded her eyes and peered into the blue, wondering what buzzards could possibly have to do with what they were talking about.

"Do you see anything strange?" he asked.

The buzzards circled slowly in a loose formation a little to the south, not very high up. They soared on an updraft, never flapping, keeping their wings rigid except for the feathers at the very end that worked the wind like fingers.

"No, I see nothing. They are just buzzards."

"Look closer. One of them is different."

Squinting, she finally saw it.

"Sí, you are right. One of them is not exactly like the others, but it's very hard to tell. It looks like his head is black where the others are bald, and there is a band of white across his tail feathers. The others are all black."

"Watch him."

The buzzards circled, shifting and drifting in a light breeze, constantly making subtle adjustments to the wind. She kept her eyes on them for a long time, thinking perhaps she had missed something until the one with the band on his tail suddenly broke formation.

Flattening his wings against his sides, the bird darted straight down at a dizzying speed. At the last possible second before crashing into the ground his wings spread to catch him and his body pivoted. Thick legs reached out and sharp talons snared a ground squirrel that had come down to the water to drink, strayed too far from cover, and saw the shadow of death a second too late. The bird bent his neck and put a swift end to the rodent's struggles with a sharp beak, then spread his wings and flew away to the trees with his prize dangling from his claws.

"That was no buzzard," she said.

"No, he is not. He is a hawk who only *looks* like a buzzard. He flies among them and makes himself look like them because the creatures he preys upon have no fear of buzzards. The ground squirrel thinks he is safe until it is too late."

Domingo let his words settle for a long moment before he spoke again, from a profound sadness.

"Cualnezqui, I could never be Amish. It would only be a lie. I was born a hawk. I could dress in Amish clothes and learn Amish ways, but in my heart I will always be a hawk."

Never in her life had she felt so divided, so torn, as in that moment. His words sent part of her spiraling into bleak depths, for a very tall fence remained between them. But another part of her heard only the word *cualnezqui*—beautiful one—and that part of her took flight like the hawk.

She took his hand again, held it softly. "I do love you, Domingo. May Gott help me, for I cannot help myself. The feelings I have for you I have never held for another man, and the hours spent with you in this valley have been like another life. Like heaven on earth. There is nothing I want more than to spend the rest of my life with you, I know that now. But if you cannot be Amish, then the only way we can be together is for me to *leave* the Amish."

Now she looked into his eyes with profound sadness and said, "Domingo, you are asking me to choose between you and my family."

He waited, watching her eyes, saying nothing and making no move toward her.

"I cannot choose," she said. "Either way lies a price I cannot bear to pay. I will need time, to think and to pray. I don't know how long. Will you wait?"

He smiled, peacefully, patiently. "I will wait forever if I must. I have no choice."

The next morning, in the pale gray light of dawn, Kyra and Miriam saddled their horses, hitched up Domingo's travois, and headed for home.

Chapter 41

Rachel missed her sister. It had been nearly two weeks since Miriam left, and she ached to see her again, longed to talk to her. She missed their late night conversations after everyone had gone to bed, a time when she and Miriam shared secrets too deep to pass between anyone but sisters, and then only whispered in the dark.

She *missed* Miriam, but she wasn't worried about her. Deep down, some part of Miriam was also part of her, and she never doubted for a minute that if anything happened to her sister she would know it. She would simply know. Until now, at least, there had been no earthquake in the Miriam part of her heart. Wherever she was, whatever she was doing, Miriam was safe. If only she could explain that to Mamm.

Mamm was inconsolable, unreachable. Dat said something cracked in Mamm's foundation the day Aaron died, and fear rushed in like water to fill the void. She tossed and moaned half the night, then sat crying and staring at nothing all day long, unable to work or even think straight. Ada, too, had become almost unmanageable without her mother's constant attention.

These were the things that filled Rachel's mind on a sunlit

Friday afternoon while she was out hoeing weeds from the kitchen garden with Leah and Barbara.

"Someone is coming," Barbara said, leaning on a hoe and gazing off to the west.

Rachel was bent over between tall, staked tomato plants. "Who is it?" she asked tersely, a little put out with her youngest sister, whose attention tended to wander from her work.

"Too far away to tell," Barbara said. "Looks like two Mexicans on horseback coming down the ridge trail way out beyond Levi's, but they don't look like bandits. One of them is dragging something behind his horse. *That's* odd."

Rachel stood up straight, but she still couldn't see around the tomato plants. "What's odd?"

Barbara shaded her eyes from the lowering sun, squinting. "Their horses. From here they look like standard bred."

Two Mexicans on standard-bred horses, coming from the west.

The Miriam part of Rachel's heart sent a shock wave up her spine. Her hoe fell to the ground between the rows as she rushed to Barbara's side, her eyes searching the shimmering distance.

Barbara pointed.

"That's Miriam," Rachel said, with a calm certainty. "Go get Mamm and Dat. Call everybody."

Then she started running.

⟨⟩

It was a joyous homecoming despite woeful stares at Miriam's clothes. The whole family swarmed around her, and then they swarmed around Domingo and Kyra. Rachel had already untied Domingo from the travois and helped him get up onto his crutches before Caleb got to him.

"You've come back from the dead," Caleb said, shaking his

hand, eyeing his wounds. "Maybe we should call you Lazarus from now on."

A blank stare. "Lazarus? I don't know this name."

Caleb laughed. "I'll tell you the story sometime. You must be hungry. Come in, let us get you something to eat."

Domingo winced. "I would, but our mother waits for us at home. She doesn't know."

"I have to go, too," Miriam said. "My clothes are at Kyra's."

Caleb shook a finger at her, eyeing her Mexican laborer's attire. "You're not going *anywhere* this night, *Señor* Miriam. All my children are staying together, under my roof, for *at least* a year. I'll take Domingo and Kyra home myself, in the hack, and I'll fetch your things back. Right now you're going to go in the house and sit with your mother until she feels better."

Miriam nodded and started for the back door, but Caleb put a hand on her shoulder.

"Go easy with her," he said softly. "Mamm's . . . not right. After Aaron, and all those babies, then Rachel got kidnapped and you were gone so long—she's just not right anymore, Miriam."

She found her mother sitting listlessly at the kitchen table, staring into space, oblivious to the clamor around her. Mamm didn't even notice when Miriam came in until she straddled the bench next to her and turned her head gently with a finger, tossing the sombrero on the table and letting her hair fall free.

"Mamm, it's me. Miriam."

Mamm's eyes widened slowly, then filled with tears. She reached out to touch Miriam's cheek and her mouth formed a quivering O. The floodgates opened as she threw her arms around her lost daughter and buried her face against an Aztec poncho.

⁓

While Miriam sat holding her mother Caleb hitched a fresh horse to the hack and helped Domingo into the back of it, propping him up with a buggy robe in an effort to make it a little more comfortable than a travois. Domingo sat up, adjusting the bandanna around his head.

"Where's your hat?" Caleb asked.

Domingo flipped a casual wave toward the western mountains. "Lost it."

"I see. Wait here."

He went into the house and came back with a wide-brimmed black Amish hat. Holding it out to Domingo, he said, "See if this fits."

Domingo took the edges in his fingertips and pulled the hat down on his head. "Fits perfect," he said. "But this is your Sunday hat, Señor Bender. What will you wear to church?"

Caleb gave the question a dismissive wave. "I'll wear my work hat, and if anyone asks what became of my good one I'll tell them I traded it to get my Rachel back. A hat is nothing. I will never forget what you did, sacrificing yourself like that. You're a hero, Domingo. I wish there was a way I could repay you. No price would be too great."

Caleb's words only seemed to embarrass the young man because he shook his head and looked away, refusing to meet Caleb's gaze. Clearly exhausted, he lay back against the bundle, covering his eyes with the hat and mumbling something in Spanish.

It sounded to Caleb like he said, *"No estoy tan seguro." I'm not so sure.* Domingo had a habit of deflecting praise as if it embarrassed him—a character trait Caleb shared and admired. No matter. Caleb gave his young friend's shoulder a reassuring squeeze and went to help Kyra up into the seat.

⌒

Miriam saw through the kitchen window when her father tied Star to the back of the hack, preparing to leave. Pulling away from her mother's embrace, she said, "I'll be right back. I must say goodbye to Domingo and Kyra."

Leaving the back door open, she ran out to the hack and gripped the side rail next to Domingo. Her father climbed up into the driver's seat next to Kyra and hesitated, giving her a minute before he urged the horse into motion.

Domingo's head turned, and his fingers came up to touch Miriam's. He smiled.

She whispered the word *Soon*, and backed away. Her father snapped the reins and clucked at the horse. She waved goodbye to Kyra and watched them pull away before she went back inside the house.

The news spread quickly, and within an hour Micah came to join the throng at the Bender house, his face lined with regret. Emma, Levi, Mary and Ezra came with their babies, and Miriam was glad for the crowd because it kept her from having to deal with Micah just yet. There was great jubilation over her return, so even though she was exhausted Miriam still spent the whole evening with her family in the living room, recounting every detail of her adventure in the Valley of the Parrots.

Almost every detail. She left out the important parts. This was not the time to bring it up, especially with Micah right there in the room and the matter still undecided.

Mamm sat close, clinging to Miriam's arm and hanging on every word, and yet Miriam got the sense that her mother absorbed very little. She just clung, saying nothing, her eyes still full of fear.

"There is news here, too," Micah said. "Freeman Coblentz came to see me when I was out in the field today. His are leaving, going back home. Hannah is just too shook up about losing little Suzie. Aaron was courting Cora too, and then all this bandit business."

"Hannah always was a little frail," Rachel said.

Mamm shook her head, dabbed at her eyes with a handkerchief.

"Poor Hannah," Miriam said. "I don't blame her one bit."

"Freeman said they'll be going back Tuesday morning," Micah added. "It's a shame. His house is half finished, and he already paid for the land. I don't know what they'll do."

⌇

Micah stayed through the evening and helped with the chores. Catching Miriam in the dark on the way back from the barn, he spoke to her alone.

"I'm mighty glad to see you back safe and sound," he said, "and I'm real sorry I didn't just go with you that night." Even in the moonlight, without a lantern, she could see genuine sorrow in his eyes, and shared in it, though for entirely different reasons.

"It's all right," she said calmly. "Everything worked out just fine. We didn't have any trouble at all. I know everybody was worried, and I never would have stayed away so long if it hadn't been—"

"I know. Domingo," he said, and he couldn't keep the fine edge of jealousy from creeping into his voice. "You already told us all about him. But, Miriam . . . that other thing—what I said about, you know, not being my wife and all—"

"Stop. There's no need to do this, Micah. You were right. It would never work out between you and me. We would never be happy together. It was wise of you to break our engagement before we made a serious mistake."

His eyes wandered, searching for words. He clenched his hat

in front of him, his fists unconsciously rolling the brim. It was a lost cause, the cold distance between them well established earlier in the crowded living room when she would not meet his eyes.

"Well, I'm real sorry about that. I wish you'd change your mind, Mir. I would still have you, you know. I didn't really mean what I said."

She stood her ground, shaking her head slowly. "No. You're a good man, Micah, and you'll make someone a fine husband. But it won't be me."

He turned away quickly, jammed his bent hat on his head and plodded quietly to his buggy. Watching him drive away, though she would never have admitted it to anyone, Miriam felt a stab of guilt. It was never her intention to hurt him.

Later, in bed, Miriam could tell that Rachel was still awake after everyone else had fallen asleep, though she'd been strangely quiet.

"Rachel," she whispered, "are you all right?"

"Jah." She didn't move, didn't elaborate.

"What's wrong?"

"Nothing."

Lying back to back, Miriam sensed a distance between them. "Rachel?"

"Jah."

"When you were telling us about what happened with the bandits—you know, the night I left—I got the feeling there was something you weren't telling us. You kept looking at me, like you do when you're hiding something."

"Oh, that. Jah, I remember. I just didn't want to say it in front of Mamm, upset as she was already, but the bandit in the

337

barn—the one Jake knocked out—he came there in the middle of the night to . . . you know. It was awful."

"Did he? I mean, did he *harm* you?"

"No. Thank Gott, Jake got there in time."

Miriam pondered this for a minute. Rachel hadn't moved or raised up and she seemed reluctant to talk—very unlike Rachel.

A slight hesitation, then Rachel's voice from the darkness, "It was no big deal, I just didn't think Mamm needed to hear that. What about you? I felt the same way when you were talking tonight, like there was something you weren't telling us. What *really* happened in the Valley of the Parrots?"

Miriam held her breath for a moment, then said, "So many things happened, it will take me a long time to remember them all."

"Really?"

Now it was Miriam who hesitated and lay too still. "Jah. It was nice there. You wouldn't believe how much Kyra knows about living off the land. She was amazing."

A long pause, and then Rachel's voice, muted, drifting. "Jah, she's quite a woman."

Chapter 42

Two weeks passed without a word from Domingo or Kyra. Caleb rode over to check on them twice, but he brought no word for Miriam apart from Domingo's rapid improvement.

"Kyra keeps a good stiff splint on that leg, and he walks with only a cane now," Caleb told her after his last visit, three days ago.

On a Monday afternoon, late in the day, Miriam was out taking down the laundry from the line when she heard hoofbeats.

Kyra trotted into the yard on Star, keeping her dust trail well away from the clothesline. Miriam did a double take when Kyra swung down from the saddle, for she had almost forgotten how beautiful Domingo's sister looked in a peasant blouse and painted skirt.

"You're a woman again," Miriam said.

"I know!" Kyra answered, beaming. "I almost didn't recognize you in that dark dress and white kapp. I'll have to get used to it all over again."

Doing her best to make it sound like a casual question, Miriam asked, "How's Domingo?"

Kyra rolled her eyes. "We can't keep him still. He wanders around in his bean field all day—leaning on a *cane*! But I guess it's for the best. We would all go crazy if he stayed in the house."

"So what brings you here?" Miriam asked, picking up the laundry basket.

"Oh, I need to borrow a pot. A *big* one. We have a lot of canning to do tomorrow—bushels. I don't know how we'll get through it, with no one to help and my mother's knees acting up."

The thought traveled from Miriam's heart straight to her mouth without a second's hesitation. "I will come help you."

"No, you mustn't do that," Kyra said. "You have too much work—" A casual glance at Miriam's face chopped off her objection. A wry smile crept into Kyra's eyes then, and she nodded slowly.

"Sí, I could surely use your help, Miriam. Perhaps you can come stay with me tonight, then help me in the morning and bring home the pot when we are done with it."

Her dat cast a worried glance at Mamm when Miriam asked if she could go with Kyra, but he reluctantly agreed. Mamm was better, though still not herself. Miriam wondered if she ever would be.

She saddled a horse and rode beside her friend with a huge pot tied to the saddle horn, bouncing as they trotted over the fields. The sun had disappeared behind the western mountains by the time they reached Kyra's barn on the back side of San Rafael.

Putting away her horse in the twilight of the little adobe barn, Miriam grew nervous. "Listen, Kyra, before we go inside, I need to talk to you about something very important. I need to know what you think about it."

Kyra shrugged. "All right. My opinion is worth almost as much as you pay for it."

She decided to just say it and get it over with.

"Kyra, you know I love Domingo."

Kyra didn't bat an eye, hefting her saddle up onto the stall rail, dusting her palms. "Sí. I saw the two of you in El Paso de los Pericos. I am not blind."

"And he loves me."

A little shrug. "I knew this long before you did. There are some things a brother cannot hide from a sister."

"Well, did you know that while we were at Parrot Pass, Domingo asked me to marry him?"

Kyra's mouth flew open in shock. "No! And did you give him your answer?"

Miriam shook her head. "I couldn't, then. It is a heavy thing, to choose between Domingo and my family. I needed time to think. I would be banned from the church, and my people would shun me."

Kyra nodded thoughtfully. "This explains much. He has said hardly a word in the two weeks since we brought him home. Have you come to a decision?"

Miriam glanced away for a moment, marshaling her courage. She had never spoken the words aloud.

"I am going to say yes," she said.

Kyra leaped into the air screaming and came down hugging her, dancing her in circles, laughing, squealing.

"You will be my *sister*! And such sisters we will be, Miriam! We will set Mexico on its ear!"

Miriam did her best to calm her excitable friend before she said, "You get ahead of yourself, Kyra. I should talk to Domingo before we celebrate."

Kyra peered out the door. "He is still out in the bean fields.

Oh, but sister, I cannot let you go to him like this," she said, touching her fingertips to Miriam's kapp. Her dark eyes lit up suddenly. "Quick, come into the house with me! I have an idea."

⟡

Life must go on, Caleb thought after he watched Miriam ride away, but it was still a hard thing to let her out of his sight for the first time since she came home. The door to life opened on infinite possibilities—including, as Caleb now knew too well, *unthinkable* possibilities. But even a father could not keep the door closed forever, so he swallowed his misgivings and let his daughter go.

For reasons he could not quite fathom, full of a pain he was not ready to talk about, Caleb struck out on foot, without a word to anyone, to the other side of the valley. In a little while, walking alone up the foot of the far ridge, he arrived at the cottonwood tree whose shade had now merged into the twilight. The western sky was still stained with blood, the east a shimmering promise of moonrise with a single star keeping watch, low over the black hills.

He sat down beside the loose mound of dirt that marked his son's grave, propped his arms on his knees and stared out over the valley. There were no words. Caleb Bender was a thoughtful man, but his bruised soul could not begin to put words to the questions life had asked him of late. Gott's reasoning was as far away as the morning. Even to grieve overlong was to question Gott. All he could do was trust, and wait. This too would pass. The light would come.

It was a tiny sound, brief as a cricket's chirp, and it came from far away. Perhaps it drifted across a mile of perfect stillness from the door of Mary's home, or perhaps it was one of Gott's little lights shined unerringly into the bleak recesses of his own soul, but for a fleeting second Caleb could have sworn he heard the faint, sweet squeal of a harmonica.

◌ᴗ◌

Night had nearly fallen by the time Kyra pushed Miriam out the back of the house with a final word of encouragement, shutting the door behind her. She could make out Domingo's shadowy figure in the dusk, hobbling out of the edge of the bean field on his cane, his new wide hat low over his eyes, his head tilted down, careful of his steps.

Self-consciously at first, she walked tentatively, pausing at the back of the garden by a fence post entwined with lush green vines. From the darkness near the ground a glint of blue-white shone up at her—a moonflower bloom. She pinched the bell-shaped flower from the vine and tucked the stem above her ear. As her fingers lingered in her undone hair, she closed her eyes and that voice came back to her, soft as a breeze in the corn, a whispered memory.

Dulcinea.

She struck out toward him confidently now, her head up, her shoulders back and daringly revealed by one of Kyra's white peasant blouses. Kyra's best black skirt—the one with the embroidered roses—swished about her sandaled feet.

She was ten feet away when Domingo finally looked up and saw her. She stopped, and he stared, the whites of his eyes showing in the dusk, surprised.

"Miriam?"

Blushing, her gaze dropped away from him.

"You didn't see me?"

"I saw," he said, "but I thought it was Kyra."

She remained motionless. Sand and rock crunched underfoot as he hobbled closer and stopped with mere inches between them. When he reached up very slowly and lifted her chin to face him, she saw hope burning in his eyes.

"Like a dream," he whispered as his hand slid gently under her hair, caressing her cheek. His eyes roamed over her face with obvious pleasure, lingering on the moonflower.

"Is this your answer?"

She nodded slowly, a demure smile creeping onto her face. "I never really had a choice," she said. "I will be your wife, and your people will be my people. But we must not speak of it until the time is right. My mother is not well, and I cannot do this to her while her heart is heavy with the loss of Aaron and the little ones. I love you, Domingo, and I will promise myself to you, but we must wait. I don't know how long."

"Then I will wait, Cualnezqui," he whispered. "For as long as it takes." His cane clattered to the ground, forgotten as he swept her into his arms.

Author's Note

For the benefit of my non-Amish readers, and in deference to my Amish kin, I feel I should point out a few things about bed courtship, or bundling (the terms are interchangeable). In the old days before the New Order came along, when a boy and girl were "going steady," after a Saturday night date it was customary for the boy to remain at the girl's house and sleep in her bed. This was done quietly and never openly discussed, even among family members, though the parents were aware of it. According to the Amish, the reasoning behind allowing such a thing was entirely practical: Their uninsulated houses were extremely cold at night, beds were at a premium because of the large families, and since the farms were some distance apart, the boy often faced a ten- or fifteen-mile buggy drive in the dark of night, in single-digit temperatures.

Bed courtship has an important (albeit secondary) role in THE DAUGHTERS OF CALEB BENDER, as it does in *Levi's Will*, but the reader should bear in mind the historical contexts of these works. While bed courtship was widely practiced until the mid-1900s, since that time most of the Amish have made a concerted effort to stamp it out.

Amish churches vary from one district to the next as to their place on the liberal/conservative continuum, but they generally fall into three categories: New Order, Old Order, and Schwartzentruber, with New Order being the most liberal group.

As far as I know, the New Order churches, which emerged sometime in the 1960s, have never practiced bed courtship. Around the 1950s many of the Old Order churches began to recognize the moral dilemma inherent in bed courtship and have since taken a stand against it. If the practice goes on at all today, it's more likely to be among the more conservative and insular sects like the Schwartzentruber. But the more conservative Amish never talk about such things, especially with outsiders, so I cannot speak for them one way or the other.

The group that went to Mexico in the 1920s was mostly members of what was then known as the Abe Troyer Church, an offshoot of the Schwartzentruber—very conservative. It is a fact that they did allow bed courtship in the early part of the twentieth century, but the church instituted a number of changes under the leadership of a man named Tobe Hostetler (they're now known as the Tobe Church) and they have spoken out against the practice for many years.

Acknowledgments

By now I have learned that the writing of a novel is anything but a solitary pursuit. There is always an army of friends and family who offer advice, feedback and esoteric knowledge in the early stages, and an army of professionals who polish and package and correct, making me look better than I am in the latter stages. Among others, who may go unmentioned but not unappreciated, I am grateful to the following:

My wife, Pam, who sees it all before anyone else and never fails to bring a feminine touch to my writing.

My father, Howard Cramer, who gives me insight into the Amish mind and culture and contributes a long memory full of wonderful stories and details.

My cousin Katie Shetler, who does her best to help me understand Amish customs and rules, and the diversity that exists among them. Thanks to her, I sometimes get it right. When I don't, it's entirely my own fault.

Marian Shearer, a local writer who grew up in Mexico, who corrects my Spanish and graciously shares her encyclopedic knowledge of Mexican life, culture and geography.

Lori Patrick, a freelance editor, friend and champion, who

writes the back cover copy and provides unflagging support through the whole writing process.

Hoot Gibson, for the monkey story.

A host of friends too numerous to list (but you know who you are), who help me shape early drafts through brainstorming sessions, fireside chats and first-draft feedback.

My editor, Luke Hinrichs, both cheerleader and coach, who brings all the various aspects of writing, editing, cover art and marketing together into a cohesive whole.

My agent, Janet Kobobel Grant, a keen-eyed editor and wise counselor.

Last, but certainly not least, this work owes a great deal to a book by David Luthy titled *The Amish in America: Settlements That Failed, 1840–1960*. To my knowledge, it is the only comprehensive written record of the Paradise Valley settlement, and it was instrumental in creating the backdrop for this novel.

About the Author

Dale Cramer is the author of the bestselling and critically acclaimed novel *Levi's Will*, based on the story of Dale's father, a runaway Amishman. Dale's latest series, THE DAUGHTERS OF CALEB BENDER, is based on an Amish colony in the mountains of Mexico, where three generations of his family lived in the 1920s. Dale lives in Georgia with his wife of thirty-six years, two sons and a Bernese Mountain Dog named Rupert.

For more information about the author and his books, visit his website and blog at *dalecramer.com*. Or readers may correspond with Dale by writing to P.O. Box 25, Hampton, GA 30228.

More Amish Fiction From Dale Cramer
Based on Real Life!

For more on Dale and his books, visit *dalecramer.com*.

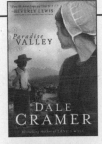

When new laws take away their freedom, one Amish community seeks religious sanctuary in Mexico. But is the road ahead more dangerous than what they left behind?

Paradise Valley by Dale Cramer
THE DAUGHTERS OF CALEB BENDER # 1

As his son's life hangs in the balance, Will is forced to return to his father's Amish farm that he fled so many years ago. But can he reconcile three generations of past events before it's too late?

Levi's Will